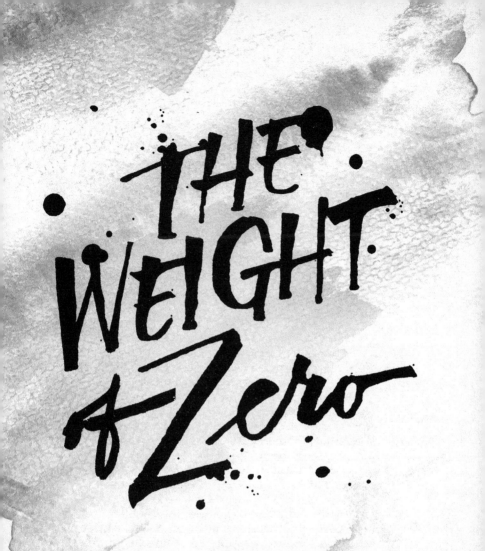

THE WEIGHT OF Zero

KAREN FORTUNATI

EMBER

Ember and the E colophon are registered trademarks of Penguin Random House LLC.

Visit us on the Web! GetUnderlined.com

Educators and librarians, for a variety of teaching tools, visit us at RHTeachersLibrarians.com

The Library of Congress has cataloged the hardcover edition of this work as follows:
Names: Fortunati, Karen, author.
Title: The weight of zero / Karen Fortunati.
Description: First edition. | New York : Delacorte Press, [2016] | Summary: "A seventeen-year-old suffering from bipolar disease wants to commit suicide, but a meaningful relationship and the care of a gifted psychiatrist alter her perception of her diagnosis as a death sentence"— Provided by publisher.
Identifiers: LCCN 2015043620 (print) | LCCN 2016019672 (ebook) | ISBN 978-1-101-93889-8 (hardback) | ISBN 978-1-101-93891-1 (glb) | ISBN 978-1-101-93890-4 (ebook)
Subjects: | CYAC: Manic-depressive illness—Fiction. | Mental illness—Fiction. | Suicide—Fiction. | BISAC: JUVENILE FICTION / Social Issues / Depression & Mental Illness. | JUVENILE FICTION / Social Issues / Suicide. | JUVENILE FICTION / Family / General (see also headings under Social Issues).
Classification: LCC PZ7.1.F67 We 2016 (print) | LCC PZ7.1.F67 (ebook) | DDC [Fic]—dc23

ISBN 978-1-101-93892-8 (tr. pbk.)

Printed in the United States of America
10 9 8 7 6 5 4 3 2
First Ember Edition 2018

For Frank, Jenna and Frankie

Most parents don't, really, know their children.

—OTTO FRANK

1

I line the bottles up on my night table. Each amber-colored warrior bears my name and its own rank and serial number: CATHERINE PULASKI—CELEXA 40 mg, CATHERINE PULASKI—PROZAC 20 mg, CATHERINE PULASKI— ABILIFY 10 mg, PAXIL, ZOLOFT and LEXAPRO—my stockpile of old prescriptions. By day, they're stationed in a box under my bed, camouflaged under old ballet shoes, un-opened packages of tights and crumpled recital flyers. But every night, I take them out. They soothe me. My psycho-tropic soldiers give me hope. There *is* strength in numbers.

My mother's bedroom door squeaks, and for the third time tonight, soft footsteps pad their way to me. There's no lock on my door; it was gone when I came home from the hospital last year. Fighting the usual Mom-induced frustra-tion, I move quickly, stashing the bottles.

Light from the hallway spills into my room as Mom

enters. "Sorry, Cath, forgot to get your number." She bends to kiss me. Before, she'd stroke the long hair off my face to find my forehead. Now, with most of my hair MIA, Mom pats my shorn head like she would a sick dog. "Well?" she asks.

"Um . . . six, maybe six and a half," I lie. Our numerical mood-report system dates back to about two years ago, right around the time I turned fifteen. The truth: I'm closer to five. Maybe even four. And I'm scared. I think I can feel Zero's black breath on my neck. Again. But I can't tell her that now.

Mom sits on the side of my bed, pulling the white down comforter tight across my chest. "So it's about the same, right? No change?"

"Yeah."

"Okay. No big changes. That's good." Mom says this more for herself than for me. "So on Monday, I'll pick you up right after school. I can leave work early."

"Mom," I say with a sigh. "That's the eighth time you've told me. I got it." Her instant smile hurts too much, so I roll to face the wall.

Mom has lassoed her hopes on Monday's appointment for my miraculous recovery from bipolar disorder. The site of the future miracle is named, appropriately, St. Anne's Hospital, which has just opened a shiny new adolescent outpatient facility right here in Cranbury, Connecticut. On the recommendation of my shrink du jour, I will be heading to St. Anne's for three hours after school, five days a week, for the foreseeable future. I haven't told him about

Zero, but since I've skipped a few classes, he's upped the dosage of my new med in addition to this intensive outpatient program at St. Anne's.

"Sorry, Cath." Mom rubs my back. Even though I'm annoyed with her, it feels wonderful, comforting, and I almost purr, my skin soaking up the contact like a parched plant takes in water. "I know we've gone over it already," she continues. "I'm so tired I don't know what I'm saying. The restaurant was packed tonight." Even her voice sounds fried. "I don't know how much longer I'll be doing this. Two jobs in one day."

We both know she'll keep doing this Friday double to pay for my doctors, therapy, meds, donations to the shrine of St. Jude (the patron saint of lost causes) and whatever else my mental defect demands.

"You should get some sleep," I say, shifting slightly in her direction. She rises and hunches over me. Her face is in the shadows, and bony shoulders poke out of her sleeveless pajama top. She could be eighty years old.

Mom tucks in the bottom corners of the comforter too hard. My toes curl forward under the pressure. "Okay, baby. Wake me up if you need anything. I love you." She clicks off my bedside lamp like I'm three.

I wait a safe twenty minutes even though it's Friday night, the night Mom passes out after eight hours of typing for a bunch of loser attorneys followed by a five-hour encore waitressing at Dominic's. I've got a couple of free nocturnal hours before she resumes watchdog rounds by my bedside.

When the silence is heavy and unmoving, I reach under my bed. Again, I line up the white-capped cylinders. I stare at their labels and pat their heads until my heart slows and my stomach unclenches. Zero is close by, sniffing and pawing, looking for a crack in my brain that the meds haven't filled. It's gotten me once before. In September of sophomore year, I turned to my brand-new bottle of lithium and took it all, with a side of a half bottle of Prozac. I failed, though, because of Mom. Somehow, some way, through some maternal telepathy, she knew, and rushed home in time to call an ambulance.

It took another nine months—when I had my first manic episode this past June—for me to get a diagnosis. Right before he retired, old Dr. A broke the news. It was the first time I'd heard the word "bipolar," with its permanent cycling of manias and depressions. I remember Dr. A was talking more to Mom than to me, explaining the "strong genetic component" of the disorder. The need to start lithium again. I remember cutting him off, asking, "So, it's the way I'm wired?"

"Yes." Dr. A nodded his fat gray head.

"And people don't outgrow bipolar disorder?" I asked. "I'll be like this *forever*?"

"Yes. It's managed like any other chronic illness, like diabetes or . . ."

In my head, the sound of the gavel crashing down drowned out the rest of Dr. A's tired voice. Oblivious to the death sentence he had just relayed, he returned his gaze to Mom, who had frozen erect in her chair like a sphinx, fin-

4

gers gouging the padded armrests. She moved only to grab hold of the cross around her neck.

It hit me then like it must've sucker punched Mom seconds earlier. The import of what Dr. A was telling us: *Catherine Pulaski is genetically defective.*

The knowledge of this permanency mutes the carousel of shrinks and their diagnoses. It makes me immune to the meds that promise to fix me, to turn me into a normal girl again. Because I know I won't ever be normal. And it's not the manias that get to me—those electric, almost euphoric phases of false clarity and vision and purpose. It's mania's flip side, the fucker I call Zero. I am petrified of him.

And now I know it's a scientific certainty, a medical fact, that Zero will get me again. Mom's saving my life was in vain.

Last year, when Zero dug in for the long haul, Mom kept asking me how I felt. *What* I felt. But there were and are no words for that particular state of hell. I couldn't tell her that I was submerged. Numbed. Unable to feel anything. My spectrum of emotions had been obliterated. My feelings, all of them, good and bad, had gone AWOL. And someone who has never felt it can never understand what the absence of emotion feels like. It is a hopelessness of incomprehensible, unspeakable weight.

Yet I'm supposed to blindly move forward? Knowing there's another wacko idea, disguised as reasonable, just waiting to take hold of my mind? To be followed by solitary confinement in Zero's black tundra? Rinse and fucking repeat? For the rest of my life? That's no future.

5

So, I've got a plan.

I arrange the bottles into a tight two-line formation with Lexapro at the front. It will be a new life for Mom. Infinitely better without Catherine sucking her dry on every level—emotional, social and financial. There's no relief for her as long as I'm still breathing. Because the bottom line is this: my bipolar life is killing her normal one. I'm a parasite, eating her alive. Almost literally. It's like the ten pounds I've put on came straight off her body. Her clothes hang on her. She's beaten down.

It's actually a pretty easy decision when you get right to it. And honorable, I think. I'm intrinsically damaged, so I'll switch out my life for my mother's.

I pick up the Lexapro bottle and gently shake it so that the four pills inside dance. I will take whatever time I have left and kill myself when Zero makes Catherine-landfall. When he's entrenched in my head and has poisoned my world alien and gray. I will do it with the contents of this shoe box. A conscious decision to refuse to live my life this way, under these conditions.

The only question is when. And the answer is unknown because Zero's ETA is basically a crapshoot. My new psychiatrist, Dr. McCallum, has spent a ton of time on the "You and Your Bipolar Disorder" lectures with Mom and me. So I know that while the mood cycles are inevitable and unstoppable, it's a mystery as to when the next one will hit.

I grab my phone and open the calendar. October. My heart pumps faster. Zero's arrival has to be imminent if it follows the same loose pattern of my first two years of high school; depression in the fall and some kind of mania in the summer. This knowledge sends twin spirals of fear and anxiety through me. I press my fingertips hard against the phone and the light illuminates them, spotlighting my bitten-down nails and tattered cuticles. But the rest of my hands are good, soft and unmarked, with long, slim fingers. A dancer's hands. And my body, heavier now from my prescription buffet, is still in decent shape. Mom likes the added weight. She thought I was too skinny before. Putting the phone down, I raise one leg high over my head. Then the other. The flexibility's still there. Must be the years of muscle memory from dance. I was good at it.

I sit up now and easily bring my head down to my knees, my hamstrings offering no resistance to the stretch. It burns me, the fact that my healthy body most likely won't see its eighteenth birthday. Sorrow starts rolling in. Over the waste of this body that didn't just dance with strength and grace but served me well in basically everything. I've run a 10K, zip-lined and rafted down the Housatonic in the spring. Biked, swum and skated. With a fingertip, I trace the outline of my lips. I've kissed. One time. At Riley's Valentine's Day party in eighth grade.

While my brain has failed me, my body's been good. Too good to be tied to such a diseased mind. It's unfair, and I mourn the things this body won't do. All the thousands of things it will never experience, from the mundane to the life altering. Dipping my toes into the Pacific Ocean, sliding behind the wheel of my first car. Unpacking dishes into the

7

cabinets of my own place. Getting married. Job. Boyfriend. College. Roommates. Recitals. Prom. Sex.

Sex. The ultimate connection. The closest possible contact you can have with another person.

I want that. At least once before Zero returns. And I should have it. It's wrong to deny my body that experience. It's wasteful to die without attempting one real, tangible connection to another human. And maybe in the time it takes to physically connect, I can shed the loneliness that I wear as a second skin. Even if just for a few minutes. A temporary escape. I click to the "Notes" section on my phone. I type "Death Day" and then delete it and type: "D-Day." Next line: "Lose virginity." I delete it and type: "L.V." I study this one and only item—the sole entry on my things-to-experience-before-Zero list.

L.V. probably won't work, though. I have no real friends anymore, girls or boys. Depression, a suicide attempt and bipolar disorder carry the same social value as leprosy, AIDS and flesh-eating bacteria. I get that. I'm not stupid or delusional. But it doesn't make it hurt any fucking less when your closest friends jump ship.

It's time. Flinging the comforter back, I grab the shoe box and gently lay each bottle down on the old tights that muffle any noise they may make during transit. I top them with more tights and a couple pairs of ballet shoes. While she has slowed up a bit, Mom still searches my room. So these guys are rotated, spending Monday through Friday under my bed and Friday night through Sunday night in Grandma's room. I feel safer with them out of my room, as

8

Mom likes to clean and organize on Saturdays before she does the early-bird dinner shift at Dominic's.

Leaving the box on the floor, I softly open my bedroom door and listen. From Mom's open bedroom door, the light of her muted TV flashes. I creep closer, avoiding the land mines of creaky floorboards. Most nights, Mom wakes up if I give the slightest cough. She used to bolt into my room, panicked. "What's wrong?" she'd cry. Now that we've passed the one-year anniversary, she'll just call out to me, "Baby, you okay?" But it's Friday and Mom should be immobile for the next couple of hours.

I hear the regular pattern of her breathing. Silently, I whip back into my room, pick up the box and lightly make my way down the steps. Who knew how handy ten years of ballet would be for sneaking around? I glide like a ghost through the dark living room and into our spotless kitchen, where the butterfly night-light glows over the sink. Fresh Italian bread from the restaurant lies sealed in a ziplock bag on the counter, but I can still smell it. Grandma's door is shut.

Her bedroom door never squeaks. I step inside. The curtains are open and the corner streetlight washes her room in light. Her twin bed is neatly made, with the yellow afghan folded at the bottom. It's been two years and three months since she died, but framed pictures still line the dresser along with her brush, Yardley English Lavender perfume and tchotchkes on white lace doilies. Her drawers are still crammed with makeup, clothes, belts and scarves probably dating back to 1940. Mom dusts everything in here, including the extra-large crucified Jesus above Grandma's bed that keeps watch over the vacant room.

I take a deep breath. Every so often, the scent of peppermint, her favorite candy, wafts by. It's Grandma, I know it is. But I'm glad that's all she can communicate from heaven. I can't bear to hear what she thinks of me now.

Avoiding Jesus's gaze (he might still be pissed at me), I lift the bed skirt and pull out the plastic box of Grandma's summer clothes. It slides soundlessly on the worn carpet. Farther back, in the black hole under the bed, my hand searches and then connects with the cracked handle of the beaten plaid suitcase. Unzipping it, I wedge my shoe box alongside packets of old letters, envelopes jammed with photographs, old jewelry and Uncle Jack's musty military jacket.

I push the suitcase back, followed by the plastic box, and fix the bed skirt so it hangs straight. I listen at Grandma's door before exiting into the kitchen. All clear. Filling a glass with water, I tiptoe up the stairs. This is always the tricky part—the possibility of having to explain to Mom what I was doing downstairs. Hence the water.

But there's no sign of Mom in the upstairs hallway, and I slip into my room. My bed is still warm. It feels nice. My new med seems to be quite effective in the slumber department; I'll definitely be able to sleep again tonight. And tomorrow I'll start looking for my first and last connection.

2

"All right, now, everybody, pair up!"

Shit.

It's third period, Monday morning. Way too muggy for the first week of October. Mr. Oleck bounces around the room, ready to crap his starched khakis over some new AP U.S. history project he's about to assign. Typical fresh-out-of-grad-school teacher. I slide down farther in my chair, the backs of my sweaty legs catching on the plastic seat. I'll just wait until Mr. Oleck orders some other friendless loser to work with me.

"Hey, dyke," a low voice whispers from behind, hot breath in my ear. "Be my partner?"

It's Louis Farricelli, Cranbury High's alpha male, senior captain of the varsity football team and resident hymen thief, responsible for the deflowering of maybe fifty percent of the vaginas here.

I don't bother to respond.

"Aw, c'mon," he moans. "I'm really digging that hair."

I had all my hair cut off this past June during a particularly productive manic episode. I had vibrated with energy those sunny young summer days. I tore through my room and the garage and attic, cleaning and organizing. I must've posted fifty pieces of crap from our basement on eBay. I thought I could easily finance a twelve-night Mediterranean cruise for Mom and me. On my emergency credit card, I charged maybe a thousand dollars worth of vacation clothes for our nonexistent trip. Online. In an hour. And then I decided that the gala cruise required a makeover. Schlepping the mile into town, I demanded that Rodrick of Rodrick's on the Green, Cranbury's snottiest salon, cut my hair. Rodrick's was the only place granted the honor of clipping the golden tresses of my former BFF, Riley, and her mom, Mrs. Judith Swenson. I can still see the pages of photographs of Audrey Hepburn and her short haircut in *Roman Holiday* that I printed off the Web, spilling from the salon receptionist's desk onto the floor.

Just my manic luck, the master was not only free but also amped to do something crazy. Rodrick was tired of the Cranbury housewives with their regulation highlights and keratin treatments. He wanted to ditch our little town for Brooklyn, but he said the money was too good here. And then he pulled my hair back into a ponytail and lopped it off. It shimmered like a glossy horse's tail in Rodrick's hand. At least twelve inches of my thick, wavy, former-ballerina hair, shining golden brown in the salon lights.

When it was done, Rodrick placed his immaculately manscaped face next to mine. Our eyes met in the mirror. "Never wear your hair long again," he breathed solemnly. "Sweetie, you were made for short hair. Look how your eyes pop, how it lengthens your neck. You're gorgeous."

Louis kicks my desk. "Hey, lesbo, I'm waiting for an answer."

Without turning around, I give a quick shake of my head and move my desk forward.

"D-day!" Mr. Oleck barks from his lectern and my head snaps up. In his plaid button-down with creased short sleeves, Mr. Oleck looks directly at me. And despite the fact that we're covering pre–World War II events, my cheeks grow warm because the only D-Day I'm thinking of is the one on my phone.

"I know." Mr. Oleck nods approvingly at me. "A project on D-day. How could it not be great?" He runs a hand through his beige crew cut, his cheeks shiny and flushed with the buzz this assignment is giving him. "This will probably be the coolest thing you guys do in high school." From behind me, Louis snorts. Mr. Oleck rushes to a canvas computer bag on his desk and pulls out a manila folder. "You and your partner will explore an aspect of D-day that you'll never get from your textbook or online. At the American Cemetery in Normandy, there are roughly ninety-five hundred soldiers interred. One hundred and thirty-one came from Connecticut. The two of you will select a Connecticut soldier who is buried there, research the heck out of him and write a biography. I want you to go all out—

track down family, do interviews, get photographs, letters, town records, school info, World War Two archives. Use primary sources if at all possible. If you run into logistical problems or transportation issues, let me know. We might be able to get some help from the history department in terms of a trip to Hartford to check the archives or genealogy records." He slaps the folder against the lectern, and I jump. "This is going to be a yearlong project. I'll be handing out the rubric in a minute, but there is one thing you need to remember." Mr. Oleck clasps his hands in a prayer position and goes still. "Honor these soldiers with your work."

Mr. Oleck remains frozen for about three more seconds before grabbing his iPad to record the research pairs. I'm tempted to take a quick look around to see if anyone else is left stranded like me, but I don't. Been there, done that. I gouge at a cuticle instead.

"Do we have any other solo students out there?" Mr. Oleck calls out.

I don't move. I won't risk the attention.

There's some murmuring from the other side of the class and then Mr. Oleck strides over to me. "Catherine, I'm going to pair you with Michael Pitoscia, okay? I think you two will work well together."

"Fine," I say. No clue who this kid is. I keep my head down when I enter any classroom now. Eye contact is dangerous, because I'm permanently tagged, the injured one in the herd and easiest to take down.

At least it's not Olivia or Riley, my former friends. I

despise having a class with them. I wasn't even supposed to take any AP classes. When I returned to school last year one of the idiots in guidance had suggested I "go easy" and avoid any unnecessary "academic stress, due to your, ahem, difficulties." So just about all my sophomore honors teachers gave me a pass on homework and sympathy-graded my tests, barely taking off for wrong answers and piling on bonus points for correct ones. Only my Western civ teacher, Mrs. Abbott, pushed for me to take this AP class. I always liked her. She never treated me any differently afterward.

Mr. Oleck claps his hands. "All righty! Pack up your stuff and find your partner. We're headed to the computer lab. I'll give you a sheet with the names of the Connecticut soldiers. Do some research online with your partner and decide which soldier you're gonna write about. Then I want you to provide me with a short summary of whatever you could find out about that soldier by Wednesday's class."

There's the herdlike shuffling and rise in volume as voices and bodies wake from the classroom coma. I don't move. And then there's a tap on my shoulder, so soft it could be a hummingbird touching down.

A throat clears. My peripheral vision detects a pair of brown cargo shorts on my right. "Uh . . . um . . . Catherine?"

My partner has arrived. So this must be what's his name. I swallow and look up from my cuticle. Please let him be civil. That's all I'm asking.

"Catherine, I'm Michael. Michael Pitoscia," he says.

My God, this kid is tall. And skinny. With dark brown hair cropped close to his skull and a goatee of maybe four hairs. I don't recognize him. I didn't go to grammar or middle school with him. He must have come from one of the other two middle schools that feed our high school of 1,800 inmates.

He awkwardly extends his hand to shake, making our introduction oddly formal. I rise to my feet and our hands make contact. His is surprisingly cool to the touch and his grip is firm and strong but not overly so. It's the first hand I've touched in a very long time that hasn't belonged to Mom or Aunt D. He gives me a quick smile. He must've had braces, because his teeth are straight and white. And while no one would say he's hot, he's definitely not gross-looking. He's just a generic high schooler. Unmarked. The type that blends into the masses. Just like me.

Or just like I used to be.

Michael stays by my side as I walk into the hall. It feels weird to have someone beside me, someone who actually walks next to me on purpose. I keep glancing at him to make sure it isn't a mistake. That he isn't keeping step with me because of some clogged traffic in the hallway. But no, there he is, voluntarily chatting away, asking me if I watch some zombie show. I don't. (Those shows aren't all that appealing when you relate more to the zombies than the humans.)

Inside the computer lab, we go through a couple of names on the sheet but come up short on any Internet info. It's actually not bad working with him. He seems nice— genuine. When the bell rings, we stand.

"Uh . . . Catherine?" Michael asks. "Maybe we should exchange numbers? I'll work on it tonight and I can uh . . . t-text you if I find somebody. If you want, then . . . uh . . . you could maybe check out that soldier."

As Michael's talking, a mottled flush makes its way up his neck. The same thing used to happen to Olivia seconds before we hit the floor for a middle school dance competition or a Miss Ruth recital. Nerves.

"Just because it's due on Wednesday," Michael is saying, "and it may take a while . . . to, you know, find somebody."

My fingers curl around the four-week-old iPhone in my shorts pocket. Mom broke her rule against using the Visa card to buy us each one. While she won't admit it, the first app she got was Find My Friends, which allows her to track me (or at least my phone).

Michael says, "My number is . . . ," and then stops and waits for me to pull out my phone. I don't want to give him my number. It's much safer to just take his.

"Okay." I pull my phone out into the light of day. "How do you spell your last name?"

As if this really matters. I have a total of six contacts on my phone: home, mom's phone, the law office, Dominic's restaurant, Aunt Darlene and Dr. McCallum.

"It sounds like 'pit-toe-sha,' but you spell it P-I-T-O-S-C-I-A," Michael answers. After he gives me his number, he says, "You know, we met freshman year. At the holiday show? 'Cranbury's Got Talent'?"

I shake my head. I can barely remember my own performance.

17

"It was before Christmas break." Michael nods, willing me to remember him. "Yeah, you did a dance thing with some girls, and me and Tyler, Tyler Connelly, did a magic act. I sawed him in half? To that old song 'Ice Ice Baby'?" His neck is scarlet now and the color is creeping into his cheeks.

December of freshman year was not a good time for me. Grandma had died five months earlier—July 3—and then Zero arrived, and the two of us entered high school together, sending my first psychiatrist, poor Dr. A, into a prescribing tizzy as he tried to combat my depression. What variety! Who knew the sheer number of psychiatric salvations? None of these prescriptions really worked but I have to hand it to the old guy—he really tried. Definite A for effort. I ended up with a lot of almost-empty bottles that I initially saved less out of any suicidal ideation than as a tribute to Grandma. She never threw anything out, recycling everything from ziplock bags to empty blood pressure pill bottles. She'd use the bottles to store safety pins, buttons and sewing needles in her underwear drawer. My collection was half a memorial to her, half a monument to the lottery of meds I'd tried and failed to improve on.

So even though my freshman year was on the mild side compared with sophomore year, it remains a painful haze.

Michael's still waiting for me to acknowledge this talent show, so I muster up some enthusiasm and lie, "Oh yeah!"

He smiles, relieved, and it makes me feel like I've done something good. I find myself smiling back at him. He pulls out his phone and, index finger poised above the screen, asks, "What's your number?"

And then, from somewhere in the computer lab, a male voice screeches, "Don't do it, Pitoscia!" And then someone else sings out in a high voice, "Cuckoo, cuckoo." A burst of laughter erupts.

I stiffen as the familiar wave of shame breaks over me. I don't have to turn around to know it's Olivia and Riley and their theater crowd. I'd recognize my ex–best friends' laughter anywhere. It roars through my head like a train.

I grab my books. I need to get away. Now.

In the safety of my cubby in the farthest recesses of the library, I lay my head in my arms while Zero pants on my neck.

3

It's beautiful out. The brilliant afternoon sun glints off the roofs of the cars as they stream out of the school parking lot. I was tempted to leave earlier because of the nightmare in the computer lab, but today is my intake appointment at St. Anne's, the home of the new intensive outpatient program Dr. McCallum recommended. Instead of scurrying home, I spent the rest of the day in the library, missing three classes. School is finally over, so now I'm shielded by a large bush and standing as far as possible from the throngs in front of the school's brick entrance, waiting for Mom.

She's got to drive me. There's no way I'm taking the transportation St. Anne's offers, with its pickup from Cranbury High at 2:45 sharp. We've only been in school for a month, but the unmarked white van is already known as "The Crazy Kids' Shuttle," "Amwack" and "The Fucked-Up

Express." I'd walk, but I'd never get there in time since the place is a good two miles away, a safe distance from our "Quintessential New England Green." Wise decision by the zoning commission: the good folks of Cranbury don't have to worry about psychotic teens roaming their quaint "shoppes" between sessions.

A cool breeze has chased the humidity out of the air and rustles the leaves, which are just starting to turn orange and red. The sky is a deep blue and dotted with thick white clouds, reminding me of the cotton ball taped to the crook of my arm after the blood draw my fledgling diet of lithium required. It's beautiful out and I'm going to another airless doctor's office at St. Anne's, where I'll sit in a stained, upholstered armchair facing yet another straight-faced doctor or social worker, going through the same Q and A for the tenth time with Mom in the other chair, a desperate, jittery wreck—all because Mom told Dr. McCallum that I had cut school.

"Cut school" is a smidge dramatic, I think. Truth be told, I just left a little early two days of the previous week. But two weeks ago, as Mom detailed the classes I had missed, a shadow crossed Dr. McCallum's face. He sighed, eyebrows scrunched, as he swiveled in his black leather desk chair to face me. I'd been seeing Dr. McCallum once a week for the last three months, and I'd learned to read his expressions. This one said, "Houston, we have a big fucking problem."

"Catherine," Dr. McCallum had said. "I've got to say this cutting classes troubles me." His fingers drummed the desk as he opened his Catherine Pulaski file. I knew what he was doing—studying Dr. A's notes. *Again.* Dr. McCallum is way sharper and more hands-on than Dr. A, whose nonstop pharmaceutical defense hadn't prevented my fall suicide attempt, or its summer follow-up: my mother-of-all manic episodes—also known as the rather expensive "Highlights of the Mediterranean" period. I hadn't said anything to Dr. McCallum about the approach of Zero, but based on my history, he wasn't taking any chances.

"Catherine, I think you'd benefit from an IOP, an intensive outpatient program," Dr. McCallum had said in the same tone a doctor suggests last rites. "These programs are ongoing. There's no start date and no end date. The particular group that I'd like for you to attend was meeting in New Haven but just moved to the new facility in Cranbury." He stopped then to gauge my reaction, and I had nodded like it was a swell idea. Like spending fifteen hours a week with a bunch of kids as messed up as me seemed downright fun.

"Will you get reports of how Catherine is doing in this new program?" Mom asked, her eyes huge. This IOP thing had to be the last thing she expected, but she wasn't going to fight him on this. Mom thinks Dr. McCallum walks on water.

"I keep in contact with the clinicians. They'll advise me of Catherine's progress," he'd answered. "There are less intensive programs, but I want Catherine to attend the daily program now, and I'll change our schedule from every week to once a month for a medication check. Of course, if anything comes up, Catherine"—Dr. McCallum turned to me again—"I'm here. Just call and we'll set something up."

Five days a week. With no end date. It's a good thing I don't have a life, because this IOP time commitment is going to be a huge drag.

It's almost three o'clock and our appointment is at 3:15. Mom said she would be here. Before I can pull up her contact, there's that butterfly tap on my shoulder.

It's Michael. "Hey."

He's the last person I want to see—the front-row spectator to my most recent humiliation.

"You didn't . . . I still need your number for the assignment. Is that okay?" he asks. His neck starts to turn splotchy again. Maybe he's embarrassed to be seen with me?

"It's all right." I turn away. "Just tell me tomorrow what you've found."

"Well . . . uh . . . it would really help if I could get your input," Michael says. He steps in front of me so I have to look at him. "We're supposed to do this together."

I shrug. It's better that he gets used to working alone. There's an excellent chance I won't be around for the project's completion.

"Cath," he says, and his use of my nickname draws my gaze up to his face, his dark brown eyes with their ridiculously long lashes. "Don't let those assholes get to you," he says in a low tone.

I give a little shake of my head and roll my eyes. Like him and his eyelashes have a fucking clue. I sidestep him to view the parking lot, eyes scanning for Mom's battered silver Accord.

23

But Michael moves in front of me again. "I . . . I passed out in anatomy class last year. During a video on heart surgery. The nurse had to wheel me out of the room. In . . . in a wheelchair. I . . . I can't stand the sight of blood. So some football players decorated my locker with heart pictures, somebody sent me links to other videos, and somebody else threw disgusting shit on my lunch table. Over the summer, they posted stuff on my Facebook page." He runs a hand through his short hair and swallows hard. "I don't care what those kids say. I asked Mr. Oleck if I could partner with you. I know you're really smart."

I study his face. He seems sincere but this could be another joke. One more prank on the crazy girl. I look around to see if anybody is watching or laughing or filming us, but nobody's paying any attention.

"I'm not asking for your social security number or anything. C'mon. I want you to look up whatever soldier I find and see if he sounds good for the project. That's it." Michael touches my arm lightly. "I won't give out your number." And then he says something else, honest and a little raw, something no one at Cranbury High would ever say out loud. "I've only got like one real friend here. Tyler."

The silver Accord flies into the parking lot. Mom will be rolling up in ten seconds.

Even though it completely goes against my judgment, there's something about this boy. He could be a candidate for L.V., at least. I take a deep breath and give him my number.

"Wait! Let me punch it into my phone." Michael moves so fast he almost drops his cell. "Okay, say it again."

The Accord is at the curb. And there's Mom. Staring at me with a look of wonder on her face.

I repeat my number. "My mom's here."

Michael yells to me as I walk to the car. "Don't forget to check your phone tonight, okay? I'll text you!"

Inside the car, Mom turns to me, ecstatic over the fact that I was talking to someone. "Is that a new friend?"

"No," I say. "Just somebody I have to do a history project with."

"Well, he seems nice," she says.

"How could he seem *nice*?" I snap. I'm not being fair, but the hope in her voice does something to me. It cranks up the guilt for the way I am. Sick. Defective. This is what she's reduced to: joy at the simplest of my social interactions. That's how little I can give her. "You saw him for what, all of two nanoseconds? And you're gonna have to call the office tomorrow. I missed my three afternoon classes."

This deflates her. As planned. "Again? Why?" Mom asks. "What's wrong?"

"Nothing," I lie. "I just had a headache and fell asleep in the library."

"Oh, Cath. Next time, baby, just head straight to the nurse's office. You can't keep getting these unexcused absences." She takes a deep breath and squeezes my hand. "I'll call first thing tomorrow. Want to take some Advil?"

A different guilt quenches my anger. She tries so hard. Always.

I turn my head toward the window and push down the lump in my throat. "No thanks," I say. "Headache's gone."

I take a deep breath. "His name is Michael. You're right. He seems pretty nice."

Mom glances over at me and smiles before turning up the volume on a Bonnie Raitt song. "This IOP thing, Cath, I have a good feeling about it. A really good feeling."

There's that hope again, but this time, I keep my mouth shut.

———

St. Anne's Outpatient Day Hospital is situated in the commercial, non-quintessential part of town, tucked behind an upscale housewife's dream strip mall: Target, Loft, White House Black Market, Whole Foods and that store that specializes in swanky fartwear, Chico's. Makes a lot of sense. While Jimmy gets his head straightened out, Mommy can bang out some errands.

The Day Hospital is a plain one-story building marked only with a number to identify it inside this small industrial park of corrugated metal warehouses and loading docks. Mom parks next to the dirty white St. Anne's van that must've just unloaded my chemically imbalanced colleagues from Cranbury High. Maybe we can all sit at one big unhappy lunch table at school. Over brown-bag lunches we can share funny stories about our suicide attempts, vomiting or cutting. Just what Mom wanted for me—new friends.

The little waiting room is empty, as is the darkened hallway with its four closed doors. A petite young woman steps from behind the reception desk. "Hello," she says, her long brown hair falling like a veil over her face. "You must be . . . Catherine. Catherine Pulaski?"

I nod.

"I'm Vanessa Capozzi. I'm a social worker and manage the IOPs," she says, smiling brightly. "I'm all ready for you." She picks up a clipboard loaded with forms. "Would you follow me?"

She leads me and Mom down the hall to the first closed door on the right. Vanessa's hair lies like brown silk on her back, reminding me that I haven't touched my hair since this morning. I run a hand through its stubby ends. It's getting a little long; I should cut it again. A return to Rodrick at two hundred dollars a cut is not in the budget, so I do it myself and Mom helps out with the back. It's not great. But I don't really care.

Vanessa swings open the door, revealing a cluttered office and fresh Ikea-type furniture. "Please, have a seat," she says. Piles of paper and folders cover the desk and floor. Empty bookcases await the contents of the large brown boxes beside them. Stepping over the crap on the floor, Vanessa smiles and shakes her head. "Sorry about the mess. We're not quite finished unpacking yet. Next week you won't recognize it." She pulls an elastic off her wrist and throws her hair into a ponytail. That movement is as familiar to me as breathing, and I feel a sudden jolt of sadness. Long hair belonged to normal Catherine.

Vanessa riffles through a metal bin on her desk and pulls out a folder. I see my name handwritten on the top tab. "Okay," she says, and takes a deep breath. She can't be older than twenty-four. "Let's talk about logistics first, get that out of the way. Our van picks up our kids right from Cranbury High at two-forty. You could take that, Catherine, or you could drive here from school. Parking is not a prob—"

"Catherine won't be driving," Mom cuts in sharply. "We have only one car and I need that for work."

Mom fails to mention the other pertinent fact: I don't have a license. I could've gotten my permit a year ago in September when I turned sixteen. But the lithium/Prozac incident put my driver's license on indefinite hold. This past summer, I brought up finally going for my permit to Mom, but she shut me down fast. I know what she was thinking. Mania plus car equals disaster.

"I don't think Cath is crazy about taking the van," Mom says, not realizing the pun.

"Ba-da-bum," I chime in, but neither woman gets the joke. So I add, "I'm not *crazy* about the van."

Vanessa smiles, but Mom almost visibly recoils from her accidental reference to my mental state. She plows forward. "So I'll just drop off Catherine and pick her up. The law office I work at is right here in Cranbury."

"Great!" Vanessa says, and embarks on the highlights of my IOP adventure: the completion of a daily mood rating checklist, the "DBT" (which means only God knows what), followed by the main event, group therapy. Vanessa explains that the group is led by a social worker and that a new topic is chosen every day. "Confidentiality is the keystone of our group discussions. We stress that repeatedly. I can't lie and tell you that in my experience there has never been a breach. But right now, I think we've got a good group of kids in that regard."

Of course, the question on my lips is: What is Vanessa smoking? Does she seriously think I would confide one measly thing to a bunch of mentally ill strangers who go to my *very own school*? The question isn't will there be a "breach" but how soon and in what manner? Text or Twitter or Tumblr? In the bathroom or the parking lot or the car on the drive home?

But I nod like it all sounds kosher. It's my standard MO. On the outside, I go with the flow. Five-days-a-week intensive outpatient program? Sure! Another new prescription? Bring it! Group therapy? I'm all in! Because the opposite would be to confide, and we all know that any meager whining on my part isn't going to unscramble my DNA and correct my abnormal brain function. And of course, the other, real reason for my Ms. Compliant act is that it raises no suspicion about my future plan involving my shoe box.

Vanessa smiles at me. "Well, unless you have any questions, you're done with me. Dr. Yu wants to have a chat with you. He's our staff psychiatrist and will do a quick evaluation. He's already been in contact with Dr. McCallum, so it shouldn't take too long. He's directly across the hall and waiting for you. See you tomorrow!"

I say good-bye to Vanessa and cross the hall into an identically messy office. A young guy in jeans and a polo shirt is glued to his phone but pops to his feet when I enter. He sticks out his hand like we're meeting at a party. "Hi, Catherine. I'm Dr. Yu. Have a seat."

And we're off. The eval doesn't take too long. Dr. Mc-Callum has fully informed Dr. Yu of my status and I know all the standard questions and answers by heart. Mom must've been hovering in the hallway because as soon as I open Dr. Yu's door to leave, she's there, fluttering her hands. "Oh . . . I just wanted to say hello to the doctor. Can you wait for me by the door?"

I plop onto a plastic chair by the reception desk. There's still not a soul in here. But then the front door swings open violently and a tall black girl with a gray newsboy cap storms in and up to the empty desk. She wears denim cut-offs, gladiator sandals and a loose, silky gray T-shirt that exposes a smooth shoulder. After two seconds, she whirls around to me. She's got one of those perfect symmetrical faces, and the dancer still in me notes that she moves with natural grace.

"Is anybody here?" she asks me. She looks frazzled as she snaps the strap on her Longchamp bag.

"Vanessa is in her office," I offer.

"Who's Vanessa?" she asks.

"The social worker. I think she's in charge here."

The girl shrugs, her shoulders brushing the gold hoops in her ears. "I don't know her. My intake was with some guy." She looks around nervously. "This is my first day. I'm an hour late."

I do a quick scan of her arms. There are no ladder scars, the cutter's signature tattoo. What's wrong with her?

Vanessa must've heard our voices because her head emerges from the office. "Hey, Kristal! Why don't you come

30

into my office? You can fill out the DBT and then head on in to Room Three. Oh yeah"—Vanessa points to me—"this is Catherine. She's new too. She'll be joining group tomorrow." Vanessa vanishes back into her office.

Kristal looks at me. "You sure you don't want to start today?" She flashes the most radiant smile I've ever seen. This girl could get signed to a modeling contract.

I shake my head and offer an apologetic smile. "Sorry."

"I don't blame you," she says, our eyes holding as her grin fades fast. She looks down the hall. "I do not want to do this."

I connect with the undercurrent of fear in her voice. "Me neither," I say softly but easily—the first two totally honest words I've said in weeks, maybe months. "Good luck."

"Thanks. I'll see you tomorrow." Our eyes lock again and she gives me a sad smile before walking slowly down the hall. "Jesus, help me," she mutters.

4

In the living room, my phone choos like a train, and I look up, startled.

The guy at the Apple Store who programmed my phone thought it was weird that I had no contacts to import. When I had to pick a chime to notify me of incoming texts, I left it up to him. I didn't care, because I knew I wouldn't be getting any. Riley and Olivia were long gone.

That still feels strange to say. We used to be inseparable, like the Three Musketeers. We met in Miss Ruth's Ballet Babies class when we were four, and that was it. Life was sleepovers and dance classes and picnics in Riley's huge backyard overlooking the Long Island Sound. We had rituals and secrets and traditions, like squeezing Olivia's cold, clammy hands for ten and only ten seconds before we took the stage for a recital, and wearing—for our entire sixth-grade year—a friendship heart necklace that Riley's mother had custom-made into three pieces. (My piece is still in my jewelry box.) Or roasting our own candy concoction (M&M's buried deep inside jumbo marshmallows) in Riley's fire pit.

In middle school, we graduated to boys and shopping and hip-hop classes. We texted furiously. Each June, we bought one new lip gloss, eye shadow and glittery nail polish that the three of us shared for Miss Ruth recitals, and we spent hours straightening each other's hair.

When Grandma died the summer before high school, Olivia and Riley swooped in, hung by my side 24-7, and even sat in the second pew, directly behind me, so they could squeeze my shoulder and pass me tissues during the funeral Mass. Afterward, they came to the house daily bearing treats—brownies, Hubba Bubba bubble gum, licorice, ring pops—fully embracing their Red Cross duties, because grief and sadness due to death were normal and expected. Catherine Pulaski was still socially A-OK in their books.

But when I failed to rebound, when I headed south into the world of lethargy and darkness, when a psychiatrist prescribed medications, I became someone who scared them.

Someone *crazy.*

That was official confirmation that I was too great a risk to my friends' social standing. And they began to slowly peel themselves away during our freshman year. It was in September of sophomore year that I realized they were gone.

My phone choos a second time, and across the kitchen table from me, Mom's head pops up from her slice of pizza, her eyes big and happy. Chimes from my phone have become extinct—audio artifacts from another age.

I open the pizza box and retrieve my third piece, sliding the reloaded paper plate along the vinyl tablecloth back to my spot. I fold the slice and take a bite. I wonder how Kristal did at the IOP today.

Mom is watching me, a thread of mozzarella hanging off her lip. "Aren't you going to get it? It's probably Michael."

My usual irritation at her meddling merely bubbles tonight. "Mom, you got cheese." I point to my mouth. "I told him I'd talk to him *tonight*. It's not even six o'clock."

Mom wipes her mouth with a paper towel since I forgot to get napkins at the 7-Eleven next to school like she asked me to. I can see her battling herself—Dr. McCallum has urged her to back off a little, to let up on her hovering. Defeated, she nods and bows her head for another bite, exposing the stripe of silver along her parted brown hair. Nice 'n Easy 6C Natural Light Golden Brown is calling. In the last year, she's gone almost totally gray. It's the accelerated aging process, aka Catherine years.

I rise from the table and head into the living room, where my backpack lies on the floor next to the sofa.

"Cath!" Mom calls out, alarmed "Where are you going?"

I return to the kitchen and Mom sits down again.

"I'll see what he wants," I say.

Michael texted at 5:47 p.m. "Hey, Cath. You free?"

"What'd he say?" Mom asks eagerly.

Deep breaths, Catherine. Deep breaths. I say, "He wants to ask you to the prom."

Mom laughs.

"He just wants to talk about our project," I add.

Mom jumps to her feet, pizza abandoned on her plate. She can barely suppress her joy. "I have some wash to do," she says, and rushes to the basement door. "Feel free to call him if that's easier than texting." She disappears down the stairs, surely congratulating herself for giving me my "space."

"Thanks for the heads-up," I mutter. She treats me like an alien now, like I need to be educated on how to act. On what's normal here on Planet Earth.

My phone choos again. Michael texts: "Found a soldier. Jonathan Kasia. From Waterbury. Has parade and Little League field named after him. Google him. Let me know what you think"

I don't text him back. The truth: I'm a little scared. I don't know if I can trust him. Even with something as stupid as texting. He might show somebody what I wrote. I better make my answers as neutral as possible. That's my plan. Yet I can't get myself to respond. Instead, I put away the rest of the pizza, take a shower, do some math homework and bring my dirty clothes down to the basement, where Mom is folding a mountain of towels and sheets.

"I need the laptop," I tell her finally, dumping the clothes on the concrete floor.

My access to the laptop is limited. Mom takes it to work and only allows me to use it at night when she's in the same room. It probably stemmed from my Mediterranean charging spree, along with Dr. McCallum's concern about "social media and its impact on our teens, especially ones who might be more vulnerable. Like Catherine." My new phone with its Web surfing capabilities troubled her, but apparently, the security of tracking me outweighed the danger. When I got the phone, she must've realized it was futile to try to police any social media attempts on my part, but she still keeps trying.

"You need the laptop for your project? With Michael?" she asks. "Just research, right? No Facebook or anything?"

"Just research," I say. Actually, I have no interest in what the Cranbury High community posts on FB, with their endless selfies and relationship status bullshit. In kindergarten, I had to write a book "All About Me." Mom helped me write paragraphs on my favorite color, hobby, animal, food, book and holiday. We taped pictures of my family—Mom and Grandma and me—to its construction paper pages. My "All About Me" white binder still sits on my bedroom bookcase, gathering dust. FB is just an online version of that same narcissistic kindergarten project. Look at me! Isn't my life great? Count my friends. *Count them.* I have more than you. This is what I'm doing this very freaking second. My Photoshopped iLife is so much better than yours! LOL!

At 8:59 p.m., Michael texts again: "Did you get a chance to look at Kasia? 😀 " It's the smiley face that does it. This time, I peck back immediately, "Looking now. Will get back to you in a few"

I type the info that Michael texted into the Google

search bar and click on a Web page filled with text and photos of a good-looking guy in uniform. Mom sits opposite me, checkbook and bills spread out before her. Her spot across the table is actually an improvement. Six months ago, she would've been seated beside me, jumpily watching each page I pulled up.

I take forty seconds to scan the information. Connecticut soldier, decorated war hero, courageous leader. Killed in action during D-day invasion at age twenty-two. Buried in the American Cemetery in Normandy. There's a link to a photo of Kasia's grave and I click on it. His gravestone is a plain white cross in an endless sea of white crosses. I imagine soldiers, boys really, not all that much older than Michael, in place of the markers. Football fields of life and potential, all wasted. I recognize that feeling and I hate it. I close out of the screen.

"Done," I tell Mom, shutting the laptop.

After completing my vocab homework, I head into the living room and curl up on the sofa, using Grandma's light blue afghan as a pillow. At 9:22 p.m. I text Michael. "Kasia looks fine." And then I add, "Thank you 😊"

Immediately my phone choos with his response and I hit the button for silent mode. "Great! Typed up short paragraph for Oleck. Should I email it to you now?"

I text back: "Can I see it tomorrow?"

My phone vibrates with his next text. "Sure! Can you stay after school tomorrow? Go over research?"

Jeez. We got this assignment ten hours ago. And it's not due till the end of the year.

Michael texts again: "Just a few minutes, nothing major 😀"

Despite the smiley face, I am sensing one major pain in the ass. I mentally remove Michael from my list as the number one candidate for L.V.

Another Michael text: "Forget that. I have Gamers Club. How is Wednesday?"

I'm tempted to text back: "Afternoons no good. At St. Anne's intensive outpatient program mon-fri for foreseeable future. 😔 Available evenings and weekends." Instead I type: "after school no good." Then I type: "job."

Michael responds with: "How about lunch? Will only take 5."

Before I can respond, he texts: "Where do you sit in caf?"

I don't. I avoid the cafeteria. I hide out in the library, avoiding the catcalls from the dementors who surround Olivia and Riley. I don't know what to say to Michael's question. How do you tell someone you have no friends? Or that you have no lunch table, and every day, you eat in your favorite cubby alone?

I shut off my phone.

"Cath, honey?" Mom calls from the kitchen.

I zip the phone into my backpack and head to the kitchen for the nightly ritual.

Mom stands beside the chipped Formica countertop. One hand holds a tall glass of water and in her other hand's palm sits my tan pill. It's Lamictal time. This pill has one of the stranger shapes, like a badge or a shield. Intentional irony by the drug company? I can hear the pitch: *When you're battling depression, shield yourself with . . . [trumpets blare] LAMICTAL!*

Dr. McCallum made some bold moves when I switched to him in June following the Mediterranean cruise debacle. He axed the Prozac Dr. A had prescribed, cold turkey, and urged lithium. Dr. A had also prescribed lithium in the summer following my freshman year, after a weird episode when I basically wanted to paint the outside of our two-story house. By myself. Not exactly a full-blown mania but screwed-up enough to clue Dr. A into thinking that a new prescription for lithium might be "helpful." Mom stalled on filling it, waiting until September of sophomore year. I was only on it for a week before swallowing the entire bottle. Mom blamed lithium for my suicide attempt and forbade any more prescriptions for it. When Dr. McCallum took over, he wanted me back on it. But even Pope McCallum couldn't convince her. They compromised with a new prescription for Abilify.

Once I was pretty stable, Dr. McCallum weaned me off that too. But due to increasing irritability (thanks, Mom), Dr. McCallum prescribed Lamictal for depression. That was over three weeks ago, and Mom, of course, was and is a wreck. She said she's just worried because Dr. McCallum told us of a possible rare allergic reaction to Lamictal—a mother of a rash.

"Stevens-Johnson syndrome," Dr. McCallum had said. "Catherine would have to be hospitalized. I've never come across it, but we'll start her out at a very low dose, twenty-five milligrams, and work our way up over a five-week period to about two hundred, two hundred fifty, maybe three hundred milligrams."

Mom had objected, saying that Dr. A had never prescribed Lamictal. Why take such a risk?

Dr. McCallum had grudgingly agreed to the no-lithium rule for the time being, but that was the extent of his med negotiations with Mom. With a firm nod, he had said to her, "I've had some really good outcomes with it, Jody." Then he focused his attention on me. Unlike Dr. A, Dr. McCallum always makes a point to include me in the discussions about my health. "I'm confident the Lamictal will help stabilize your mood, Catherine," he said. "And more important, it won't make it worse. But because we have to raise the dose gradually over five weeks, you shouldn't expect to wake up one day and suddenly realize you're no longer depressed. Instead, if you respond like most kids, after six to eight weeks you'll slowly notice that you don't get as down as before, or that little things that used to irritate you no longer seem as big of a deal."

So Mom was overruled and I began Lamictal. And every night, after I swallow the pill with a rush of cold water, Mom inspects my arms and legs for the rash that has yet to make an appearance. Her brows knit together as she leans in close, eyes running the length of my arms, legs and back. But her extraordinary inspection skills are about more than some itchy red bumps. I know my mother. This new prescription is undeniable proof that things are not fine with her daughter. It's confirmation that Zero could circle again. Time to buckle your seat belt, Jody.

Mom returns the Lamictal bottle to the large pink-and-black polka-dot makeup bag that contains all the house medicine like Tylenol and Pepto-Bismol along with my personalized goodies. Ever since my attempt a year ago, she carries that bag with her, inside an enormous purse, day in and day out. Obviously, this makes it much harder for me to recruit new troops for my shoe box.

Luckily, I began collecting my current stockpile that eighth-grade summer, in my strange and misguided attempt at a tribute to Grandma's own pill-bottle collection. I didn't use them on the first Saturday of September, sophomore year, when Zero sucked me dry. When Zero bore down, I chose lithium, whose element-y name alone screamed its alpha position in the psychopharmaceutical pecking order.

Post-attempt, everything changed. All pills remain under lockdown in the traveling polka-dot bag. I haven't been able to stockpile any newbie Lamictal yet. Mom insists on hanging out with me for at least a half hour after I take it so she can watch for allergic reactions, and even if I didn't swallow it, the damn thing dissolves in my mouth anyhow.

Mom follows me into my room to give me a good-night kiss. "Number?" she asks, her hand ruffling my hair.

"Six. Six and a half."

"Okay, babe. Pretty stable, I think. Right?" Her eyes, shadowed in black, beg me to agree that yes, I am stable.

I want her to sleep well tonight. "Yeah," I lie.

She shuffles out and I wait until the silence from her room falls like a thick blanket. Ever so gently, I shut my door. After spending the weekend in Grandma's room, my shoe box is back under my bed. I pull it out and feel immediate relief just touching the cool, smooth plastic of the bottles. I stare at them in their line, and their presence quiets that falsetto *"Cuckoo, cuckoo"* that has echoed in my head throughout the day. Riley's laughter. The shock and pity in Michael's eyes. The dark hallway to Room Three. Vanessa's long brown hair. Mom's gray roots.

Everything will be okay, my soldiers tell me. We're here.

5

Oh God. It's Tuesday and Day One at St. Anne's. The waiting room is filled with five other kids—two girls and three boys. No Kristal. Shit. Maybe she dropped out already.

I recognize one of the kids, a boy from grammar and middle school, Thomas Reardon. Everybody called him Lil' Tommy because he was always the tiniest thing, barely reaching the shortest kid's shoulder. Even in middle school, the girls would pick him up and carry him around. He catches my eye and waves. I give a short nod and look away quickly but it's too late. He plants himself in front of me, head tilted up, his Harry Potter–like glasses reflecting the overhead fluorescents.

"Hey, Catherine," Lil' Tommy says. "Funny meeting you here. Ha ha."

Poor kid has grown maybe an inch since eighth grade, so I'm a sumo wrestler next to him. Puberty hasn't laid a hormonal finger on him yet—his face is still downy smooth.

"Hi, Tom," I say.

"First day, right?" he asks. "Nervous? Don't be. This is a really cool group of kids. You at Cranbury High?" Without waiting for a reply, he says, "I'm at St. Joe's."

Smart move for Lil' Tommy to be at the all-boys Catholic high school in New Haven. He would be eaten alive at Cranbury.

The door at the end of the hall swings open and a woman around Mom's age appears on the threshold. She's got on high-waisted mom jeans, possibly bought before they became "in" again, a short-sleeve sweater and flats. Her frizzy blond hair is pulled into a short ponytail. She calls out cheerily, "Hi, everyone! C'mon in!"

Room Three is open for business. My heart thuds heavily in my chest.

We head down the hall and into a large room. As I pass the woman in the doorway, she pats my arm. "Welcome, Catherine. I'm Sandy. I'm a clinician, and I'll be running our group."

Four sofas arranged in a square take up most of the room. There's a large coffee table in the middle, and a long table with a couple of folding chairs hugs the wall with the large picture window. The two girls, after eyeing me warily, snag one of the sofas. Lil' Tommy and the two other boys take another sofa. The sofa with a pile of clipboards appears reserved for Sandy. So it's just Catherine Pulaski, stranded like a shipwrecked sailor yet again, on the last island.

"Everyone, let's welcome Catherine to the group,"

Sandy announces as she sits down. "Why don't we all introduce ourselves?"

Lil' Tommy shouts out, "We already know each other! We went to the same grade school and junior high. Right, Catherine?"

I nod and attempt a smile, but my mouth is dry and my lips snag on my teeth.

The stocky Hispanic boy outfitted head to toe in Red Sox gear alongside Lil' Tommy talks next. "I'm John. Hi."

The other boy, a blond stoner in a black hoodie and skinny jeans, gives the bare minimum. "Garrett."

It's the girls' turn. They look at each other and stay silent.

Sandy turns to Thing One and Thing Two. "Is there a problem?" she asks, her tone indicating that no shit will be tolerated in our happy little group.

"Uh," Thing One with the long blond hair starts, "I'm Alexis."

The uglier, scrawny, brown-haired Thing Two stares at me, and I'm amazed at the size of her head. It's ginormous, somehow balanced on a pencil neck that juts out of a huge, thick, long-sleeve sweatshirt. She's a human bobblehead. Finally, she asks, "Did you go to cheerleading camp? For girls starting high school? At Laurelton Park? You're a junior now, right?" Her mouth forms an almost snarl.

"Um . . . yeah," I say. I hated that camp. I didn't even like cheerleading, but Mom had signed me up to get me out of the house, shake me out of my "funk." Grandma had died only a few weeks earlier.

In front of me.

I blink hard. "Do you go to Cranbury?" I ask.

"No, we go to Immaculate Conception," Thing One/ Alexis answers. With something resembling a smile.

Lil' Tommy bursts out laughing. "That never gets old! *Immaculate* conception? Classic organized-religion bullshit!" He sits straight up on the sofa, his little Docksides barely scraping the floor. "Am I right?"

Thing Two snaps at him, "What? You have to tell that same joke like once a week?"

In a surprising show of solidarity with Lil' Tommy, Garrett says, "Good one, little man." He raises his fist for a bump but they stop, fists apart about an inch, and make no contact. An air–fist bump.

Huh. I assumed Garrett the stoner would be too cool to partake of the festivities here inside the four walls of St. Anne's.

Sandy shakes her head. "C'mon, guys. Rule number one—*respect!*"

Alexis makes eye contact with me, smiles and points to her ridiculous sweatpants, the ones with the word PINK emblazoned across the ass. "We change out of our uniform before we come here."

Thing Two, aka Bobblehead, stays silent in her sweats.

"We go to Cranbury," John volunteers, adjusting his Sox cap. "Me and Garrett. I'm a sophomore and Garrett's a senior."

I nod while simultaneously launching a silent prayer: *Please, God, let us never run into each other at school.*

Garrett slides down the sofa as he stretches out his legs, his hood falling farther over his head. "You catch a ride here or something?"

"My mother drives me," I say.

Sandy pops to her feet, clipboards in hand. "All right, let's get to the diary cards." She passes out the clipboards; when she gets to me, I see a manila folder with my name on it. "Let me know if you have any questions about it, Catherine," Sandy says. "These are not shared with the group. Vanessa reviews it and follows up with you in her office if you want to discuss anything."

Everyone is opening their manila folder and getting poised to write with the pen from the clipboard. Inside my folder is a sheet of paper mysteriously titled "DBT Diary Card." I still have no idea what DBT stands for. Don't Bullshit Them? The paper has a grid with the days of the week running across the top and a list of ten emotions ranging from "angry/irritable" to "good/happy" down the left column. We're supposed to fill in how we feel for each emotion using a number scale (0 = extremely low; 9 = very high). I'm a pro at fraudulent reporting, having all that excellent practice with Mom every night. I fill in a six and a seven on the two positive emotions and for the negative ones (like "empty/alone," "disconnected/unreal" and the tricky "ambivalent"), I score them low—ones or twos.

Catherine Pulaski is doing swell according to her DBT Diary Card.

On the bottom of the sheet, it's fill-in-the-blank time for the phrase: "Today I felt an urge to . . ." This box is a

47

little more serious because it wants the number of times you thought about self-harm and the number of times you acted on those thoughts. It also asks for the stats on your drinking, drug use, bingeing and purging, or "other" (you fill in the blank with your own personal poison). The final question asks whether you need to speak to a clinician today and provides a yes-or-no check box. I fill in all zeros, of course, and check "no" on the speaking to anyone.

Me and my shoe box troops are just fine, thank you very much.

Sandy collects the forms and Vanessa walks in. Her hair is pulled into a gorgeous high pony and she's got on capris and a cute sleeveless shirt. After a friendly hello, she grabs our folders. The boys' eyes follow her as she glides out the door.

Sandy sits back on the sofa, crossing her legs. "Okay, today's topic is bullying. Have you been targeted? What happened? How did you handle it?"

Lil' Tommy immediately raises his hand. "Can I start? Okay, you guys all know that I get picked on for my size." The sofa crew nods sympathetically and Lil' Tommy continues, "So today, I'm in the boys' room, you know, doing my thing. Scrubbing away. It's right before lunch, no big deal. People are supposed to wash their hands before lunch, right? So this big asshole comes up to me and starts cursing that I'm taking too long, what's my problem, lunch is gonna be over by the time I'm done, the other sink's broke, whatever. And then"—Lil' Tommy's voice cracks and his eyes water—"the fucker picks me up—*picks me up*—and moves me aside. I wasn't even finished!"

Sympathetic murmurs come from the girls and John shakes his head while Garrett growls, "Asshole. Sorry about that, dude."

"How did you feel, Tom?" Sandy asks slowly. "When he did that?"

I want to say, "Duh, Sandy, how do you think he felt?" but Tommy answers like it's a valid question.

"Like complete shit," he says, his hands rubbing the tops of his thighs over and over. "Worthless. I . . . I missed lunch. It took me so long to finish washing my hands."

Tommy must be OCD, probably with a germ phobia, if that air–fist bump with Garrett means anything. Tommy's little-kid hands are bright red, chapped and raw from the relentless onslaught of soap and hot water. I should've recognized it before. My roommate in the hospital had OCD.

"That's rough," Sandy says. "I understand how upsetting that was for you. I'm sorry that happened."

And then, starting with John and traveling around the circle, everyone says to Tommy, "I'm sorry that happened," or some other version of it. I say, "I'm sorry, Tom."

Tommy nods, already recovering his composure. His hands stop their nervous travel up and down his legs. "Thanks, guys."

"I want to get to anyone else who wants to share, but first let's talk about Tom's situation," Sandy says. "Any suggestions on how to handle it? How to avoid it or defuse it?"

Just then, the door swings open. It's Kristal. Looking stunning in a miniskirt, copper metallic flats and belted tank top. I feel sloppy in my denim shorts and T-shirt from Old Navy. Kristal shakes her head and mumbles, "Sorry." Then

49

she sees me on the sofa and makes a beeline straight to the empty spot beside me. The ten silver bangles on her wrist sing noisily as she sits. "Hey," she whispers. "You made it."

I'm about to whisper back, "Unfortunately," but Thing Two whines loudly at Kristal, "Group starts at three," as her bobblehead shakes back and forth, threatening to snap her neck.

Kristal snaps, "I'm coming all the way from Chapman. I can't get here any faster."

Chapman. The expensive private school for the area's most elite families. A pipeline to Yale and the other Ivies. It's all the way in Hampton, on the other side of New Haven, a good half hour's drive from here. A girl from my junior high got accepted there and that whole spring of eighth grade she wore only Chapman shirts and sweats. It's a ticket to the good life.

Sandy raises a hand to Thing Two. "That's enough, Amy," she says. "If you have an issue, you'll need to say it in terms of how *you* feel, okay? No attacks. This is a safe zone." Sandy turns to Kristal. "Welcome, Kristal. We're glad you're here."

And as with our apologies to Tom, we go around the circle like pre-K robots and say hi or hello to Kristal. Unaware that we met yesterday, Sandy makes a point of introducing me to Kristal. When it's Thing Two's turn, she says, "I'm sorry. It's just that when you . . . *I* sort of lose focus when you . . . when people come in late." Her huge head dips down as if that neck is getting fatigued. "It, like, disrupts stuff."

Kristal nods and asks Thing Two defiantly, "What's your name again?"

Thing Two takes a second, sizing up the room's altered dynamic now that Kristal is here, realizing that maybe she'll be dislodged from the alpha girl spot. Then she says, "I'm Amy."

Kristal says, "Well, I'd hate to disrupt *Amy's* therapy. Maybe I shouldn't come here. I doubt I can make it any earlier." And it's clear she likes this idea because a smile spreads across her face. She catches my eye and winks.

Sandy shakes her head. "We'll work something out, Kristal. We want you here. Now, we were discussing an incident that happened to Tom today." Sandy gives a quick summary of Tommy's bodily ejection from the restroom sink. What follows is a free-for-all of advice coming from Garrett, John and the Immaculate Conception girls that ranges from bringing a bigger bottle of Purell to finding a new bathroom.

I offer nothing. After about ten minutes of this bathroom-crisis summit, Kristal asks Tommy, exactly how long does it take you to wash your hands? Tommy ponders that and answers, if it's just before a meal or something, maybe ten, fifteen minutes. Kristal then asks, does it ever take you longer than that?

Lil' Tommy's feet beat a pattern against the sofa as he answers, "Only after I . . . um . . . do my man thing." He gives a naughty smile. "Hey, sorry, but a man's got his needs. We're supposed to be honest here, right?"

The room explodes with laughter, shouts of "TMI"

from Amy and Alexis and air–high fives between the boys. Kristal turns to me, the stunned grin on her face matching my own. Then her warm hand is on my wrist, squeezing it as she whispers, "Fucking A, Cat. Fucking A."

Only to me.

6

Michael waits outside my locker Wednesday morning holding a sheet of paper in his hand. He's wearing baggy black shorts, a Nike T-shirt, tennis sneakers and a baseball hat with the brim facing forward. His neck is bright red.

I'm in a crappy mood. For the first time since Grandma died I think, Mom started in on what I was wearing. "You are not wearing those shorts for the fourth day in a row," she had snipped at breakfast. I denied it, but she actually yelled back that I had worn them to church on Sunday, and school on Monday and Tuesday and told me to take them off and put them in the wash.

"Hey, Cath," Michael says, shifting back and forth. "I just wanted to give you what I wrote on Kasia."

I look at him blankly. What the freak is Kasia?

"You know, Jonathan Kasia, the soldier we're doing the biography on?" he asks. "You took off so fast after class yesterday I didn't get a chance to give it to you. And I didn't see you in the cafeteria."

Michael offers the paper to me and I take it. "Thanks," I say, turning my back to him and opening my locker.

"Maybe you can look at it tonight and text me if you want any changes or anything."

I turn suddenly to face him, paranoia kicking in. "How did you know where my locker is?"

Michael points a thumb over his shoulder at the row of lockers opposite mine. "Mine's right there." His brown eyes cloud over with what looks like hurt that I don't know the location of his locker. I guess I should know who's around my locker. I feel bad, but I rarely look up when I'm stuck in this hellhole. I just concentrate on getting to class and avoiding all interaction with the nightmares who dwell here.

"Oh . . . that's right," I say, but Michael looks bummed. So I ask, "Do you want to walk to history?

He nods, a shy smile creeping up. "Sure."

Again, it's odd to have someone beside me in the crowded halls, especially someone who wants to tell me every—and I mean *every*—detail of his quest for a soldier for our project. I tune back in when he announces grandly, "And *then* I found Kasia. I thought *you'd* especially like him."

Was Jonathan Kasia crazy too? I want to ask. "Why?" I ask instead.

"Didn't you read about his mom?" he asks, his eyebrows arching in surprise.

"I . . . I'm drawing a blank," I mumble. "Sorry."

"Kasia's mother was Polish. She ran a Polish bakery in Waterbury," Michael says triumphantly.

I stare at him. I have not a clue where he's headed with this one.

"You're Polish, right? Pulaski? Is your dad Polish?" he asks as we enter the classroom.

Ah yes, my father. Or, the man who merely stayed around long enough to get Jody Pulaski pregnant. Mom was twenty-three, he was nineteen. They dated up until it was confirmed I was growing like a mutant seed inside her. And then he left. To this day, I still don't know who he is, because Mom won't give it up.

My grandfather had just died and Grandma was living by herself when Mom got pregnant. With no other kids besides Mom, Grandma swooped in and took over. Mom moved back to her childhood home, a small Cape with two sloped-ceiling bedrooms upstairs. Grandma kept hers, and Mom and I shared the other. At some point, the dining room was converted into Grandma's bedroom so that I could have my own room.

"C'mon, c'mon, let's get seated," Mr. Oleck barks from his desk. He's wearing a pink bow tie with his pressed white button-down today. "Got a ton to cover."

"Bye, Cath," Michael says.

I give Michael a slight nod as he heads to the other side of the classroom. My seat is the second from the front, one row in from the left. Louis Farricelli is spread-eagled in the desk behind mine, leering as I approach. I slide into my seat.

"Those shorts are hot," he whispers in my ear, lofting a

nauseating garlic cloud around my head. "I'm getting hard right now."

Of course the pig would like them. They're about two sizes too small. I send a silent, sarcastic thank-you to Mom for making me change this morning.

I scoot my desk up, trying to get away from him. I could ask Mr. Oleck to switch my seat, but the risk that I'd be closer to Riley or Olivia is too great. Sucking it up and sitting near Louis Farricelli is the lesser evil here.

"Hey, crazy, don't run away," Louis breathes into my neck. "I'm not gonna bite unless you want—"

"Mr. Farricelli, is there a problem?" Mr. Oleck walks over. Despite the bow tie, Mr. Oleck is pretty tall and stocky. He's also the JV wrestling coach. Looming over Louis, he says, "Push your desk back and keep it there, got it? If it moves an inch, you've got detention."

"Not a problem, Mr. Oleck," Louis says smoothly. "Just chatting with . . . Cathy here. Sorry."

Mr. Oleck strides back to the lectern. "Okay, before we get started on the new chapter, a couple of housekeeping things about the D-day biography project. On Monday, I want a preliminary list of sources—both primary and secondary—on your soldier." Somebody groans from the back of the class. "You don't have to do any legwork. I just want you to begin compiling your sources so we can start figuring out logistics—who needs to go where, how many of you, et cetera. I spoke to the history chairperson yesterday. We're going big with this, you guys." Mr. Oleck strides up and down the aisles, his voice rising. "We're going to do a blog. The local and online papers are going to carry it. Each week there'll be a new installment with one of your bios featured. Maybe some of you can submit to some World War Two periodicals."

The rest of the day passes without too much pain. At lunch, one of the librarians, Mrs. Markman, stops by my cubby to say hello. I like her because she never gives me any grief about eating in here, just checks in, asks if I'm reading anything good. I'm not, even though I spent the past summer volunteering at the Cranbury Public Library. Mom insisted, desperate to fill up the empty, friendless hours of my long summer days. I was waist-deep in books Monday through Friday at the end of July and all of August, my fingers constantly grasping the smooth, slick covers as I reshelved the books and arranged the "Hot Arrivals" on the display tables at the entrance. But I have a hard time reading—I'm too nervous to lose myself in a story again.

It stems back to a year ago, September of sophomore year. "The Lithium Incident." Spurred on, at least in part, by a book. After that, I self-imposed a book ban that I know is stupid because there are a gazillion different books out there. But it's just the way it is now. The new, curtailed normal of my bipolar life. Like no unchaperoned Internet access, no driver's license, no plans to take the SATs because college is not an option. I won't even bring that up with Mom. If she won't let me drive, there's no way she'll let me leave the house. Attempt to live on my own? Not in this lifetime. So, no reading turns out to be one of the less dramatic prohibited activities for Catherine Pulaski.

7

The book was *The Perks of Being a Wallflower*. Old Dr. A had recommended it during our appointment on a Friday, just one week before my sixteenth birthday. I was sitting on the sofa in his office, the warm September sun making me sweat. The same tired sofa I had sat on for the past year.

"You should read this," Dr. A had said, smoothing back some lank gray strands of hair from his lined forehead. "The main character's got some issues, but it's really uplifting. Has a positive message." True to form, he spaced out for a few seconds and then refocused. "Oh yeah. Hermione was in the movie. You know, from Harry Potter?"

I had actually heard of the book already, and I wasn't interested in reading some bullshit story of teenage psychiatric angst, some la-la feel-good crap. But I'm a good girl, manners-wise, and I couldn't say no when Dr. A slid the book across his desk.

"My granddaughter gave it to me," he said. "Go ahead. Tell me what you think of it."

At home, I read the first page and was hooked. I got the main character, Charlie. He felt so real to me in his confusion over why he was the way he was—different. In how he related to other kids, how he saw the world, how things affected him, how he felt. And in his isolation. I breathed isolation too. Charlie had entered high school without a friend, and my friends were defecting throughout my freshman year and following summer.

So that Friday, I couldn't put *Perks* down. I was halfway done that night and Mom was thrilled to see me *doing* something and not just going through the motions. And the next day, that first Saturday of sophomore year, I sat on our living room sofa fully engrossed in the story and Mom left for her shift at Dominic's with a lighter heart.

I tore through the book until the end, when it was revealed *why* Charlie was the way he was. There was a reason. An objective fact. An event. A fucking *incident* that had skewed the way his brain and psyche had evolved.

That crushed me, because I had connected with Charlie. I had recognized myself in him, but then everything changed. Because an event was the origin of Charlie's problems, his healthy mind reacting to a bad thing, it meant we were no longer the same. He was an innocent victim.

But me? Nothing had *happened* to me. I was born with a defective mind. As my father's sole contribution to my life knifed its way into my mother's egg, it unleashed a faulty genetic code that warped the normal brain development of fetus me, growing wrong inside my mother.

I was a thing that should never have been.

The book slipped from my fingers to the floor. I remember feeling bewildered at first. And then betrayed.

Charlie's friends had liked his oddness, valued the quirkiness and perception that his abnormal mental state had spawned. They had *embraced* him while he was hospitalized. Charlie emerged from the psych hospital straight into the arms of his large, loving family, his friends and teachers all ready to gently cradle him back to life.

That's not how it works.

Friends run. My friends had run.

Olivia, Riley and I had still been texting sporadically that summer. They typed quick, three-word courtesy responses to my more lengthy overtures. The past week, Mom insisted I invite them to the dude ranch in upstate New York she and Aunt D had planned on taking me to celebrate my birthday. But neither one responded. Years of best-friendness, sisterhood, reduced to a complete communication blackout.

I lied to Mom. I told her they really wanted to come but had stuff going on. That the three of us were going to celebrate my big sixteenth, we just had to get around to planning it. This soothed Mom, and she threw herself into scheduling horseback riding, skeet shooting and spa treatments.

So on that first Saturday in September, my new reality sunk in. And it was nothing like *The Perks of Being a Wallflower*. Friends evacuate. They don't want a trace of fucked-up you or your birthday on their hands. The most profound loneliness takes up residence in your gut. The house is screamingly silent, absent of grandmother or friends. And it doesn't get better.

The grief finally filleted me, tearing vents in my head and skin to let Zero in. And in he rushed, capsizing me. I recognized him then as that emptiness, that nothingness, that absolute wasteland. And I understood his permanence.

It suddenly became clear then. There was only one way to end it.

Only one way.

I rose from the sofa and neatly folded Grandma's blue afghan. I took the paperback to the bookcase in my room and inserted it into the binder of that other work of fiction, my kindergarten "All About Me" book.

There was a roaring in my head, a white noise that blotted everything else out, even my own heartbeat. I walked slowly back down the stairs, my hand skimming the wooden banister, and entered the living room. It seemed like the house knew. The air stilled as I cut through the rooms, the molecules ceasing their manic movement around my body; I was already dead.

In the kitchen, I swallowed my fresh, full, amber-colored bottle of Catherine Pulaski's lithium and my half-empty bottle of Prozac. Then I rode on waves of NyQuil to that place of peace that smelled of Yardley English Lavender.

Inside Grandma's room, the silence stopped its screeching. Grandma's sheets were cool as I lay down. I hugged her yellow afghan and apologized to my body for any pain it would have. It had always been good to me, allowing me to dance when my brain had functioned. I asked the extra-large crucified Jesus to forgive me. And then I closed my eyes and waited for Grandma.

But she never came.

My lithium/Prozac/NyQuil cocktail began to circulate through my veins, bringing a sleepy haze and stomach pains that curled me into the fetal position. Then Mom was there, shaking me and screaming. I vaguely remember tears streaming down Aunt Darlene's cheeks and paramedics hoisting my stretcher roughly into the ambulance. Then bright lights and IVs and monitors beeping and people in green scrubs and masks asking, shouting, "Catherine, can you hear me?"

"Catherine, what did you take?"

And that was that.

8

It's Friday afternoon and Mom is late again. It's already 2:55 and she's not picking up her phone. How hard is it to leave at 2:15 each day? It's not like she's doing brain surgery. Cath, she said yesterday, it's not that easy. There's always something going on, a closing, a client meeting, a deposition. I'm the only secretary in the office.

Tonight's football game is away, so the front of the school emptied out quickly. All decked out in a shirt and tie today, Louis Farricelli was too distracted by groupie drool to harass me much. A lone school bus enters the driveway and stops at the curb in front of the school, completely blocking my view. A hand shoots out a window and waves in my direction, but it's clearly not for me. I ignore it and walk to the rear of the bus so I can watch for Mom on the curb.

"Catherine!" a male voice calls.

I stiffen defensively until I see that it's Michael, with a shorter kid in tow.

"Hey!" He walks up, smiling shyly. He turns to the kid beside him. "This is my friend, Tyler."

"Hi," Tyler says, quickly looking at me but then shifting his gaze to just over my shoulder.

A lot of kids who know my history act like this. No real contact, just vague, distanced comments. They avoid meeting my eyes. As if what I have can be passed to them by a mere verbal exchange. They're the nice ones.

But I'm not getting that sense from Tyler. Because Tyler is tagged. Like me. There's not one centimeter of clear skin on his face. It's the worst case of acne I've ever seen. His face has been attacked, *invaded,* by fat, angry red welts topped with ripe whiteheads that stretch from chin to forehead. The onslaught continues past the border of his blond hair and onto his scalp. The only peaceful zones are the white circles of skin surrounding his blue eyes.

"Hi," I say.

I get Michael now. He's a fixer—one of those people who likes to collect the wounded and heal them. I feel myself unclench even more. I think Michael's safe and not looking to publicly embarrass me. At this point, I'll take being someone's project versus their target. Something like relief flows through me.

Michael smiles full-on at me and looks surprisingly cute. I return him to the number one candidate spot in the L.V. sweepstakes. "Ty's the one I sawed in half at the talent show," he says. "Remember?"

"Oh yeah!" I smile back. It's his eyes. The way Michael looks at me. Could that be bona fide interest instead of just Good Samaritan–ness? "Your act was great," I add.

"You're a good dancer," Tyler says to my right ear.

"Thanks," I say. And then, "But I don't dance anymore."

"That's too bad," Tyler says, now studying his sneakers.

"Headed to work?" Michael asks me.

"Um." Brain freeze. Shit. I told him I had an after-school job. "Yeah. I help out at the law firm my mother works at," I lie again. "Just filing and copying stuff. Nothing major. I'm just waiting for her."

"Cool," Michael says. "So, uh . . ." His neck sprouts red patches near the collar of his T-shirt that blossom upward along his neck. "Since you're busy after school during the week, do you want to meet tomorrow at Starbucks? Or the Cranbury library? Not too long. Just try to bang out that list of sources? It's due on Monday."

"Umm . . ." The Accord rounds the wide curve to the front doors of the school, barreling toward us. I'm suddenly nervous to meet Michael. I haven't done anything with a kid my own age in almost two years. Since that freshman-year talent show.

Michael studies me. "My mom could give you a ride," he says. "I have my license, but I still can only drive my family."

In Connecticut, you can get your license at sixteen and a half, but you can't drive your friends around until you've had it for at full year. Which is a nonissue for me, given the lack of both a license and friends.

"No," I say quickly. "That's okay. My mom doesn't work until later in the afternoon. She can take me."

"Okay, how's one-thirty?"

I swallow. "Sure. Let's meet at the library." This is just in case Mom can't drive. The library is close enough for me to walk to.

"It's a plan." He smiles broadly. He doesn't say anything else; he just looks down at me like we've accomplished something great. Tyler elbows him, jolting him out of his triumph. "Okay, Cath, see you tomorrow," Michael says. "Let's meet on the front steps?"

"Yeah. See you then. Nice to meet you, Tyler."

In the car, Mom gives a restrained hi, but happiness oozes out of her. Her little Catherine was talking to not one, ladies and gentlemen, but two, count 'em, *two* new friends! Mom sits erect in the driver's seat, her fingers tapping in time to a Bonnie Raitt song. It's always Bonnie Raitt. The eject button broke and that CD has been held hostage for the past two years.

Through her barely suppressed smile, Mom babbles excuses for picking me up at 2:55. "Cath, I'm sorry. It was a closing from hell. They're still waiting for the bank to wire the funds. They weren't going to let me leave. Are you sure you don't want to take the van?" she asks, before quickly retracting that question. "No, no, that's okay." She shakes her head. "I'm giving them an extra unpaid hour for this arrangement," she says, speeding past the strip mall. "And Aunt Darlene will pick you up tonight. I'm headed straight to Dominic's after work."

I despise arriving late to anything and I know Amy will probably say something snarky, but the anger that I would normally feel is surprisingly absent. Maybe it's because I have plans for tomorrow. With Michael. The number one (and only) candidate for L.V. Could he be the one I connect with? The boy who holds me so tight it's impossible to get any closer?

This thought soothes me. As we race into the parking lot, I realize I'm not dreading St. Anne's anymore. It's not quite as hellish as I expected. On Wednesday, Sandy continued the bullying discussion. Lil' Tommy advised us that the school nurse is letting him use one of the bathrooms in her office to wash his hands. John, still in the Red Sox gear, wanted to talk about his wrestling teammates and how they were all over him last year to cut weight for matches. His supportive buddies had pushed puking, laxatives, extended sauna visits and spitting (I had never heard of that one—just constant spitting into a Gatorade bottle), all of which had kick-started his bulimia. Kristal managed to arrive on time and chose to sit next to me on Wednesday and Thursday, even though spots on the other sofas were still open.

Kristal is recovering from an eating disorder. I learned this when she told John her strategy for handling her "touch of bulimia." Kristal said, "Every time I was stressing, about school or my weight or something with my friends, and I wanted to just slam everything down my throat, I would just say fuck it. Fuck it. Two little words. Simple yet effective. I'm telling you, you've got to try it."

Yesterday, Garrett ran the discussion on drugs. Garrett volunteered that he's on probation for selling his Adderall to finance a pot habit. He even sold to a few of John's wrestling teammates for weight loss. I still haven't said a word, but Sandy hasn't pushed me with any dumb comments like "Why don't we hear what Catherine has to say?"

The Immaculate Conception girls and Kristal are absent today. Alexis and Amy are off at some retreat, and Kristal is headed to Boston for freshman parents' weekend at her brother's college. So Sandy returns to bullying. "Today I'd like for us to discuss how we handle bullies. John and Tom have told us their experiences, and Tom has found a way to avoid confrontations, but what can John try? Any thoughts on how he can handle the upcoming wrestling season?"

"Yeah, take up swimming!" Tommy shouts.

I stay quiet. I have no advice on this practice of cutting weight. When I was dancing I never had to worry about weight like Riley and some other girls did. But at break time, while Garrett and Lil' Tommy chow down on chocolate-covered raisins, John ventures up to my sofa and sits down next to me. He asks me what I think of the IOP so far. And it's weird because I feel surprisingly okay talking to him. It's like the public knowledge inside these four walls that we are all damaged in some way liberates me. And while I don't feel I can speak completely unguarded to John, for at least three hours a day, five days a week, I do feel a lot of the layer of shame slipping away.

Aunt Darlene is waiting for me after the session, her red Mini Cooper illegally parked in a handicap space directly in front of the door. Aunt Darlene isn't my real aunt; she's my mom's best friend since high school. She never married. Her parents bought a Dunkin' Donuts back when no one had ever heard of the chain around here, and now Aunt D owns and manages a small empire of them in Cranbury and the surrounding towns.

Inside the car, we run the same affectionate Friday-night dialogue, our lines perfected over the previous forty consecutive Friday nights that Aunt D has babysat me while Mom works at Dominic's. I slide into the front passenger seat and Aunt D bear-hugs me ferociously. "Hey, baby! How are you?"

Kissing her on the cheek, I disentangle myself. "Fine."

Aunt D gives me her usual appraisal, beaming like perfect Kate Middleton is beside her. "Ready to eat? I'm starving!"

"You can just take me home. You don't have to hang out with me tonight. I'm fine."

Aunt D puts the car in reverse. "I know you're fine. But who else am I gonna hang out with? My cats?" She backs up and drives out of the parking lot. The interior of the Mini Cooper is permanently infused with vanilla and coffee. It's delicious. I take a deep breath as my faux aunt turns to me with her trademark grin. "How does Mexican sound?"

The house is still and dark when Aunt Darlene drops me off. Mom forgot to leave the lamp on for me this morning.

After the music and crowds at Casa de Amigos, the silence presses on my ears. Flipping on the living room lights, I take the to-go burrito Aunt D ordered for Mom and put it in the fridge.

I text Mom that I'm home, and two minutes later she replies: "Should be home by 10. Hopefully earlier. Slow nite here. Xoxo" followed immediately by "Please don't forget ur pill. Call me asap if u see a rash."

One lone Lamictal lies on the counter next to an empty glass. I promised Aunt D I'd take it, and surprisingly, she agreed not to come inside this time to witness it for Mom. I palm the tan pill and head upstairs. Pulling out the shoe box, I line the troops up on my night table. I open the Lexapro bottle and drop today's Lamictal inside it. It's slightly OCD, but I like to keep the *L*'s together. I lie back on my white down comforter, drowsy from my enchilada and fried ice cream. My bed feels good.

A choo from my phone startles me, and I realize I fell asleep. I'm having a much easier time falling asleep lately, but now is definitely not the time I want to do it.

Shit.

I bolt out of bed, heart slamming against my rib cage. The troops are still out in the open and it's 9:51 p.m. Michael's text woke me, thank God. Mom's not home yet. Ignoring the text, I toss the troops into the shoe box, cover them up and hustle downstairs to Grandma's room. I can't take that chance tonight, leaving them in my room with Mom prowling around all weekend. In the darkness, I whip the plastic box out from under Grandma's bed and struggle with the zipper on the old plaid suitcase. I'm sweating. Every little sound could be the key in the front door.

I tuck the troops inside the suitcase, slide everything back into place and fix the bed skirt. Shaking, I rest my head on Grandma's favorite yellow afghan. I burrow my nose into it, seeking her scent, the Yardley English Lavender we could never find in a store, only online. She'd always ask the salesclerks at Kohl's why they didn't carry it. My throat tightens. I'm tired. Tired of being scared. Tired of this life. I want to go back to when Grandma was alive and I was okay. It's too hard for me now. I start to cry.

Where are you, Grandma?

No answer.

9

Michael sits next to me at a scarred wooden table in the first-floor reading room. This is where I spent most of my summer volunteer time, and I note, a little smugly, that whoever's doing the "Hot Arrivals" display doesn't have my artistic touch. This is my favorite room in the Cranbury Public Library, large but still cozy, with a beamed ceiling, fireplace and scattered Oriental rugs. High shelves of DVDs, audiobooks and magazines give most of the tables privacy, but Michael dumped his backpack on a table right in the center, so we're in plain sight of everybody entering the room this Saturday afternoon. Octogenarian Gary, one of my fellow volunteers, gave a wobbly thumbs-up when he spotted me from behind the circulation desk.

Flipping open his laptop, Michael logs on to the library's Wi-Fi. He glances at his phone to read a new text. "My mom said it's no problem to drive you home."

I smile politely. But inside I'm furious with Mom.

Michael jogged up to the Accord as Mom and I pulled up to the curb, and before I could shut the door behind me, Mom had already called out hello to him. Michael bent down to speak with her through the passenger-side window.

"I'm sorry for changing the time today," he said. That was his text to me last night, the one that woke me up and saved me and my troops from discovery. He had texted that he had to meet at two today and not one-thirty, like we originally planned. "I can give Catherine a ride home if you're leaving for work," he told Mom, unknowingly touching a live wire.

A short battle between Mom and me had erupted this morning, with Mom wanting to call Aunt D to pick me up from the library and me begging to walk the two miles home.

Ignoring the terms of the treaty we had agreed upon (I could walk but needed to text her every five seconds), Mom jumped on Michael's offer to drive me home. "Oh, that would be great! Thanks, Michael. And please tell your mom I appreciate it," she said, not even checking with me to see if that was okay, if I wanted to drive home with Michael and his mother—which I definitely did not. I turned my back on her and started up the steps. I heard her yell, "Cath, hon, I'll be home around seven. See you then!"

I didn't turn around. Instead I hurried up the stone steps away from her.

Michael had bounded up the steps in front of me,

stopping in front of the ornately carved door more fitting for a church than a library. He smiled at me, the sun catching and highlighting the chocolate-brown of his eyes.

"You even run gracefully," he said.

This threw me. "What are you talking about?"

"You run like this." Michael stuck both arms out perpendicular to his body, his long fingers pointing up to the sky, and flapped. He resembled a turkey, a not very graceful one, and a laugh burst out of me.

"Can you still do those turns? The ones where you spin on one leg and the other leg twirls you around?" he asked.

"A fouetté turn?"

"Uh . . . I don't know. Why don't you do one here?"

I laughed again. "Here? On top of the library steps? I don't think so."

"Well, that's my goal, then," Michael said, pulling open the door. "To get you to do a *fwetay* turn for me."

"Good luck with that," I said, still laughing at the image of me doing one in front of the library's double doors. What if Riley or Dr. McCallum drove by at that very instant? Jesus.

Now Michael opens a Word document on his laptop. "Here's our list of primary and secondary sources so far. I thought you could take a look at them, see if they're good. And then maybe we can check out what they have in the history section downstairs."

"Sounds good." I can't in good conscience let this guy do all the work. It doesn't feel right anymore. Even if the odds of me seeing this project completed are basically nil. So instead of just eyeballing the sites and sources, I grab a couple of sheets of paper and a pen from my bag.

"Is this where you work?" Michael asks, picking up a sheet of my scrap paper with the embossed letterhead. The thick, expensive paper is from Mom's law firm. The printers not only got the zip and area codes wrong but also made gross errors in spelling—"The Law Offices of Hefferman & Schletz" morphed into the cheesier "Hosserman & Schlitz." Mom rescued the boxes of rejected stationery dumped next to the office garbage cans and brought them home. We use this whenever we can to conserve my school loose-leaf.

I nod in response to Michael's question about my fictitious employer and then turn to the computer screen. Michael did a great job with "our" sources. There are three books by local authors on Jonathan Kasia, and a couple of websites highlighting the annual parade, the baseball field in his honor and the statue of him on the Waterbury Green. Michael also listed two non-Kasia names with Waterbury addresses.

"What are these?" I ask, tapping my pen on the names.

"Those are possible Kasia relatives," Michael says proudly. "I used my mom's Ancestry.com account to look them up." He leans forward and says, too loudly in the cavernous room that amplifies every sound, "We can interview them. See if they have any pictures or letters. Maybe there's an old uniform up in the attic? Wouldn't that be cool? I found some phone numbers. We should try calling them later, okay?"

A timely shush comes from Gary. He winks at us as he puts a finger to his lips. Michael flushes guiltily, so I distract him with a suggestion that we check out the books in the history section to fatten our bibliography. On the library's research computer, I find a couple of books on Normandy and write down their call numbers on my Hosserman and Schlitz letterhead.

"How do you know how to do that so fast?" Michael asks, pointing to the computer screen with the research results.

"I volunteered here during the summer," I say. "I had to help out with research sometimes."

"Wow, Cath," he says, looking at me with a scaled-down version of awe. "So you worked here in the summer and now at the law firm? Impressive."

His comments make me feel sweet and sour, because one part of my résumé is the truth and the other is a defensive lie. I wish I had never told him about the law firm. I wish I didn't have to.

We're the only two people downstairs in the dusty history stacks. Michael reads out the call numbers as I hunt the shelves. I'm taking the last book off the shelf when I get a mother of a paper cut.

"Ow!" I cry out before popping my right index finger in my mouth. I hate these little lightning strikes of pain.

Ever the do-gooder, Michael says, "Don't worry. I've got a Band-Aid on me. You really shouldn't put it in your mouth." He crouches down and rifles through the small pocket on the outside of his backpack. "Here it is," he says, a small ziplock bag swinging in his hand. It has Band-Aids and, dear Lord, a tube of Neosporin. This makes me laugh. Out loud. For like the third time today.

"Wow. You're prepared," I say.

"Here." Michael has ripped open a Band-Aid and squeezed a dot of Neosporin onto it. "This has got a pain-killer in it. Paper cuts are the worst." He looks away as he holds the Band-Aid out for me. "Sorry. I am not good with blood."

I bandage up my finger. "Thanks."

He's gone a little pale.

"Let's sit down for a sec," I suggest. "Look at these books."

Michael nods and slides his back slowly along the wall to the floor, where he lands Indian-style.

"Do you need some water?" I ask. "Or I can wet a paper towel and you can put it on your neck?"

Somehow, I've morphed into my forty-year-old mother.

He closes his eyes, leans his head against the wall and smiles. "No, I need a stronger stomach. I don't know how to get over this. It's gotten worse since that anatomy class."

"There wasn't any red stuff," I say. "No worries."

His eyes remain shut but his smile grows bigger. "I think you might be lying about that, but thank you." And then, as if he forgot his manners, he sits upright, eyes snapping open. "How's your finger?"

His concern over my lousy little paper cut gets to me somehow. A wave of feeling rises inside me that's unfamiliar but good. I can't identify the emotion.

"It's fine," I say.

Suddenly, I have no doubt. My first and last connection will be Michael. He is kind and gentle. Safe. I feel so grateful that he appeared in my life like a parting gift. Just in the nick of time. My clock is running down, and I have no idea when the buzzer will sound, but I know that I *have* to do this. I have to have my first and last connection, before Zero drives me off. And now I don't need to search for an L.V. candidate. I've found him. He is sitting right here, two feet away, and smiling at me like I'm healthy. I feel my lips turn up, returning the smile. What would his arms feel like around me, pulling me close?

Unexpectedly, a riptide of loss courses through me, shattering the moment. What might there have been with this boy, if I were normal?

"I'm . . . lucky you had your first-aid kit," I say, battling the sudden flare-up of Zero anxiety. Of grief taking small bites out of me.

"My mom packed it. I think she hopes that if the catastrophe strikes—you know, like me getting a cut—I'll slam a Band-Aid on it and lessen my chances of fainting."

"Sounds like a good plan," I say.

"I'd rather just get over it," he says.

We waste the rest of the afternoon in the history stacks, Michael telling me in detail his unsuccessful efforts to desensitize himself to the sight of blood.

"I stopped trying once I barfed on my laptop. This is a new one," he says, patting his backpack as the overhead lights blink to inform us of the library's five p.m. closing time.

Listening to Michael talk all afternoon has taken my anxiety down a level, so I'm actually feeling pretty com-

78

fortable sitting next to him in the backseat of his mother's Subaru as we pull away from the library.

"Never call me *Mrs.* Pitoscia," his mom is saying. "That is my mother-in-law." She twists to face me in the backseat, to make eye contact with me, to underscore the importance. "I'm Lorraine, okay?" She turns back to the road. "Catherine, I need to make a short pit stop before dropping you off. Won't take more than a minute."

Michael, seated directly behind his mother, glances at me. "Why, Ma?" he asks.

"Gotta stop off at home first. Nonny needs garlic," Lorraine says quickly. "She's making gravy and she said the garlic went bad. She can't do the gravy without the garlic."

Michael leans forward slightly. "Let's just take Catherine home first."

"Michael, she texted me four times already," Lorraine says. "I could kill your father for teaching her how." Lorraine angles her head toward me, explaining. "My Italian mother-in-law refuses to speak English correctly but texts like a twelve-year-old. Look, I'll just get out of the car and run it inside. Won't take more than thirty seconds."

Michael looks over at me and shakes his head. "Sorry, Cath."

"No problem," I say. I'd like to see where Michael lives.

Lorraine weaves the Subaru around the Green, past the restaurants and "shoppes" and Rodrick's on the Green, the site of my long-hair execution. We drive in the direction of the Long Island Sound, where the houses and the egos of their occupants grow bigger as the water gets closer.

Lorraine turns onto a street where identical colonials with symmetrical driveways line up in perfect precision. It's not a McMansion neighborhood but it's nicer than mine. There are sidewalks on both sides of the street and a community basketball hoop at the end of the cul-de-sac.

"Uh-oh," Lorraine says as she slows down. In the middle of the driveway of a white colonial on our left, an old lady sits on a metal folding chair. Her arms are folded over an enormous mountain of breasts and her spindly legs are crossed at the ankles.

Michael slides a little lower in the seat.

Lorraine sighs and then says in her best Navy SEAL commando voice, "You guys stay put. I'll handle Nonny."

Nonny stands and folds the chair as the Subaru gets closer. Lorraine pulls into the left side of the driveway, closest to the flagstone walkway to the front door. The old lady darts past the driver's-side window, nimbly sidestepping Lorraine's outstretched hand that frantically waves a yellow plastic ShopRite bag. Nonny raps her knuckles hard on Michael's window. She's about as tall as Lil' Tommy.

Michael clicks down his window. "Hey, Nonny."

Nonny sticks her head inside. She's got gray hair pulled into a low knot at her neck, and glasses that must have a solid inch of lens. Behind them, her brown eyes are magnified about ten times, making her appear like a geriatric Powerpuff Girl.

"This your friend, Michael?" she asks, staring unsmiling at me. An enormous gold medal of Jesus or somebody dangles from her neck and through the open window.

Lorraine jumps out of the car and places a hand on Nonny's back. "C'mon, Nonny. Here's the garlic."

Nonny ignores Lorraine.

"Nonny, this is Catherine. We're d-doing a school thing together," Michael says.

Nonny hasn't taken those mega eyes off me. "Where's her hair?"

I stiffen and my hand flies up to my head as Michael exclaims, "Jesus, Nonny!"

Lorraine says, "Nonny, that sounds rude. That's the fashion now. All the movie stars have that style."

Nonny nods and then sticks her head farther into the car. "I got braciole and ravioli and gravy." She taps Michael's chest. "You bring your friend inside."

"Thanks, Nonny, but she's got to get home," Michael says, his face flaming red.

"Well, Michael, why don't you ask Catherine?" Lorraine says, trying to gently pry Nonny away from the car. "If her mom is working, maybe she'd like a quick bite."

That is truly the last thing I want to do. Go through the standard getting-to-know-you drill and all the lying that my life entails. I just don't have the energy right now.

Michael turns to me, sweaty and anxious. "Cath, I'm so sorry about this. I know you probably have stuff to do. I'll get my mom to drive you home now."

Before I can nod yes, my door flies open. It's Nonny, with the brilliant afternoon sun behind her. She looks like an Italian prison matron in a black skirt, white short-sleeve button-down blouse, knee-high panty hose and lace-up shoes. She reaches down and grabs my clenched hand. Her hand is wrinkly and veiny, the skin worn shiny smooth. But it's warm and strong.

Like Grandma's hand.

Nonny works my fist open. "C'mon. I got icebox cake," she says, those eyes boring into mine.

I get out of the car.

10

The kitchen table is set for six. Foil-wrapped dishes, a long loaf of Italian bread and a plate of olives and cheese crowd together tightly in the center of the red tablecloth. On the stove, tomato sauce bubbles in a pot so big you could wash a small child in it. It smells divine in here, better than the kitchen at Dominic's. My stomach roars.

Michael is a nervous wreck. "Uh, Cath, you can sit anywhere," he says, weakly waving a hand toward the table. Then he turns on Nonny, who's donned an apron and stands on tiptoe stirring the pot on the stove. "I thought you couldn't make gravy because you needed garlic," he accuses her.

"I'm out of garlic now," she says evasively. "I need it for Sunday dinner tomorrow." Putting the spoon down, she hollers, even though we're all standing two feet from her, "Everybody sit down! We don't wait for the other two.

Let's eat!" Nonny bangs the top of the wooden chair closest to her. "You," she says, looking at me. "Sit here."

I slide into the chair and she pushes me in easily. I say, "Thank you."

Michael grabs a chair opposite me and mouths the words "I'm sorry."

I mouth back at my D-day partner, "It's fine."

And it actually is. Nonny has ripped the aluminum foil off the dishes to reveal a smorgasbord of Italian food. There's ravioli, a bowl of chilled shrimp, a platter of steaming rolled-up beef things and meatballs, a plate of thinly sliced tomatoes wedged between slabs of mozzarella and a bowl of Parmesan cheese, shredded paper-thin.

"You," Nonny says again, her big eyes focused on my face. "You got those allergies? Like Tyler? He can't eat no nuts. Every time he come over, I make sure no nuts. I don't know about you, so I make nothing with nuts."

"I'm not allergic," I say. "But thank you anyway."

"For you," Nonny says, piling my plate high with ravioli, meatballs and one of those rolled-up meat things. She adds shrimp and tomatoes and mozzarella, splashing them quickly with balsamic vinegar.

"This looks great," I say to Nonny as she deposits the heavy plate in front of me. "Thank you."

But she doesn't take a step back. "Go ahead. Try the braciole," she says, pointing to the meat roll-up. "I make it the best."

The beef falls apart under my fork and I can feel her eyes on me as I bring the first bite to my lips. The meat is tender and rolled inside it like a pinwheel is some kind of amazing cheese mixture. "Mmm," I say. "This is awesome."

This might be all I need to do to earn Nonny's approval. She squeezes my shoulder before seating herself in the chair next to me.

"You like dogs?" she asks, deftly inserting a braciole into a hunk of the crusty Italian bread. Before I can answer, Nonny commands, "Michael, go get Mitzi."

"I don't think that's a good idea, Nonny," Michael says, "You know how she is with new—"

He's interrupted by the sound of the front door opening followed by a guy yelling, "Yo, I'm home."

Lorraine yells back, "Anthony, we got dinner on. C'mon and eat."

Heavy footsteps clomp down the hall and a young guy who sort of resembles a shorter, stockier Michael walks into the kitchen and straight to the table, snatching a piece of bread out of the basket.

"Anthony, wash your hands and pull up a chair," Lorraine says. "We got company. This is Catherine, a friend of Michael's from school. Catherine, this is my oldest, Anthony."

Anthony gives me a friendly smile as he half turns to the kitchen stove and dunks his piece of bread into the pot of tomato sauce. "Nice to meet you," he says.

"Anthony, sit down," Nonny barks, while Lorraine starts filling a plate for her son.

Anthony slams the bread into his mouth and shrugs

apologetically while pointing to his grass-stained jeans and filthy green Paoletti's Landscaping T-shirt. "Can't right now," he says with a full mouth. "I gotta shower first. Going out tonight." He swallows and then says proudly, "Did seven houses today. All-time high! I got two hundred twenty bucks just for today. And it'll probably be like that until, like, early December. Chris said once fall cleanup starts, we'll be raking it in."

"I hope your father sees some of that," Nonny mutters.

If Anthony heard Nonny, he ignores her and focuses on me. "So, you a junior like Mike? Go to Cranbury?"

I nod. "Yeah." There's an awkward silence, so I ask, "Did you go there too?"

Anthony drops his eyes to the table and says quickly, "Yeah, graduated a few years ago." He bites off half of his sandwich. "So why do you hang out with Mikey here?" he asks. "I can't stand the kid." He smiles, stuffed mouth and all, and Michael whips a balled-up paper napkin that hits Anthony squarely in the face.

"All right, enough!" Lorraine says. "Anthony, either sit down and eat like a human or go take your shower."

Anthony raises his hands. "Okay, I know how to take a hint."

"It's not a hint, Ant. You reek," Michael says.

"I'm going, I'm going," Anthony says, walking backward out of the kitchen, hands raised in mock surrender. "Catherine, nice to meet you."

Lorraine calls to him, "Anthony, where are you going tonight and who's driving?" Her voice carries an undercurrent of something. Anger? Fear?

Anthony continues down the hall, yelling back, "Hanging out at Rob's. Elliot's driving."

"It's okay." Nonny nods to Lorraine. "Elliot a good boy. An Eagle Scout." From her skirt pocket, Nonny whips out an iPhone cradled in tissue like a gyro sandwich. Peeling back the Kleenex, Nonny pecks at the cell phone. "I'm texting you brother," she tells Michael, eyes glued to the phone screen. "Go . . . get . . . Mitzi."

Michael bursts into laughter. "No, don't do it, Ant!" he yells up at the kitchen ceiling.

Nonny waves at Michael. "She in her crate for over an hour. That's not right."

Lorraine taps Nonny's hand. "Let's not bring Mitzi out yet. I'd hate for her to bite Catherine the first time she's here."

"Oh yeah"—Michael nods emphatically at his mother—"the second time would be just fine." He rolls his eyes at me and a small laugh escapes me.

That may be my what? Fourth? Fifth laugh of the day? It feels good and weird and foreign all at the same time.

"Mitzi just need to warm up, that all. And all she got is one tooth anyhow." Nonny shrugs, apparently sensing defeat. "But nobody don't have to worry. I'm going to my girl." Nonny grabs a small plate and takes two meatballs, one shrimp and one ravioli and dices them up so finely a baby could gum them down. She stands and yells loudly, "Here I come, Mitzi girl!" She then focuses those jumbo eyes on me—she's so short we're just about eye to eye even though I'm sitting and she's standing. "Bye, Michael's friend. I'm going," she says. "I gotta feed my baby. You meet her next time." She walks out of the kitchen bearing the gourmet mush.

Lorraine smiles at me and then shakes her head. "I'm sorry about Nonny. I love my mother-in-law, but she is certifiably crazy."

Certifiably crazy. Her words are lightly said but they slice me, sudden, hard and deep.

And just like that, Zero seeps inside the Pitoscia kitchen and wraps around me, weighing me down and sucking out the color so everything fades to gray. It makes no difference where I am or who I'm with or what I'm doing. I can't escape; I can never forget that I am sick. That my illness will always be a joke for normal people. Or a clever line for a pop song. (Riley used to sing a line from an old song, "Hot N Cold," whenever I walked by: "Got a case of a love bipolar.")

No, Lorraine, I want to say. *I am the crazy one.*

Suddenly I'm exhausted. I want to burrow deep under my soft white comforter and go to sleep.

And never wake up.

Michael's chair screeches loudly as he bolts to his feet. He looks alarmed. He must know a little something about my mental health history because he hurries over to my side. "Hey, Ma, Catherine and I should make a phone call for our project before you drive her home. Is it okay if we do that now? Cath, you up for that?"

I stand. "Um, Lorraine, can I help you clean up?" I ask. Meet Catherine Pulaski, the world's most polite depressed-bipolar dinner guest.

Lorraine shakes her head, unaware of the abrupt deterioration of my mood. "Oh no, sweetie, not necessary. Anthony will eat after his shower and my husband should be home pretty soon. Go ahead and do what you have to do for school."

Michael leads me to the center hallway, its walls covered with annual school portraits of the Pitoscia boys from kindergarten on. He opens the door to the basement. I can feel my phone buzzing through the canvas skin of my backpack. Oh shit. I never texted Mom.

"I just need to check my phone," I mumble to Michael, pausing at the top of the carpeted basement steps. There are four texts from her. The last one, from five minutes ago, reads, "I can pick u up from Michael's. Text me time."

Undoubtedly she has tracked me here with her handy-dandy phone app.

I text, "Come in 10 min"

Mom immediately responds, "See u soon! xoxo"

I say to Michael, "My mom has to pick me up in ten."

He nods grimly. "Should we even try to call those Waterbury people?"

"Sure," I say, and we head downstairs to the finished man cave of a basement.

There's a beat-up sofa facing a ginormous TV that's wired to some kind of gaming system, a Ping-Pong table, darts and a foosball table. We sit down on the huge, squishy sofa. Michael takes out his phone and folder and stares at them for a second before abandoning them on the coffee table. He groans as he leans back heavily against the sofa and runs his hands through his short hair.

"Oh man . . . ," he begins. "Cath, I am so sorry about

tonight. I know you didn't plan on coming over, but then Nonny traps you and makes you stay for dinner." He sighs. "My parents, Nonny, my brother, they're always in my face. Wanting to know everything. And my mother . . ." He doesn't finish his thought. "You probably have had way too much of the Pitoscias today." He shakes his head and squeezes his eyes shut as if to block out the dinner scene. "I bet your mother can't get here fast enough for you."

I know Lorraine meant nothing by her comment about Nonny, but I so get what Michael is feeling. That forced intrusion, well-meaning but constant. Do this. Don't do that. Try it my way. Trust me, it will be better any freaking way but yours.

Seeing Michael almost physically cringing from the memory of the dinner does something to me. Zero's body slam of heaviness lightens.

I tap Michael's bony knee with my bandaged index finger and feel the warmth of his skin radiating through his jeans. "If you think your mother is bad, mine is a thousand times worse," I say. "Don't even worry about it. Nonny is a great cook. It was nice."

Michael studies my face closely to see, I think, if I'm being straight with him. "My mother—" he begins.

Lorraine cuts him off by yelling from the top of the basement steps. "Michael, somebody just pulled up in front of the house. Is that for Catherine?"

Michael rolls his eyes and yells back, "Yeah, it's her mother."

"Oh shit," Lorraine yells, still apparently somewhere

on the first floor. "Cath, honey, we could've brought you home. You didn't have to call."

"It's no problem," I holler.

"Just don't leave without saying good-bye to me. . . ." Lorraine's voice trails off.

I swing my backpack over my shoulder and head for the stairs. Michael follows me.

"Hey, how's the finger?" he asks as I start up the steps.

I stop and turn around. He's only a step behind me so our faces are level, mere inches apart. I'm surprised but I don't move. Neither does Michael. My heart begins to pound as we stare at each other. His pupils are larger now in the dimness of the basement and his lips part slightly in a small smile. His cheeks are flushed and he looks older. His expression changes then, it *opens,* and I know now that he truly likes me, wants me somehow. To heal or to help me, maybe. But that's fine. Because I need him too. This boy will be my first and last connection. Before Zero comes back for me.

I lean forward, placing one hand on his shoulder. Everything moves in slow motion. His eyes widen as I tilt my head and put my lips on his. His lips are so much softer than I could have imagined, and warm. I rest my hand on the back of his neck and feel his skin boiling under my fingers. My heart pounds as Michael presses his mouth against mine and we move closer.

It is amazing. This contact. Strange and exhilarating and delicious. So much better than my one other kiss in eighth grade. Michael's warm hands are on my waist now—

"Catherine, I got something for you!" Lorraine yells from somewhere above.

Snapping my head back from Michael's, I quickly turn around and hike up a step to put some distance between us.

"Catherine, I want you to take some icebox cake home," Lorraine says as she appears in the doorway. "You didn't have dessert."

"Oh, thanks," I say. I climb the stairs. My hand shakes a little as I reach for the paper plate covered in plastic wrap.

Nonny emerges from the kitchen as Michael joins me in the hallway. "You ever have it, Michael's friend? Icebox cake?" she asks.

"Uh, no," I say.

"It's just graham crackers between layers of pudding and whipped cream," Lorraine says. "It's got to go in the fridge, okay?"

Nonny adds, "It's Michael's favorite!"

Lorraine puts her arms out as I walk toward the door. I guess I have to hug her. She gives me an Aunt D hug, squeezing me hard and fast, and then lets go.

"Thanks for coming, Catherine. Come over again, okay? And tell your mom I'm sorry I didn't drive you home."

"It's no problem. Really. She was finished at work, anyway," I say. "Thank you so much for dinner." I look back at Nonny. "The food was great."

Michael, flushed and red-necked, hasn't moved from the basement doorway. Nonny grabs his arm and pushes him toward me.

"What you standing there for? Go say good-bye to your friend. Walk her to the car!"

Michael shrugs off Nonny and follows me out the front door. We walk in silence to the Accord at the curb. Mom's at the wheel on her phone but clicks it off as Michael and I approach.

Opening the passenger-side window, Mom yells to Michael, "Hi, Michael. Please thank your mom again for me."

"Not a problem," Michael says quickly.

I turn to Michael. "Well . . . uh . . . ," I say.

Mom's face looms larger in my peripheral vision as she leans farther across the passenger seat to get a better look at us. Jesus.

But then Michael smiles and I can read the wonder and disbelief in his healer eyes. "Good night, Cath."

11

It's 4:07 on Monday afternoon and I'm not at St. Anne's. It's my monthly med-management appointment with Dr. McCallum and should take fifteen minutes, twenty tops. I've got the drill down pat: greeting—I am fine, thank you, no side effects—and a hop onto the scale. A few quick questions and then it's sayonara. The plan is for Mom to drop me off at the IOP after so I can make the last half of the session.

Today I give Dr. McCallum a generous seven on my numerical mood scale, up a whopping point from last month. This good news is followed by more questions and more answers: Yes, St. Anne's is fine. Yes, I am sleeping. Not too much and not too little. Yes, I am eating. Yes, I am attending class. Yes, I am completing my homework. No, I am not feeling hopeless. No, my thoughts are not racing. No, I am not thinking of killing myself. No sir, everything's just swell. I scoot to the end of the chair, ready to rise to my feet. But Dr. McCallum sits back and stretches his long legs, settling into the armchair opposite me. Wait a sec, we're not supposed to have a therapy session now.

"I've had a cancellation, Catherine, so I figured we'd use the time to chat a little," he says, patting the top of his balding head as if checking to see if anything has grown. "Your mother emailed me. She said things seem to be going pretty well."

Christ Almighty, Mom! She'd Instagram a particularly hearty poop of mine if she could. *This is Catherine's BM last night. Normal for someone on Lamictal?*

Dr. McCallum rests his Catherine Pulaski chart on his knees. "How would *you* rate things?"

"Um . . . fine," I answer, slightly bewildered by the lack of dismissal. "Like I said before."

"What's fine about them?" he asks.

Well, if we're being honest, Dr. McCallum, not a whole hell of a lot. I'm bipolar if you haven't forgotten, and I'll be that way for the rest of my sorry life. But short-term-wise, things have been surprisingly tolerable. If I dare to be completely honest with myself, the number on my numerical mood scale is probably a six. But I don't like to dwell on that, because it's hardwired not to last. And I know what's waiting for me.

"Um . . . I met this kid," I say. "He's pretty nice. We're doing a history project together."

Of course, Dr. McCallum wants details, like Michael's name and the project and what we've done together. I tell him how we spent Saturday at the library and that I had dinner at Michael's house.

Dr. McCallum nods. "And how did you feel while you were there?"

"Fine. We had fun," I say, omitting the kiss, *that* kiss, the one I can't stop thinking about. How great it was to touch someone and be touched. I even recorded it on my D-Day List as entry number two: First Kiss, Michael. On Sunday night at 9:48 p.m. he texted. Something short. But so damn sweet it sent a swell of good feelings swirling through me. "I'm glad we finally met this year! 😀 😀 "

It's quiet for at least a minute. Dr. McCallum does this. Allows these gaps of silence so that I'll keep talking. But I don't. I just sit and wait. He breaks first, asking me how I feel about hanging out with Michael. If I think we'll hang out again. And how I feel about that. Et cetera, et cetera. I give my usual generic responses and then I lean forward, hoping my body language indicates that our appointment is over.

But he ignores it and springs this on me, "How are you feeling about your grandmother?" He is forever asking me this, at every other session, as if she died yesterday instead of two years and three months ago.

I shift in the chair. I refuse to cover this territory with him.

But he pushes. "You were alone with her, right? When she died?"

Dear God, I pray, make him stop. It's times like these that I long for Dr. A's laissez-faire attitude.

"Catherine?" Dr. McCallum persists. "I know this is hard to talk about."

Why don't you try chatting about your loved one stroking out right in front of you? How at first you think it's a joke. That she's trying to be funny with that weird face and . . . and . . . those sounds. But then you see the animal terror in her eyes. Spot the ropy string of drool dangling from the corner of her mouth. And you know it's no joke. And there's nothing you can do as she pitches forward like a redwood and hits the bedroom carpet face-first and goes still. And it's all happening so fast that calling 911 hasn't even crossed your mind.

I sit there, mute. I cannot unleash this. Not today. Not ever. How do I explain the fear? The grief in witnessing her dignity demolished. That rude string of saliva. She would've especially despised that. Because Grandma was always impeccable—clothes, hair, jewelry. She never emerged from the bedroom without her makeup on. Her lipstick fresh at 6:30 a.m. Oh God, that part hurt the worst. The stroke stealing her dignity.

"We talked about this before," Dr. McCallum says. "You know your mother would like to clean out your grandmother's room." Adrenaline surges through me. *Holy fuck! Did she start already? Did she find my shoe box?* I sit straight up in the chair, my heart racing triple-time. I can't breathe awaiting his next question.

Dr. McCallum watches me closely as he says, "She said she doesn't want to upset you. She said when she tried last year you were very unhappy about it. How do you feel about that? Cleaning out some of your grandmother's belongings?"

I exhale. Okay, I know where he's headed with this—emptying out Grandma's room and converting it into a "cozy study," as Mom had proposed. But it still feels bad. Wrong. Disrespectful. I don't want Mom touching one lace doily in there.

Dr. McCallum leans forward, done talking. It's my turn to say something about erasing all traces of my grandmother's monumental existence from the house.

"I'm not ready," I say, the truth a foreign, bulky thing on my lips.

He nods. "Your mom is fine with that. She told me it wouldn't happen until you say so. You understand that, right, Catherine? Nothing happens with your grandmother's room until you say so. How does that feel to you?"

I nod as a sliver of relief flows through me and then make quite the show of looking at the small clock on the table. I really need to get the fuck out of here.

Dr. McCallum waits a beat before beginning. "Catherine, mourning can be a long, long process. Especially when the circumstances are particularly traumatic, like what happened to you. I know you're not ready to talk to me about it, but I am here for you when the time comes. And the time should come at some point."

I nod again, but I know I'll never be able to talk about it.

After the session, I have no interest in going to St. Anne's. On the ride home, Mom asks me to run into Walmart to buy napkins while she gets gas. I'm feeling shaky, unmoored. Dr. McCallum lifts up the boulders in my head and shines a flashlight on stuff I do not want to see. I don't like thinking about Grandma. How her brain weakened and betrayed her. It reminds me too much of my own defect. It reminds me that my future is damned. Regardless of how fine and dandy things can be, I'm still in Zero's crosshairs. He's coming for me. My permanent mental sucker punch. With all the resulting loss of dignity. So once inside Walmart, I stride straight to the pharmacy department and select a one-hundred-tablet bottle of Tylenol with the twenty dollars Aunt Darlene slipped me after our Mexican dinner. I pocket the bottle inside my sweater before exiting the store with the napkins.

Tonight, my shoe box gets a little more crowded.

12

It's Tuesday at St. Anne's. Week Two. The intensive out-patient program runs for three hours, three o'clock to six o'clock, with a ten-minute snack break, usually around 4:15. As soon as group guru Sandy announces break time and everyone stands and stretches, Kristal catches my eye and does a subtle head tilt toward the door, her long silver earrings swinging.

Outside Room Three, Kristal gently takes my elbow and steers me toward the girls' bathroom. The others remain clustered around the Costco-sized jar of animal crackers and the bottled waters on the table. Inside the bathroom, Kristal plants her back against the door, blocking entry from the Immaculate Conception girls. "You've got to give me a heads-up when you're not coming, Cat. It is unbearable when you're not here." Then, whipping out her iPhone, she asks, "What's your number?"

What's your number? What's your number? What's.
Your. Number. A surge of happy floods me. It is the second
time in two weeks I've been asked for my number.

As Kristal pecks in my number, she asks, "Why'd you
miss yesterday?"

"Medication check," I say, astonished at how easy it
is to be truthful with this girl I barely know. Maybe it's
the free-to-be-fucked-up vibe at St. Anne's. Maybe it's the
new nickname—Cat—that Kristal has christened me with,
making me feel like somebody else. Or that she willingly
makes physical contact with me—digging her arm into my
side during discussions, taking my elbow, grabbing my
hand to make a point. Or maybe it's that a girl like her, rich
and polished and smart, seems to want to hang out, at least
here at St. Anne's, with Cat Pulaski.

Kristal rolls her eyes. "Don't you hate all this? Shrink,
IOPs, therapy . . . it's endless."

"God, yes," I say, loving how phenomenal it is to confide in somebody who understands completely. Especially
on the heels of yesterday's hell session with Dr. McCallum.

Somebody raps hard on the bathroom door, and both
Kristal and I jump. A girl's voice urgently shout-whispers,
"I need to come in!"

"It's Amy," Kristal whispers, bracing herself against the
door. "Just a minute!" Kristal calls out sweetly before telling me, "Always text if you're not coming. 'Cause if you're
not coming, neither am I. The only person I want to do a
freaking collage with here is you."

We roll our eyes about the arts-and-crafts project

Sandy has planned for us today. We're going to cut out pictures from magazines to make special "self-soothing" collages. We have to select images of things that soothe our five senses when we're stressed. Sandy had offered up examples, such as a cozy blanket, hot chocolate, scented candles, relaxing music. Oh goody. All I need is for Mommy to hang it on the fridge.

Amy raps again. "C'mon already. I don't feel good," she says in a low voice.

Kristal flings open the door and Amy barrels in. In the fluorescent light, the blue shadows under her eyes make the rest of her face a pale, greenish hue. She clutches her lower belly.

"Uh . . . would you mind giving me some privacy?" Amy asks, not quite making eye contact with us. She looks longingly at an open stall. "I'm sorry. It must be something I ate."

These three sentences are the most Amy has ever spoken to me. And the sole thing she's ever said to Kristal was how disruptive Kristal's late arrival was that one time. Since then, she only talks with Sandy, the boys, or her Immaculate Conception sidekick, Alexis.

"Oh jeez, sure!" Kristal says, moving toward the door. "Can we get you anything? Water?"

Amy shakes her head and gives a forced smile. "Don't tell Alexis. Or anyone. It's embarrassing." She moves quickly into the stall, slamming the door behind her.

As I follow Kristal out, there's an incredibly long, loud wet-sounding eruption from Amy's stall.

I start to smirk, but then Kristal says, "That's why I

never use a public bathroom. No dignity." Instantly, I'm brought back to yesterday's session with Dr. McCallum and Grandma, and I get an image of me rambling in the chair at Rodrick's salon about wanting to look like Audrey Hepburn for my fantasy trip to Italy. The happy buzz from Kristal wanting my number ebbs until Kristal whispers, "I actually shit in my pants in my mother's car. She was furious. We were at the mall and I had to go but wouldn't use the bathroom there. On the drive home, I just couldn't hold it in any longer."

We both begin to crack up outside Room Three.

"The car reeked for weeks. Oh my God, Cat," Kristal says softly, laughing and holding her stomach. "It was horrible."

"When?" I ask, thinking it had to be a kindergarten kind of event.

Kristal grips my wrist, tears of laughter filling her eyes. "Don't tell a soul! Summer before sophomore year!"

We almost fall over laughing.

"It gets worse," Kristal says between laughs. "My mother made me take off my shorts and underwear in the garage. I . . . I still have this image of her running to the garbage can with this . . . this *laden* pair of Victoria's Secret black lace undies."

The two of us slump to the hallway floor. I'm laughing so hard, my stomach muscles cramp in the best kind of pain. Both Sandy and Vanessa come out to check on us.

For the rest of the afternoon, Kristal and I cannot control ourselves, pasting ads for toe fungus medicine and Depends next to the puppies and beach sunset pictures on our "self-soothing" collages. Cleaning up the mess on our table, Kristal leans close and whispers, "I have never told anyone that story, Cat. Not anyone. You're the only one."

Her words make me forget that last night I added a new bottle of Tylenol to my shoe box. They make me forget that I am terminal.

This hour and a half has to be one of the best afternoons of my life.

13

As soon as I get home from St. Anne's, my phone choos. It's Kristal. "Still!!!! laughing!!!! 😂 💩"

"Me too!!!!" I type back immediately.

Mom turns away from the kitchen sink, where she's scrubbing out a tall Tupperware container that held the chili she made on Sunday. She mouths, "Michael?" with her eyebrows raised questioningly.

I shake my head, ignoring the slow burn that ignites with every micromanagement of my life. I move to the living room.

"Are you missing any more this week?" Kristal writes.

"No. You?" I answer.

"Here all week but missing next Friday to check out colleges. 😔 Would rather go to IOP! Hahahahahahaha!!"

Mom scurries into the living room and stands over me, drying her hands on a kitchen towel. She stage-whispers loudly, "Who are you texting?"

"You do realize that I'm *texting,* right? Nobody can hear you when you text," I say.

Mom asks in her regular voice, "Who're you texting?"

"Kristal," I answer, and look back down at my phone. Mom returns to the kitchen and bursts into song. Jesus help me. I type Kristal: "You a senior?"

"Yes. Only seven months of chapman hell left. Counting the minutes. Haha," she writes.

Wow, I can't believe she hates Chapman, the Yale of Connecticut high schools, maybe all of New England. I write: "You are so lucky you are almost done with high school!!" And then I add, "I hate it"

"Felt the same way too. Don't worry. It goes by even when it doesn't feel like it."

Then she texts this: "Have to go to DC next weekend to look at schools. Waste of time. Want UConn. Are you around this weekend?"

My heart speeds up. *What?* What did she just ask? Am I around this weekend? Should I tell her I've been around for the last one hundred and sixteen weekends without one pathetic invite? We bipolarites generally have light social calendars. I'll keep it short and simple. "Yes"

"Have museum thing for my mother's work on Sunday. In new haven. Do you want to come with me? New exhibit opening. We can get froyo next to museum."

Jesus! A positive rush roars through me. *Kristal wants to hang out with me. Outside of St. Anne's.*

I text back: "Sounds like fun"

My phone choos right away with her response: "Awe-

some Cat! Will give you details tomorrow at St. A. 🌰🍦
🏛"

I feel something that must honestly fall somewhere high on the happy scale. Definitely eight or nine territory. This definitely matches the kiss. And today's shit-in-my-pants story time.

Wait a sec. Maybe I misread her text. Maybe she wasn't really inviting me. Maybe she was just bitching about going. Uncertainty floods me. Quickly, I reread the conversation. *Yes.* There it is: "Do you want to come with me?"

Humming, I click on Michael's Sunday-night text: "I'm glad we finally met this year! 😃 😃" I had responded with a "ME TOO" and a smiley face. I keep reading the texts over and over. And thinking about that kiss. I'm so ready for another one.

"Cath, honey, dinner!" Mom calls.

She has set the table with two bowls of chili, a small pile of mini corn bread loaves and two salads. She's laid out at least five different types of Wish-Bone salad dressing. Our glasses of water are filled with ice *and* a lemon slice. She makes a production out of dinner most nights. It's our only real time together, she'll say.

And every night as I approach the dinner table and see this, her grand gesture, darts of guilt fly at me. Mom shouldn't have to make culinary amends because she works her ass off and can't be with me every second of my nonschool day. She shouldn't have to pour every ounce of her love into me, her emotional and financial black hole of a daughter.

I force a smile that she instantly returns. "I made plans for Sunday, okay?" I say, sprinkling shredded cheddar on my chili.

"With Kristal?" Mom asks, eyebrows arched.

I nod, my mouth full.

Mom does a good job of repressing any whoops of delight. She just smiles, but it reaches her eyes and takes ten years off her face. Another dart. "What are you doing?" she asks ever so nonchalantly.

"Her mom works at a museum in New Haven and there's some event there," I answer.

"Well, I'm off, so no problem driving you in," Mom says. "What time?"

"Kristal will let me know tomorrow." I sip some water. "Maybe you can do something on Sunday? Maybe a movie? With Aunt D?"

Please, please do something for yourself. For once.

Mom shakes her head. "Nah. I can do the food shopping and clean the bathrooms. I'll get a head start."

"What about Bill? You could give him a call?" I suggest.

Mom flushes and shakes her head quickly, picking up a corn bread and buttering it with the precision of a surgeon transplanting a new kidney. Eyes glued to the task, she asks lightly, "So Kristal, is she a junior too?"

I grab a corn bread and dip it in my chili. "A senior."

Mom suppresses a little smile. "Is she in one of your classes at Cranbury?"

"No. I met her at St. Anne's."

The buttered corn bread en route to Mom's mouth stalls. She puts it down untouched next to her bowl, her face transformed into a mask of worry. "Kristal is a patient at the intensive outpatient program?"

I already know where this is going. She's going to shoot it down. Oh no! Not her precious Catherine mixing with the other mentally unstables. Especially when it's not an official therapeutic program sanctioned by Pope McCallum.

"Yes. She is. And she's really nice."

Please, Mom, let me have this. Let me have this piece of normal before Zero hits again.

"Oh, I don't know about this, Cath," Mom starts, dread filling her eyes.

"What?" I ask, placing my spoon down, suddenly no longer hungry. "What don't you know?"

"It might not be the wisest of ideas," she answers.

I rise from my chair. Suddenly, I am furious. And desperate. "Why? Why the fuck not? We're not shooting up heroin. We're going to a museum!"

"Catherine, please sit down," Mom says, also standing. "Can we try to talk about this?"

"There's nothing to talk about!" I'm shouting now. "I'm going!"

"Catherine, please. I don't want to fight with you." Mom sits down and picks up her corn bread, attempting to resume normalcy. "Just hear me out. Can you at least tell me a little about her?"

Oh my God. Normal kids never have to deal with this shit. Their parents would be jumping over the freaking moon that it's a museum and not a dumb mall. But still I answer her.

"Kristal's nice. She's a senior. She goes to Chapman." I swallow, trying to calm myself down. "I really want to go. We have fun together." I leave out that I know this thing with Kristal, this fetal friendship or whatever you want to call it, has a shelf life. Once this girl gets to know me—Catherine, not Cat—and the fact that I have a mood disorder that affects how I behave rather than something that stays hidden behind closed doors like cutting or vomiting, she won't stay around. No one does. Because my disease is a public one. Just ask Rodrick. Any friends I might have are guaranteed to see and feel the impact of it too.

Mom doesn't understand. She doesn't know that I told Riley and Olivia about my diagnosis this past summer. Ten months after my suicide attempt and one month after the mania-inspired shopping spree—more than one year of basically no contact from them—and suddenly, out of the blue, they both texted me, asking to come over. They had heard I got my hair cut, that it looked "really cute." I was pretty stable by then. Courtesy of my then-new shrink, Dr. McCallum, and a prescription for Abilify. Of course I said yes. I was desperately lonely. I could ignore their defection; I could repress the memory of their radio silence after my sweet-sixteenth birthday invite. This would be our friendship 2.0. Yes, it had shattered in the wake of Grandma and Zero, but I thought it could rise like a phoenix, in time for the last two years of high school.

Riley and Olivia came to my house and we sat on the

floor in my bedroom. Just like old times. It seemed like they cared again. Why else would they come see me? So I told them. I did. I allowed the word "bipolar" to leave my lips. I thought they'd get it.

Riley picked up her phone and Googled "bipolar" right in front of me. She glanced a couple of times at my hair and then, with barely a word, she and Olivia both left. For good. But armed with fresh info to report to their theater friends, a small group of nasty, spiteful people collected freshman year when Riley and Olivia were in the chorus in *Fiddler on the Roof.*

Mom has no idea what that did to me. Now, she runs her index finger up and down her water glass, obviously debating her next move. "And . . . um . . . what's wrong with Kristal?"

There it is. *What's wrong with her?* The ugliest of questions hangs in the air, filling me with the familiar sickening realization of what my life is. Damaged.

I look at Mom. "She likes me." I exit the kitchen slowly, like an old woman, and mount the stairs to my room, toward my soldiers.

14

My fingers itch to reach under my bed, to push aside the barrier I've constructed of books, magazines and mateless socks, and retrieve my shoe box. But it's too dangerous with no lock on my door.

"What's wrong with her?" Mom's question has lodged itself in my chest.

Mom raps on my door. "Catherine? Can I come in?"

"No." I don't have the energy for this.

"Please, Catherine," Mom says. "I know I majorly fucked up."

This gets my attention. Devout Catholic Jody Pulaski dropping the f-bomb? In front of her mentally challenged daughter? This has never happened. Ever. I'm beyond stunned, and even worse, I feel a laugh gurgling up from somewhere inside me.

Mom opens the door. Our eyes meet, and I can't

help it. I have to smile. "I cannot believe you just said 'fuck.'"

"It fit the crime," she says, leaning against the door-frame but not entering. "I wish . . . I wish I could just delete our whole conversation downstairs." She shakes her head. "I did not mean for it to come out the way it did."

"It's okay. I'm not going," I say, the goodwill between us evaporating. Breaking eye contact with her, I lie down on my bed and roll away to face the wall.

"Oh yes you are," she says, moving forward to drop my phone on my bed. "You have enough on your plate without adding my baloney to it."

What does that mean? "My baloney"?

"Look, Cath." Mom sits down on the side of my bed and places her hand on my upper arm. She seems a little angry. "You *are* going with Kristal on Sunday. End of discussion. I . . . I think I'm going to start therapy."

I roll back toward her and sit up. "*What?*" I ask.

"Dr. McCallum has been telling me for a while that I'm extremely anxious. You know that. I need to stop hovering, lighten up, all that stuff. And based on what just happened downstairs, it's clear I need to get a grip. You're moving on. Your life is picking back up. I refuse to be the one who . . . who is bad for you."

Who are you and what did you do with my mother?

"So you're going because of me?" I ask.

Her answer sends me reeling again. "No. I am going for me," she says. "You are going to be fine, Catherine. Dr. McCallum is really happy with how you're doing. He thinks you're especially perceptive and observant, and that is really going to help you in accepting your condition. He keeps telling me I need to trust you, and I am going to start doing that. Right now."

Two emotions flare inside me. The first is a perverse pride because Dr. McCallum thinks I'm observant and perceptive. But there's also a deluge of guilt over my fraud in Dr. McCallum's office and, even worse, Mom's new campaign to trust me. There's a shoe box not twenty-four inches below us chock-full of my deceit.

She nods. "Okay? And when I asked about what was wrong with Kristal—"

"Forget it," I say. I don't want to hear this.

"No. I need for you to hear me." Mom's voice rises. "I know that you're meeting kids with different issues like eating disorders or cutting or bulimia—"

I interrupt her. "Bulimia is an eating disorder."

"I know that," Mom says huffily. "It just came out wrong. I worry that you'll be vulnerable to them. That what they're saying will sound good to you and that you'll . . . uh . . . start doing it." She takes a deep breath. "But I will not go that route. I'm trusting you, Catherine, and you will go on Sunday and you will have a great time whether you want to or not." She leans forward to hug me and I break the hold quickly. Her hugs usually feel desperate to me, too intense, like all her worry and anguish is transferred into her shoulders, arms and fingers. I try to avoid them. But she takes it in stride, used to it by now.

To soften the blow, I tease her. "You better get yourself over to confession, Miss Potty Mouth."

Mom stands and points at me. "I've learned from the best. C'mon downstairs. I'll heat up our chili. I'm hungry again."

After dinner (take two), homework, shower and two Lamictal tablets (Dr. McCallum upped my dosage again so that I will peak at the targeted 250 milligrams by the end of the month), I check my phone. There's one text from Michael and one from Kristal.

I click on Michael's text. He wrote "Hey," so I type back my standard smiley-face emoji.

Right away my phone choos. Michael has sent two smileys back.

I type: "See you in history tomorrow," with another smiley.

Kristal wrote: "Do you want me to pick you up on Sunday? 🚐"

New, "trusting" Mom would still probably veto a ride from a girl, a St. Anne's one at that, so I text back: "It's ok. Will get a ride. What time and what museum"

Kristal: "New haven museum of history. On chapel st. 2:00"

I type, "Great—thx for asking me," but then delete the "for asking me." Too pathetic-sounding.

Kristal: "Great! Have to study physics now. Did I mention I hate high school? See you at St. As 😃 😃 😃"

In bed that night, after the parade of my troops, I open up the D-Day List on my phone and add a third entry.

1. L.V.
2. First Kiss, Michael Oct. 11
3. New Haven Museum Kristal Oct. 19

And something weird happens. Looking at this list, actually staring at the two newest entries, calms me. Maybe even more than my shoe box. Because it's proof, tangible proof that I might be able to experience some really good things before Zero moves up the Catherine coastline. After the troops are secured under my bed, I stand in the middle of my room and try a couple of fouetté pirouettes just for the hell of it. Just to see. And surprisingly, they're not too shabby.

15

As soon as Michael and I walk into history class on Wednesday, I can feel it. Everything looks normal, but there's a tension, an undercurrent of something in the air. Michael, oblivious to it, gives me a quick, "See you after," and heads to his seat on the other side of the room. Something's off and it's not just the blessed absence of Louis Farricelli's Incredible Hulk body looming behind my desk for the second day in a row. There's a tittering that increases as I approach my seat. A folded sheet of paper is waiting for me. "Catherine" is written on it in block letters.

I knew it. It's from those theater fuckheads again. Instinctively, my eyes fly to Riley. She's got her white-blond head on her desk, shoulders spasming with laughter. I shift my gaze to Olivia. Her cheeks are flushed and her head is turned to hiss something to Riley. Next to Riley, some skinny guy with dyed black hair openly smirks at me. I spin to face front and slide down fast in my chair, trying to hide the burn in my checks. Mr. Oleck stands at his podium with another student, momentarily lost in the cyberworld of his iPad.

I unfold the paper. It's a photocopy of a DVD cover, *Girl, Interrupted,* an old movie about psycho girls in a mental hospital. The hum of white noise rises in my ears and the surface temperature of my skin rises to scorching. Who are Riley and Olivia now? Doesn't our history count for any decency? Why couldn't they just scrape me off their lives like I was a piece of shit on their shoes instead of inflicting this constant torture? Maybe our history does play a part, because they can't quite let me go. Like I turned bipolar and depressed on purpose. Like *I* rejected *them.*

The paper wilts where my hot fingertips make contact. I want to crumble it into a ball and whip it right at Riley's face. I swallow compulsively to loosen the lump in my throat and slip the poisonous sheet into my binder.

Maybe I should bring this to St. Anne's today. Sandy would undoubtedly ask her typically dumb question, "How did this make you feel, Catherine?" And Tommy would get all riled up and curse a blue streak. Since the IOP started, I've passed Garrett a few times in the school hallway and he always acknowledges me with a polite "Hey, Catherine," giving me an unexpected sense of solidarity. Maybe the Cranbury High contingent of St. Anne's—me and Garrett and John—could gang up against Olivia and Riley and the theater geeks. John could enlist his wrestling buddies, Garrett could get the stoners and, atop the roof of St. Anne's dirty white van, we could all do a sing-off or something to prove my worth. Just envisioning this twisted *Pitch Perfect* scene cools me down.

The classroom door swings open. It's Louis Farricelli, stiff and awkward with a thick white brace encasing his neck and one around his right knee. He moves slowly, crutches wedged firmly under his muscled arms. An aide, a woman in her forties, trails him like a serf, lugging his weighty backpack. The class is stunned into silence. Even the theater demons in the back are still. Cranbury High's Moses, perched to lead the Hornets to the promised land—a second consecutive state football championship—has fallen.

"Jesus, Farricelli, what happened to you?" is pitched from a boy behind me.

Another yells, "Tell me you're not out for the season? We need you, man!"

Instead of basking in the spotlight of their concern, Louis Farricelli ignores them. I don't turn around as he passes and apparently he's having trouble sitting down be-cause the aide is saying in a tense whisper something like, "Put the crutches aside and I'll help you," to which Louis growls a typically classy, "Back the fuck off. I got this."

Mr. Oleck gives the aide a little shake of his head as she exits the classroom in a huff. Good for her for not putting up with Louis Farricelli's spew. In a low voice, Mr. Oleck asks Louis, "Want me to tell them?"

Louis grunts and Mr. Oleck interprets that as an affir-mative response because he says, "People, Louis cracked a vertebra in his neck and tore his ACL. It happened during a workout. Freak accident kind of thing. He's gonna be out for the rest of the season."

Immediately, the room resounds with the herd's horrified reactions.

"What the eff happened?"

"Can you even play anymore? What about your scholarship?"

"But it's your senior year!"

And the lone, reasonable: "You're so lucky you're not paralyzed."

There's not a word from Louis until some guy spouts, "So that freshman, Gordon, he the new quarterback?"

Louis Farricelli responds in a tight voice, "I have no fucking clue, dude. This happened like two fucking days ago. Why don't you go ask him yourself?"

"All right, Louis," Mr. Oleck says, displaying a new-found tolerance for Farricelli's favorite and maybe only adjective. "Now that we've gotten that out of the way, let's talk about your biography projects."

My moronic classmates have a hard time refocusing after the earth-shattering news, their fingers alerting the rest of the Cranbury High community via text, Twitter, FB and a few covert photos of the injured hero on Snapchat. Michael and I make eye contact, and he subtly rolls his eyes. I feel the corners of my mouth lift.

After some repeated commands to focus and then threats to confiscate everyone's phones, Mr. Oleck finally gets the class to shut up. Before returning to the scintillating topic of the rise of the consumer pre–World War II, he rattles off another biography assignment. "I want a detailed outline on your soldier, with all the basic stats that we talked about before, like birthday, birth city, schooling, childhood, family, job and military service, including length of service, locations of service and specific rank. Was he a gunner aboard a B-17 or a paratrooper, a member of the infantry? Include any details regarding his death. And then I want a road map. Give me the next steps of your research: What do you need? Where is it? Stuff like that. The more detailed it is, the easier it's going to be to write this."

"When's this due?" Sabita Gupta asks. In seventh grade, Sabita and I were elected co-captains of our Girl Scout Cadette troop. We got along great, but I was always too busy with Riley and Olivia to develop anything with Sabita outside Scout meetings. After a slew of rejections, she gave up on me. And she did just fine for herself as an honors student, gifted pianist and tennis player, with a wide circle of friends. Little did she know it was her lucky day when I blew her off.

Mr. Oleck answers her. "This is due on Monday, October twentieth." The class groans and he adds, "Look, it's only Wednesday. For the rest of the week, I'm just assigning you reading. And not a lot of it, either. This is AP U.S. History, remember! You guys can handle it!"

After class, I rush for the door to avoid the hordes that instantly throng Louis Farricelli. The aide hasn't returned, and the boys jostle each other for the honor of schlepping the Great Horny One's backpack. Michael appears next to me in the hallway.

"The sky is falling," he says softly, and we both smile. "Hey, about the assignment due on Monday, we're going to have to do it before Friday. I'm leaving for D.C. for a Model Congress conference this weekend. Can you stay after school today so we can work on it?"

A wave of kids crashes its way down the hall, causing Michael and me to split and then rejoin. My shoulder hits his arm and he presses it lightly into me, a secret hello. It seeps into me like psychic Neosporin on my latest cut.

"I'm sorry," I say. "Work."

"You work every day after school?" he asks, eyebrows raised in surprise and admiration.

I nod, my eyes shifting away. I hate lying to him now.

"Wow, that's really great. Racking up the bucks for college?" he asks.

"Yeah," I lie again.

"Man, my folks would love if I did that," he says, high-fiving some short kid who just greeted him with a high-pitched "Hey, Pit Man!" Michael focuses his brown eyes with their unfairly long lashes on me. "Well, I'll just bang out the assignment for us, then," he says. "Sounds like you're really busy with work and all." He gives me a goofy smile and from my vantage a couple of inches below him, I can see the cut on his chin from his shaving there.

"No, I'll do it," I say. "You've done mostly everything so far."

"Cath, that's okay," he says as we approach our lockers. "I don't mind."

"What? You don't trust me?" I say in a tone that sounds dangerously close to flirting. *WTF? Who is this girl?*

Michael flushes in response, a slow grin spreading across his face. "All right then, it's all yours. Just remember that you'll be held to the almost impossibly high PLA standard."

"You mean MLA?"

"No." He shakes his head. "The PLA—Pitoscia Language Association. Only a select few are invited to apply."

"And how many members are there?"

"Just me and Tyler," he says. "As I said, it's very select."

"I'm honored," I say.

And actually, I am.

It's 3:02 and Mom, as usual, is late. The buses are gone and only a few stragglers loiter near the front doors of Cranbury High. As I'm punching my passcode into my phone, I hear "Catherine! Cath!"

Michael jogs up to me waving some white papers in his hand. "Here!" He pushes the papers toward me. "I just printed out all of our work so far. You can use this for the biography."

"Thank you." I take them. "You could've just given them to me tomorrow. You didn't have to rush."

Michael shakes his head. "I have a Model Congress meeting, maybe during Oleck's class. And then we leave for D.C. first thing on Friday. I didn't want to forget."

With one hand, I unzip my backpack and retrieve my history binder. As I open it, the fucking DVD recommendation from Olivia and Riley floats to the ground. The paper stays folded, but good gentleman that he is, Michael automatically bends to get it for me.

Dropping to my knees, I shout, "I got it!" as my phone and the stack of papers he just gave me fly out of my hand. I snatch the paper with its ugly block-letter "Catherine" and jam it in my backpack as the Accord screeches to a stop at the curb.

With her usual impeccable timing, my warden arrives. "Everything okay?" Mom shouts to us from the open passenger window.

"Fine!" I yell to Mom, grabbing the papers and popping to my feet. "I'll see you tomorrow," I say to Michael, barely looking back at him as I dive into the Accord for the trek to St. Anne's.

Kristal is waiting for me outside the front door, even though it's 3:15, armed with two copies of the exhibit flyer from the New Haven Museum. "That's Kristal," I tell Mom as she pulls the Accord into the parking spot directly in front of Kristal.

As if our fight over Kristal and the museum never happened, Mom puts down her window. "Hi, Kristal!" she yells as I cringe. "I'm Jody, Catherine's mom. Nice to meet you!"

Jesus.

Kristal walks over, says hi to Mom and gives her a flyer and a brilliant smile.

Inside, Sandy's scheduled a therapy dog to visit our happy group today, and after completing our DBT mood rating forms, the rest of the time is spent lounging on the floor, playing with a white fluffy schnoodle named Lucky Boy. When Sandy declares today's session "open discussion"—anyone can talk about anything they want—I'm tempted for a nanosecond to bring up the hate note from Olivia and Riley. But then Lucky Boy drops to his belly in front of me and rolls onto his back, his legs sticking up in the air.

His trainer, Marcy, explains, "Catherine, he's asking you for a belly scratch."

I comply, and Lil' Tommy immediately rushes next to me and assumes Lucky Boy's pose on the floor, flat on his back with his stumpy legs and red, chapped hands cycling in the air. He even play-pants, "Pet me too, Cath!" The room pops with a laughter that carries away the rest of the note's sting.

By 6:12, the sun has basically set, but even in the murky light, I can easily see a large brown envelope sticking out of our mailbox. Mom pulls into the driveway and I jump out of the car and rush to the front door to pull the envelope out, my gut cramping at the site of unfamiliar blocky writing. *Catherine*. No last name, no address, no return address. *Not again*. It feels weighted. Like there's something more than paper in here. All of today's good stuff—Michael's smile, Kristal waiting for me, Lucky Boy and Lil' Tommy—dissolves.

I am pulled down. Weighted again.

Mom is next to me. "What's that?"

I don't answer her. I need to open it in the privacy of my room, but I can't now that she's seen it.

Mom weighs the heft of it in her hand. "Feels like a phone or something."

My hand flies to the pocket of my jacket, the place I usually store my phone. It's empty. I see my phone on the sidewalk outside of school as I crouched down to grab the *Girl, Interrupted* note before Michael could see it. I rip open the envelope. It's my phone.

I turn it on to a text from Michael: "You left this at school. Text me when you get this so I know you got it"

I type back immediately, "Thanks so much!!!!!!" I have a lump in my throat from relief. And gratitude for Michael and his kindness. I type, "You are the absolute best!" and add the smiley face with the hearts for eyes.

16

"Lord, I am not worthy that you should enter under my roof, but only say the word and my soul shall be healed," intones fat Father John. He's at the altar prepping for the Sunday magic trick of transforming the wine and wheat hosts into Jesus. It is always here at Our Blessed Shepherd, with my ass going numb on the hard wooden pew, that I feel the furthest from God.

Mom and I, along with the rest of the flock, robotically follow the routine each Sunday: sing, kneel, sit, stand, shake hands and deposit the check or cash into the collection basket that comes around not once but twice during Mass. Our Blessed Shepherd even accepts credit and debit cards. Welcome to religion in the twenty-first century.

During Father John's homily, Mom starts to nod off. I can't blame her. With his mind-numbing abilities, the man rivals a high dose of NyQuil. Even cranky babies sleep. I spend my time gazing at the back of two perfectly coiffed heads located way in the front. They belong to Riley and her mom, Mrs. Judith Swenson, who are seated in their usual position of honor in the first pew on the left-hand side. It's almost always just the two of them. Mr. Angus Swenson is away on business 99.9 percent of the time.

The Swenson clan basically founded Cranbury. There's a park near the water named after a hallowed ancestor, and I'm pretty sure they funded a huge part of the rectory's remodeling a couple of years ago. In the caste system that comprises Our Blessed Shepherd, the Swensons and other rich and generous benefactors make up the top. Their names are engraved on small, gold plaques that line the pews, raining hosanna in the highest on them and their wallets. Occupying the thankless middle are the families who donate only a shitload of time doing menial labor, like answering the rectory phone, teaching CCD and cleaning the church. Mom and I flounder in the lowest caste—the faithful who donate neither a huge chunk of change nor talent. We come only to pray (or at least, Mom does), and that's not quite good enough for Our Blessed Shepherd.

As usual, Mom insists on staying until the bitter end, after the last choir song and the grand exit by Father John, his cross raised high, trailed by an entourage of lackeys and small altar boys and girls. It's raining this Sunday morning, so he pauses in the foyer while the elite crowd around him, peppering him with invites to brunch at "the club." The worker ants scatter to clean the pews, count the collections and set up the coffee urns and stale pastries for the post-Mass refreshments in the basement. Mom and I slink out as fast as our legs can carry us.

Which is not very fast—the river of early exiters moves slowly past the priest. The Swenson ladies are on the periphery of the Father John horde, and Mom and I are close enough to see Judith pass a bottle of Purell to Riley. God knows what germs her little angel might have picked up during the sign of peace.

My eyes follow Riley as she squeezes her way toward fellow youth group members. They are the chosen ones— hand-selected to do the readings in their Sunday finest, their high, breathy voices amplified by the lectern's microphone as they spout "A reading from the First Letter of St. Paul to the Corinthians" or some variation. They never miss the retreats with the breakout sessions on "Jesus in Your Life" and "Living a Life with Grace." Behold, parishioners, here are Blessed Shepherd's Varsity Christians, who wouldn't know mercy if it hit them in the face.

It's the hypocrisy that makes me want to hurl. The Riley Swensons who'll feed the homeless but only while wearing gloves. The ones who'll read the Gospels on Sunday and write nasty notes on Monday. And unlike Jesus, these are the ones who shun Cranbury High's lepers. Like me.

Mom drifts next to Judith Swenson and calls a cheerful, "Hi, Judith. Good to see you."

Judith, clearly uncomfortable but trapped by a wall of devotees, gives Mom a rushed, "Oh hello, Jody. Forgive me, but I really need to speak to Father John about the mission trip to Appalachia," before turning her back to Mom and me. Typical. Another good Catholic more comfortable with a handpicked charity-at-a-distance, the type where you do your good deed quickly and get out. Scheduled at your own convenience. No pesky emotional commitment.

Mom flushes at the snub but says nothing to me. Not a fucking word. Inside the Accord, the silence is broken only by the swish of the windshield wipers. Usually this double-edged injury—the snub and then Mom's silent acceptance of it, her penance for having me—would bother me. The Swenson/Blessed Shepherd Affair would normally lodge deep in my chest and fester for days, piled on top of the *Girl, Interrupted* note and other assaults. But instead of turning onto our street, Mom guns the car toward Route 1.

"I need about three double-chocolate doughnuts this morning," she says, her knuckles white as she squeezes the crap out of the steering wheel. These doughnuts are my mother's Lamictal. "How about you?"

Dunkin' Donuts chocolate-cake doughnuts dipped in glaze and then thickly topped with chocolate icing are the only things that Mom and I will never, ever fight about. Aunt Darlene owns the DD closest to our house and if she knows we're coming, she'll add extra frosting to the batch.

Mom glances over at me and I smile back at her. "Roger that," I say.

The Accord's tires squeal as she turns into the parking lot.

"Okay, I'll be back at five. Text me if anything changes," Mom says.

We're parked in front of the New Haven Museum of History, a large redbrick building nestled on Chapel Street alongside quirky clothing stores and an artsy-fartsy bookstore necessitated by its immediate proximity to artsy-fartsy Yale. I look at the entrance, and little spasms in my stomach tumble the digested remains of three and a half, yes, three and a half double-chocolate doughnuts. Kristal texted me that she'd be waiting outside the front doors but no one's there.

Maybe she changed her mind? Maybe she got wind of my social pariah status? Maybe her mother doesn't want *her* daughter hanging out with a St. Anne's IOP girl? I should tell Mom to just drive us home.

Suddenly the front door is opening. It's Kristal waving excitedly at me. I recognize the relief in her eyes; it must match my own. My stomach cramps vanish as I exit the Accord. Kristal flashes that grin and pulls me inside to the grand foyer with its black-and-white-checked floor and graceful, white-banistered spiral staircase. Museum hipsters scurry back and forth carrying wires and boxes and tools, urgently speaking into their phones and darting into the large room on the other side of the foyer.

Kristal has on skinny jeans, Converse high-tops and a long black sweater that's unbuttoned to reveal a vintage T-shirt. And a very cool scarf that's arranged perfectly, of course, around her neck. She fits right in here. I think I'm okay in my jeans and black H&M sweater.

"It's always like this on the day an exhibit opens," Kristal says softly to me. "It's like everything gets done in the hour before the doors open to the public."

"I've never been here before. It's really cool," I spout nervously. *Well, gee whiz, I'm just a little Cranbury country girl in the big city.* But I do like the dark, musty feel of the building, the rooms just beyond my view packed with things that each tell a story.

"My mother has worked here forever. I basically grew up here. Come see the New Haven gallery," Kristal says.

We enter the gallery and browse the exhibits on New Haven's claims to fame like Yale, Eli Whitney and the Amistad trial. Kristal gives me a "Kristal Tour" with her own thoughtful tidbits: Cinqué from the *Amistad* was hot and Benedict Arnold cheated on his wife and had an illegitimate child in Nova Scotia. She points out the display of a mannequin wearing a corset and wire hoopskirt thing. It's for a New Haven business that was the first in the country to manufacture corsets in the 1880s.

"Listen to this," Kristal says, reading the label. "Dr. Scott's *electric* corsets promised to cure *nervousness.*" She grabs my arm, her eyes wide in mock revelation. "Maybe that's all we need? Screw the meds. Let's just squeeze the shit out of our lungs all day."

All this smiling is giving my facial muscles a workout. *This is fucking fun.* Laughing and joking with a girl my own age, this is what my life used to be.

"C'mon, Cat," Kristal says. "It's time for the opening. My mom will freak if we're not there when she speaks."

Kristal's mom is the executive director of the museum and gives a short welcome speech. I zone out on what she's saying; I'm too focused on looking at her. Her hair is cut short like mine, but she wears her bangs down and swept to the side. She's all urban coolness mixed with the Yale art-fart vibe in her black turtleneck and black-and-white houndstooth pencil skirt. She's one of the five people in the U.S. who could wear a beret and pull it off.

But I didn't expect her to be so short and petite. She and Kristal look nothing alike. The rhythm of her speech is slow, measured and strong. She looks supremely comfortable speaking to the crowd in the lobby. I'd feel more intimidated, but thanks to Kristal, I now have the visual of her mom running to the garbage can with Kristal's underwear to counterbalance the cool.

Kristal's mom finishes to a rousing round of applause, and Kristal and I flow with the current of bodies to the other room. A placard over the door reads "Civil Rights and World War II: The Struggle for Freedom at Home." I wonder if Mr. Oleck is here. I scan the room for a stocky dweeb wearing a bow tie.

"I have to do a project on World War Two," I tell Kristal as we step inside the room. "A biography of a soldier. I wonder if there's anything on him here." An urge to text Michael sweeps through me, but I let it pass.

"Well, if he's white, he's not going to be in here," Kristal says. "This exhibit is only on the shit that was going on during the war."

I'm afraid to ask what shit she's talking about. I can't look dumb to Chapman senior Kristal. So I nod like I understand and we head to the first display. Immediately, I start reading the label. It only takes one line to clue me in. It's good old American racism right here on the home front. For the first time, I think about the difference in our skin colors. What goes through Kristal's head when she's reading about these horrors?

Huge black-and-white photographs show clusters of Japanese-American citizens locked behind barbed wire fences in internment camps. The camps look like they're made up of small, cheap buildings plopped on dry, dusty ground in the middle of freaking nowhere with mountaintops in the distant background.

Kristal points to the photos. "These were taken by Ansel Adams."

I freeze. Should I know who Ansel Adams is?

"He's that nature photographer," Kristal explains, glancing at me with a slight frown. "He did all those black-and-white pictures of places like Yosemite."

I can only shrug stupidly.

Kristal sighs and shakes her head. "Jesus, I sound like my mother." She takes my hand and lifts it. "Slap me really hard, Cat."

Laughing, we turn the corner to the next display. This one's bigger. It's got a TV monitor running a grainy black-and-white video that shows row upon row of women soldiers marching down an almost empty street. The women are wearing uniforms of long, double-breasted winter coats with hats that look like inverted canoes, tilted slightly to the side. Their arms and legs move in synchronized precision, heads held high.

The view changes and now the parade of women passes

what looks like an English policeman. This new angle allows for a close-up of the women soldiers. Many of them are African American. My eyes move to the display's title: "The 6888th Central Postal Directory Battalion."

"This is my favorite one," Kristal says, holding up her hands in surrender. "I promise I'm not gonna say anything else except that these ladies truly rocked."

"What did they do?" I ask, my eyes veering back to the video.

Kristal says, "The Six Triple Eight"—she points to the blown-up black-and-white photos—"was the first totally black female unit to go over to Europe during World War Two." She looks at me. "They didn't fight. What they did was to totally revamp the mail system. It was a mess when they got to England. None of the soldiers were getting their letters. They were like a year behind in delivery. These letters were the only contact from home. And this unit just kicked ass. They—" Kristal stops abruptly.

I smell Kristal's mom before I see her. A floral-citrus scent wafts around me. Up close she's even more beautiful. Her clothes, perfectly tailored to her tiny frame, scream class. Large brown eyes, a flawless complexion and a full mouth covered with just the right color lipstick—it's almost hard to take in. She smiles at me and extends her hand. "Hello, Catherine. I'm Kristal's mom, Beverly Walker."

"Hi." I jut my hand out a little too hard and shake. My mind drains of anything else to say. I feel like the words "Property of St. Anne's" are branded on my forehead.

"Please call me Bev," she says. "And thank you so much

for coming. You're the only reason my daughter has decided to grace us with her presence today."

Kristal rolls her eyes.

"Uh . . . thanks for having me," I manage. "I've never been here before. It's great."

Bev cocks her head at me. "Let me know what you think about the new exhibit," she says. "Now, I'm serious about this. If you think something works well, great, but I'm more interested in something that's not working. Like if a label has too much text. Or if something in the text is unclear. Or we need a bench somewhere. Or better lighting. Kristal is great at this kind of stuff, but she doesn't like working with her mother anymore."

"I've spent every single summer here since I was seven," Kristal says to me, her arms folded tight across her chest. "I'm a little museumed out."

"Well, you're smarter than most of my grad students," Bev says, and then turns back to me. "I just love getting a pair of fresh eyes on this. Any feedback would be great."

There's a definite tension between Kristal and her mother, and the lull in conversation threatens to become awkward, so I turn to the 6888th exhibit. "This is really amazing," I say. "What these women did."

"They just give me the chills," Bev says with reverence. "You think about what these ladies were facing. It was a double whammy of prejudice—they were women and they were black. I always ask myself, would I have done that? Would I have enlisted? Given everything that was going—"

A young guy wearing an apron taps Bev's shoulder. "We've got a problem in the kitchen," he says. "There's coffee leaking all over the floor."

Bev looks at Kristal and the tension breaks. They both smile. "You were right, baby," Bev says to Kristal. "Time for a new one. You see why I need you here?" Bev turns to me. "We've got this one coffeepot that only behaves for Kristal. Would you excuse us for a minute?"

"I'll be right back," Kristal says. "And then we'll hit froyo, okay?"

They leave and I return to the video. It's looped around to that close-up again. These women can't be much older than me. Next to the video screen stands a mannequin dressed in a dark gray double-breasted winter coat that matches the coats the soldiers in the video wear. The small card on the floor says it belonged to PFC Jane Talmadge.

I move closer to the wall to read the labels there. They say that there were two women from Connecticut who joined the 6888th. Encased in a plastic box is a yellowed handwritten letter covered with a faded spidery script. The small card says it was written by the same Jane Talmadge who owned the coat. She was from New Haven.

February 17, 1944

Dear Mama,

I don't know how much more I can take. Things are bad here. They give me looks and say nasty things when I walk by. I hurt so much. It doesn't matter

*what I do. How hard I try. I'll never be good enough.
And there's nothing I can do about it. I can't change
the way I was born.*

The letter goes on, but I freeze. Then read these lines
again. I could've written this. *I don't know how much more
I can take. I hurt so much.* Jane Talmadge's words are déjà
vu familiar. These are my words. *I can't help the way I was
born.* I stare at her coat.

"Powerful stuff, huh?" Bev has returned to my side.

I struggle to focus. "Yeah. I . . . I wish I could do my
project on her," I spout uncensored, then point to the mannequin. "I have to do a biography on a soldier from Connecticut who served in World War Two."

Bev seems confused. "Jane Talmadge did serve in
the war."

"The soldier has to be buried at the American Cemetery
in Normandy," I explain.

Bev takes a deep breath. "That's where Jane is."

17

"Uh . . . wait," Michael says. "Who is she?"

"A soldier from New Haven," I tell him as I boot up the laptop at my kitchen table. "Her name is Jane Talmadge."

It's Sunday night. I actually called Michael to tell him of the change in plans for the project. That it's now going to be on Private First Class Jane Talmadge of the 6888th Central Postal Directory Battalion. But Michael is uncharacteristically resistant.

Mom is lurking in the kitchen, eavesdropping as she makes our meals for the upcoming week. Smells like something Mexican, maybe meat for tacos, and lentil soup.

"She was in the Six Triple Eight," I explain again, stepping into the living room. "That unit served overseas in England and France. And she died over there. She's buried at the American Cemetery."

"How'd she die?" Michael asks.

"In a jeep accident." I had felt a stab of sadness learning this. After Kristal and I returned to the museum following our froyo break, I glued myself to the exhibit and read everything that there was. I must've reread the sentence on the accident five, ten times. Bev must've noticed because she came over again.

"Cat decided to do her history project on Jane Talmadge," Kristal told her mom. "Do you have any other stuff on her?"

"This is music to my ears," Bev had said with a huge smile, one hand on the silk knit of her turtlenecked chest. She then flew into executive director mode and retrieved two books as well as her business card and the museum curator's card for me. I was to reach out to the curator and see if the museum had anything else I could use. And Bev demanded a copy of the bio when I finished it.

I'm pretty sure that Cat Pulaski, an official St. Anne's IOP girl, made a good first impression on Bev.

Michael's talking and I zone back in. "But she didn't actually fight or anything," he's saying. "I think Oleck wants us to do a bio on somebody who died in battle. Like storming the beach at Normandy. He called this project the D-day Project, right? Did she have anything to do with D-day?"

This is the response I expected. And I'm prepared for it. "I'm pretty sure the only requirement is that the soldier is buried in Normandy. Oleck probably didn't even consider a woman being there. There's, like, only five women total buried there."

"I don't know," Michael says stubbornly. "I mean, this Jean lady only delivered mail, right? I'm not sure this is what he was looking for."

"Look, it's okay if you're not into it, but I really want to do the project on her," I say, growing irritated. "She was from New Haven and the museum is really close, like fifteen or twenty minutes away. Your Kasia soldier is from Waterbury. That's a major hike from here. And for *Jane*, most of the research is already done. I've got a couple of books and the museum's got her coat, some letters, a couple of photographs." This last bit about the photos is a white lie, but I'm sure I'll be able to dig something up. "Oleck will understand," I add. "You can still do your project on Jonathan Kasia, if you want. We'll just explain to Oleck before class, and I'll take the blame about your summary on Kasia not being ready."

"We're not splitting up," Michael says with some heat. And this gives me a little rush of happy. "We're a team. It's just . . . I don't know," he continues. "Why do you want to do it on her so badly?"

"Because . . . because . . ."

Because I feel like I know her somehow. She's somebody I think I would've been friends with if there weren't seventy or eighty years between us. But I can't say that. *Cuckoo, cuckoo.*

Kristal's and Bev's comments come back to me and fill in the gap. "Because these women rocked. They faced all kinds of prejudice and still wanted to serve."

Man, that sounded good. Mom emerges from the

kitchen and gives me a thumbs-up. I can't keep down a smile.

"Okay," Michael says. "History's first period tomorrow. Can you get there a little earlier so we can talk to Oleck? I just want to make sure it's not going to affect our grade."

"I'll ask my mom," I say, but Mom is already nodding from the kitchen door, not even knowing the question.

Michael's not the type to hold a grudge, and for the next twenty minutes, I hear every minute detail about the Model Congress conference in D.C. As he chatters, I scroll the Internet for photos of the 6888th and find a good number of websites. I copy and paste the URLs onto the bibliography I've created. When Michael and I say good-night, he seems on board with Jane as long as we don't get penalized grade-wise for the switch.

Sunday-night dinner is scrambled eggs with onions and peppers, toasted Italian bread from Mom's Saturday shift at Dominic's, and finished with two double-chocolate doughnut survivors from this morning. While Mom cleans up, I pull the laptop back in front of me and continue my online search.

In only an hour, I've compiled a decent bibliography to show Oleck tomorrow; it lists the websites, the two books from Bev (*To Serve My Country, to Serve My Race* and an autobiography of Major Charity Adams, the 6888th's commander), the coat and letter at the museum. I print it out on the printer in the living room.

Mom joins me at the table. "Sounds like a great project."

I look up from the screen. "It is," I say.

"And they have a coat of this woman's? At the museum?" Mom asks.

I nod.

She tilts her head and her eyebrows cinch together. "You know, I'd bet anything we still have Uncle Jack's uniform somewhere in Grandma's room."

My shoe box radar goes berserk as Mom rises to her feet. I know exactly where that jacket is. My small battalion is hiding inside it in the plaid suitcase under Grandma's bed. Per Catherine protocol, I moved them Friday night from under my bed (after jamming the *Girl, Interrupted* note inside the shoe box) to their current weekend location in Grandma's room. "We don't have the uniform anymore!" I say, and stand. "I saw Grandma give it to Goodwill." My heart races.

Mom looks at me skeptically. "Grandma would never donate anything to Goodwill," she says. "You know that. That's why our basement looked the way it did. She could've been on one of those hoarder shows."

Mom's got that look on her face when she wants to prove me wrong. *Oh shit.* She takes a step toward Grandma's door.

"I didn't mean Goodwill," I say. "It was some veterans' place. They were asking for uniforms or something. For a museum." I shrug. I'm sweating now. Desperate times call for desperate measures, and I pull the Grandma death card. "It was right before . . . you know."

A combo of compassion and sadness washes over Mom's face. For the final piece of faux evidence, I add, "I think she was nervous to tell you, that you'd want to keep it or something."

"Huh," Mom says, and sits back down. "Who knew?" She laughs a little. "Figures. The one thing we could've used, she gives away."

Later on, after the Lamictal rash inspection, Mom and I head upstairs. From behind me on the staircase, she says, "Oh, I meant to tell you. I won't be working anymore on Saturdays at Dominic's. And I'm scaling back on Friday nights too. Probably working every other weekend."

I stop and turn around. "Why?"

"Well, first off, it's a pretty brutal schedule," Mom says, running her hand through hair that she still hasn't colored.

"And?" I ask, prompting her to finish. Because I have an inkling as to the second reason, and it's pissing me off.

"I want to spend more time with you," Mom says. "We see each other what? An hour on Friday? Half of Saturday? It's not enough."

I can't help myself. "Or is it that you don't want to impose on Aunt Darlene anymore? And you've run out of Friday-night babysitters and Lamictal monitors?"

Mom squeezes past me and heads to her room. She spins around at the door to face me, her face red. "Actually, Catherine, I'm exhausted. What part of that don't you get? I cook, I clean, I do laundry, I fold clothes, I shop, I don't ask you for any help. Not one thing!" She's yelling now. "I'm working full time and then a second job for most of the weekend. You know why, right? Because it's just me, Catherine! It's just me supporting us! I don't want to blow through everything Grandma left us in the next five years.

I'll start the Friday shift up again. It's just right now, I need to take a little break. I want to leave the office on a Friday and just come home. Have two whole days to myself. Is that so hard for you to understand? Is it possible for you to *ever*"—her voice cracks on that word—"cut me some slack?"

She's right. Sometimes I stun myself. All I ever see is how her working makes *me* feel. Jesus Christ. Who knew how many facets guilt has? I ache that she works double-duty to pay for all my extra bipolar expenses, that she's stuck in a shitty job because it gives her the flexibility to shuttle me everywhere, that she agonizes over time spent away from me because of work, and now let's add this one, the physical toll of working so much. Sure, I've noticed, but not once have I done a fucking thing to lighten her load.

Mom hurries into her bedroom and I follow her. Her bed is unmade and I can't take my eyes off it. It is always half made, only one side ever occupied. Because of me. It's wrong that I absorb her so much, there's no room for any-one else.

There should be. She should have room for Bill, at least, but I ruined that, too. It happened maybe three weeks after I came home from the hospital, on one of those brilliant early-autumn evenings with the sky an impossibly deep sapphire blue streaked with pink.

I was camped out on the sofa, and Mom was her usual two feet away from me. We were sloppy in sweats and T-shirts, a congealing pizza that neither of us could swallow on the coffee table. A strong rapping on the front door punctured the canned laugh track of whatever lame sitcom we weren't watching. Mom jumped up, almost like she was expecting it.

Peering through the picture window, I spotted Bill's black F-150 at the curb in front of our house. Mom and Bill had been dating for ten months. He was a contractor, divorced with twins he got on alternating weekends. Despite the fog of Zero, I liked Bill. I liked his strong, steady presence, his quick smile and his black curly hair with gray at the temples. He was in a different league from Mom's past boyfriends, who had never lasted longer than a couple of months.

Bill genuinely cared for Mom. I saw it in his nightly call to make sure all was well (or what could pass for well in the Pulaski household at the time). And in the way that he listened to Mom, head cocked, a slight smile on his face. The tender way he watched her when she wasn't looking.

Mom greeted him on the stoop and pulled the front door almost shut. Almost. That inch of space allowed their voices to flow back into the living room and over to me. Bill's voice was raised in a pitch I had never heard before— stressed. Asking, "Why, Jody? I don't understand."

Then Mom's gentle murmurs. "Catherine . . . I just can't . . . all my time has to be . . . needs me now . . . so sorry." She was crying. I crept closer and peered through the crack and saw they were holding each other. Saying good-bye.

And Mom has never, not once, thrown that back in my face. She's never mentioned his name again, never talked about his adorable kids, or sailing on his little boat. She's never even brought up that trip to the Florida Keys that never happened.

She's better off without you, Zero whispers in my ear.

"You're right, you should have your weekends off," I say to Mom, and move toward her bed. I straighten the sheet and then grab the crumpled comforter.

"What are you doing?" Mom snaps.

"Just fixing your bed," I say.

"I'm going to sleep in fifteen minutes, Catherine. Don't bother."

I return to my room, seeking refuge in my own bed. I just need Mom to fall asleep and then I can creep downstairs and get the troops of bottles. I need to hold them tonight.

But twenty minutes go by and Mom still hasn't clicked off her light. And then she's beside my bed, extending a glass of water like a peace offering.

"Look, I'm sorry—" she begins.

I cut her off. "*You* don't have to apologize. Please. I was wrong. You deserve to have a full weekend off. And I can help out too. You don't have to do everything."

"But I jumped down your throat. I shouldn't do that," Mom says. "I'm stressed too. Aunt Darlene's been on me to quit everything and manage one of her stores, but I can't take advantage of her like that." Mom forces a smile. "I'm gonna try this, cut back my hours and see how we do. Forget what I said about money. We've got plenty. How about we start Sunday-night movie night again?" She smiles, and my Grinch heart cracks even more.

"Sounds good." Dear God, please make her leave now. I need to go downstairs. I feel off-balance without them here, under my bed, supporting me.

Kissing me on my spiky hair, Mom exits and putters around in her bedroom. And keeps puttering. Her TV's on and I can hear the hiss of the iron.

I can't get to my stockpile, so reviewing my list will have to do. I slip under my comforter and gaze at my phone's screen until the day's fatigue presses down and pulls me under. In a dense twilight haze, I hear Mom shut off my light and whisper, "I love you, baby girl," her lips soft against my forehead.

"I love you," I whisper back. "I love you. And I'm so sorry."

I sleep the entire night.

"It's freaking brilliant!" Mr. Oleck shouts, waving my bibliography in his hand. "Yes, yes, yes!" The classroom is lit with the early Monday-morning sun that streams through the bank of windows.

Michael's face falls at Mr. Oleck's reaction to my proposed switch from Jonathan Kasia to Jane Talmadge. "Well, we were worried that it's not quite what you wanted," he says. "You know, this isn't a soldier who fought in the D-day invasion."

I throw a look at Michael. *We* were not worried.

He adds, "You know, it wasn't a soldier who died in battle."

"Oh no," Mr. Oleck responds quickly. "Look, this soldier, Jane"—he looks down at the bibliography title—"Talmadge. She gave her life. She enlisted and did her part. She wouldn't have gotten killed in an Army jeep in France any other way. There's no doubt about it. She was there for her country. It's the ultimate sacrifice." Mr. Oleck takes a deep breath. "This is really awesome. You'll be telling a chapter from the war that gets next to no attention. I've never even heard of the Six Triple Eight. But these were Americans who faced incredible obstacles like legalized prejudice, and yet still wanted to enlist and help America. Well done, you guys! I can't wait to see what you come up with."

Mr. Oleck rushes off to get coffee from the faculty room, and I start to laugh a little. Michael looks like somebody just sold his puppy.

"Nice try," I say with a grin.

"What?" he asks.

"Trying to get out of doing the project on Jane," I answer. " 'We were worried'?"

He shrugs. "Nothing against her," he says, looking down. "Oleck is right. She did her part. I was just into doing it on Kasia. It seems more exciting. More epic."

"Why don't we just split up, then?" I ask. "It's no big deal. I won't be mad."

Michael's head pops up and he looks me in the eye. "Is that really it?" he asks. His neck is getting splotchy. "That you don't want to partner with me? Is this just an excuse? To break up?"

To break up? Wait a second. We're going out? I can't say any of this. I'm the one who kissed him. "No. I mean, no, not to break up," I sputter. "Uh . . . I just . . . I really don't know. I just clicked with Jane somehow."

I shift, uncomfortable. I didn't plan on spilling my connection with Jane, but Michael doesn't even seem to catch the weirdness of it.

"So it's not me?" he asks, still uncertain. "We're still good?"

Something inside me unclenches even more and I reach out to squeeze his hand. "Yes," I tell my first official boyfriend. "We're still good. Definitely."

18

It's Friday afternoon and all hell is breaking loose in the girls' bathroom at St. Anne's. Kristal and I just walked right into a big-ass brouhaha between the Immaculate Conception girls.

Amy, pale and slight in her oversized sweatshirt, is shrieking, "It was just this week, Alexis! I swear!"

Alexis, waving a small, silvery packet of something, screams, "You are so full of shit! You are a pound and a half from a feeding tube!"

"I am not!" Amy says, but there's a glint of something in her eyes—something twisted and triumphant.

I look over at Kristal, but Kristal is staring straight at Amy with a shocked and almost fearful expression.

The bathroom door swings open. Sandy enters, followed closely by Vanessa. The St. Anne's behavioral SWAT team. *We've got a 109 in the ladies' washroom. All units please respond, stat.*

"All right, everybody, let's calm down," Sandy says in a soothing voice.

Vanessa asks with some intensity, "Is everybody okay?"

Alexis's head whips toward Sandy and Vanessa, her blond hair flying. "No! Everybody is not okay. She"—Alexis points at Amy, who has retreated behind a stall door—"is popping laxatives again." Alexis shakes the silver packet again. "I knew she was losing weight! I kept asking her and she kept lying her fucking head off to me!"

Alexis plows toward the stall in which Amy is cowering. Vanessa inserts her body between the two girls.

"You *promised* me!" Alexis screams past Vanessa. "We made a pact." Her voice is breaking now. "We were done with it, right? Isn't that what we said?"

Sandy turns to Kristal and me. "Girls, can you please return to the room?" she asks.

"Sure," I say, and obediently move to the door. Kristal hasn't budged, transfixed by the scene, so I lightly take her arm and pull her with me.

Amy begins mounting her defense from the toilet. "It was only this one time! Just yesterday!"

In the hallway, Kristal whispers to me, "That wasn't the first time. That's what we heard her doing last week."

Sandy steps back into the hallway and says, "It's all right, girls. We're handling this. Why don't you wait inside the room for me? I think—" Sandy stops abruptly, studying Kristal's face. There's silence in the bathroom now, and then the soft rise and fall of Vanessa's voice as somebody cries. "Catherine, I'd like to talk to Kristal privately for a few minutes. Would you please excuse us?"

I glance over at Kristal. She's clearly shaken: her eyes are wide and she bites her lower lip. For somebody getting over bulimia, it must hit too close to home. Without a word, Kristal follows Sandy into Vanessa's office and shuts the door.

Inside Room Three, Lil' Tommy bounds over to me. "What the fuck is going on in the girls' room? A fight?"

I don't think I should be talking. At least, not without Sandy here. But I can't deny it either. Everybody has ears. "Alexis and Amy were arguing," I say to Lil' Tommy, Garrett and John. "That's all I know." I sit down on a sofa and pull out my phone. I don't want to talk to anyone. I'm worried about Kristal.

When Sandy returns with a somber Kristal fifteen minutes later, she refuses to talk about what happened.

"But I thought we were supposed to be honest here," Lil' Tommy complains. "It's a safe zone and all that."

"It is, but it's for the girls to discuss if they want to," Sandy responds. "Now, if anyone needs to discuss how the incident is affecting *you*, then by all means, speak freely. But I can't discuss what happened between Alexis and Amy."

Lil' Tommy looks around the room, but everyone stays mute. Sandy turns the topic to resilience, asking us to think about what it means and how we achieve it. I say nothing. Resilience is not in my DNA. Kristal too stays quiet, lost in thought. I nudge her elbow and raise my eyebrows. "You okay?" I whisper.

She gives me a very small, unbrilliant smile.

After group, I stop her in the empty waiting room. Through the glass front doors, I can see Aunt D's red Mini

Cooper illegally parked in the handicap spot again. "Are you okay? You look really upset."

Kristal sighs and keeps her eyes on the parking lot. "Thanks, Cat. I'm okay. I just hate seeing that with Amy. It freaks me out."

I nod, uncertain of how much more to ask her. "Because . . ."

"Because," Kristal picks up my unfinished question, "I don't know, it makes me feel nervous." She looks at me and says firmly, "I'm done. I stopped doing that a while ago. I'm in recovery." She looks away again. "It's just . . . you hate to see other people . . . slide back. Amy's done with us here. Did you know that? She'll probably have to go to a *hospital* now. She'll probably be admitted tonight. This is bad. *Really* serious."

I'm glad Kristal is confiding in me, but her comments about having to go to the hospital—that it's really serious, really bad—scare me. I don't like how she said them either. The gravity in her tone. An Amy-versus-us mentality just starting to form.

Can I ever tell her that I was hospitalized? Can I ever tell her the reason?

Some kind of luxury sedan pulls into the spot next to Aunt D and a man steps out from the driver's side. "That's my dad," Kristal says. A new expression slides down, masklike, to hide the anxiety in her face. Opening the door, Kristal yells an introduction, "Dad, this is my friend Cat!"

My friend.

Kristal's dad is tall and is wearing a jacket and tie. He

walks around the front of the car to shake my hand. "Nice to meet you, Cat."

"Have a great time at Amherst!" I tell Kristal. She's going tomorrow to check out a cluster of schools there.

"I don't think that's possible. Those tours suck. But at least I'm driving," Kristal tells me from the open driver's-side door.

"Wish me luck," Kristal's dad says to me.

"Have a good time at the museum!" Kristal calls out. "I want all the details." She winks at me.

Kristal knows Michael and I are headed to the New Haven Museum tomorrow to check out the 6888th exhibit.

"All the details!" Kristal says again before sliding into the driver's seat. She gives a short beep and a wave and then backs out like Grandma—exceptionally slowly, with liberal use of the brake.

I feel a pang of jealousy as Kristal steers toward a future. Mom will never let me learn to drive. I won't ever be checking out colleges. All I'll ever have are short, fleeting bursts of color in a genetically preordained gray life.

I'm not in the mood for dinner tonight with Aunt D, but, as usual, she insists, and we wind up at a Lebanese place, the Cedars. It turns out to be great for many reasons—food, company, but the highlight is her offer of a job at Dunkin' Donuts.

"When do you think the IOP ends?" Aunt D asks, dipping a falafel ball into the hummus.

"No clue," I say. "Whenever Dr. McCallum cries uncle."

"Well, the job is waiting. Just let me know when you're through and we'll get your training started. I don't know if your mother told you"—Aunt D pauses while our waiter brings us stuffed grape leaves and labneh dip—"but I want her to manage one of the stores. Tell those a-holes at Heffer-man and Schletz to take a hike. What do you think? That would be better for her, right? I'd have two Pulaski women on my team!"

At drop-off, Aunt D keeps the engine running, just like last Friday. "I told your mom it was ridiculous me coming inside anymore. You're right, Catherine. You don't need any 'Lamictal monitors.'" She makes air quotes for the last two words and then smiles at me.

At that moment, I swear to myself that I will swallow my pills once I get inside.

But the house is dark and cold and empty. Inside the kitchen, my tablets and empty glass call to me. I think of my future job and seeing Michael tomorrow. But then I remember Kristal and what she said about hospitalization. And that she has a driver's license and she's going to college. Things that are not options for me. With no Lamictal monitor looking over my shoulder, I ignore my pills and get the troops from upstairs. In Grandma's room, Friday's two tablets join their brothers inside the Lexapro bottle.

19

Nonny twists all the way around to look at me from the front passenger seat of Lorraine Pitoscia's Subaru. Who knew her aging vertebrae had so much flexibility?

"Why you wear your hair like that?" she asks.

"Oh man, Nonny," Michael groans beside me in the backseat.

"It's okay," I say. And it is. Nonny doesn't mean anything by it, and she seems sincerely interested in my hair. "I saw that movie with Audrey Hepburn. *Roman Holiday,*" I tell her. "She cuts her hair short. I just liked it." I omit the small detail that the haircut occurred during the apex of a manic episode.

"Oh, I love *Roman Holiday*!" Lorraine says. "That movie is why we went to Rome for our honeymoon." She throws a glance at Nonny. "Nonny, why don't you turn back around? You'll be more comfortable."

"Me too," Michael mutters under his breath.

Nonny ignores her and continues questioning me. "What you think? I get my hair cut short too?"

A vision of Nonny getting her hair snipped by Rodrick flashes through my head. Two worlds colliding. Her eyes are expectant, demanding an answer.

"My grandmother always wore her hair short. It looked great on her," I say. I have no idea where that just came from. I never talk about Grandma. It must be some residual Lamictal loosening my tongue.

Nonny nods and then directs her gaze onto Michael. "*That's* why I had to come. I need some girl advice." She readjusts herself to face front. "Lorraine, you take me to Supercuts after we drop off the kids. I'm gonna be Nonny Hepburn." She pulls out her iPhone, peels away the Kleenex encasing it and begins pecking away.

"Michael, call and make a reservation for Nonny at Supercuts," Lorraine says. "It's a zoo on Saturdays."

"And Michael's friend comes over for dinner tonight. She see my hair!" Nonny shouts as her phone chimes. It sounds like a foghorn. Holding the phone as far as possible from her face, she slowly reads aloud the text message she just received. "Sylvia wants a picture of my new hair."

"Hey, Nonny," Michael says, "maybe you should have your own Instagram account. I can start it for you."

"Don't you dare, Michael!" Lorraine yells.

Nonny isn't in the car when Lorraine picks us up at four o'clock. "She wants to surprise you," Lorraine tells me.

So I'm headed back to Casa de Pitoscia. At least it's not a dinner ambush like last week. Still, Nonny's tactics make me like her all the more. Grandma did the same thing once.

I was in fifth grade, and Mom had started dating an orthodontist she'd met at the law office—he was being sued for malpractice. He'd come inside the house whenever he picked Mom up, but Grandma and I never spent any time with him.

One Friday night, Grandma finally snagged him by cooking her best dish—fried chicken. She also whipped up the lightest mashed potatoes and brown gravy, along with my favorite dessert, apple pie. But the real hook was the chicken. It was early evening and the scent of the chicken had wafted into the living room and out the front window screens. Dr. Scott was drooling on his Ralph Lauren polo by the time his penny loafers cleared the first concrete step to our door. And that's how we spent our only evening with Mom's first steady boyfriend. So when the balding douche broke up with Mom, Grandma said with authority that she had known something was wrong with him and that Mom was better off.

That was the way Grandma worked. She was never in your face about anything, just a subtle, steady presence at every breakfast, after-school snack, dinner and good-night hug. Snapping pictures from the front row at every recital. Religiously saving my report cards, ballet flyers and artwork. Singing as she folded clothes warm and soft from the dryer. She was as constant as my breath. Our house was always well lit and warm with the great smells of whatever she was cooking or baking.

So the truth is, I don't mind returning to the Pitoscias. Mom is working a longer shift today, anyway—somebody called in sick, so she won't be home until nine. The Pitoscia household with Nonny in the garlic-scented kitchen and the loud voices, well, it seems a hell of a lot more appealing than the empty Pulaski Cape on Maple Drive.

This will also be the longest stretch of time Michael and I have hung out. And so far, so good. Borderline great. He was the perfect museum companion this afternoon: not too chatty, not clingy, stayed within view and only called me over to point out something especially amazing or heartbreaking. He saved the exhibit on the 6888th for last.

"I have to get myself in the mood," he explained, half-serious, half-joking, during our froyo break. "I'm ready to meet your Jane now."

His lips lifted in a half smile, and in that moment, sitting on a stool looking out onto Chapel Street, he looked beautiful to me. Maybe it was a sugar rush from the yogurt. Or the fact that he acknowledged this project meant something to me. Whatever it was—the way his face looked, that Mona Lisa boy-smile, his brown eyes holding mine—it was one of those moments that imprints itself onto the brain. I felt my cheeks warm and knew I was blushing.

"Thanks again," I had said, realizing then that I never thanked him in the first place. "For agreeing to switch soldiers. That was really great of you. I know you were into Kasia."

"It was hard," Michael had admitted, spooning strawberry yogurt with chocolate sprinkles into his mouth. "I still have my G.I. Joe and Rescue Heroes. I won't let my mom donate them yet."

Then, at the 6888th exhibit, he just soaked it all in, reading everything, studying Jane's coat, watching the looping video for at least four full runs, all the while typing notes into his phone. When he got to Jane's letter under Plexiglas, his eyebrows drew together and his fingers rubbed his chin. I joined him there, and Jane's words still sang to me: "I can't change the way I was born." We stood side by side and that was when he laced his fingers in mine.

We dropped hands as soon as an attractive brunette approached us. It was the curator, Jenna. I had emailed her on Monday per Bev and asked about any other items she might have on Jane, and then I let her know about our Saturday visit. After introductions, she told us that she might have more materials, that another library was loaning them a whole box of letters and that once they arrived, she'd shoot me an email if she found anything. As soon as Jenna walked away, Michael reached for my hand again.

"Let me go inside first," Lorraine tells us now as she pulls into the driveway. "And tell Nonny that you're here."

But the front door is already swinging open and I can see Nonny's short, stocky frame silhouetted in the doorway. Just as we reach the door, Nonny flips on the foyer light. "What you think?" she yells.

Gone is the center-parted knot of gray hair at the base of her head. Now her thick hair is short, side-parted with long bangs, and tapered to her neck. I might actually need to check out Nonny's stylist.

"You don't look like you just landed on Ellis Island anymore," Michael says, hugging her.

She turns to me. "So, Michael's friend, you like it?"

"It's fantastic! What a great cut," I say.

"No, I went to Supercuts," she corrects me. She about-faces and marches into the kitchen. "I made pizza. Come and eat now."

Anthony and Mr. Pitoscia are already seated at the table, eating. Anthony waves and gives a friendly, "Hi, Catherine."

Michael's dad pats his mouth with a paper napkin and then rubs his hands together as he rises to his feet. He's maybe five foot nine—so that's why Anthony's so much shorter. Michael towers over both of them.

"Hello," Mr. Pitoscia says to me, hand outstretched. "I'm Tony, this guy's dad." With his free hand, he squeezes the back of Michael's neck. "I've heard a lot about you. And your hair." He grins and I can see Michael's smile in it.

We shake hands, and Mr. Pitoscia pulls out a chair for me next to Anthony.

"Hey, Dad, I'm thinking putting Catherine right next to me is not the greatest of ideas," Anthony says. "I worked today and haven't showered yet." He looks at me with an open grin. "I do wash. We just always meet when I've gotten off work." Anthony's baseball hat is on backward, revealing sweat-dried hair, and his green Paoletti's Landscaping T-shirt looks damp and threadbare with small bits of grass and leaves speckling it.

Michael pulls out a chair on the opposite side of the table for me, next to Lorraine. "Hey, Michael's friend," he teases. "You sit here."

On the kitchen table are two cookie sheets of misshapen, clearly homemade pizza. Holding a pair of heavy silver scissors, Nonny wedges herself between Anthony and Mr. Pitoscia.

"You two slow down and let Michael and"—she looks at me—"his friend eat first. You already went through two pies."

Then she picks up the corner of one of the pizzas and cuts it into large squares.

"She uses those scissors on everything," Anthony tells me. "Cutting coupons, pruning her tomato plants, even trimming Mitzi's hair."

Michael and Mr. Pitoscia burst out laughing. Lorraine looks at me and rolls her eyes. "She definitely does not use them on the dog," she says.

Nonny slides two large squares onto my plate and then steps back, watching me, so I pick up a slice and take a bite. Maybe it's the dog-hair seasoning or the newspaper-print flavor, but Nonny's pizza is awesome.

"Catherine, we can drive you home tonight," Lorraine says. "Is your mom working?"

Before I can answer, Nonny spouts, "Where your father?"

I can handle this, my answer automated from years of practice. "My parents split up when I was young." *In utero, to be precise.* I add, "I never really knew him." *Or his name.*

Lorraine's face is a mask of sympathy that turns to horror when Nonny speaks again.

"That's okay, Michael's friend," she says, while scissoring into the second pizza. "My grandmother hated her husband. Spent forty years of her life with that ass. She better off without him."

"Jesus, Ma!" Mr. Pitoscia reaches for his mother's hand. "Settle down."

Lorraine quickly repeats her earlier question about whether I need a ride home.

"My mom can get me," I say. "She's hoping to get out around nine."

That's kind of late. For a second I worry that I'm overstaying my welcome, but then Michael asks, "Can she pick you up later than that?"

Before I can answer, Mr. Pitoscia asks me where Mom works and I tell him about both her day and night jobs. Big mistake, because Lorraine then says proudly, "And you work at that law firm too, right, Catherine? Michael told me."

Oh Jesus. "Um . . . yeah . . . just when they need me," I say.

Mr. Pitoscia nods. "I love to hear when kids get experience like that. What do they have you doing?"

I'm overheating. I'm trapped, locked into this lie for good now that I've scammed Michael's entire family. What makes it even worse is that they're all looking at me expectantly, waiting to be impressed. When the truth is that I'm not doing anything brilliant—psych rehab is pretty much the complete opposite.

"Like, filing stuff," I say slowly, looking down at the pizza square on my plate. The lies are like mud on my tongue, thick and heavy.

Just as I'm about to attempt a conversation hijack by asking about toothless Mitzi, Michael reroutes the discussion with a loud, "Let's open an Instagram account for Nonny." He must know his mother's going to flip, because I can see a flush bloom near the neckline of his T-shirt.

Lorraine indeed flips out as Nonny withdraws her phone from somewhere within the top half of her torso and drops its tissue cocoon to the table.

"No!" Anthony says. "Facebook! I'll get my laptop."

Anthony bolts from the kitchen and Mr. Pitoscia heads to the refrigerator. He's halfway back to the table, beer in hand, when Lorraine scolds, "Tony!" Her tone is soft but sharp-edged. Without a word, Mr. Pitoscia returns the unopened can to the refrigerator.

We spend the entire night at the kitchen table, on Anthony's laptop, creating Nonny's FB account. For the relationship status, Michael types Nonny is "in a relationship" with Mitzi. For her profile picture, Anthony puts his baseball cap sideways on Nonny's newly stylish head and calls her "'90s Nonny." For a favorite quote, he types in some Italian profanity courtesy of Google until Nonny makes him delete it. Michael adds Muse for favorite music (Nonny likes the "orchestra parts") and *People* magazine for books.

The only slightly awkward part is when they want to send a friend request to me and I have to tell them that I'm not on FB. Obviously I can't say the reason why, which is that Dr. McCallum has outlawed it.

When Mom texts me at eight-thirty to tell me she's in the driveway, I'm stunned. The hours flew by and I laughed as hard as I did that day at St. Anne's with Kristal. A surprisingly awesome day, even if Michael and I didn't get any alone time in the basement. I have a feeling another opportunity will present itself soon.

"So, you spent a long time with this boy," Mom says inside the Accord, a minute into our drive home. "Anything going on I should know about?"

"Nah, not really," I say.

I can't tell her that Michael and I are technically "going out." My mother would take it too much as a sign of progress, when I know this won't last. Michael doesn't know *me*. God knows how many defensive lies I told his family tonight. I sat there at their table, served by Nonny, and lied to all of them. Lies I can never undo or explain. Shame rises hot and fast. They're such good people.

Anxiety, my constant companion, wakes up to further erode the day's goodness. My heart picks up its pace as I think about Dr. McCallum's warnings. He often babbles about a "game plan," something we'll devise together because, as he has explained, "patients with bipolar disorder often get depressed again after a period of stability and even after doing everything right—establishing a good diet, good sleep patterns and exercise habits, and taking their meds. It can be really discouraging."

No shit. It's infinitely more than discouraging. It's catastrophic.

On the verge of tears, I look out the window so Mom

can't see. It's so brutally unfair. I want more time. I really like Michael, and I would love to let this, *us,* unfurl naturally. But as Dr. McCallum has warned, Zero is coming, maybe preceded by a manic episode of God only knows what. An image of me revved up and hyper in front of Michael pops into my head. I shut my eyes. He can never, never see that.

I have no choice. I need to squeeze out as much good as I can with Michael. In whatever time remaining.

20

"Oops," Louis Farricelli says as he deliberately flicks his pen off his desk and right in front of me. After I picked the same pen up off the classroom floor and returned it to him not three seconds ago.

He leers at me. His cheeks and double chin are compressed upward by the neck brace so he looks like a perverted Pillsbury Doughboy. "I *love* to make you bend over," he whispers.

He's turned darker since his injury. There's something ugly and angry percolating under that mass of muscle and flesh. His celebrity status at Cranbury High is already declining, accelerated by the freshman quarterback, who, according to Michael, is completely kicking ass. Before our eyes, Louis Farricelli is atrophying into an eighteen-year-old has-been.

I ignore him and his pen and sit down as Mr. Oleck turns on the Smart Board.

Louis Farricelli hisses like a serpent, "Heard crazies like you are complete freaks in the sack. Maybe we—" But by hyperfocusing on Mr. Oleck's voice, I can mute the asshole behind me. Just like I can completely not see Riley and Olivia and their crew at the back of the room. They've backed off from the heckling and pranks, for now at least.

I think it might be Michael. He's like my Patronus Charm.

After history class, Michael and I walk together to our next classes. It's a routine now. Today, Monday, he has AP physics and I'm off to non-honors precalculus with the poorly named Ms. Stinkov. Some days, Tyler walks with us because he has U.S. history near our classroom. He still doesn't say a whole lot, but as soon as I walk away, I hear him resume his normal conversation with Michael. I get it.

After school, as usual, I'm stuck waiting for Mom. I don't see Michael on the sidewalk out here anymore. He's in a bunch of different clubs—Model Congress, the newspaper and, I think, a gamers' one. It's a little lonely without him.

I stare at the parking lot entrance willing the Accord to appear. Nothing. I text Mom three question marks followed by three exclamation points. This is getting freaking ridiculous.

I really don't want to be late to St. Anne's today and miss any wrap-up of the Immaculate Conception meltdown. It was all Kristal and I could text about last night. She's sure that Alexis will come but that Amy has been transferred to a rehab center or hospital.

The Accord barrels into the parking lot at the same

time my phone choos. It's Michael. "What are you doing on Friday? Can you come over? Help me give out candy to little kids?"

That's right. It's Halloween in four days. The past two Halloweens have been anti-holidays. Burning orange reminders of everything that's been tsunamied by the gray of Zero. Out of all the holidays, Halloween is the most friend-centric one. And for someone who had lost her friends, it was best ignored, with the TV in Mom's room cranked loud, the door shut tight so as not to hear the laughter on our street, or the joyous shouts of "Trick or treat!" And Mom, beside me on the bed, eyes blankly staring at the screen, silently praying that the bowl of candy outside our front door would stave off the ringing of the doorbell.

But now, it feels different. I can actually remember, in my body, that Halloween feeling. That jangly, twitchy buzz from candy corn, popcorn balls and the jumbo Hershey's chocolate bars that Mr. Willetz from two doors down always gave out. The exquisite selection process of the costume. The world turned upside down—in a good way—for one black velvet night.

I slide into the front passenger seat. "Michael asked me over to his house for Halloween," I tell Mom.

Mom glances at me before accelerating, but I can't read the expression on her face. "Oh," she says. "Do you want to go?"

"Yeah," I answer.

"You know, he can come over to our house too," Mom says. "I'm not working this Friday."

I see Michael and me on the living room sofa with Mom

orbiting around us, offering food, drink and Jenga. Our three voices would never match the volume at the Pitoscia house. "Um . . . well, he asked me to go there first," I say. Knowing Michael, I'm sure he'd come to my place instead if I asked. But I don't want to.

"That's fine, Catherine," Mom says quickly. "But just please invite him to our house sometime, okay?"

I study Mom's profile. Her eyebrows are scrunched together as if she's not sure how to navigate this change to our Halloween protocol. "So, are you guys like dating or going out?" she asks.

I want to lie and say we're just hanging out, no big deal, but I'm not feeling it. Lying to her so much is tiring sometimes. So I tell a half-truth. "It might be going in that direction. . . . We'll see."

Mom gives me a smile, but the usual exuberance is missing. Her worry is almost palpable inside the tight confines of the Accord. *What if this boy hurts her?* she's thinking. *Catherine is still so vulnerable. She can't take any more rejection.*

Don't worry, Mom, I think. *I can't be hurt anymore. I've got a plan.*

I can't say that, though, obviously. So I'm silent and Mom is silent. But when we roll up to St. Anne's, Mom pulls me close for a hug, and I let her.

Pulling gently away from her, I say, "You should make plans for Friday night. Do something fun with Aunt D."

"Maybe I will," she says, and her smile reaches her eyes again.

When I enter Room Three, Kristal looks up from her

DBT card to give me a small, serious nod. I do a quick inventory of my IOP colleagues. Amy is missing, and Alexis sits alone on their sofa, just as Kristal predicted. And today, for the first time, Alexis hasn't changed into sweats. She's still in the Immaculate Conception uniform of plaid pleated skirt, white polo shirt, maroon knee socks and loafers.

I whisper to Kristal, "This is not good," and take my spot next to her on the sofa to supply the usual BS on my DBT form.

Everyone finishes in record time of course because of our missing member. Nobody makes a peep, not even Lil' Tommy, whose Docksides beat a rapid rhythm against the sofa. *Ba da. Ba da. Ba da.* We all look at Alexis.

Sandy takes a deep breath. "Well, I hope you all had a good weekend. Does anyone need to talk about anything?"

Again, nobody says a word. John clears his throat and adjusts his Red Sox cap. Garrett cracks his knuckles. Alexis stares at the floor. The room is quiet except for *ba da. Ba da. Ba da.*

Sandy nods as if expecting this. "Okay, well, first I need to make an announcement. Amy will no longer be in our group. I can't tell you any more than that. I know you understand why."

I glance at Kristal. She's holding herself rather rigidly, staring at Sandy.

"Okay," Sandy continues. "Some housekeeping notes. We're starting a new step-down program. The first week of December. Instead of five days a week, the step-down group will meet two days, from three o'clock to five o'clock. The step-down program follows the same format that we use here: group discussion, activities, exercises. At this point, it looks like I'm running that group. So, we've already advised your treatment providers. It's up to them to give the okay for you to join that program."

Wait, what? There's an end date to our happy little group? I feel a surprising amount of disappointment.

Sandy goes on about how another group will be starting in December. Their session will probably begin at the same time that the step-down program ends—five o'clock. So to avoid any delays, the step-down program will be taking place in a different room. "It's a great space. They're finishing it up now," Sandy says, pointing to the wall opposite the Room Three door. "Right next to this one. I just poked my head in today. Real pleather sofas," she says, and this gets the appropriate chuckles.

Sandy takes a breath and picks up her Starbucks cup. After two gulps, she looks around at us. "Okay, let's open it up now. Does anyone want to share anything?"

Alexis raises her hand. She looks at us, her face a mixture of embarrassment and defiance. "So, about last Friday . . ." Her hands in her lap have suddenly mesmerized her. The pause stretches out. She seems to have lost her chutzpah.

"It's okay," Kristal says. "You don't have to talk about it."

I can't believe Kristal said that. She's always encouraging people to share. Me especially. And this particular topic was all she could talk about last night.

Alexis looks up quickly. Her eyes are brimming with tears that avalanche down her cheeks at the sudden movement of her head. Kristal rises and joins Alexis on her sofa. And then Kristal does a not very covert head tilt, indicating that I should hop aboard the Alexis Consolation Train.

This is not my thing. Alexis doesn't even like me that much. I can't get up and walk over there. But Kristal is giving me big eyes that scream "Get your ass over here." And Lil' Tommy and Garrett and John are all looking at me now, expecting me to move. Even Sandy offers me an encouraging smile.

I'm not doing it. Alexis is going to ask, "What the freak is Catherine doing here?" And then she'll demand that Sandy order me back to my designated sofa.

Alexis gives a big sniffle and Kristal is almost glaring at me now. *Fine.* I get up and move across the square created by the four couches, bump my shin against the coffee table and sit next to Alexis, who actually shimmies closer to Kristal, farther from my lame carcass, and leans into her shoulder. I knew it. Jesus Christ. I thought this was supposed to be a safe zone.

But just as I'm urging my feet to propel me back to my sofa, Alexis's right hand reaches out and grabs my left hand. Her hand is sweaty and cupping a soggy Kleenex, but I hold on to it as she cries out her history with Amy.

After Alexis is finished, Kristal does the most talking. She is kind and encouraging, but there's a strange formality to her speech. Like she's reading a script. I don't know if the others sense it. I'm guessing it's because Amy's re-lapse has scared Kristal, made her feel more vulnerable.

"I know exactly how you feel, Alexis," Kristal says, the bangles on her wrists silent as she grips her knees. "Trust me, it feels unbelievable to move on with your life and stop obsessing about food. That sense of control you get while you're doing it? It's a crock. It only lasts as long as the bingeing and purging do and then all the bullshit just rolls back in. You get that now, right?"

Alexis nods, her eyes holding Kristal's.

"If I can stop doing it," Kristal says, "you can too."

It's 11:15 p.m. and Mom is doing God knows what in her room. Every night, after my regular homework is done, I read the books on the 6888th that Bev Walker gave me and take notes on the laptop. And every night, without fail, Mom shuts me down at 10:30.

Last week, Mom freaked out when she came to kiss me good-night. I had taken *To Serve My Country, to Serve My Race* upstairs with me. The book talks all about the women of the 6888th, or WACs as they were called. (WAC stands for Women's Army Corps. That was the unit in the army that women could belong to.) I had gotten to the part in the book where the first group of WACs was sailing to En-gland. As they got close, a German U-boat engaged them, forcing the converted cruise ship they were on to do all kinds of evasive maneuvers. It must've been scary as any-thing, with alarms ringing and the boat swerving left and right. The WACs could've been blown to smithereens before setting a toe on English soil. I couldn't put the book down. I wondered if Jane was on the ship, or if she had come over on the second one.

Of course, when Mom saw me on my bed with the book, she completely overreacted. Instead of being grateful that I was reading again, she had barked sharply, "Catherine, you need your sleep!" and then snatched the book out my hands like it was a bomb. So now, our new nighttime ritual, in addition to the Lamictal rash check, includes her locking down the laptop and taking both of my books hostage for the evening.

I'm waiting for Mom to fall asleep. She's already been in my room twice to kiss me good-night, but I'm not ruling out a third visit. Her nocturnal sentry duty is amping up, no doubt due to her worry over Michael. But I have things to do, like get my own troops out. They need to be in formation on my night table when Monday's cuts roll through my head: Louis Farricelli's insults du jour (on today's menu: the spicy "I like to make you bend over" and a new classic, "crazies are freaks in bed"), the disgust on Riley's face when she spotted me in history class (my unseeing eyes do see) and that scooped-out feeling (Zero's angel Gabriel) when I joined Alexis on the sofa and thought she was recoiling from defective Catherine Pulaski. It was a reality check, a sudden and swift sword jab that reminds me of who I am and the limited distance I can go.

I did manage to smuggle one thing up tonight, though, and I pat the small square of paper in my front jeans pocket, retrieving my contraband reading material. It's a printed-out email from Jenna, the curator at the New Haven Museum. She had transcribed the full letter from Jane, the one under Plexiglas, and sent it to me today. I've read it about ten times already, these words my only connection to a dead girl I think of as my second friend.

February 17, 1944

Dear Mama,

I don't know how much more I can take. Things are bad here. They give me looks and say nasty things when I walk by. I hurt so much. It doesn't matter what I do. How hard I try. I'll never be good enough. And there's nothing I can do about it. I can't change the way I was born.

Why in the world would we be assigned to South Carolina of all places? Fort Jackson is full of Sergeant Jim Crows who take any chance to put us down. We're called WAC Detachment #2. #2 always stands for colored. They got separate barracks for us #2s to sleep in. They've got us working at a hospital. Some girls here have medical training and they're cleaning out bedpans. I've got one year of college under my belt and here I am washing walls. Some girls got in big trouble for trying to change things here. There's some meeting coming up, but I don't think it's going to help much. But don't worry. You didn't raise a quitter. Just keep saying your prayers for me, Mama. Most

*of the girls are nice and we try to look out for one
another. Give a big hug to Petey for me and tell Mari
to stay out of my things! (Give her a hug for me too.)*

*Your loving daughter,
Jane*

Mom's coming down the hall again, so I stash the printout
under my pillow. "Catherine, are you going to get ready
for bed?" Her tone is anxious rather than pissed. "Can you
not sleep?"

"I'm fine," I say, but I know I look a little weird just sitting on my bed, still dressed in my regular clothes, doing
not a damn thing as far as Mom can tell. I retrieve a pair of
shorts and a T-shirt that I use for pajamas.

"Are you sleeping okay?" she asks. For maybe the
fourth time. Her anxiety is really skyrocketing. I hope she
starts therapy soon.

"Fine," I say. And for once, this is the truth. The Lamictal is continuing its job in the slumber department; for the
first time since maybe late September, I can actually fall
asleep and stay asleep.

"Number?" Mom asks, and it sounds like she's holding
her breath.

"Holding steady at . . ." I pause. Because the truth is
that I seriously think I'm at a seven. It was a decent, no,
a good day. Even with all the Farricelli and Riley junk.
Alexis confided to the group her and Amy's unholy alliance in the bingeing-and-puking underworld and how

competitive Amy was regarding their weight. Alexis had said, "Amy would always brag that even her name weighed less than mine."

After Alexis and Kristal were done talking, I just held tight to Alexis's hand and she squeezed right back. So yes, it was a good day.

Still, it's best not to give Mom false hope. There's no way this seven will last. "Six," I say. "Six and a half."

She nods, and I can practically see the wheels in her head spinning. *If this boy Michael hurts her,* she's thinking, *Catherine might dip to a three or even worse.*

And we both know that those numbers are not survivable.

When the silence in Mom's room gets loud, I get on my hands and knees and reach under my bed. And then my phone choos, scaring the absolute crap out of me. I never muted it, so it sounds like an Amtrak Acela roaring through my room. I slide back into bed as Mom's feet hit the wood floor of the hall.

My door swings open and Mom stands at the threshold. "It's quarter to midnight! No more texting, Catherine, or I'm taking the phone."

"Okay," I say, glancing at the phone. "It's from Kristal." It's probably the thirtieth text of the night. We had to do a recap of today. "I'll tell her I'm going to bed. I promise."

Mom gives me another kiss and leaves. I read Kristal's text: "Am going to the new step-down program only if you are. Ask your shrink and let me know asap"

She texts again: "And remember—no red flags!!!!!!!!"

I smile. Lil' Tommy advised us at break today how to ensure we all move on to the step-down program. He wants our group to stay together, and the way everybody nodded back at him, it seems to be unanimous. I know I do. In a hushed voice over Flavor Blasted Goldfish, Tommy said that as long as, unlike Amy, we raised no red flags, contributed in group, avoided meltdowns, took our meds and kept going to school, there was no way anybody's insurance would allow them to stay in the five-day program. No way.

"Will do," I text Kristal. My fingers hover over the screen. I want to ask her why she has to continue treatment. She said she was over her bulimia.

But then again, maybe she'd say the same thing about me. Maybe she's just as good at hiding the bulimic's equivalent of Zero. I type: "Goodnite! See you tomorrow!"

21

On Tuesday, I don't get to see Kristal or anyone else in group, because Mom has scheduled yet another appointment with Dr. McCallum. This one is an ambush.

I should have known something was up when Mom arrived at 2:45 on the dot to pick me up. "But why?" I ask, after she tells me. "I just saw him like two weeks ago. It's only supposed to be once a month for med checks now that I'm in the IOP program. And why didn't you tell me last night?" I swallow my frustration. I know Mom is worried about Michael. This visit is more for her than for me.

"I'm sorry, Cath. I didn't know. He had a cancellation today, so I thought it would be a good idea to touch base," she says evasively.

"Is it Michael?" I ask her. "Is that what you're worried about?"

"That's not it," Mom says.

"Well, then what is it?" I ask, and she curls her lips in,

physically barring herself from saying anything. "I guess I'll find out when I get there," I mutter to the passenger-side window, and then send a quick text to Kristal to let her know I'll be a no-show.

Already seated in the armchair opposite mine, Dr. McCallum smiles at me as I walk in. "Catherine, how are you?"

"Fine," I say.

"How are you making out at the IOP?" he asks, running a hand over his bald head.

"Good," I answer. Dr. McCallum keeps his trap shut, obviously expecting me to provide a little more detail. "The kids are nice," I offer. "I'm becoming friendly with one of the girls." That should do it.

Dr. McCallum nods. "I'm hearing good things for sure." And again, nothing more from the lips of the good doctor.

I cut to the chase. "Is it Michael? Is that why I'm here? Is that why my mother called you? He's not my boyfriend," I lie.

Dr. McCallum shakes his head. "Your mother is worried that you may be getting manic."

WHAT. THE. FUCK.

"I have no clue what she's talking about," I snap. "I haven't painted any houses or charged any vacations lately."

Dr. McCallum studies me and then says, "No, no, it's nothing like that. She was worried about warning signs. She feels bad for missing them before and she wanted us to touch base. She says you're working a lot on a school project. Staying up late."

So that explains Mom's Gestapo attitude toward my

project. Shit. How could I have missed *Mom's* warning signs?

"You look upset," Dr. McCallum says.

"I am," I say, leaning forward in my chair. "Why couldn't she just tell me herself?"

"I think it's hard for your mother, Catherine," he answers. And he lets that zinger hang in the air over my head, a floating anvil of guilt.

We both know why it's hard for Mom. Because on top of every other horrific emotion my condition has spawned in her, she was (is?) also racked with guilt. I heard her. It was this past summer, early July, soon after Dr. A and his arthritic body had hightailed it to the wretched humidity of Florida. I had gone to the bathroom after my session, and Mom was inside Dr. McCallum's office. I moved soundlessly in the reception area so I could listen.

Mom's voice was high, and I could hear her pleading with Dr. McCallum. Something like, "What kind of mother does that? Tell me, please! Who leaves their child alone? She tried to kill herself, what, two hours after I left? To not know the pain she was in?" Self-loathing dripped from each word.

Dr. McCallum responded softly. So softly I couldn't catch all of it over Mom's sobs. "It's so difficult, Jody. . . . Many adolescent suicides and suicide attempts . . . impulsive acts."

Mom's voice grew louder, "How could I have missed it?"

And Dr. McCallum responded in the same way. "If you feel you missed the signs, it's possible there weren't any red flags to see. Often kids seem fine, but then something triggers a change in the way they think about themselves, the way they think about their lives. And then they impulsively act on it."

Mom said something else. I forget what it was, but I remember how compressed her words had sounded. As if they had been held in for so long, and the guilt was still hissing out of her, almost ten months after the fact.

She still feels guilty. It is this guilt that must power her, making her hypervigilant, afraid of missing the slightest clue in my world. My anger dissolves and I lean back in my chair.

"This history project," Dr. McCallum says. "Can you tell me about it?"

I take a deep breath and explain exactly what it is and the exact amount of time I'm putting into it. "It's not the same," I say. "As the other times."

The manic times.

And it's really not. I felt buzzed during the "Highlights of the Mediterranean" episode. A little less so during the attempted house painting. But each time there was a strange electricity coursing through my body, fueling my actions and igniting the thoughts that sparked lightning fast through my head. An irrational elation. I don't feel that way now—not at all.

"I just like the project."

"What do you like about it?" he asks. "What exactly is it?"

So I tell him. For the first time since beginning treatment with Dr. McCallum, I talk uninterrupted for at least five minutes. It's easy, because it's nothing about me. It's about that day at the museum with Kristal and her mom and discovering Jane Talmadge and the 6888th. I do allow myself to tell him that Jane hit a nerve with me somehow. He asks about the letter and I tell him she wrote about how hard it was to be a black woman in the army in 1944.

After a couple more questions about sleeping and eating and my general mood, Dr. McCallum leans back in his chair, stretching a little. "Catherine, I'm in agreement with you. I don't think you're getting manic." He says it confidently, and for the first time, I feel like I might have an ally in him. Yes, he pushes and prods and pokes me, but he's much more in tune with me than Dr. A ever was. New questions form and flutter through my mind: What would've happened if I'd started with him right away? Would Zero have gotten me last year if I'd had McCallum on defense? If I'd been on Lamictal then?

He leans forward now, closing the distance between us. "I do think it's a good idea for us to review your condition. Have a refresher on being proactive. That okay?" I nod. "Would you mind if I called your mom in?" he asks. "It might help with her anxiety if you're together for this."

I nod again. "Sure."

Mom enters the room, her body just about visibly trembling. Dr. McCallum gives her a reassuring smile. "I think Catherine's doing just fine."

Mom blinks quickly, fanning away tears of relief, and I feel a prickling of tears in my own eyes. I reach over and gently rub her back and she looks at me, surprised by the contact. Then she takes my hand and squeezes it.

"I think it's wise to periodically review things," Dr. Mc-Callum says. "As you both are well aware, Catherine's condition, bipolar disorder, is chronic."

Dr. McCallum leans back in his chair. "Now, a chronic condition requires monitoring. Catherine, if you had diabetes, you'd be checking your blood sugar. Jody, if you had hypertension, your blood pressure would be monitored. For bipolar disorder, we monitor by checking both emotional and physical symptoms."

This has to be the fifth freaking time I've heard the "You and Your Bipolar Disorder" lecture. I take a deep breath and try to block the fact that I'm missing Lucky Boy for this. My favorite therapy dog is supposed to be at St. Anne's right now.

"One of the biggest red flags that may *signal* an oncoming manic phase"—Dr. McCallum slows down his speech—"is changes to sleep patterns. If you find that you don't need as much sleep as usual, you'd be best off checking in with your psychiatrist. For now that's me, but in college, it'll be someone else. Your mom told me that you'll be taking the SATs in the spring."

I sit up in my chair. Wait. What? Mom is planning for me to take the SATs? For college? Sure, I took the PSAT but that was because school mandated that all juniors sit for it. I figured it was a wasted exercise for me.

"I would like for you to keep a sleep journal, Catherine. Nothing big," Dr. McCallum is saying. "I'd like you to note the amount of time you think you're sleeping and the quality of your sleep. You can keep a log on your phone or in a notebook on your night table. If you see an irregular pattern over a couple of days, give me a call."

I turn to Mom. "Is this why you keep coming into my room five times a night?"

She nods.

Jesus Christ. No wonder she looks exhausted.

Dr. McCallum says, "It's also critical for you, Catherine, to continue getting enough sleep. Every night. Never short-change yourself on sleep if you can help it. Staying up late for a couple of nights in a row may make it harder for you to fall asleep when you want to sleep and that could *trigger* a manic episode."

Dr. McCallum goes through the other warning signs of a manic episode. He finishes up with the trinity of anger, hostility and irritability that seems to be more a trademark of my relationship with Mom than a precursor to a manic episode. Mom and I glance at each other as Dr. McCallum lists the three emotions.

"I know"—he nods, a rare smile lighting up his face—"not always the easiest to spot between a seventeen-year-old and her mother." He gives a second, brief smile before moving on. "The other pole is depression." He ticks off the well-known symptoms and holds my gaze when he gets to the last one—suicidal thoughts. I feel like he can see the shoe-box guilt on my face somehow. I shift in my chair.

Dr. McCallum leans forward. "Any condition, *any condition* requires a proactive approach. Eating right, getting enough sleep, exercise, taking your meds, it all works to keep you feeling stable. And of course, the other big one is avoiding any and all types of drugs and alcohol. I always like to remind my patients, especially my adolescent ones, that *any*, I mean *any* drug or alcohol usage is bad. Really bad. Catherine, alcohol and drugs will affect you differently from other teens. You'll get high or intoxicated more quickly. And you won't realize it. The other issue is that you're at substantially greater risk of addiction, which, I don't have to tell you, can be catastrophic."

I glance over to see how Mom's taking this news. Her hands are gripping the chair, her nails almost digging holes in the leather. Well done, Dr. McCallum, you've just hiked up Mom's anxiety about a thousand degrees.

Oblivious, Dr. McCallum forges on. "Catherine, alcohol and drugs are obviously issues in high school. But when you get to college, without supervision, the temptation will be even greater."

Jesus. He just said "college" again. When did he and Mom decide that sick Catherine Pulaski was capable of handling college?

"It might feel a little early to start talking about this, I know. You've just started your junior year. But I want you to keep this in mind. When you start looking at colleges. Dorms. We'll make sure that we have everything in place for you at your school—doctor, counselor, things like that. Also, I Skype with some of my patients when they're away at school and it works just fine. But again, I know we've got time."

Mom is abnormally quiet, probably trying to figure out if it's possible for her to be assigned my roommate at Bipolar U. On second thought, this SAT thing is just for appearances, knowing Mom. I'm sure she's thinking, *Oh yes, let Catherine take them because the community college in New Haven probably requires them anyway.*

But Dr. McCallum is going along with it, and he's not a bullshitter. This medical professional truly believes I'm headed to college. That I've got a future.

That feeling I had earlier, of him being my ally, drains away. I feel the urge to shout at him that I've got a shoe box of meds because he's drilled it into my head that I cannot escape Zero. I've been sitting here for months, nodding and answering his questions, all the while planning my death. The success of my deception astounds me.

"What do you think about college, Catherine? Is it something you want to do?" Dr. McCallum asks now.

I answer honestly. "I haven't thought that much about it."

"Why not?" he asks.

The words are in my throat, then on my lips. I push them out. "Because . . . because I'm bipolar."

Dr. McCallum nods. "Is college something you'd like to do?"

This time I tell the truth, even though the goal is unattainable. "I'd love to go."

"Good." He nods like it's a done deal. "I'm trying to stress something to you both. And it's that this condition is *manageable*. Staying alert and watching for changes, like changes in sleep patterns, is the main challenge. But it's a doable challenge."

He turns to me, his eyes laser-locked on mine. "Catherine, what you've got to believe is that people with bipolar disorder live productive, happy lives. This is not a death sentence."

I know Dr. McCallum is sincere and that he believes what he's saying is true.

The only problem is that I don't.

22

Michael and I can't stop eating them. They're these little orangey-scented cookies with a vanilla glaze that the Pitoscias are giving out for Halloween; Michael calls them "Nonny cookies" because he doesn't know their real Italian name. Anthony filled a whole Tupperware to take with him before getting picked up by his friend Elliot to play video games somewhere. Right now, there's a brief lull between the throngs of trick-or-treaters, so Michael and I chow down.

We're seated on folding chairs outside the Pitoscias' front door, travel mugs of hot chocolate at our matching Converse-clad feet. Nonny is carting out an endless amount of these cookies fresh from the oven with the glaze sweating down the little mounds. In the chilly air, the fragrance alone is temptation enough, but with the warm trays on our laps and the cookies mere inches from our fingertips, Michael and I are eating as many as we're handing out.

And that's a lot—these cookies are a Nonny tradition in Michael's neighborhood, and both costumed kids and adults steadily stream up to the front door. Lots of them pop inside to say hello to Nonny and her cookie-drone Lorraine, who keeps the baking assembly line rolling. Mr. Pitoscia, aka Tony, creates adult treats with a Keurig coffeemaker, a bottle of Baileys Irish Cream and a paper coffee-cup column.

My boyfriend is in his element. I've never seen Michael so relaxed. He's even wearing a red-and-white-striped Cat in the Hat hat with his jeans and sweatshirt. (We agreed not to wear costumes, so I wore black skinny jeans, a black-and-red flannel shirt and a fleece. But when I got here, Michael gave me a yellow beanie with a propeller on top. I put it on. When in Rome . . .) Everybody greets Michael with genuine warmth and I get a secret buzz every time he introduces me as his girlfriend. Even to the handful of Cranbury High kids who arrive to snag some cookies. I recognize only one of them, a Bryce McSomething. He's in student government, I think.

After snatching the last of the cookies off our trays, Bryce says to Michael (and actually makes eye contact with me), "Hey, you know about Robbie's party, right? You guys should come."

His words sink into me: You guys. You *guys*. Plural. It feels strange—both good and sad—to hear those words. I am beginning my third year of high school and this is the first time I've been invited to a party. The constant loneliness of freshman and sophomore year comes back to me just as the wind kicks up, gusting over my ears and neck, which were shielded by my long hair last October. Like a phantom limb, I can still feel its heavy softness. I shiver.

"Thanks," Michael says, his eyes on my face for a moment before returning to Bryce. "Maybe we'll stop by."

After the Cranbury High group departs, Michael stands up and removes the empty tray from my lap. "I'll get reinforcements," he says. "Need anything?" He flicks the propeller on my hat softly and I hear it spin.

I shake my head and smile; and when he returns, he's wearing another sweatshirt and carrying a jacket. "You look cold," he says, holding out the thick, fleece-lined coat. "It's Anthony's work coat, but Nonny just washed it." Michael flips the jacket around to show me PAOLETTI'S LANDSCAPING in fluorescent extra-large-script blazed across the back of it. He taps the words and says, "Works like an ID badge. To soothe the rich people, so they don't freak out when they see some strange guy in their yard waving a Weedwacker. It's the mark of a minion."

I'm a little surprised by his sarcasm, but I like it. There's more to Michael than meets the eye.

His comment stirs memories of all the gardeners and support staff in Riley's neighborhood during summer. They were all nonwhite men who moved silently among the built-in pools and patios and stone fire pits to clip and cut and mow on every day but Saturday and Sunday, when the gentry were present to lord over their manors.

Ever the gentleman, Michael holds the jacket up and I stand and turn to back into it. As Michael slips it up onto my shoulders, he gives me a quick hug, his breath warm and vanilla sweet on my ear. It feels better than a Nonny cookie tastes, this fleeting physical contact. I hope we get some basement time tonight.

I tug the zipper up and my fingers graze the embroidered letters on the front of the jacket. I read Anthony's name and trace the letters.

"Wow," I say. "This really is an official work jacket. Are you sure Anthony won't mind my wearing it?"

Michael shakes his head. "Nah."

"I'll be very careful with it," I kid.

"You don't have to," Michael answers, and then glances back at the door. "My parents would probably thank you if you lost it permanently."

"What do you mean?" I ask, but Michael doesn't answer because Tyler is walking up the flagstone path.

Tyler wears a Darth Vader costume, but he's holding the mask up to reveal his identity.

"Hi, Catherine. How's it going?" Tyler asks, and gives me a real smile. He's definitely loosening up a little around me.

If Webster's Dictionary needed a photograph to put next to the word "guileless," they could use Tyler's. There's an innocence about him and I can see why Michael takes on the big-brother role with him. But there's friendship too. That day at the museum, Michael told me he had a bad stutter through second grade and that Tyler was the only kid who never made fun of him. They've been best friends since.

I feel a jab of loneliness as I see the ease they have with

one another. Tyler doesn't have to ask Michael for a chair; he just goes into the garage and grabs one from the spot where he knows the Pitoscias keep their chairs. I used to have that—a certain comfort and familiarity with friends.

Well, maybe not with Riley. There was always the invisible, unspoken class thing separating us.

But it was there with Olivia. At least I think it was. With Olivia, I didn't worry about being cool enough or if my clothes from second-tier, not-Abercrombie stores like the dreaded Justice, and then Target, and then Forever 21 were good enough. Around Olivia, I always felt like I could exhale.

Fully costumed and in the dark, Tyler is a different person. He's teasing the little kids and his jokes are fast and smart but nice. I find myself joining in, relaxed and uncensored. We joke and drink hot chocolate and eat more Nonny cookies in the cool air. And under all those layers of gray, I feel the colorful confetti of happy bubbling up out of me. How could I have forgotten this feeling? I am a . . . what?

I can say it. It's only to myself.

I am a nine.

Right now, right here, on October 31, I am a nine. Thank you, God and Jesus and Mary and all the saints. Grandma, can you hear me? I am happy. And it may not be a fluke emotion artificially triggered by my meds.

How many more of these shimmering moments do I have left?

The trick-or-treaters eventually peter out, but the three of us stay on the front stoop until ten-thirty when Nonny shoos us inside because of the dropping temperatures. Inside the foyer, Nonny grabs my hand and leads me down a short hall.

"C'mon, Michael's friend," she says, opening her bedroom door. "You see this."

As soon as my Converse make contact with the beige carpeting, a yippy growling begins. It's coming from a small, locked dog crate that sits between a recliner and a low bookcase crowded with paperbacks and magazine holders.

"It's okay, Mitzi girl," Nonny says, and leads me to the crate. "Let her sniff you." She pushes me forward. "I won't let her out."

The top of the crate doesn't even reach my knee. I can barely see through the holes in the gray plastic, but inside is a rat-sized thing with gray and black and brown hair that's howling now. As Nonny bends over to reassure Mitzi, I do a quick scan of the room. There's the crucified Jesus over the twin bed—mandatory Christian-grandparent decor—and on the brown wood dresser stands an elaborate Jesus statue complete with puffy papal crown, fabric gown and mini-globe in one outstretched hand, the other hand held up in a Scout's honor kind of pose. It's so excessive that I have to wonder if American Girl came out with a new character: Jesus, the carpenter boy from Bethlehem.

"Look at this," Nonny says over the Mitzi din. She points to a small desk next to an open door that leads to a bathroom. In the glow of the bathroom's night-light, I can see a tube of CVS styling gel on her sink. Clicking on the metal desk lamp (circa 1950), Nonny points to a pile of *People* magazines, the pages of which have been tagged with slim, fluorescent pink stickies. There must be thirty stickies. She flips open to the first one. "See?" Nonny taps a photograph of the latest celebrity to cut off her locks. And then to photo number two, and number three, and so on. It hasn't even been a full week since her Supercut. I don't know when she had time to do all this research, especially while producing massive amounts of cookie dough. "Me and you. We're just like the stars," she says, her eyes glued to the glossy pages.

By photograph twenty-two, Mitzi has yipped herself into a coma, but Nonny is still going strong. Michael knocks on the door and enters. "Is Michael's friend in here?" he asks.

"I'm just showing her the movie stars' hair," Nonny says. "We look just like them." She turns to me, her face tilted upward, and those eyes, magnified a thousand-fold behind the thick lenses of her glasses, hold mine. "My friend Sylvia getting her hair cut too. She like mine so much. Thank you," she says before charging out of the bedroom. "Now c'mon," she yells over her shoulder, "I got cookies for you and your mother!"

"This is a little frightening," Michael says, gesturing toward the tagged magazine pictures. "Maybe she should take a class or apply to profile serial killers for the FBI or something." He tilts his head. "Now, that would make a great TV show. *The Secret Life of Nonny Pitoscia: FBI Profiler.*"

I jump right into the joke. "The opening scenes could be her baking and sewing by day, while at night she's got a whole computer lab behind this room that she accesses by twisting the Jesus statue's hand or something."

This *CSI: Cranbury* riff continues until we reach the kitchen. The large tins that Nonny and Lorraine have filled with cookies for Tyler and me sit on the table. In the light and without his mask, Tyler has withdrawn a little, but he's still pretty relaxed. Lorraine is asking him, "You sure you don't want to go with Michael and Catherine? You've known Robbie since you were babies. He's only four doors down."

Michael says, "Ma, I'm not even sure we're going to the party. I haven't talked about it with Catherine yet."

Lorraine turns to me, a dish towel dangling from one hand. "Honey, do you want to go to Robbie's? I can drive you home. Whenever you want. Your mom doesn't have to come out now."

Yikes. I haven't checked my phone since I got here. There are three texts from Mom and one from Kristal.

Kristal is at a Chapman event. At 9:23 p.m., she wrote, "This sucks! Escaping now!"

The first two texts from Mom are questions about pickup time; the last one, in all caps, says she will be here at eleven. Fifteen minutes from now.

I text back: "Can I go to a party? At michael's friends. 4 doors away. Only for an hour. Can you get me at 12?"

At least two full minutes pass with no response from Mom. I imagine her in the bathroom with nervous diarrhea. Her Catherine at a high school *party*? With the "catastrophic" drinking and drugs?

I text again: "Don't worry. I'm not stupid!"

My phone choos loudly. It's a text from Aunt Darlene. "Go Baby! Have FUN!!! I am sitting on ur mother to restrain her from running to car ;) She'll get u from M's at 12!"

Thank you, Aunt Darlene. Aunt D basically strong-armed Mom into attending a Halloween party at her condo complex tonight. I can trust her to keep Mom busy for an hour.

While I go to my first party!

I text back five smiley faces (a record for me) and look up at Michael. "We can go to the party if you want. My mom is coming in an hour."

Despite living close by and having grown up with Robbie, Tyler still doesn't want to come, so we say good-bye to him on the front stoop, then grab our chairs and return them to the garage. Mr. Pitoscia is on his knees in front of the open refrigerator. Spread around Michael's father are bags of bread, plastic containers of mozzarella, pepperoni sticks and foil-wrapped trays. I can see the bottle of Baileys wedged way back on the lowest shelf of the fridge. Tony Pitoscia is building a firewall around it using the food by his knees.

I recognize that move. He's hiding the bottle.

Michael calls quickly to his dad, "Hey, just dropping off the chairs." It's a definite alert of some sort. I glance at Michael. There are some red splotches on his neck, a tell-tale sign of discomfort.

Tony Pitoscia hops to his feet and slams the refrigerator door shut. "Mom said you were headed to Robbie's?" he asks.

"Just for an hour," Michael answers.

"My mom will be here to get me," I add, so Mr. Pitoscia doesn't have to worry about driving me home.

Michael seems flustered as we walk in the cold to Robbie's house. "That was weird, I know," he says. "My dad . . . He and my mom don't really like to keep alcohol in the house anymore." He looks at me, gauging my reaction.

I nod. Like I'm one to talk about abnormal behavior. And that's not even abnormal.

"If I tell you something," Michael says, slowing his pace, "you can't tell anyone, okay?"

I want to say I have only one friend and she doesn't even live around here, but I keep that to myself.

"Michael, you really don't have to tell me anything. That's your family's business."

"Well, I want to tell you," he says, and stops walking. He takes one of my hands from the pockets of the Paoletti's Landscaping jacket and holds it in both his hands. "You're gonna be at my house, so you should know. Anthony might have . . . He *has* a drinking problem. He was going to Sacred Heart University last year and got kicked out in November for underage drinking. And then a couple of months ago, he got a DUI. That's why his friends are always picking him up. He can't drive anymore. And that's why my mother is kind of hyper about what he does on the weekends. So, he's got no license, no college, and he's doing landscaping work. Lost the full first-semester tuition, which was like over twenty grand. My parents are freaking out about it. He was on the lacrosse team. He was a good student." Michael shakes his head. "There's nothing wrong with being a landscaper, but he was thinking about law school. Or teaching."

"That really sucks," I say.

"Tonight my dad was . . . he was hiding that bottle of liquor in the back of the fridge so Anthony doesn't see it. And they keep like five beers in the fridge just to sort of monitor whether he's drinking." Still holding hands, Michael and I begin walking again. "It's so strange to think that this is my brother. None of us saw it coming."

I'm not sure what to say. Part of me wants to help put it into perspective for him. Maybe something like, "If you think alcoholism is bad, try bipolar disorder!" Of course I'd never say anything of the sort. Michael will never know that about me. He probably just heard that I went through a depression or something last year. But I'm wondering, *is* being bipolar really worse than being an alcoholic? To be honest, they seem pretty balanced on the shit scale.

"I'm so sorry," I say instead. "That's really sad."

And I do know sad.

Michael lightly bumps my shoulder. "Sorry to be such a downer," he says. "I just thought you should know."

We're already at the place. We stop in front of a brightly lit colonial, a clone of Michael's house. A pounding bass beat leaks through the basement windows, and they must have a strobe light down there because it looks like an electrical storm is taking place.

"Do you know Robbie?" Michael asks.

I shake my head. He will soon learn I know no one. But that too can wait.

"He's a good kid," Michael says. "He's one of the presidents of Model Congress. Math club, swim team. Wants to go to Yale." Michael takes a deep breath. "But he loves to party. That's why Tyler didn't come tonight."

Maybe Tyler had the right idea. I can hear screams and laughter coming from the basement. What if Riley and Olivia are here? What if they say stuff about me? My heart beats a faster rhythm.

"Let's just say hi and get out of here, okay?" Michael asks. "I'm not really into a party tonight."

I nod, and my mouth goes dry as we walk up the concrete path to Robbie's front door. Michael's still holding my hand and I'm sure it's slick with sweat. Should I tell him that I don't drink? That it would fuck with the delicate balance that my Lamictal has just established? I'm at full strength now, Dr. McCallum's targeted two hundred fifty milligrams. I'm sure the two and a half tablets I took tonight are trapped in the bottom layer of sediment in my stomach, buried under the avalanche of Nonny cookies.

I take a quick glance at Michael and he smiles at me. With blatant adoration. *For me.* And it stops me in my tracks. Has anyone ever looked at me like that before? Besides Mom and Grandma? I squeeze Michael's hand, and then the front door is opening and somebody is yelling, "Yo! Pit Man!"

Inside the living room, there are maybe twenty kids. I don't recognize a soul and relax the tiniest bit. Michael introduces me to Robbie's parents, who say hello and continue with their anxious surveillance. Michael greets somebody else and then we head to the basement. The temperature and noise increase as we descend. It is packed down here and it's hard to identify anyone with the seizure-inducing strobe lights.

A burly redheaded guy comes up to Michael, and Michael introduces us. It's Robbie, the host, and he's holding a nuclear-blue-colored sports drink that he offers to Michael and then to me. Michael puts a hand up to decline and gives me a little headshake that translates to "Don't take it." Robbie is hyper and loud, his movements sloppy, his laugh hyena-like—it's pretty clear he's drunk. Whatever he's drinking must be camouflaged in the Gatorade bottle. I take a quick look around the room. The lights are off except for the strobe light and strings of white Christmas lights that run the perimeter of the low ceiling. Kids are everywhere, playing Ping-Pong at one end of the room, sprawled on the two sofas and dancing in a corner that's furniture-free. I can feel the bass of the rap music vibrate in my bones. The people seem to be a cross section of high school achievers—athletes, honors kids, student government—who like to party. Almost everybody is drinking a brightly colored sports drink/cocktail.

Once Robbie lurches away, another boy, a non-drunk, Model Congress friend of Michael's, comes over to talk. That's when almost-friend Sabita Gupta walks past. Our eyes meet and a smile flashes across her face—the smile real, instant and unforced, with nothing evil or pitying behind it. It's the same smile from when we were kids. Sabita and I talk for about twenty minutes, catching up—her telling the truth, me not telling the truth—and then move on to the much more comfortable territory of schoolwork.

Sabita is exactly how I remember her—always ready to chat about classes regardless of the setting. We take turns basically screaming into each other's ears about our history projects. She's blown away by Jane's story and thinks Michael and I have a guaranteed A.

"Mr. Oleck completely digs stuff like that," she says, taking a small sip from her full, bright red Gatorade and then shuddering. "I hate vodka." She tilts the bottle my way, but I shake my head.

"No thanks."

She screws the cap back on and places the bottle on the floor. "Good move. It's like cherry Robitussin mixed with turpentine."

The one time I almost freak is when I catch sight of a Red Sox cap on a tall, stocky, dark-haired kid not more than five feet from me. It's one of the kids from group—wrestling John. I lose track of the conversation between Michael, his friend, Sabita and some other girl and try to shrink into the shadows next to Michael. He misinterprets the move and wraps an arm around my shoulders.

What's the protocol outside the institutional walls of St. Anne's and school? Do group members acknowledge each other? I decide to ignore John, figuring that's the smart thing to do. But when Michael and I say our good-byes and make our way to the basement steps, John is parked right there. He puts out his hand for a high five and my heart stops beating.

Please, please, God. Don't let him say anything about seeing me on Monday.

Of course, the music has stopped briefly and Michael

is sure to hear any exchange. "Hey, Catherine. How's it going?" is, blessedly, the only thing John says.

And instead of slapping his palm, I give it a little squeeze. The secret handshake of the St. Anne Society. He squeezes right back.

Michael and I wind up staying until ten minutes to midnight, and I am pumped when we walk outside. I have been a solid nine for at least three hours tonight. Participate in first high school party? *Check.* Not curled into the fetal position in a bathroom? *Check.* Not rocking myself in some remote corner? *Check.* Talk to seemingly nonjudgmental peers who didn't seem surprised that crazy Catherine Pulaski was in attendance? *Check.*

Michael and I swing hands as we walk down the path to the sidewalk. In the light of a brilliant almost-full moon, I can see the Accord idling in Michael's driveway four houses away, the cold creating a trail of steam from the exhaust pipe. "My mom's here," I say.

Michael stops walking. "Already?" He drops my hand and starts trotting backward into the dark abyss between Robbie's house and Robbie's next-door neighbor's. "Cath, come here a sec." He waves me toward him as his feet crunch the leaves on the ground. "I want to show you something."

I join him under a half-naked maple tree. We're now officially trespassers on private property.

"I lied," he says, and shifts from foot to foot, smiling, expectant. Then he wraps his arms around my waist, pulling me close, and it's thrilling. "So, w-was it okay that I called you my girlfriend tonight?"

"Absolutely." I lift my chin to smile up at him.

"I can't believe it," he says softly. "My girlfriend is Catherine Pulaski." His obvious pride makes my heart dip into my reservoir of grief. *I don't want this to end.*

"Can . . . can . . . I kiss you?" he asks softly, hijacking my attention. "C-c-can I?"

His boyhood stutter reprising itself makes something inside me melt. I nod and he places his warm hands on my jaw and neck. That alone feels delicious. He leans down, but our heads are tilted the same way and we bump noses. At the same time, we reverse direction and then reverse again, likes mimes doing a mirror act. We laugh, and it pushes down my sense of impending loss.

This time, Michael holds my head tenderly yet firmly in his hands. "You stay like that. I'll go this way," he instructs with a little laugh. "Like I know what I'm doing." And then his beautiful face is looming closer and his lips are touching mine.

And for someone who doesn't know what he's doing, it's a great freaking kiss.

23

I slide into the passenger seat of the Accord at four minutes past midnight. My lips feel warm and tingly, like the
rest of my body. Mom is not quite so warm. In a clipped,
almost clinical tone, she greets me with, "Bear with me,
okay, Cath?" and clicks on the interior light of the car to
probe my face with laser eyes. Her nostrils even flare as she
takes a few investigatory sniffs for pot smoke. "Did you
drink anything? Take anything?" she asks.

I don't answer immediately. I'm waving to Michael,
who stands on the front stoop of his house, watching us.
Watching *me*.

The fury that Mom and her questions normally trigger
in me is absent, and the scene doesn't culminate with one
of my typical snarls. Because as Michael waves back, I feel
magnanimous.

"No worries, Mom," I say, still on my own personal

cloud nine from both the kiss and my first successful social outing as a bipolarite. "There was alcohol, but I stayed away." And I graciously add, "Michael doesn't drink either." *Because his twenty-year-old brother might be an alcoholic.* I keep that last detail to myself.

After texting Kristal, I wait for Mom to pass out so I can complete the Friday-night transfer of my shoe box to Grandma's room for the weekend. I don't think it's safe to take the bottles out and line them up like I usually do. Mom is too much of a wild card tonight. Instead, I click on my phone and open my D-Day List.

Immediately, I feel a sense of peace. But I hate the first entry now. The L.V. part. It seems so cold and impersonal— the total opposite of Michael.

Michael is . . . brown eyes and warm hands and quick smiles and arms I want to dive into.

Before, he was just supposed to be my first and last connection, but now he's something more: my boyfriend.

Zero whispers that it's not real. That Michael doesn't know the real me.

I shake my head, clearing away those black thoughts for now. *It's okay.* He likes what he sees so far, and that's more than I could've ever hoped for.

I delete L.V. and type "1st/Last Connection." Written out, it looks even more stupid than L.V. I delete it and type "Michael." That's all the secret code I need.

Without turning on the light, I search for the Nonny cookie I know is on my night table and find it next to the propeller beanie Michael gave me. Mom loves these cookies too. Dealing with post-Catherine-at-party anxiety, she had me pop the lid off the cookie tin on the drive home.

I finish the cookie and lie back on my bed. It feels great tonight. Warm and cozy and sweetly scented from the fabric softener Mom uses. I click my phone to refresh the Notes page. In the month since I started the list, it's grown to a whopping five entries. I read them for the millionth time:

D-DAY:
1. Michael
2. Meet Kristal at Museum Oct. 19
3. Museum with M Oct. 25
4. Halloween with M

And now I type in:

5. Sleepover at K's Nov. 7

Kristal had texted a few minutes ago to see if I wanted to sleep over after Friday's group. I responded yes with a smiley face and three exclamation points without asking Mom. There was no way I was going to request permission tonight. The poor woman was still wrapping her head around the idea of her unbalanced daughter at an honest-to-goodness high school party. And also, I'm anticipating a battle about the sleepover. I haven't slept over at someone's house since eighth grade. I doubt Mom will be on board given she has never met Kristal's parents or seen her house.

In savvy preparation for the impending debate, I answered Mom's mood scale question tonight with a confident, "Seven." I'd never, ever tell her the truth, that I had hit a sustained nine. I don't want to get her hopes up.

And why not? Because . . . My eyes fall on the title of the note: D-Day. Death Day.

True, my one-item to-do list has morphed into a record of all the things, all the *great* things, that I'm experiencing. It's so beyond what I thought was possible, I'll take it. I'll gladly take whatever I can get.

But that doesn't change the fact that I know it will end when Zero returns.

I wonder how much time I have. I haven't felt Zero breathing on me for a few weeks now. But he's not gone for good. I am chronic. And that's why I add to my shoe box when I can. I need the reassurance these bottles give me. I know that I will never again have to deal with Zero's bottoming me out, flattening me into a numb, hollow nothing.

After the surreptitious journey downstairs to deposit the shoe box in its triple-layer vault, I tiptoe up the stairs, alibi glass of water in hand. I pause midway to study one of the fifteen or twenty framed recital photographs, illuminated by the glow of the night-light, that line the staircase wall.

Here I am at four years old with some horrific floppy bunny ears and tail; there as a five-year-old Doc from *Snow White and the Seven Dwarfs*; then, at age seven, wearing a plain pink leotard and sparkly tutu, with a braid that Grandma had twisted into a high bun and circled with a pink velvet ribbon. I still have that ribbon taped on a page in my "All About Me" book.

That was a big year dance-wise—it was the year I was anointed a soloist. From then on, I had solo performances in every recital until I was thirteen. Olivia was always thrilled for me and would stand beside me as we waited for Miss Ruth to post the roles, but I don't remember Riley ever being there. She was the first to quit Miss Ruth's School of Dance, about thirty seconds after I had taken my solo bows and walked off the stage with a big bouquet of flowers for the *Sleeping Beauty* recital.

We were twelve. I'll always remember it because it was the first time any of us cursed. "This fucking sucks," Riley had said. She was waiting for me backstage in full pout mode, her eyelids heavily colored with the metallic silver-blue shadow the three of us had bought together at Walgreens. "I think we're done with this baby stuff. Let's do hip-hop someplace new." Olivia had abdicated with Riley to the Dance Studio, a new place on the Cranbury Green, but Mom felt a sense of loyalty to Miss Ruth, and so did I.

Riley's jealousy-inspired move to the new place turned out to be pointless. Because my dancing career at Miss Ruth's came to an abrupt end just a year later. After July 3, when Grandma died, I never danced in one of Miss Ruth's recitals again.

Mom and I both oversleep on Monday morning; she has to call school so I don't get detention. We had stayed up late

Sunday watching an old movie, *Jerry Maguire*. It's one of Mom's favorites, and I have to admit, it was surprisingly good. We polished off almost all the Nonny cookies, saving three each for our lunches today.

I enter history class. Mr. Oleck is lecturing from the podium and, without stopping his verbal flow, holds out his hand to accept the pass I got from the front office. I glance at Michael and then Sabita, my Halloween-party comrades, and they both grin. I approach my desk and Louis Farricelli looms like a rotting mountain of flesh behind it. The neck brace still encases his thick neck and he's got a twisted smile as his eyes lock onto my pelvic region. I'm tempted to give him the finger at the zipper level of my jeans, but he'd probably take it as an invite. As I turn to slide into my seat, I realize there's another fucking note waiting for me on my desk. It's got the same block letters spelling out "Catherine," but this time it's taped shut. I hear Riley's distinctive snort-giggle.

And with devastating familiarity, Zero flutters by me.

I don't want to open the note, but my fingers have a mind of their own. It's another psycho-movie recommendation: *A Beautiful Mind*. I crumple up the paper and cram it into the pocket of my hoodie.

Humiliation washes over me, and I feel my throat clog up. Mr. Oleck's voice is white noise. My life is hard enough without these goddamn sucker punches. I sit there, overheating from the stress, and then realize there's another, stronger emotion beginning to surface: anger. Because they'd never be doing this if I had something physically wrong with me like cancer. They'd be the first to jump on the Help Catherine bandwagon, blanketing the Cranbury coffee shops and stores with colorful flyers for whatever fund-raising event they were holding in my honor.

I want to walk right over to Riley and rip her stringy blond hair out. I want to make her little blue eyes shed tears. I focus only on the anger for a change. Because it feels a hell of a lot better than dwelling on the pain of this latest betrayal.

The class blurs to an end. Behind me, two boys jockey for control of Louis Farricelli's backpack. Farricelli is taking full advantage of the extra travel time he's allotted between classes because of the injury. He hasn't leveraged his bulk out of his seat yet but sends the two off with his backpack.

Riley skates past me surrounded by a gaggle of theater geeks. I do a quick search for Olivia. She usually trails Riley like an indentured servant. Today, though, she's nowhere in sight.

Suddenly, Sabita is standing beside my desk. "Hey, Catherine," she says kind of shyly as the rest of the class shuffles out. Michael makes eye contact and tilts his head to indicate that he'll wait for me outside.

"Hi," I say to Sabita.

Sabita offers me a book. "I was doing research for my soldier project at the library yesterday and found this. For you. And Jane." Her eyes crinkle in a smile.

I'm floored. This almost-friend actually remembered what I told her Friday night about Jane, and here she is making the effort to check out a book and give it to me. Her kindness is a balm to all the bullshit with Riley.

Sabita runs a hand through her long black hair. "There's a couple of pages on the Six Triple—" She stops short because a pen has just flown past her and hit the floor.

I turn around. Farricelli is leering at Sabita. "Oops. My bad. Would you mind picking that up for me, Sabita?"

I stand up. "Don't do it. He just wants to see you bend over."

Sabita actually laughs. It's not a flirty, oh-Louis-you're-a-naughty-boy-I'm-laughing-*with*-you laugh but an oh-Louis-you-are-such-a-pathetic-creep-I'm-laughing-*at*-you laugh. Suddenly, I get the ridiculousness of Farricelli and his pen. I laugh too.

And even though he's a disgusting lech, he's not stupid. Louis Farricelli understands our mockery, and that current of malice I've felt percolating in him since his accident rises to his eyes. It makes both Sabita and me hurry out of the classroom and into the hall, where we join Michael. Looks like I'm not the only psycho in AP U.S. history. Note to self: Stay the eff away from that dude.

At 7:34 p.m. my phone choos. It's an email from Jenna, the curator at the New Haven Museum. She's been going through a box of letters and has found a second one from Jane. Not only has she sent me a photo of the letter but also transcribed it for me. My heart ratchets up a notch, as if I'm getting a letter from someone I actually know. Mom sets up the laptop for me on the kitchen table and I open the document attached to Jenna's email.

It's dated June 19, 1944. So Jane wrote this only a few months after the one displayed in the museum in which she complains bitterly of the prejudice at her South Carolina base.

Dear Mama,

You'd better sit down to read this. It's good news, but I know you, Mama. Get yourself a big glass of water or maybe even some of that sherry you use for cooking. And whatever you do, do not start hollering. Hollering these days is only bound to scare somebody. And this is good news, Mama. Your daughter, Jane Louise Talmadge, is going to Europe! Yes, yes, yes! I've been picked to be part of the first WAC unit assigned to overseas duty. Now, please don't start worrying. As I'm writing this, I can see the tears falling down your cheeks.

First off, I'm not sure we're headed to Europe. It's just the gossip that's flying around down here. Second, I don't even know when we're going. With my luck, by the time they get around to sending us, the war will be over. Now, you know I want the war to end. I don't mean that the way it sounds. It's just for the things that are the most important to us, it always takes forever and a day to get done. And third, we won't be too close to the fighting. We'll be assigned driving and secretarial duties and not that escort business for our Negro soldiers over there. Please just put that nasty thought out of your mind.

I am so excited, Mama! I never thought I'd ever get to Europe. I don't know how I was chosen. A group of officers came around and interviewed a bunch of us, and I guess I must've said something right. Maybe because I have that year of college, I don't know, but I am thanking God for sure. I need to get my hands on some books on Europe. I need to do a lot of reading so I know what I'm looking at when I get there. I'm keeping my fingers crossed for England or France. I still can't believe it. It's a dream come true! When I'm teaching, I'll be able to tell my students that I served in Europe.

Give Petey and Mari a big hug and kiss for me and tell them that their big sis will bring home lots of souvenirs from Europe for them.

Your loving daughter,
Jane

Mom wants to hear the letter, so I read it aloud. Then I read the letter three, four, five more times to myself. And each time, my eyes drag on that last sentence: . . . *bring home lots of souvenirs from Europe.* I feel sick and sad. Because I know Jane will never bring home those souvenirs, that she'll never be a teacher, that she'll never set eyes on her mother or brother or sister again. She died in the jeep accident only a year after she wrote this letter, with the vast Atlantic Ocean separating her from her mama.

Tonight I don't take out my shoe box—it feels disrespectful in some weird way. My sleep is disturbed with vague dreams of a big gray ocean. And Mom drowning in it.

24

John walks into group late Tuesday afternoon, a good fifteen minutes after Sandy has collected our DBT mood forms. It's the first time I've seen him since the Halloween party. I was a little bummed he was absent yesterday. I had felt some ridiculous sense of kinship with him at Robbie's, like we were part of some underground society, not an intensive outpatient program.

John looks like shit. First clue: not one thread of Red Sox gear on his body. Second clue: unwashed, greasy hair and dark shadows under his eyes, emphasized by his pale skin. Third clue: Sandy. She pops off the sofa, puts an arm around his shoulder and escorts him to the sofa he shares with Garrett and Lil' Tommy.

"Hey, man," Lil' Tommy instantly says. "What's wrong?"

Garrett stands up and gives John one of those emotional guy handshakes—an almost high five that melds into a hearty grasp lasting a moment longer than the standard shake. "Not your fault, dude," Garrett says.

Kristal nudges me as a "Shit, man," bursts forth from Lil' Tommy. His small hands begin their nervous travel up and down the tops of his thighs. "What the hell is going on? What's not your fault, John?"

Sandy interrupts. "All right, let's all take a deep breath for a minute, okay? I know some of you are worried about John. As you can see, John is here and managing, and he'll decide if or when he wants to talk."

Everyone's studying John, and he gives a small shake of his head, crosses his arms over his chest and drops his eyes to the floor.

"Okay," Sandy says, "I'd like to open a discussion on peer press—"

"Wait a sec," Lil' Tommy whines. "How are we supposed to concentrate on anything if we don't know what's wrong with John?"

"Jesus, Tommy, shut up," Alexis snaps. "He doesn't want to talk." Since Amy's defection, Alexis seems different, more engaged. At break, Alexis, Kristal and I usually chat in the ladies' room. I mean, Alexis and I aren't friends by any stretch, but it's a lot more pleasant without Amy. Especially since we'll all be continuing on in the step-down program. Dr. McCallum was quick to okay my participation.

"Yeah, Tom, don't you understand the meaning of giving somebody space?" Kristal adds.

"But he doesn't look—" Tommy's anxious objection is silenced by Garrett.

"Tom," Garrett says, his head whipping toward Tommy, "for once in your life can you just fucking chill?" It's the first time I've seen Garrett react to anything.

The words almost physically lash Tommy and he abruptly sits back on the sofa.

Everyone is trying to support John, but I think they're blind to something. I can see the tears gathering in Tommy's eyes.

"You guys, he's just worried about John," I say. And then I look to Tommy. "It's okay, Tommy. It's okay." My voice sounds abnormally loud in the brief sliver of silence, but somehow it calms everyone down. The effect makes me feel like an idiot savant who has just figured out the cure to Alzheimer's.

"Thank you, Catherine. Well said," Sandy says. "I think we all need to take a deep breath. Remember, all of this, everyone's reaction, is born out of something good. And that's our concern for John." Sandy turns to Tommy. "It's really wonderful, Tom, that you care about John. But you know that sharing here will always be a *choice* for each of you. We can't force—"

"It's okay," John interrupts her. "I can talk about it. Thanks, little man." John does an air–high five with Tommy. He turns back to the group and his eyes drop to the speckled gray carpet. "I . . . I quit wrestling. . . . Something happened yesterday. . . ." He rubs his hands together and then squeezes his eyes shut.

Tommy says, "It's okay, buddy," and then his little

Purelled hand actually pats the unsanitized cotton fabric of John's gray flannel button-down. Real, voluntary, physical contact. The shock is enough to pull John out of his private hell for a moment. He raises his head to look at Tommy. "Dude, did you actually just touch me? On purpose?"

Tommy nods, slightly dumbfounded. For a germophobe with OCD, this is major progress. Ignoring the minor victory, Tommy graciously concedes the floor. "So, John, what happened yesterday?" he asks, resting the renegade hand conspicuously still on his leg like it's covered with Ebola virus.

John swallows, his Adam's apple moving with the effort. "I broke a kid's shoulder. During practice." His eyes return to the carpet.

"But isn't it too early in the season to be practicing?" Tommy asks.

"Objection, relevance," Kristal barks, and I have to stifle a laugh. "Tom," Kristal continues, "can you *please* let the kid speak?"

Tommy nods. "Sorry."

We all wait, but John doesn't say anything. A full minute passes. When John finally raises his head, his eyes are tortured.

"Something went wrong during a takedown . . . he moved wrong. . . . And I landed on him funny . . . I . . . I felt the fucking bone snap." John twists his hands around each other, over and under. He continues in a raspy voice. "And we both froze for a second and I looked at his shoulder, which was, like, two inches from my face. The shape was all wrong—distorted—and something white—the bone, I guess—was sticking out of the skin." John drops his head into his hands. "Oh my God. I can't get it out of my head."

The rest of us sit there, stunned. Alexis and Tommy stare at John, their eyes wide and mouths slightly open. Garrett's hands are pleated together on top of his head and he keeps looking up at the ceiling and shaking his head. Kristal covers her mouth with one hand. I'm suddenly cold.

"That wasn't the worst part," John says, still cradling his face in his hands.

I feel the prickling of fear, a premonition of what he's going to say. I don't want to hear anymore. I want to walk out of Room Three right now. Instead, I pull my knees up to my chest, as if to defend myself against John's words.

"When it happened . . . ," John continues. "When the bone snapped, the kid went quiet. He stopped moving. And then . . . and then . . . he made this . . . this noise. It was so sick. I keep hearing it. It wasn't human . . . it wasn't human." John's crying openly now.

Garrett pats John's knee, but Tommy doesn't get it. "What? What do you mean?" His voice is high and chirpy. "Not human? Like what?"

I can feel the blood pulsing in my ears, the pressure in my head elevating.

John doesn't respond and Tommy repeats his inane questions. He won't stop.

"Like an animal," I say. "An animal in pain."

I heard that same sound July 3 when I rolled Grandma over and saw her open eyes and bleeding nose. Her mouth, the mouth that had sung me silly songs and kissed me and told me she loved me, was making awful noises. My beautiful grandmother reduced in seconds to a tormented creature dying on the bedroom floor, and I knew that sound was the last I'd ever hear her make.

"I know it," I tell John, a floodgate finally opened in my core. "I heard it too. My grandmother made that noise when she died. . . ."

I feel Kristal's arms encircle me and John's eyes are holding mine. I am crying now, too. I see thirteen-year-old me calling 911 and then wrapping Grandma in her favorite yellow afghan, holding her as the keening ceased and she slipped away from me.

It's break time in Room Three. The mood is hushed and we all tread lightly around the table with pretzels and apple juice. I think Garrett was the only person in the room who didn't cry. Even Sandy was dabbing her eyes as she came over to sit beside me and pull me close. I cried again when John said in a deep, trembling voice, "Thanks for sharing that, Catherine. It helps me. . . . I'm sorry you went through that. But I . . . I feel better knowing you know what it feels like."

I nodded. "Me too."

And it's true. I never told anyone about those sounds. Not Mom, or Dr. A, or Dr. McCallum. This memory has haunted me for years because I didn't think anyone would understand. But John does.

Kristal is still huddled over me, armed with extra tissues. "Jesus, Cat," she says. "That was the fucking saddest thing I've ever heard. Your grandmother dying right in front of you."

It is the first time someone has said this to me point-blank. I have run from these words for the past two years and four months. And then Alexis pops up and sits beside me. I am sandwiched between my two IOP comrades on the sofa. Alexis gently pats my back.

I can only respond, "It was horrible." There's more, but I can't say it just yet. Yet speaking those three words aloud shifts something inside me. I feel a little lighter. I realize now the enormity, the weight of that secret memory, is part of what keeps Zero tethered to me.

Sandy forges ahead with discussion even though the fifteen-minute break isn't over. She directs us back to our sofas to "process" our emotions.

"So we've all just heard the events that happened to Catherine and John. The freak accident while John was wrestling and his opponent so horribly injured," Sandy says. "And Catherine witnessing the death of her grandmother. Extraordinarily traumatic, painful things. So how do we deal with this? *How do we deal with pain?* We are human. We suffer. No one, *no one* escapes that fate." She pauses and her eyes travel to each of us. "So this is the question for all of us: how can we ride out the bad times? And I'm using the phrase 'ride out' on purpose. Because our lives are in constant motion, and everything in life passes. The best of times don't last, as much as we'd like them to, but the worst of times don't last either. Even though it may feel like they do."

Sandy leans forward, her elbows resting on her knees, as if to get closer to us. "Everyone in this room has experienced pain. You each have your challenges. But I don't think that's necessarily a bad thing. In a way, I think you guys are a little ahead of the game. Lots of people don't deal with their issues until much later in life when, believe it or not, it gets even more complicated. I like to think that *because* you're handling these tough issues, you will be stronger and better for it."

This is a novel spin on the IOP experience—Sandy pitching our mental illness issues like they're black badges of courage. *The few, the brave, the bipolar.*

Tommy does a few enthusiastic claps, which makes the rest of us break out into small smiles.

Sandy scoots forward on the sofa so she's perched on the very edge. I've never seen her so intense. "My goal is for you to leave this program with not only a greater degree of honesty with yourselves but also a greater willingness to be honest with others. And with greater coping skills to handle what happens next in your lives. I want you to think about the safest ways for you to deal with pain." She pauses and then continues in that deep, slow tone. "Whether that pain comes from anxiety or loneliness or a traumatic event or a condition, it doesn't matter. Pain is pain. This is the reason you're sitting here in this room today. The bottom line for all of this is to learn to safely deal with your pain."

25

"Are you a virgin, Cat?"

It's two-thirty in the morning on Saturday, and Kristal and I are in her bedroom. I'm stretched out on the luxurious daybed and Kristal sprawls under the covers of her queen-sized bed with its upholstered headboard. Kristal's question has not quite come out of left field, since the topic of conversation is Michael, but it still throws me a little. She left the light on in her walk-in closet, so the room is pretty well lit and I'm worried she'll be able to see the red heat in my cheeks.

"Uh . . . yeah," I say.

Kristal and I haven't stopped talking since Aunt Darlene dropped me off tonight loaded with two boxes of doughnuts. Incredibly, Mom had offered no resistance to the sleepover plan—perhaps a by-product of the new anxiety support group she's just started attending. She took a Friday-night shift at Dominic's since I wasn't going to be home and Aunt D was headed to New Haven anyway for dinner. So Aunt D's dropping me off at Kristal's only a few miles away was a no-brainer. I stalled on taking the doughnuts, but Aunt D said it was good manners to bring something for the host. So I walked in carrying my duffel and twenty-four wheels of iced, sugary goodness. Kristal dropped a dozen on the granite island in the Walkers' grand kitchen and hurried the second box upstairs to her bedroom. "Shhh," she had said. "This will be our reserve. Don't tell my mom."

Kristal kicks off her covers now. "Sorry. Was that virgin status question a little too personal?"

"No," I say, even though I'm thinking, *Kinda*. I forgot about this girlfriend intimacy. With no topics off-limits.

"How long have you guys been going out?" she asks.

"We had our first kiss on October eleventh," I say. I know this from studying my list. I also just added entry number seven: Michael's first scheduled dinner at the Pulaski household for later today, Saturday, November 8. Mom had insisted.

"Congrats!" Kristal gives a low whistle. "You're coming up on your one-month anniversary. Do you celebrate stuff like that, or is it too middle school?"

I rest my chin on a pillow. "I have no clue. I've never had a boyfriend before."

"Wow, I'm surprised," Kristal says, the relief obvious from her tone. "You're so pretty. You seem like one of those girls who always has a boyfriend."

227

"That's what I think about you!" I don't share that my bipolar disorder has majorly impacted my desirability to the opposite sex. Or that Zero is terrific at pulverizing one's sex drive. "Are you dating anyone?"

"No," Kristal says.

A silence falls, and I don't know if she's getting sleepy or doesn't want this discussion to go any further. I lean back against the pillows.

"It's . . . it's hard for me," she begins. "I've had these issues for a while. . . ."

Another silence. I have to say something. It feels rude not to.

"It is so hard," I say. "It's much harder for people like us. Dealing with the regular bullshit of high school and then adding all this extra crap—psychiatrists, counseling, IOPs."

"I'm so glad I met you," Kristal says. "Just so fucking glad. I don't know about you, but I just don't feel connected anymore to my friends at school. I can't tell them anything. They're really nice and all, and I'm sure they'd be okay with it. A couple of them go to counseling too. But it's for stuff like divorce. It's just . . . I don't know. It doesn't feel right. I hang out with them and do stuff on weekends but it feels kind of superficial. But with you . . . we're in this together. You understand. I don't have to edit myself."

"Oh my God, me too," I say. I can't tell Kristal the full truth, so I give a watered-down, edited version. "A lot of my friends left when I . . . when things got bad. It was rough." It feels safe in the dim light of Kristal's room. I feel safe. So I add, "It still is rough. They're pretty mean to me now."

"That sucks, Cat. I'm so sorry. But you have me now. I'll be your new BFF." Kristal sits up. "You never really talk in group, about yourself. What's going on with you?" she asks softly. "Depression? From your grandmother dying in front of you?"

God. She says it so openly. So easily. I'm still getting used to the very publicness of my most private pain.

"Yes," I whisper. Another partial truth.

I know I could tell her right now that I have bipolar disorder. She's asking. Part of me reasons, *The IOP gang doesn't give a shit about your diagnosis. Kristal will be fine with it.*

But Riley and Olivia asked too. I remember Riley studying her phone and then glancing at my hair, the glaring evidence of my instability. I remember how her mouth opened in shock, and how quickly she scrambled to her feet after probably reading Wikipedia's take on bipolar disorder. She couldn't get out of my house fast enough.

So I decide not to tell Kristal. I couldn't handle her rejection, couldn't bear the way it would destroy the safe zone of St. Anne's forever, especially in my final chapter, when things are going so well. Being blacklisted at group would definitely accelerate Zero's arrival.

"I have anxiety," Kristal says. "Horrible anxiety. That's why I got bulimic. I thought it was a way I could control things. Or so says one of my eating coaches. But that's over. I'm done with that. It's really disgusting to me now. I hope

I helped Alexis a little. Amy really screwed her up. I felt bad for her, didn't you?"

"Definitely," I say. "She must've felt betrayed in a way."

"Good point," Kristal says. "You know, you should talk more at group. Don't be afraid to share. Rule number one at St. Anne's: Don't be stingy with the wisdom, Cat. That's why they want us together, right? Peer support." Kristal sighs and grows quiet.

Okay. She wants support. I can ask this. "You said you have anxiety. What are you anxious about?"

"Everything." In the dim light, I can see Kristal lean against the headboard. "School. Friends. Guitar. I quit guitar. Got rid of that stressor. But I can't quit school. Or college. Get this, my brother is a freshman at Harvard."

"Shit," I say. "Do your parents put a lot of pressure on you?"

"Not at all," Kristal says. "They'd be happy with me at community college as long as I stop putting my finger down my throat. Which I *did*. It's all me, Cat. It's me who inflicts all the pressure." Her voice sounds small and defeated. "We were supposed to look at schools in D.C., but my mom doesn't want me that far from home. *Just in case,* she keeps saying."

"You really want UConn?" I ask.

"No, I just told you that because . . . I don't know why. I guess to make you think I didn't care. I really want Vassar. But I don't think I'll get in."

"You go to Chapman," I say. "You have a great shot."

"It's probably better if I stay in Connecticut. I've got other stuff going on. . . ." Her voice trails off.

What else could she be dealing with?

"Do you want to talk about it?" I swing my legs off the daybed so my toes scrape the plush Oriental rug. I lean forward. "You can trust me."

"I know. I do trust you. I told you my poop story." We laugh a little and then there's silence. I hear Kristal sigh. "It is just so fucking, mind-bogglingly, insanely humiliating, Cat. Only my parents know." The sadness in her voice is almost palpable.

I lean forward, whispering urgently, "You don't have to tell me. But I'm here whenever you want to talk. If you ever want to talk about it."

Kristal inhales deeply. "Okay, then. Here it goes. My body doesn't work right," she says quickly. "Down there."

"Uh . . . what do you mean?"

"I'm like a Barbie doll."

WTF does she mean? "You don't . . . don't have a vagi—" I can't finish the rest. Maybe she's a hermaphrodite.

Kristal laughs. "Sorry, that came out wrong. Yes, I have a vagina. But it doesn't work right. Due to my anxiety."

I have no clue how to respond. What does she mean by "doesn't work right"?

"God, I'm so sorry," I say. "Do you need surgery or something?"

"I wish," she replies. "That would be awesome if they could just *do* something. I have vaginismus. Ever hear of it?"

"No."

"It's where the muscles inside your vagina completely tense up. It feels like the Berlin Wall down there."

Shit. Could I have that too? "How did you know you had it?" I ask.

"I could never get a tampon in. Never. Finally, my mom took me to the gynecologist. It was bad. I had to have an ultrasound since there was no way for her to do an exam."

"Oh my God, Kristal. That is horrifying."

"You have no idea, Cat. It is beyond humiliating. On top of everything else, I get stuck with *this*? An anxious vagina?" She pauses. "That would make a good name for a band, right? The Anxious Vagina."

We burst out laughing.

"I won't be sharing this at St. Anne's. There's no zone safe enough for this one," Kristal says, chuckling and wiping her eyes. "It just really sucks. I have to go to a physical therapist who specializes in this kind of stuff. Pelvic floor dysfunction. I still can't believe this is my life."

"I am so sorry," I say again.

"I hate that my body doesn't work right. It feels so unfair."

Her words vibrate inside me. Yes, yes, yes. I know that feeling. I live that feeling. I want to tell her I understand the pain of a body malfunctioning. I could tell her that my brain doesn't work right. But the confession hides low in my gut, nowhere near ready to be released into the realm of public pain.

Kristal gets out of bed and opens the box of doughnuts on her desk. It looks like she has one in each hand as she climbs back into bed. An alarm bell goes off in my head. I hope it's just what Mom does, stress eating. And that the food stays put, in her stomach.

Kristal says, "My mom calls it 'nature's chastity belt' and thinks it's just gonna relax on its own all of a sudden. But when? You know what it's like to go shopping for period stuff? I have intense tampon envy." She finishes the first doughnut and starts on the second. "And I'm jealous of you. You have a boyfriend. You can be with him without worrying about something like this." Her voice trembles. "How am I supposed to go off to college like this? With this fucking vagina . . . vagina lockjaw?"

"Well, what does the therapist or your doctor say?" I ask. "Maybe it will be gone by then?"

"They won't give me a time frame. They just said to focus on the therapy and it happens when it happens. And not to worry because it's completely curable. But who the fuck knows when the miracle cure will happen? Ugh. Enough of this." Kristal gets up for another doughnut. "What are you doing with Michael this weekend?"

"He's coming over tomorrow, well, technically tonight, for dinner. With my mom. I'm dreading it, actually. It's just me and my mom, and compared with Michael's noisy house, it will probably be so damn awkward. Michael's kind of shy and my mom . . . God knows what will pop out of her mouth. She already started pulling out the board games." I cringe in the semidarkness. "She'll be hovering the entire time."

There'll probably be no alone time with Michael either. But I don't mention that. Why rub salt into Kristal's wound?

Kristal wants details on Michael—height, weight, eye color, build. Then she tells me about the guy she's been crushing on for all four years of Chapman. We strategize ways for her to get to know him better for at least a half hour, but around 3:10, I start to fade, my eyelids heavy and the daybed just too perfect with its fluffy pillows and cozy blankets. The ceiling fan blows a soft breeze.

I'm awakened around 3:30 by the sound of the shower running in Kristal's adjoining bathroom. Her bed is empty and I can hear low, coughing sounds. Like someone's throwing up. Instinctively my eyes go to Kristal's desk. The box of doughnuts is gone. Oh Jesus.

The shower runs until four a.m. I pretend I'm asleep as Kristal emerges from the bathroom. I don't know what to say. I can't jeopardize this friendship. Before getting into her bed, Kristal slides something under it.

Does everyone hide their darker selves under their beds?

In the morning, before we head downstairs to breakfast, Kristal turns to me. "Don't say anything about the doughnuts. I just threw them out last night after you fell asleep. My mom gets all weird about food and stuff now."

We're standing at the top of the back staircase that leads directly to the kitchen. Kristal won't meet my eyes. She runs a hand along the white paneling that rises halfway up the wall.

I don't say that I heard her coughing in the bathroom at 3:30 or that the shower ran for almost a half hour. I don't say that she's lying about being recovered from bulimia. She's entitled to her secrets just like I am. But I'll watch her. And maybe, if the time is right, I'll say something. I'm not sure she'll be receptive to any words of wisdom coming from me, though, regardless of what she said last night.

Bev makes us banana-and-strawberry pancakes at the six-burner mega-stove. We sit around the island and chat about school and Jane and her letters. It's nice, but all the while I'm aware of Bev stealing glances at Kristal and Kristal's plate. The expression in her eyes reminds me of Mom.

——

D-DAY LIST
1. Michael
2. First Kiss, Michael Oct.11
3. Meet Kristal at Museum Oct. 19
4. Museum with M Oct. 25
5. Halloween with M
6. Sleepover at K's Nov. 7
7. Michael Dinner #1 @ Pulaskis' Nov. 8

——

Mom and I are in Walmart. We drove here straight from Kristal's. "I cleaned and went grocery shopping last night," Mom had said as soon as I slid into the Accord. The twenty questions, sleepover edition I anticipated were not on the morning's agenda. "It was slow, so Dominic let me go early," she'd said. "Do you think Michael will like that chicken dish I make with the artichoke hearts and mush-rooms? And I'll do roasted potatoes, string beans and an apple pie. With vanilla ice cream." She was abuzz with nervous energy. Dinner at the Pulaskis' with Bipolar Cath's new boyfriend!

We split when we got inside the store, Mom headed to Housewares in search of a new tablecloth, me to the Women's Intimates linoleum quadrant. My bras are all pretty new. The silver lining to my weight gain was to go up a cup size, necessitating a trip to Kohl's with our Kohl's cash and coupons in hand. But I really need underwear. My existing stock is worn, and now that I have a boyfriend, the status of my underwear has become more relevant.

But then I realize that, duh, there's no way I can buy underwear. Could I be any more fucking obvious? *Hey, Mom, thanks for cooking dinner tonight and, oh, would you mind shelling out for these new undies I plan on wearing for Michael?* I guess I'm stuck with my aging tie-dye bikinis from Target.

At home, I help Mom with peeling the potatoes, and then cover the table with the new tablecloth. Mom tells me about her first session with the anxiety support group, how initially she was petrified, but the people are really nice and have family with all kinds of issues—addiction or alcoholism, bankruptcy, criminal activity, Alzheimer's. Only one other person has a loved one with mental illness. Mom didn't recognize anyone from Cranbury and that made her feel better.

"Jeez, Cath, I understand now why you were so worried about going to St. Anne's," she says as she rinses the chicken breasts under the kitchen faucet.

"I was freaking out when I walked in that first day," I say, surprising myself with my honesty. "I was praying I didn't know anybody." And then I realize that I have to tell Mom about my lying to Michael about work. Michael could bring up the topic tonight at dinner. "Michael's asked me a few times to stay after school for our project," I say. "I told him I couldn't, that I work at your law office."

Mom puts a chicken breast down to look at me. Then she shocks me. "I was wondering about that. He used to be there a lot when I picked you up. I wondered if he ever asked you."

"I couldn't tell him about St. Anne's," I say.

Mom brushes her shoulder against mine and returns to the chicken. "I don't blame you. So how many days a week do we work together?"

"Five," I say, and we both start laughing.

"Industrious," Mom says. "I'm impressed." She moves to the refrigerator and gets the eggs. "You know, Cath, if things seem to be working out between the two of you, you'll eventually have to tell him, right?"

"Sure," I say. "But I barely know him. Let's see what happens." I don't tell her the truth, that Michael will never know about that part of me.

"I get it now, Cath. How hard it is to go to these group sessions. How hard it is to say your problems out loud. I'm so proud of you." Mom wraps an arm around my shoulders and I allow myself to lean into her. "You tell Michael when you're ready, baby girl. If you do decide to, we'll buy some doughnuts for moral support."

I think of last night and Kristal. Her anxiety and bulimia and vagi-whatever. How it all just sucks.

"Yikes, I forgot about the laundry," Mom says suddenly, moving to wash her hands under the faucet. "I put in a load last night and it will smell if I don't move it to the dryer."

"I'll do it," I say. "Finish up here."

"Wow," Mom says, sending a dart of guilt through me—that my doing the laundry warrants such shock and awe. "Thank you."

In the basement, I empty the dryer and transfer the wet towels and sheets into it. There are huge mounds of clean clothes in the two laundry baskets on the floor. Their sweet fragrance dances up to me and I suddenly remember Grandma, bending to pull the clothes out of the dryer. She'd always sing the same song, "You are my sunshine, my only sunshine, you make me happy when skies are gray. . . ." She'd fold the clothes, sometimes draping me in a warm towel or blanket fresh from the dryer while I'd lie on my stomach on the braided rug, coloring or drawing.

I hum the tune as I fold all the clothes in the baskets.

In addition to Michael, Aunt D joins us for dinner. Those awkward silences punctuated by Mom's ramblings that I feared never happen. Aunt D skillfully keeps the conversation hopping from one fun topic to another as Mom bustles around serving a dinner on par with Nonny's cooking. I need to remember to thank Mom for that. I also need to thank her for giving Aunt D a heads-up about my lie about working at the law firm.

Following dessert of apple pie and vanilla ice cream, the most unexpected development occurs.

"I'm stuffed," Aunt D says, her hand resting on the pudgy stomach that swells slightly over her belt. And in a rehearsed fashion, Mom replies, "Why don't we try to walk off some of our dinner?" Aunt D responds with the enthusiasm of an infomercial hostess. "Great idea, Jody!"

I raise my eyebrows. It's beyond bizarre. My mother would sooner go for a Brazilian bikini wax than meander through our dumpy neighborhood at eight at night. But the two of them are already zipping up jackets and wrapping scarves around their necks and heading for the front door.

"How long do you think we'll be walking?" Aunt D stage-asks Mom while covertly winking at me.

"A half hour," Mom says, checking her watch. "We should be back around eight-thirtyish. Maybe we can play Jenga or Taboo when we get back?" And then Mom gives me a little smile that says, "Have fun but not too much."

I feel a surge of love for the two of them. A whopping thirty minutes of private time—what a freaking unexpected bonanza!

As soon as the front door closes, I hit the overhead light so just the one lamp is on. Michael stands stock-still, clearly silently freaking out. I sit on the sofa and pat the cushion.

"Why don't you sit down?" I ask, trying not to sound

like a cheesy porn star. Thirty minutes is the most time we've had alone. Maybe I should've bought new underwear at Walmart.

Michael sits down next to me and stares straight ahead. I can see red blotches on his neck. I lightly touch his cheek and then his chin, pulling his face toward mine. Leaning over, I kiss him. The race to connect crosses my mind, but I don't want to think that anymore. It's cheap and wrong now that I actually know Michael. It's more that I want experiences *with this boy* before Zero returns. But that may be another lie I'm trying to sell myself. Because the bigger truth may be simply that I like him. I just really, really like Michael Pitoscia.

26

Our kissing has progressed from sitting on the sofa to lying down. Not very smoothly accomplished, since I kind of tugged Michael down by the front of his flannel shirt, but here we are, his long body on top of mine.

Michael explores my ear with his tongue, giving me delicious shivers. I could do this all night, but we are seriously running low on time. According to my Timex, we've been kissing for seven minutes. This only leaves us a solid ten minutes, fifteen max. Undoubtedly, Mom will be at the front door at 8:30 on the dot or maybe even five minutes before. Aunt D wouldn't allow an arrival any earlier.

Michael is kissing my neck. "You are so beautiful," he whispers in my ear. His breathing is faster, but his hands have stayed locked on my waist, superglued to the nubby fabric of my sweater.

I bring both my hands up to his neck. I love the way

our bodies feel, pressed tightly together like this. I love this closeness, and the warmth of this contact. I lift his shirt and run my hands up his back. His skin is hot, smooth and a little sweaty. I'm surprised at how his back widens from those narrow hips. The twin columns of muscle running along his spine are firm and I like the way they feel under my fingers. He moans a little.

"We should probably stop, Cath. Your mom is coming back."

"Five more minutes," I whisper.

We kiss some more. Michael moves his hands, tucking them under the small of my back. I wrap one leg around his and this brings us even closer together down there. I can definitely feel a pressure buildup in his zipper region. This is getting better and better. My hands slide down to the jean pockets on his butt. And that is where I err. With a deep gasp, the boy rises horizontally like he's been electrocuted, jackknifing into a sitting position a good foot away from me on the sofa.

"Whoa," he breathes, his face a brilliant red. He leans over as if in pain. "Where's your bathroom?" he asks. I point to the door off the living room, and, slightly hunched over, he hobbles out of the room.

Oh God. My heart picks up its pace and I feel the tiny needles of anxiety. Was it too much, too soon? But we have been dating a month. I feel a shadow over me, the evening's goodness growing tainted. Did I fuck up in some way? Miss Manic acting inappropriately again?

Michael returns to the living room, his shirt no lon-

242

ger tucked into his pants. He smiles as he slides beside me on the sofa. He wraps his right arm around my shoulders and kisses my cheek. "Sorry about that, Cath. You are so hot." He nuzzles my ear. "I'm just worried about your mom walking in on us. It's eight-twenty-two. Let's snuggle for two more minutes."

"Snuggle"? He just seriously used the cutest word in the world in a sentence. With me.

With his free hand, he plays with my fingers. Then he says, "You know, our one-month anniversary is coming up this Tuesday." He is a total mush right now, and Zero's shadow vanishes. "We should celebrate next weekend. Saturday night, okay? Let's plan something good."

27

I should've known that Mom's Saturday-night gift of privacy with Michael would come at a price. It comes on Tuesday, my official one-month anniversary of dating Michael.

We are en route to St. Anne's when Mom announces a little tentatively, "Dr. McCallum is supposed to call before the IOP. He wants to check in, see how things are going."

"Well, if he calls while we're in the car, can you pull over so I can get out and talk to him alone?" I ask. I'm grateful that she's not dragging my ass into his office again.

"I'll get out," Mom says. "It's too cold to be walking around outside. I could run into a store depending where we are."

We're in front of a strip mall with a dollar store, a craft place and an Xpect Discounts when my phone buzzes and the screen flashes: Dr. McCallum. Mom hangs a hard right into the parking lot. "Text me when you're done," she says, opening the car door.

"Hello?" I say as Mom jogs into Xpect Discounts.

"Hello, Catherine. It's Dr. McCallum." His voice booms out of my phone. I check to make sure all the car windows are fully closed.

"Hi," I say, sliding down in my seat. I'm hoping this base-touching won't take more than ten minutes.

We go through the preliminaries: I feel fine; yes, I am sleeping; yes, I am eating; no racing thoughts, no depression; all cool in Catherine-land. And then he broaches the real topic—my meltdown at last week's IOP.

"Catherine," Dr. McCallum says, "I was in touch with Sandy. I understand that you were able to talk about the circumstances of your grandmother's death." In his typical modus operandi, he pauses after that opening salvo and waits for me to fill the silence.

"I wasn't planning on it," I say. On today's menu: the truth. It's a little easier when Dr. McCallum's not directly in front of me. It's almost like talking to myself, here inside the Accord. "Something happened to one of the kids. . . . He was really upset . . . and he said something that I remembered about Grand— . . . my grandmother . . . when she died."

"How did it feel?"

I pause. "Mostly awful. But . . ." What do I tell Dr. McCallum? That it feels better to have brought this memory into the light, diluted by the compassion of others? Better but also worse at the same time, because it lessened my link to Grandma. That raw, primal connection was weakened and she feels further away now.

"But what, Catherine?"

I put my feet up on the dashboard. "Well . . . a little lighter, I guess." I can't go into the twisted aspect of my feelings. That the more intense the pain, the more alive Grandma remains to me. That may be a bipolar thing.

Dr. McCallum says, "It's hard to bear something like that alone. Sharing it doesn't change that it happened or what it felt like or what it feels like now, but at least you know that others have experienced that pain and you're not alone in that regard."

Dr. McCallum rambles a little bit and I watch as Mom exits Xpect Discounts. She points to Harley's Craft Palace and I give her a thumbs-up. She hustles inside. My ears perk up when Dr. McCallum mentions Michael. He pauses again. That's my cue. And I missed the question. I go with a generic "good."

That seems to satisfy him and I chuckle to myself a little. But I stop short when Dr. McCallum says, "Birth control. I urge all my sexually active adolescent patients to begin birth control."

Whoa. I obviously missed a *huge* topic transition during my brief space-out.

"Uh . . . we're not . . . ," I begin.

"Catherine, you don't have to tell me if you don't feel comfortable. Let me just say this: Drugs are classified into categories depending on their known risk of causing birth defects."

Jesus—I can't even wrap my head around this concept of me becoming a mother. It's like Dr. McCallum said I could live on Mars if I wanted to.

"You're taking Lamictal, which is not commonly associated with birth defects, but it's also not risk-free. Lithium is in a different category. If we feel the need to begin lithium at some point and you are sexually active, birth control is absolutely mandatory."

I can't wait to tell Kristal all of this. Well, on second thought, I'd better not, given the fact that she's sexually challenged for the time being.

"So, if and when the time comes and you are engaging in sex," Dr. McCallum continues, "you should be taking birth control. It is not safe enough to rely solely on condoms. I'm recommending to both you and your mom that you see your pediatrician . . . you see Dr. Coughlin, correct? Of Cranbury Pediatrics?" Dr. McCallum says, and I can hear some static like he's shuffling papers. No doubt scanning his Catherine Pulaski file for my info.

"Yes."

"I'd like for you to touch base, find out if there would be an issue with the Pill. The Lamictal that you're taking lowers the Pill's effectiveness. But there are other options. An IUD might be a consideration. You wouldn't have to worry about taking another pill every day. You can discuss that all with Dr. Coughlin."

"Okay." Our Father, who art in heaven, when is this conversation over?

"One more thing, Catherine," Dr. McCallum says, sensing my impatience. "I'll be brief. I don't want to make you too late for group, but I do want to remind you of something. The holidays are coming up. They can often become stressor events, like anniversaries of painful events. I'd like you to be especially on guard, so to speak, in terms of monitoring your emotions and sleep cycles, watching for any blips in the regular patterns, okay? Keep up with your sleep journal."

"I will."

After confirming our next appointment for sometime Thanksgiving week, we say good-bye.

As usual, Dr. McCallum stirs up shit I try to avoid thinking about. An innocent third party to the Catherine Pulaski saga? Not happening. No way. Don't worry, Doctor. I'll take whatever over-the-counter precautions I need to.

I don't text Mom that the phone call is over. Instead, I rush into Dollar Daze. In the back of the store, I find it. Red "satin" underwear, Silkeez Intimates. A buck each. I scoop up three in size large, pay at the register and stuff them into my jacket pocket.

Back inside the car, I text Mom: "ALL DONE"

I'm trapped in my seat as Louis Farricelli pants his dog breath on my neck. "Hey, dykie," he whispers. It's Thursday morning, two days after the Dr. McCallum phone call. The call must've been triggered, at least in part, by Mom after she saw Michael and me sitting together on the sofa, flushed and a little disheveled, on Saturday night. I've quarantined the McCallum pregnancy discussion to the No Admittance office in my head, but Mom has already attempted an "us girls" chat about it. "I'll call Dr. Coughlin when I'm ready," I told her, amazingly calm. Of course, I won't ever be scheduling that appointment. I'm sick of spewing forth my every thought and emotion, my sleep and eating cycles and every other bodily function for someone's clinical examination and dissection. I'm tired of questionnaires and health form updates and drug histories. I'm sure other girls, *normal* girls, have no problem chatting with their doctors about sex and birth control. But I want this one potential jewel in my life to be private. Just mine. My first and last connection is reserved for me alone.

Behind me, Louis Farricelli whispers my name again and I lean forward to escape his pocket of putrid breath.

"I want a rough draft of your biographies before Christmas break," Mr. Oleck is saying, looking especially spiffy in a navy bow tie, starchy white button-down and polished loafers. There are the usual groans about the assignment, but it's no problem for Michael and me. I already have five pages typed up.

A boy with a brand-new deep voice whines from the back of the room, "But I thought this wasn't due until spring."

I glance back to see who just graduated from puberty and spot Riley tapping away on her phone. The seat behind her, Olivia's usual spot, is empty. Weird. Scanning the classroom, I spot Olivia. She has relocated to the opposite side of the room, to the first desk in the aisle closest to the wall. She leans her head into her hand, her mousy brown hair lying flat against her cheeks. Olivia must feel my gaze because she glances over at me and we make accidental eye contact. In the millisecond it takes for my ocular muscles to snatch my gaze away, I detect the beginnings of an Olivia smile, a smile I have known for most of my life. And so rare now it could be on an endangered species list.

Mr. Oleck slams his hands against the podium in delight. "People, we are fast-tracking the project. Big plans for your biographies. The school will be doing an all-out blitz in getting these stories into local papers and magazines and on websites. Your projects will now be completed by February. So, I'll also need updated bibliographies as well as a game plan for project completion, including interviews to be conducted and your finalized timelines for these interviews. *Before* we leave for Christmas break." He glances down at his iPad. "Oh yeah. Sabita found a great oral history collection online." He moves to the blackboard. "Copy this link down."

"Mmm, I like *oral* histories," Louis breathes, his rancid breath again tainting my airspace. I lean farther forward, but he continues in a wheezy tone, stretching toward me now that his neck is free of the brace. "You must be especially good at that, right, Catherine? That's what ladies like you specialize—"

I jerk my desk forward. It screeches loudly and Mr. Oleck stops talking. He sizes up the situation in one glance. "Louis, I'm pretty sure your neck injury didn't give you any cognitive impairments. So why are you leaning so close to Miss Pulaski?"

The class chuckles, but there's no corresponding smile on Mr. Oleck's face, no good-ol'-boys' camaraderie that's usually evident between Cranbury High's faculty and the elite male athletes.

Mr. Oleck continues, "The next time I see you lurching over any student, you are out of my class. For good. Got it?"

The class goes silent, astonished at the public execution. Can Louis Farricelli fall any further?

While I appreciate the save from Mr. Oleck, I brace myself for Louis's wrath. It comes when the bell rings. Louis rises from his seat and, using the end-of-class exodus noise as camouflage, hisses the worst of all curse words as he passes me: "Cunt."

Instinctively, I cringe. But it's not the stark ugliness of the c-word that unnerves me. It's the black malice in his tone. This is the kind of kid who snaps, someone who "out of the blue" brings his dad's gun to school.

The news reports would give the glorified stats: honors student and All-State football captain, sidelined by a career-ending injury. *Aha!* the older readers would say, desperate for a reason. *That had to be it.* But their high school memories have been repressed or dulled or grown outdated. Only the younger ones would know. They're well aware of the pressure and jabs and cuts and slices. The insults and ridicule complete with photos and videos flying at cyberspeed to reach greater audiences of "friends" of "friends" of "friends." It happens every fucking day inside these hallowed halls.

I wait until Michael comes over before exiting the classroom.

"Is Farricelli bugging you?" Michael asks immediately, his eyebrows furrowed with concern.

"Nah. No big deal." I want to hug him right then and there. "I can handle it."

Michael's face flushes. "I'm . . . I'll go talk to him. I don't want that asshole hassling you."

That is literally the last thing I want. First, I do not need a knight. Second, Farricelli has at least sixty pounds on Michael. Sixty pounds of muscle and percolating volcanic fury. Farricelli would absolutely relish a fight to reestablish his place in the Cranbury High pecking order. Michael would get hurt.

"It's really just his breath," I lie. "He must eat poop for breakfast."

"Oh, he's doing the Mitzi diet?" my boyfriend says, flashing a smile. But then he turns serious again. "Cath, for real, you'll let me know if he bothers you?" he says. "That kid is such a damn bully. Anthony and his friends despise him."

I nod and then take Michael's hand. "Thanks for the offer," I say. We walk down the hall, linked.

Michael wants me to sit with him and Tyler and some other boys at lunch. On another day, I might be tempted. But there's a new email on my phone from Jenna the curator. I'm hoping she's found a third letter from Jane. I tell Michael this and he wants to come with me to read it. He loves the other two letters that Jenna sent.

But I don't know how to explain that he can't be with me right now. When I lay eyes on Jane's words, I need to read them in private, at least for the first time.

"I have other homework too," I say. "I didn't finish it last night. I wonder why?" Michael gets it. We stayed up till after midnight texting. He's got a surprise planned for Saturday night.

In my favorite library cubby, I click on the email.

Jenna thinks this is the last letter of Jane's that she'll be able to locate. I click on the photograph. I can tell that the paper Jane used to write this letter is a different shade of white, and it looks like she wrote in pencil; her graceful, even script appears more smudged and faded compared with that of the other letters. Once again, Jenna has transcribed it for me.

April 29, 1945

Dear Mama,

I love England! I truly do! Your daughter sailed in high style on the finest cruise ship around, the Queen Elizabeth. She's a beauty even though she's been painted a dreary gray and her main job is moving troops back and forth. I'm happy to report that it was very smooth sailing for us. Not like the first group of 6888s. They were chased by a U-boat and the girls tell me that everything was flying off the shelves in their rooms and people were screaming and the boat was rocking this way and that, with all the bells and sirens going. Some girls said they'd rather go after Hitler himself than get themselves back on another boat. But please don't think it was a vacation for me. They had us constantly doing drills and tons of exercise, which you know I do not like.

Birmingham is a big city pretty much in the center

of England. We're about three and a half hours from London. We can still see the damage from the Luftwaffe bombing. London got hit the hardest and Birmingham came in second. It is a real shame. Especially because the people here are so nice, Mama. It is so much different from at home. They are so kind to us. Families invite the girls inside their homes for "tea." Dorothy and I are especially lucky. Mrs. Spencer wants us to spend the weekend with her again. She said she's lonely and loves how lively the house feels when we visit. She's got a big garden filled with roses and lilac just about to bloom. You would love it, Mama. And if you need more proof that we are treated well so you can sleep at night, listen to this. Some girls went into a pub and there were white American soldiers there. They didn't welcome the 6888s at all. Instead, they started yelling nasty things like how dark the room got 'cause the girls came walking in. It was awful. But then the local people told the white soldiers to stop and they wouldn't, so they got kicked out of the bar. Wasn't that amazing? It made me so happy but it also made me sad. I thought our being here might change things.

I am slowly getting used to living at the King Edward School. It almost feels like a real base now instead of a temporary accommodation. I still hate the showers outside in the courtyard. Good news is that I now bathe pretty darn fast. I know you will be hoping/praying that I will continue that new habit when I get back home.

I hate to grandstand, Mama, but we are doing a fine job with the mail. Nobody expected us to get it sorted so fast. I bet we would go even faster if the windows weren't blacked out and we had some decent working space in this drafty gymnasium. On some days, I still wear my ski pants, it's so chilly inside.

Bet you didn't expect such a long letter from me. I have just been missing home a little. Please don't worry anymore. We are all safe here. Everybody's saying only just a couple more weeks and Hitler will be caught. The war is going to be ending.

Give Mari and Petey and yourself a big hug from me, Mama. I miss you and can't wait to see you all!

Your loving daughter,
Jane

The same sadness envelops me again. I hate knowing the end to Jane's story. The jeep accident happens on July 13, 1945, so she's got only about five weeks to live after this letter was written. She and Dorothy will be in the jeep when it crashes in France after the 6888th is transferred there. The girls will be killed in a town called Rouen, the same town where Joan of Arc was killed.

There's another emotion in addition to my sadness. I'm *pissed*. How could those assholes in the pub treat them that way? Weren't we all supposed to be on the same side?

All through Ms. Stinkov's class, I simmer.

28

Amy might be returning to group. That's what Sandy has just dropped on us this Friday afternoon with only a half hour left to go. "I'd like to see how you all feel about that," Sandy says. "Anyone want to share?"

"I don't want her here," Alexis says curtly. "It's better without her."

Lil' Tommy nods. "Yeah. I don't think she's right for this group. She kills the mojo. We've got our own thing going now."

Sandy looks at me. "Um, I can see what Alexis and Tommy are saying," I say slowly. "It definitely feels a little more relaxed without her here."

"What?" Kristal bursts out, looking at me like I'm an idiot. "Really?"

Where the freak did that come from?

"Here's my two cents," Garrett says. He's going Rasta,

his long blond hair now a mass of dreadlocks. "I don't think we should block her from coming. If she wants to come, that's fine with me. If she acts like a bitch, you guys should just tell her that."

"That's easy for you to say," Alexis says sharply. "She was always flirting with you."

"Sorry, guys, but I've got to agree with Garrett," John says, his mental state stable again if his full-body Red Sox attire means anything. "It's not right to exclude her."

"This is an IOP, people! An *intensive outpatient program*," Kristal bristles at Alexis and Tommy. And me. "Right? People with issues are supposed to come here. You can't turn this into a clique and exclude her. That's just wrong. And mean." Kristal's eyes travel around the room to land on me beside her. She sniffs scornfully. "Just because it's more *relaxed*? Get over yourselves."

"It wasn't just that she wasn't friendly," I say, irritated at Kristal's righteousness, at her overreaction. It's not like we're saying no to Kristal. "She does change the group dynamic."

"Cat, she's got *serious* issues." Kristal gives me a long look.

Did she just imply that I *don't* have serious issues?

"You don't get it, Kristal," Alexis joins in, really pissed now. She leans forward, eyes wide, hands squeezing the sofa edge. "Me and Amy, we were a 'team.'" Alexis makes air quotes. "You know, me and her were in this IOP long before you got here. And we *bonded*." Sarcasm drips from Alexis's words. "In the beginning, we did all our fucked-up eating shit *together*. We shopped for broth and yogurt and cereal. We kept track of how many hours we'd exercise. And we'd binge together. And puke together." Alexis's voice cracks. "I already have to see her in school. I don't want to see her here. She's gonna get into my head again."

"But we can't just shut her out," Kristal says obstinately. "She needs help too. It is not cool what you guys are saying."

"Jesus!" Alexis shouts. "What don't you get? I'm glad for you, Kristal. That you're cured. That you're totally over it. I'm jealous to be completely freaking honest. Because even though I haven't done anything in forty-two days, I still want to. I am still tempted every fucking day. Have you forgotten what that feels like? Can't you *try* to understand that it's bad for me to have Amy here?"

I'm waiting for Kristal to admit that she isn't cured. The opportunity is right here, right now. Perfect open door. But she says, "I still think it's wrong not to let her come back. I just do."

Alexis rolls her eyes. "I'm leaving if Amy comes back."

Sandy reaches forward to take Alexis's hand. "I understand how you feel, Alexis. And I thank everyone here for sharing his or her thoughts. It's a highly emotional issue and I see everyone's point. But due to the unique circumstances of this issue, the prior unhealthy relationship between Alexis and Amy, I don't think it's wise to have Amy return to this particular group."

Kristal whispers to me, "I cannot believe you voted her off the island, Cat. That is cold."

"We have other programs for Amy, so, Kristal, you

don't have to be concerned about that," Sandy continues. "We've only got two more weeks left. Our final meeting is on the last Wednesday in November, right before Thanksgiving. The following week, the first week of December, you will all be starting the step-down program in the new group room. We're calling it Group Room B. As I told you, we have another group starting around that time using this room. You'll enter the same way, use the same door and foyer area, but instead of heading to this room, you'll be turning left."

After group, Kristal and I walk out together as usual. There's an awkwardness between us that I've never felt before. The first cracks in my first post-diagnosis friendship. Is this the start of another Riley-and-Olivia situation? I'm so glad that I didn't tell Kristal I was bipolar.

I spot the Accord a couple of rows away and start to walk toward it.

"Cat." Kristal grabs my arm on the concrete sidewalk outside the door. "Wait a sec." We say good-bye to Garrett and John. And then Alexis walks out. Kristal spontaneously hugs her. "I'm sorry if I hurt your feelings, Al. I get what you said."

"Al" is stiff and barely returns the gesture. "Have a good weekend, Catherine," she says, and gives me a wan smile.

"Shit," Kristal says. "I . . . I really fucked up. I shouldn't have opened my mouth."

She's waiting for me to say it's okay, but I don't. I can't. She was wrong.

"Are you mad at me too?" she asks.

The question hangs in the chilly air. I could just say no and blow the whole thing off. She's already kind of apologized. But I can't. "Why did you say that? About some people having serious issues? Were you hinting that I don't?"

"No, Cat," she says. "Not at all. Having your grandma die in your arms, I can't think of anything worse. Of course anybody would be totally messed up from something like that. It's just that . . . well." Kristal stops.

I don't fill in her gaps of knowledge about my other "issues." Instead I ask, "What? It's what?"

"Sometimes you don't seem that sympathetic to the stuff other people are going through."

"What?" I force myself not to shout. "How can you say that to me after what you just did to Alexis in there? Saying that Amy should come back when it's so obvious she's bad news for Alexis?"

"I wasn't thinking about Alexis. I was thinking about Amy, about her wanting to come back to group and not being able to. I felt bad for her. And I told you, I was wrong. I should have been more clued in to what Alexis was saying. But, Cat . . . Never mind. This probably isn't the right time."

"No. Tell me."

"Sometimes I get the feeling you think your shit is, like, the worst and no matter what any of us go through, it will never compare to yours. Does that make sense?"

I'm stunned. "How can you think that?"

"Please don't be mad. It's just . . . you keep your distance. Like that time when Alexis was crying about Amy and it took you forever to come over to the sofa just to sit next to her as she basically hyperventilated. And when Tommy or Garrett say stuff, I get the feeling that you don't think it's really a problem for them. The only time you got involved was when John's wrestling accident happened. It was great that you . . . I don't know . . . engaged, shared what had happened to you. It really helped him. But usually . . ." She trails off.

I'm on the verge of asking her why she didn't "engage" with Alexis today about not being cured of bulimia, but I can't. Because it suddenly slaps me that I brought two dozen doughnuts to a girl with bulimia. My God, what was I thinking? Not about Kristal, that's for sure. I was thinking about how the Walkers would perceive the gift. And me. And worrying that maybe it was a little low-class for them. Kristal's eating disorder never even crossed my mind. What kind of friend am I? I should've told Aunt D no.

Kristal places a hand on my arm. She has the most open expression on her face. "You're my best friend, Cat. I always want us to be totally honest with each other. I'm so sorry if I hurt you because of my diarrhea mouth."

Best friend. Best. Friend. The words twinkle inside me like Christmas lights under snow. I move in and we hug. "You're the best thing to come out of this IOP," I say to her.

Inside the Accord, on the way to celebrate Aunt D's birthday at Casa de Amigos, something sharp pokes into my happy. It's Kristal's observation that I'm some kind of mental-health illness elitist. The Judith Swenson of St. Anne's. I think of Garrett with *just* his kids-will-be-kids addiction issues that have already garnered him a juvenile rap sheet that jeopardizes his future. And Kristal and Alexis and John with their eating disorders, which I know can last a lifetime. Going into a restaurant for them is no leisure activity. It is an obsessive calorie-counting, exercise-planning nightmare that sometimes ends with the meal winding up in the toilet later. And my roommate in the hospital, and poor Tommy. I admit thinking his OCD is kind of cute, but what happens when he gets out of high school, when he's a fully grown man with a beard and chafed, red, raw hands that can't touch anyone? How could I have never acknowledged their pain, when pain is the one thing I understand? I carry the unbearable weight of secrets.

Just like they do.

My throat tightens. Amy. That sick, sick girl. The one who was basically starving and shitting herself. To death. Right in front of my eyes.

Where the fuck is my heart? Do I still have one? God, Mary, Jesus, Joseph, anybody up there, help me.

All day Saturday, I do penance. To Mom, to Amy, to Garrett and Alexis and all my IOP comrades. I clean my room, empty the dishwasher, and dust and vacuum the downstairs.

Mom feels my forehead twice and then finally blurts out the worry that's been creasing her brow all morning: do I have any racing thoughts? Because a four-day cleaning binge was the prelude to my "Highlights of the Mediterranean" episode. I tell her the truth, no racing thoughts, but then modify it: I feel a little guilty, I say. I feel like I ought to be doing my share around here. You shouldn't have to do everything. I don't tell her that the chores relieve the shock of last night's revelation in the Accord.

After the house is clean, Mom and I watch three episodes of *House Hunters International*. Each show, we agree on the same place to buy: the one-hundred-year-old Tuscan villa, the grand Prague apartment with the brick kitchen, and the impossibly tiny apartment in Tokyo with the washer-dryer unit on the balcony. Duh, we said. The washer-dryer trumps everything.

In a lighter mood, I begin my body prep for tonight's anniversary surprise that Michael has been planning. In the shower I take my sweet time shaving. In the moist mugginess of our tiny bathroom, I slather on moisturizer and add perfume to my wrists, cleavage and the back of my neck. Finally, I step into my one-dollar Silkeez Intimates and snap on my nude lace bra. Tonight's outfit: a strategically chosen button-down flannel shirtdress and leggings. Slightly sloppy but easy to move if Michael's hands feel like exploring. I'm ready for my anniversary surprise.

The Pitoscia house is quiet as I pass through the fragrant wall of warmth and garlic in their foyer. Lorraine, Tony and Anthony are all out and only Nonny is patrolling the kitchen. She says she didn't cook tonight, but there are two steaming plates of ravioli and sausage on the table that she must've ladled out just as I rang the doorbell. She's adorable in black leggings (which look scarily similar to mine) and an oversized sweatshirt that comes down to her knees. Aside from the Crocs with sweat socks, Nonny is definitely amping up her style game.

"So your mom, she a good cook," Nonny says as she plants herself down opposite me and Michael and our plates. So much for an intimate dinner with Michael. "You cook too?"

"Uh . . . not really," I say.

"Michael say she make chicken and mushrooms," Nonny continues. "You bring me the recipe, okay, Michael's friend?"

After twenty more minutes of chitchat/interrogation and an appearance by a leashed and muzzled six-pound Mitzi, Nonny finally leaves us alone. I help Michael clear the table, and after we rinse the dishes, he asks in a husky voice, "Ready for your surprise?"

He looks especially cute tonight in a white T-shirt and jeans and thick, gray flannel socks that he uses to slide around on the tiled kitchen floor. I think there's even pomade in his hair, and he's shaved his chin. The skin there is smooth and clean, and I fight the urge to kiss it.

"Sure," I say, smiling back.

"Let's go in here," he says, and takes my hand in his warm one. Our fingers are so comfortable together, greeting each other in only the way hands can, I am learning. Saying things that we can't.

Michael leads me to a room right off the kitchen that's dominated by a huge TV and a U-shaped leather sofa. He sits me down in the center of the sofa, and I can't help it—I wrap my arms around his neck and pull him in for a kiss.

It feels great—warm and soft—and I breathe in his delicious shampoo-and-soap boy scent. But he kisses back for only a few seconds before pulling my hands from his hot neck and straightening up.

"Hold on a sec, Cath," he says, backpedaling out of the room. He returns beaming and holding a small box gift-wrapped in dark blue glossy paper and topped with an elaborate white bow.

Shit. I didn't get him anything. Not even a card. I'm sensing a theme with me.

Memo to self: Withdraw head from asshole. Start thinking of others.

Michael looks proud and excited when he hands me the present, which makes me feel even worse.

"I feel awful for not getting you anything," I say. "Can't you hold on to it until I can get something for you?"

"Didn't your mother tell you that's not the way gifts work?" He sits down next to me. "Go ahead." He rests his hand on the small of my back and I can feel its heat through my dress, warming my skin. I hesitate and he says, "Please, Cath. I wanted to get this for you."

I feel awkward. I've never been good with presents. With Riley, I always worried if my gift choices were Swenson-worthy.

"C'mon, Cath," he says. "Open it." He rubs his hand up my back and neck and caresses my earlobe with his thumb.

265

I raise the little, lightweight package to eye level. The wrapping is perfect. "Did you wrap this yourself?" I ask.

"No way. My mom saw what I had done, ripped off the paper and started from scratch."

I'm careful not to tear the paper, and once I gently peel off the tape, I smooth out the sheet and fold it like Grandma used to do. The small white box screams jewelry.

Michael sighs impatiently. "Cath, if you don't open it, I'm going to do it for you!"

I lift the lid. Resting on the stiff white cotton square is a pair of small silver snowflake earrings. They're kind of modern with a high shine, and they're beautiful—exactly what I would pick out.

My fingers graze the cool smoothness. "I absolutely love them," I breathe. "How did you know?"

"Seriously? You really like them?" Michael asks, joy raising his voice a notch or two. "Anthony was with me and said I should've gotten this other pair, with these tiny little fake diamonds. But these seemed more you. More Catherine."

"You shouldn't have," I say.

"It's a guy's prerogative if he wants to buy his girl-friend something," Michael says, reaching for the earrings on their little plastic card. "Put them on."

He hands me the first earring. I haven't worn earrings in two years and four months, and I'm worried that my holes have closed up, but the post slides right through, pain-free. I click the back in place and then put on the other earring.

Michael whistles. "They're even better on. Go look!"

He grabs my hand and we head to the foyer, where a mirror hangs next to the front door. He's right. They are spectacular. Perfect size, maybe two-thirds the size of a dime and just right with my short hair. The shiny silver catches the light.

"Oh my God, I love them. I really do." I turn around and hug him. "You are the best."

Michael pulls away to look at me. "You know why I got you snowflakes?"

Uh-oh. I'm sure I'm forgetting something of importance to Michael. Something he confided in an earlier conversation when I would sometimes zone out.

I search and come up blank. I shrug.

"Because it snowed the first time I saw you," he says. "Remember? The night of the holiday talent show? Everybody was worried it was going to be canceled and there wasn't a snow date because it was too close to midterms and break."

Of course, I have minimal recollection of that freshman-year event. But the fact that Michael remembers that night because of me—*me*—makes me want to cry a little.

I matter to someone besides my mother.

"Your hair was long then and you had it in a ponytail with a red ribbon, and you were wearing a really short red skirt. You were so beautiful," Michael continues, his voice almost hushed. "That one girl, Riley, and the other one, I forgot her name, brown hair, they were always moving to the front, but you stayed in the back. Even though you were the best one on the stage."

I feel my throat tighten. I guess perception is everything. Michael only saw this: a girl with a long chestnut-brown ponytail wrapped with a red ribbon. And he liked her. Liked the way she looked, the way she danced. If only he knew that that girl was zoned out from a desperate prescription roulette to fend off Zero. He never suspected that for that girl, life as she knew it had ended along with her grandmother's.

Yet here I am. Still standing. From somewhere deep inside, I feel the tiniest swell of something like victory.

"Stay here," I tell Michael, and run into the kitchen for my phone. "I need a good picture of us. For my home screen." After finally getting a good shot, Michael and I use the same photo on our phones. Now, every time I turn my phone on, our two smiling faces pressed together will be the first thing I see.

We're about to return to the TV room when Michael halts me. "So, Michael's friend," he says, holding both hands out in front of him, palms facing up and pressed together, cupping them, as if preparing to receive a gift. "I'm ready for my present." He closes his eyes. "Tell me when I can open my eyes."

I start laughing. "Oh man, you're great at this guilt thing. Stop! I already feel bad enough."

He opens his eyes and smiles. "You can do one thing for me. To make up for your appalling lack of manners."

I smile and walk closer, rising on my toes and tilting my face up to kiss him. But just before our lips meet, he pulls away an inch. "Oh no," he says. "I want to see those pirouette-y turns. Just one, Cath."

"Seriously?" I ask.

"Yeah, just one," he says, making puppy-dog eyes. "They're so cool."

"I think I can manage that." The floor in the hall is tile and there's enough room here. My heart picks up its pace. I've actually been practicing a little, ever since that day at the library. Still, I can't believe I'm doing this.

I take a deep breath, center myself, chin up, feet turned out in first position, shoulders back and squared. I bring my right foot up to my left knee, passé position. And then I do seven fouetté turns. Automatically, my body instinctively remembering how. I spin on the tiled foyer of Michael Pitoscia's house during our Saturday-night date, my new earrings catching the light. My boyfriend counts each turn, clapping as I spin.

I could've never predicted that scene in a million years. Later that night, it becomes entry number eight on my list.

29

"How about a four-way? Me, you guys and this Jane chick?"

Sabita had come over to my desk following the end of history class. To see if her book had helped with my project. "Was there anything on Jane?" she'd asked.

And then Farricelli leaned toward the two of us and launched that line, the latest winner from his sexual harassment tour.

For a microsecond, Sabita and I can only stare at Louis Farricelli, our minds resisting comprehension. Around us, kids file out of the room. Sabita says something first. "You know Jane is the subject of Catherine's project, right? Jane was a soldier in World War Two?" She pauses and lets the unspoken "you fucking idiot" hang in the air.

Louis at least has the decency to flush.

Sabita laughs that patronizing laugh again, but I can't

join in. I'm still disgusted by Farricelli's comment. I just stand there, shaking my head. Not Sabita, though. She's laughing harder now, and attracting the attention of the remaining kids. "Oh my God, I didn't think . . . you could pull it off, Louis. But you did. You outdid yourself today." She slides into a desk, doubling over. "Just brilliant . . . really."

Farricelli, accustomed to the spotlight and admiration, flounders. Gathering his binder and iPad, he has nothing to say, only growing redder and redder by the second.

"What . . . what I want to know is this." Sabita wipes under her eyes, glancing at her fingers for smudged mascara. "How did you even get into an AP class?" One of Sabita's friends arrives, a tall senior who also plays football, and I take this as my cue to leave. Sabita is protected by her big friend, but I have no allies inside the room right now. Michael left while I was talking with Sabita.

I catch Sabita's eye. "I'll talk to you later," I say.

She shakes her head and smiles at me before turning to her friend. "What's the deal, Steven? Do all you football players get free rides in upper-track classes? Make you more appealing to the scholarship committees?"

At the door, I can hear Sabita's clear voice ringing through the classroom. "Listen to what Louis just asked me and Catherine. He wants—"

Damn, that Sabita is fearless. What must it be like to have confidence like that?

In the hallway, I walk into an amicable yet heated debate between Michael and Tyler on how they'd prepare for a zombie apocalypse. They're both pumped about the new zombie blockbuster opening Thanksgiving weekend. The three of us have planned on seeing it together.

"An RV is just flat-out dumb," Tyler is saying. "Runs on gas. You think there's gonna be working gas stations every two hundred miles?"

"But it's mobile and a lot better than your fortified compound," Michael busts back. "Like a moat is a good defense?"

"It's one of those flaming moats," Tyler responds. "Lit with the gas from your RV."

Just then, Farricelli limps out of the classroom alone, cane in hand and his backpack hanging off one broad shoulder. Mid-laugh, my eyes connect with his and hold, and something dark crosses his face. Maybe he thinks I'm telling Michael and Tyler about his stupid four-way comment and we're laughing at him. Who knows? But he comes right over to us, almost snarling like a feral dog. He stares at me and I swear there's heat coming off him. I'm waiting for a string of curses to rocket my way. Michael takes a step forward and diagonally so he's partly shielding me. "What's your problem, Louis?" he asks.

But Farricelli stays silent.

His beady eyes move quickly over Michael and then lock onto Tyler. With no warning, Farricelli unleashes a barrage of words at Tyler. Words that cut to Tyler's core, the beating heart of his greatest tragedy: his skin. "Dude, do us all a favor," Farricelli hisses. "Just fucking get homeschooled. Think of it as your community service requirement." Tyler shrinks into his hoodie as Farricelli's voice rises. "You know why? It's your face, man. It's beyond repulsive. Nobody can look at you while they're eating. I'm ready to puke just standing here."

It is horrifying, all of it. Farricelli's astonishing malice, the pain in Tyler's eyes, the morbid interest of the crowd that gathers to watch this act of verbal terrorism.

I can't take it. And neither can Michael. Just as I'm screaming, "Shut the fuck up, Louis!" Michael steps forward and takes a swing at Farricelli. But the punch never lands. Farricelli effortlessly blocks it and then lightly pushes Michael backward. And that's when things get really bad. Michael's heel catches on a backpack on the floor and he falls sideways. The open metal door of the bottom half-locker catches Michael's chin as he falls to the floor, slashing it wide open. Immediately, there is a deluge of bright red blood down Michael's gray shirt. His hands cup his chin and look like they've been dunked in a bucket of red paint. He slumps against the lockers, blinking a thousand times a second.

I fall to my knees beside him just as his eyes started to roll backward. I quickly lay him back. Mom always told me to put my head down if I ever felt faint, to get more blood into my head. I talk to Michael the entire time, telling him it's okay, everything is going to be fine. Mr. Oleck appears next to me and waves smelling salts under Michael's nose. Unlikely Good Samaritan Olivia presses a roll of paper towels into my hands and I use it to sop up the blood as we wait for the school nurse to arrive. Given that we don't know if Michael has a concussion, she calls an ambulance. Through it all, Michael's eyes hold mine, only breaking contact when he gags a few times.

I refuse to turn away when he does that. When his body humiliates him in public. I would not do that to him and further compound his loss of dignity. I didn't do it to Grandma and I will not do it to Michael. By not turning away, I hope he knows that it's okay and that I won't be turned off. That I understand the body's rebellion and its social malfunction. Because that acceptance is exactly what I wanted from Olivia and Riley and never got.

This is the third time in less than three years that I'm at the Yale–New Haven Hospital Emergency Room. And I am mentally kicking myself. Because the warning signs were there. I had been feeling the change in the Farricelli atmosphere like a barometer detects the drop in air pressure due to an incoming storm. I should've said something to Michael. Maybe things would've ended up differently if I had. For now, I can only keep squeezing his icy fingers as we wait for the doctor to come.

"You're doing great," I say to Michael for the fiftieth time. "Really great. The worst part is over."

He gives a small nod, his face bleached of color and almost blending into the white sheet on the examining table. He's still shaking underneath the blue hospital blanket and blood seeps through the white square of gauze on his chin, saturating it, but I won't tell him that. The minute he crashed to the ground and his chin began gushing, his eyes latched on to mine and clung. He looks at me like he's drowning.

And Catherine Pulaski is his life raft.

A nurse in green scrubs walks in, a stethoscope looped around her neck like a towel. "How you holding up, Michael?" she asks. "Still feeling woozy?"

"Okay," is all Michael says. I know he's afraid to talk too much and make himself bleed even more.

I squeeze his hand again.

"Just a few more minutes," the nurse says, collecting new bandages from a cabinet. "Let me freshen this up. Maybe you want to look at your girlfriend or close your eyes." She knows that Michael loses it at the sight of blood. I told her as soon as we got here.

"I'm really proud of you," I tell him again. Michael squeezes my fingers harder as the nurse replaces his bandage. He covers his eyes with his free hand. This is pure hell for him.

Michael's phone buzzes in my lap. It's Tyler. I answer. "Hi, Tyler. It's Catherine. We're just waiting for the doctor in the ER."

"Holy shit!" Tyler shouts, still rabid. "I still can't believe it. Is he going to be okay?"

"Yes. Absolutely," I say in my best everything-is-fine Mom voice. "He's just got the cut on his chin." Michael is listening, so I omit the fact that stitches are a certainty. Many of them.

"Are the Pitoscias there yet? Anthony's gonna freaking

kill Farricelli. What I did to him today was nothing. Maybe I better tell Anthony myself. He cannot get into any more trouble. His probation office—" Tyler cuts himself off, unclear as to how much I know about Anthony and his DUI arrest.

"That's probably a good idea," I say, and then quickly fill Michael in.

Michael nods and says in a raspy tone, "Anthony can't do anything. Tell Tyler to tell Anthony I said not to do a fucking thing."

Lorraine and Tony Pitoscia should be here any minute. In the ambulance, Michael gave me his phone and his new passcode (1011 for our October 11 anniversary) and had me call his mom. Technically, I shouldn't have been allowed to ride with Michael, but one of the EMTs had graduated with Anthony and said it was okay.

Lorraine flies into the room and blanches as she absorbs the scene: her youngest son lying on a gurney and me sitting alongside him, the sleeves and front of my pink sweater stained with the dark maroon of Michael's blood. I recognize the raw fear in her eyes from having seen it so many times in Mom's. But Lorraine doesn't fold. She leans over Michael, her hands smoothing his hair from his face. She croons softly, but there's steel in her voice. "I am going to neuter the son of a bitch who did this to you, okay, baby?"

"Jesus, Ma," Michael moans. "Relax."

Lorraine comes around the foot of Michael's bed to me. I stand and she further takes in the mess on my sweater.

She gives a little head shake and pulls me in close for a hug. "Thank you, Catherine," she says, her voice trembling. "Thank you for being here and taking such good care of Michael." She pulls away, her eyes watery. "Soak that sweater in cold water when you get home. Do you have any of that OxiClean? It works really well on bloodstains. Now tell me what happened. Who did this to my son?"

Michael tries to sit up, but both Lorraine and I gently push him back down. I don't want him blacking out.

"Was it Louis Farricelli?" Lorraine asks like a Mafia don, casual but with deadly intent. "That's all I want to know."

"I don't want to talk about it," Michael says.

Lorraine turns to me. "It was Farricelli, wasn't it?"

I don't want to annoy Michael, especially now, but there's no way I can avoid Lorraine's question. "Yes," I say. "Sorry, Michael. Your mom wants to know."

"Son of a bitch," Lorraine breathes, pecking a text on her phone. "I told your father he was too soft on those Farricelli turds."

I'm totally confused. Why did Tony Pitoscia talk to the Farricelli clan? And when?

Lorraine reads my face. She explains, "That asshole Louis used to bully Michael. All freshman year." Michael groans with embarrassment. "Michael, hush now. My husband, in his infinite wisdom, wanted Michael to handle it, but that didn't work. Not really. So Tony went to speak to Louis's father."

"Ma, stop it. You're making me look like a complete loser in front of Catherine," Michael says angrily.

"It was Anthony who got Louis to back off," Lorraine continues.

"Can you just fucking shut up already!" Michael's words rip the air, and Lorraine takes a step back, her face awash in hurt.

She doesn't understand yet that Michael has been humiliated again by Farricelli. "I better text my mom," I say. "Let her know what's happening." I exit so Michael doesn't have to say in front of me how he got hurt.

Outside of the examination room, I text Mom to let her know I'm not at school. I tell her Michael had an accident and that I'm at the hospital with him. She calls immediately and I give her a quick rundown. She asks two questions— "How is Michael?" and "How are you?"—and that's it.

I tell her I'll text when I'm ready to get picked up, and before we hang up, Mom tells me she's proud of me.

Before group, Mom and I stop off at home so I can change my shirt. I take the bloodstained sweater downstairs and sprinkle it with OxiClean powder and soak it in cold water in the laundry sink, just like Lorraine told me to.

Michael was weird when I said good-bye to him at the hospital. He was beyond embarrassed and could barely look at me. It was a little before two in the afternoon, and Mom was waiting in the front lobby for me. Michael had just gotten fourteen stitches, so I wasn't expecting him to be his usual jolly self, but this was still surprising. Before I left, we had watched the video Tyler had sent that some kid had taken of the incident. Tyler actually punched Farricelli twice after Michael went down, his blows rage-fueled and effective against the cane-dependent Farricelli. But Michael took no joy in Tyler's vengeance.

"I'm really sorry about this, Cath," he said. "You missed a full day of school and your sweater is ruined. I'm sorry I'm such a wimp."

Minutes later, once I was inside the Accord, after an awkward hug in front of Lorraine and Tony, he had texted: "Im sorry you had to see me like that"

I texted back that I was proud of him and that he was really brave to defend Tyler and not pass out or anything when he got hurt. He responded with only :(. I texted that if I didn't have to work this afternoon, I'd come over and hang out with him.

There was no response.

30

"Why can't you come over?" Kristal asks for the second time. It's our break at St. Anne's and we're in the girls' bathroom. Alexis is still blowing off Kristal and stayed in Room Three for the Fig Newtons and orange juice.

During discussion, John asked me about today's kind-of fight that my boyfriend was in. John hadn't actually seen it, but at least three Cranbury students posted videos, so he was able to give me some details that I had missed from my distance of three feet away.

Kristal heard the whole gory story, so I feel okay telling her that I'm not sure what's going on with Michael and that I don't want to make any weekend plans yet. I know for sure I'm headed to the Pitoscias' on Friday. Nonny had texted Lorraine while we were waiting for the plastic surgeon and demanded that I come over on Friday for a special dinner for "saving" Michael. And I want to keep Saturday open.

Before today, I had never seen Michael like that—angry and humiliated. Maybe I thought he wasn't capable of those emotions. It's ridiculous to me now, that I could think he's this one-dimensional personality. I'll ask him to come over on Saturday. Mom would love that.

"But, Cat, it's Wednesday," Kristal says. "He only got some stitches. He'll be fine by the weekend. You can't be seeing him the entire weekend, right? What about Saturday afternoon or Sunday afternoon?"

"I'm not sure."

"I need to show you what I ordered off the Internet." Kristal whispers, her lips centimeters from my ear. "For my vaginismus. I'm freaking out."

"What?"

Kristal reaches for my wrist and squeezes. "It's insane!" she whispers. "It's a dilator kit. With different sizes—"

"Wait. What's a dilator?"

Kristal drops my wrist and looks at me like I'm an idiot. "You don't know what a dilator is?"

I shake my head and Kristal says, "Jesus, Cat. What century have you been living in?"

I stare at her. She's like sandpaper on a rash right now.

"Just go home and Google it." Kristal shuts down. "It sounds stupid, me telling you. I don't even want to talk about it here." She takes a step closer and stares at my neck. "Tell me that's not a hickey."

In the mirror, I see a small red smear on my neck, close to my collarbone. It comes off with a wet paper towel. "It's blood. From Michael."

"That's a relief. That hickey stuff is so trailer park," she says. A double-edged-sword comment—not only is she callous about Michael's injury but she's pulling a class thing, asserting her superiority.

The bitch in me snaps to attention. "Did you see the earrings Michael bought me?" I ask brightly. "For our anniversary?" I despise girls who parade their boyfriends around, trying to rack up points in the "I'm Better Than You" sweepstakes, yet here I am.

Whatever. This is a defensive maneuver to negate the class comment.

But it lands on Kristal like a direct-hit drone strike.

"They're beautiful," she says slowly, and I can almost see her brain working, thinking how she's got a new set of dilators and I got new earrings. *Which one of these is not like the other?*

"I've got to make a phone call before we start up again," Kristal says suddenly, pulling open the bathroom door. Her bangle bracelets chatter. "See you in there?" Without waiting for my answer, she exits, leaving me alone.

And for the first time in at least a month, since the *cuckoo, cuckoo* incident in the computer lab, I feel something on the back of my neck. It's the breath of my old acquaintance, Zero. That shrewd fucker has been waiting in the wings, biding his time for the inevitable cracks to appear. So he can seep back in and flood me. He's getting bolder again.

Not now. Not yet. I lean close to the mirror and whisper loud enough for Zero to hear, "Fuck off."

31

"Catherine, you sit here." Nonny beckons me to the chair at the head of the table. Michael, Anthony, Lorraine and Tony all freeze in place.

"Did you just call Michael's friend by her real name?" Anthony yells. "Catherine, you've broken the land-speed record. Nonny never calls any non-Pitoscia by their first name until at least one full calendar year has passed along with a lunar eclipse. Jesus, Michael, you should've tried to take out Farricelli like three weeks ago."

The last comment wipes the fake smile right off Michael's bandaged-chin face. Something is definitely wrong. I haven't seen Michael since Wednesday. He missed school yesterday and today. All his texts were one-word responses to my questions. Then tonight, he greeted me at the front door, dressed in a ratty old Paoletti's Landscaping T-shirt and baggy sweatpants, with a lukewarm hello, his eyes glued to a spot right above my eyes. I thought for sure he'd notice his snowflake earrings. Before I put them on, Mom helped me polish them with her silver cloth to make them extra shiny. Michael didn't notice, he just turned his back and left me to follow him down the hall to the kitchen. I halted, the tail of his shirt in my hand. He had to stop, but he only turned halfway to face me.

"Hey," I said softly, pressing my cheek against his shoulder. "You okay?"

"Sure." Bland. Generic. No eye contact. He pulled away and began walking again.

No connection. After two days of no physical contact, he still won't look directly at me. The world feels off-kilter.

And now there's no quick smart-ass comeback to Anthony's Farricelli comment. Instead, Michael drops into his chair and spoons a heap of rigatoni onto his plate. No one else has even sat down yet.

"Oh, bro, this is getting really old. You've got to drop this sad-sack shit, like, now," Anthony says.

Lorraine immediately referees, "Ant, just leave him be."

"Can you all please just stop?" Michael asks, his eyes not leaving his plate. "I mean, Catherine's here. Do we have to start this again? If anybody says another word, I'm leaving."

Of course it's Nonny who says a bunch of words. Words of the surgically precise kind that peel away the layers of denial and doubt and expose the raw nerve. Nonny says loudly, "Michael, he feel *bad*. He *embarrassed*. He want to hit the Farricelli boy and he *miss*. I say good. Michael don't break a fingernail for that *stronzo*."

The legs of Michael's chair screech on the tile floor as he whips back from the table. "Jesus Christ!" He charges out of the kitchen. A door opens somewhere, then slams shut.

What the fuck? Is he going to leave me here? The Pitoscias, all of them, study me with expressions of pity. The cloth of my blouse must be vibrating, my heart is beating so hard. My face is on fire, and I start to sweat, but inside, I feel cold. Is Michael breaking up with me? Right here in front of his whole freaking family?

And then the moment is over. Michael yells, "Catherine!" and in his tone, I can hear it. The way it cracks a little on the *rin* part of my name. It's not me. He's just beyond mortified. That he failed spectacularly not only in front of me and Farricelli and Tyler and the rest of the school but also in front of Anthony, the cool, take-no-shit older brother with the college expulsion and DUI arrest who, paradoxically, Michael will never live up to.

What is it that Sandy said? How do we deal with pain? This is Michael's pain. And he's not dealing very well at the moment.

I so get it.

"Excuse me," I say to Michael's family.

"I'm sorry about that, Cath," Lorraine says. "Get him calmed down and come up whenever you guys are ready to eat."

Anthony shakes his head. "Michael's a drama queen. Everyone knows Farricelli isn't fully charged. The kid runs at like fifty-eight percent. It's no big deal—"

Tony puts up a hand. "What about this don't you get? How many times do I have to explain that your brother . . ."

I don't hear the rest. Michael is waiting for me, red-faced, on the basement steps. He lets me pass him and closes the basement door behind me. Downstairs, the room is dark, lit only by the giant TV on the wall. It is black velvet down here, the exact cozy cave that I need. I slink onto the soft sofa, my heart slowing. Michael joins me, but he's still wound tight. I can feel the rage inside him, radiating from him in waves.

I reach for one of his balled fists and work my fingers inside it. Once again, our hands talk before our mouths can speak.

"Cath," Michael starts, and then shakes his head. "How can you even stand to come here tonight? How can you still want to see me? Didn't you see any of the videos? I'm such a loser." His voice is ragged.

I move closer and rub his back. "Stop saying that. I think you were great. Defending Tyler like that."

He rolls his eyes. "Like a complete wimp? Who couldn't even hit Farricelli's fat fucking head? I mean, Jesus Christ, his forehead alone is like a freaking billboard."

I don't mean to start smiling, but his description is cracking me up inside. "Nah, it's smaller. I'm thinking minivan."

He looks at me and a slow grin forms above the huge chin bandage. "Gee, thanks. I feel better now."

"You should. Seriously." I rest my forehead against his. We're so close that his eyes merge into one. "Even if you were a Cyclops, I'd still want to be your girlfriend." I kiss the tip of his nose.

Michael pushes me back gently so he can study my face. "So you're telling me what happened doesn't turn you off? You're not, like, skeeved out or anything? When I almost passed out? And almost *threw up*?"

I start to massage the tops of his shoulders, which are knotted tight with tension. "I especially like that part." We both laugh. "This doesn't change my feelings for you at all. The part that sticks with me is that you're a loyal friend. Got that, Pit Man?"

"Got it," he whispers.

I scoot closer and we come together. Michael pulls his head back and we start to kiss, sweet and light. But then it deepens. Ignites. Like all the worry and stress of the last couple of days, all the negative energy is rechanneled. We're kissing with a new intensity, and between the warm lips and tongues and hands, I only vaguely register the cotton gauze of his bandage against my own chin.

Michael pushes me back so we are lying on the sofa. His back is damp with sweat and his mouth is moving lower, down my neck, my collarbone, going even farther. Then his hands are under my shirt. He's pulling me even closer to him, unhooking my bra. It has never been this way between us before—rushed, fast. But it feels so good.

"You are so beautiful." His breath is deliciously hot on my ear.

His weight on top of me feels so solid, so right. We fit together perfectly. He lifts himself to gaze at me, intense lust in his expression. As he unbuttons the first two buttons of my shirt, his dark eyes hold mine. With that same Mona Lisa boy-smile. And in the flickering light of the TV, the image of his face imprints itself on my brain. Permanently.

"Is this okay?" he whispers huskily, reaching for the third button.

It strikes me that I could love this boy. I could really love him. And then the second truth hits: I can never be with him that way, experience sex with him. It would be beyond cruel to share that with him, to be so intimate, when he's only met the facade of Catherine Pulaski. The real Catherine has to die when Zero crash-lands, and I don't want to hurt or scar him forever.

I feel cold suddenly. I button my shirt and manage to separate from him. "No, we better not. Not now." I stand up.

Nonny calls to us from the top of the basement steps, "Michael! Michael! You done being a baby now? Bring Catherine up. I got dinner here for you. It's getting cold."

"Jesus," Michael mutters, before yelling to her, "We'll be up in five."

He stands and moves close to me, cupping my face gently in his hands. "Cath, I've never felt this way before. I think—"

"C'mon," I say, cutting him off. I can't hear this. I don't want to know how he feels about me. It cannot be said out loud. I'm not ready to let him go yet, but I can't add any more to the cloak of guilt I wear for Mom. It's too heavy for me now. "Nonny is waiting for us."

32

I leave my phone off the entire weekend. I'm confused and sad about Michael.

What started out as a quest to experience has turned into a bittersweet entanglement—something that majorly complicates my plan, which makes it no longer possible. And that knowledge shakes me. I've been thinking about breaking it off with Michael, a preemptive strike that will hurt him less in the long run.

And hurt me less too. I know I can never tell him I'm bipolar. I could not bear to see his face.

And there's Kristal. I know I damaged our friendship last week. With that comment about the earrings. She's stopped asking about getting together, and soon she's going to start asking herself, *Why bother with Cat?* If she hasn't already. It's only a matter of time.

I'm trying to adjust to their future absence, so I shut off my phone to get myself used to the inevitable.

This turmoil is accelerating Zero's arrival. I felt him last week, breathing on my neck in the girls' bathroom. I saw him in the kitchen at the Pitoscias', circling like a shark. For the first time since starting Lamictal in September, I couldn't fall asleep Friday or Saturday. I know Dr. McCallum would tell me to note it in my nonexistent sleep journal. *To tell him.* But I trust my shoe box more than that.

I don't know what to expect when I turn on my phone this Monday morning. As I hold my breath and type my passcode, I avoid looking at my home screen photo. There are three voice mails from Michael and ten texts, three of which are from Kristal.

First one: 10:16 a.m. Saturday. "Hope M ok and you had a good time last night." The next one: 4:37 p.m. Saturday. "In CVS feminine care aisle. Major envy. Ha!" The third is from last night: 10:51 p.m. Sunday. "Are you ok?"

I take my first full deep breath of the last fifty hours. I've been tightly compressed all weekend, breathing shallowly. I respond first to Kristal. "So sorry. Not good weekend," and then I stop. I don't know how much more to say.

She responds right away. "You ok????? Was so worried"

I almost lose it right then and there, at the top of the steps, with Mom waiting at the front door. Kristal's concern is exactly what I need. But I can't tell her the truth. So I type, "M not great but things better now. He is hugely embarrassed. Can't come to group today. Dr appointment"

Kristal texts back, "Will give you big hug tomorrow! Hang in there! 😃 😃 😃 "

"Catherine, c'mon! I can't be late today," Mom calls

from downstairs. "I want to warm up the car. Don't forget to lock the front door."

I feel a million pounds lighter. So much so that I almost laugh at Mom's reminder. Don't forget to lock the front door. I've been doing that every single day since freshman year. Mom always starts the car and loads it up with her paisley lunch tote, the traveling polka-dot bag/medicine cabinet and, up until two weeks ago, the laptop. (She leaves the laptop in the kitchen now—unguarded and available. It is an unspoken leap of faith.) Regarding my door-locking task, Mom stubbornly refused to relieve me of it, even in my darkest hours, unwilling to acknowledge that I might not be capable of the simplest of functions.

I grab my backpack, open the front door and freeze. Because Mom's not in the Accord. She's standing on our cracked concrete walkway, talking with Michael. *Michael.* Who nervously shifts from foot to foot. A flesh-colored Band-Aid covers his chin. Our eyes catch. In my peripheral vision, the tailpipe of Lorraine's Subaru at our curb blows a steady stream of white into the morning air.

"Catherine." Mom wheels around. "Michael asked if he could drive you to school today."

"Uh . . . okay," I say, trying to tamp down the relief and happiness flaring up in my chest, tugging up the corners of my mouth.

"Is this legal?" Mom asks Michael. "Has the required time passed for you to be able to drive friends?"

Michael tears his eyes from me and back to Mom. "Yesterday. As of yesterday, I'm allowed to drive friends. And

I'm a good driver. My mom would have never given me her car if I wasn't."

"Does she know you're driving Catherine today?"

"Yeah." Michael flushes.

This is new territory for both Mom and me: Catherine driving with another seventeen-year-old. Jody is yet again pushed out of her comfort zone. And must handle the latest issue all by herself.

"Can I go with Michael?" I ask.

Mom's expression asks me if I'm really okay with Michael. As my eyes tell her yes, I notice that she looks old this morning. Older than she did when she handed me my toasted and buttered English muffin fifteen minutes ago.

I throw my arms around her. Mom is stunned, and before I pull back, I kiss her on the cheek.

Dear Lord, when was the last time I've kissed my mother?

"I'll see you at two-forty-five? On time, okay?" she asks, the code for "Don't forget we have a Dr. McCallum appointment at three."

I nod. And then Michael takes my backpack and slings it over his shoulder. He opens the passenger door for me. It's so awkward between us. I slide onto the passenger seat and Michael takes the driver's seat.

"I have a lot to say, Cath, but let me concentrate and drive to school first and then we can talk in the parking lot. Is that okay?"

I nod. I'm not sure what to do. He must be mad at me for blowing him off all Saturday and Sunday.

But then he says, "That's for you," and points to a

Dunkin' Donuts bag on the floor. I open it to find two double-chocolate doughnuts. "That's your favorite, right?" Michael asks nervously. "I thought that's what you said."

"But there's no jelly—your favorite," I say. "Did you eat it already?"

"Nope," Michael says, his eyes glued on the road. "Couldn't eat this morning."

When we get to the student parking lot, Michael pulls into the spot farthest from the school. He turns to me, his face red and eyebrows rammed together. "I . . . I . . . had my speech all planned out. But . . ." He takes a deep breath. "I am so sorry about Friday. If I pushed you in any way. If you felt pressure. If I—I m-m-made you uncomfortable in the basement."

Oh my God. He's agonizing over *that*? And has been since Friday when I didn't return his texts or calls? Instantly, I feel like complete shit. "No, Michael, please don't apologize." And even though I told myself the entire weekend that I would limit contact with him, I find myself moving closer, wrapping my arms around him, hugging him. "No, I wasn't upset about that. I was just . . . I don't know." And then this comes out, "I was having a tough weekend. It had nothing to do with you. I'm so sorry if you thought that."

Michael pulls back to study my face. "Really? Oh my God, I was completely freaking out. I thought I had blown it with you." He takes both my hands in his. "I still cannot believe that you're my girlfriend. I've liked you since freshman year. Since that show. You probably don't believe it, but the minute I saw you, that was it for me. I haven't looked at another girl since. Tyler sent this to me almost two years ago." Michael takes out his phone, taps away and then hands it to me. It's a video. "Go ahead. Watch it."

It's a clip of me dancing in the talent show. Just me. Riley and Olivia twirl by occasionally, but the camera is focused on me. Michael was right about how I stayed in the back. The music, the number one pop song for that year, a song I despised, sounds cheap and tinny.

"Tyler saw my face. He took the video while we waited in the wings and sent it to me for Christmas," Michael says.

I can't speak. My heart thuds. My cheeks feel like they're on fire. I can't take my eyes off red-ribboned, chestnut-ponytailed freshman me. The gleam of my red satin miniskirt catching the light as I move. I was good. And damn, I was skinny. Too skinny. Mom was right. I look a little bobbleheaded, my head a tad too big for my frame. I have a mellow smile on my face, slightly zoned out from whatever Dr. A was prescribing me. And even though I hated the song Riley chose, I loved that routine. In fact, I don't think I ever met a routine I didn't like. I remember dancing now. This particular show and all the Miss Ruth recitals. The joy of it. The music enveloping me. My body moving purely from muscle memory. Performing in the heat of the spotlights. Thoughts on mute. Only music and motion.

Peace.

I miss it.

"Cath?" Michael asks. "Are you creeped out? Is it kind of psycho for me to have this?"

"I can't believe it," I whisper, mesmerized by freshman me. Because I know this girl's story like I know Jane's. This skinny, dance-loving freshman is less than a year away from her lithium and Prozac overdose. I want to cry for her. Because she looks okay right then and there. She's *dancing,* for Christ's sake.

I don't want her to die.

"Do you want me to delete it?" Michael asks.

"No," I say, dragging my eyes from the screen to Michael, who studies me with worry and concern. Michael, a complete stranger eight weeks ago, who has kept a video of me, *me,* on his phone for two years. "Don't delete it. I'm . . . I don't know. Just really touched, moved really, that you have this. Of me."

Michael groans a little. "This is my proof, Cath. So you know how much I like you. You're like . . . perfect." He swallows. "Last week was such a mess. . . . I was such a jerk to you." He stares at the roof of the Subaru. "I kept thinking you were going to dump me. And then Friday night, you were so great. You made *me* feel great. And then I thought I blew it again with you. This time for good.

"You said you had a rough weekend," Michael continues. "High school . . . well, it hasn't been the best experience for me. Not at all. With Farricelli hassling me and then my passing out in anatomy class and now this. Can you understand?" He's staring at me with a questioning intensity. I nod. "I should've told you what I was feeling. What happened with Farricelli in the past. So you'd understand a little. It wasn't fair to you." Michael takes my hand. "I want us to be completely honest with each other, okay?

I want to be able to tell you things and for you to tell me things. To trust me. I want that kind of relationship with you. I really want something with you. Something big."

I nod, blown away. By him and by the fact that he has these feelings for me. "Me too," I whisper.

"Now your turn," Michael says. "Why was your weekend bad?"

I shake my head. "It was nothing, really." I lie. "Just stuff with my mom. Just fighting, the usual."

"Cath, I'm here for you. I'm not going anywhere. You didn't run from me. I'm loyal, remember?" he says. He must know something about me from the gossip last year at school. I think that's what he's getting at. There's an urgency to Michael's voice, a question he's not asking on his lips. "You can trust me," he almost pleads. "It had to be pretty bad if you shut off your phone the whole weekend."

Again, I shake my head. It's too much to tell him. Where I really go after school. Why. What medicine I take every night. Would he take out his phone and Google "bipolar"? No, I can't do it. I'm entitled to the little peace, the enjoyment, the *absence of shame* that my lies allow.

Disappointment crosses Michael's face and he pulls away from me. An expression I don't recognize slides over his face, something guarded and distant. He grabs the Dunkin' bag. "You ready for your doughnuts?"

"You eat them. I'm kind of full," I say. But the truth is I'm a little nauseated. Because something has shifted between us. Something big. I can feel it.

"Well, we should go in now," he says, biting into a doughnut. "Don't want to be late, right?"

I feel like crying as he gets out of the car. I am so fucked. By a disease that isolates me with its stigma. That not only taints my reasoning but also limits any relationship that I could have. It's so not worth it, a life like this.

Slipping on my everything-is-just-fine mask, I walk into school with Michael.

33

I'm hunkered down in the black leather chair, with Dr. Mc-
Callum opposite me. He's grabbed his coffee mug and
placed a bottled water on the small end table between our
two chairs in his office. He's making himself comfortable
for the long haul. Shit. I was hoping I might be able to split
a little early and get to St. Anne's. After today, there are
only two more IOP days left, Tuesday and Wednesday; this
week's sessions are cut short due to the Thanksgiving holiday. After that, we are officially in the step-down program,
which seems to basically be the IOP minus three days of
meeting.

"So, how are things?" Dr. McCallum asks.

Bad, I want to say. The full extent of my disease is
really sinking in now, the scope of Zero's destruction wid-
ening in ways I didn't expect. It not only kills existing relationships but also, I'm learning, stunts new ones. Things

with Michael and Kristal are deepening and the effort to conceal is exhausting. I'm sick of the hiding, and I'm sick of constantly anticipating Zero. He went away for a while, but I know he's back, circling ever closer. And now one of Zero's four horsemen, disrupted sleep, is here. But I don't say any of this.

"Things are okay," I answer.

"What's going on, Catherine?" he asks. Jesus, he's perceptive.

I shrug. Dr. McCallum sits like a stone Buddha, just watching and waiting for me to spill the contents of my chemically imbalanced mind. Oh, screw it. "Just some stuff with my fr—Michael and Kristal."

Dr. McCallum nods.

"I haven't really told them anything about me . . . you know, being . . . b-b-bipolar," I stutter.

"Why not?"

"Why do you think?" I snap.

"I know what I think," Dr. McCallum says oh so wisely, like he's fucking Dumbledore. "I'd like to hear what you think."

"Because . . . because . . . they'll be like Riley and Olivia." Oh my God. That was brutal. The first time I've even hinted at what their leaving did to me. "I think . . . I think it's . . . safer not to tell them."

My first month with Dr. McCallum, this past July, he wanted to talk a lot about my former friends and their abandonment of me, and how I felt about it. It was unbearable, fending off the weekly tearing away of that scab.

Dr. McCallum leans forward, elbows on his knees. "I understand why you feel this way. But you won't know until you try."

I'm waiting for him to turn on the sound track to *Rocky* and give me a pep talk about trusting people, blah blah blah. Instead, he leans back and crosses one long, gangly leg over the other, exposing his sock and two inches of hairy shin.

"And *before* you make that decision to confide, you need to evaluate the friend and the relationship. Have they proved themselves worthy of you?"

I almost fall off my chair. Did I hear him correctly? "Worthy of me?"

Me? My head is exploding with this novel concept.

Dr. McCallum smiles gently. "Yes, Catherine. Worthy. Of. You. What do you think?"

"I don't know. I have to think about it."

Dr. McCallum nods. "You know, what we have to do here is separate the wheat from the chaff, separate the symptoms of your bipolar disorder from typical adolescent issues. I can't tell you how many of my patients who lose or terminate friendships in high school—maybe eighty-five to ninety-five percent. It's a common thing, especially for girls. Now, for you, this loss of Olivia and Riley . . ."

I hate and love how familiarly those names roll off his tongue.

"That loss seemed to be tied directly to two things: the traumatic death of your grandmother and the onset of your bipolar disorder. I understand how you might feel that your condition defines you and *caused that loss*. But what I'm trying to stress to you, Catherine, is that while you are dealing with managing your bipolar disorder, you are also tackling the normal highs and lows of being a teenager. And I have a strong suspicion that your relationships with Olivia and Riley would have ended regardless of your condition. That is most often the case, that the friends you have entering high school are very often not the same ones you have at the end of it."

I find myself nodding. Because lately, that same renegade thought has been orbiting my head. The kindness of Michael and Kristal and their genuine concern has exposed the fault lines in my relationship with Riley. And I feel like I never really knew Olivia, despite all our years together. By the time the bipolar thing happened, our little trio had probably long passed its sell-by date.

"I want you to remember that very common pattern of relationships and not let the pain of Olivia and Riley hold you back from engaging in other friendships," Dr. McCallum continues. "Use your judgment in deciding whether Michael and Kristal are worthy of you to confide in."

Dr. McCallum moves the conversation to the next topic on his agenda: Zero. Or his clinical name, *depression*. "I want to discuss something that we touched upon at the beginning of treatment. You're doing well, Catherine, really well, and I think it's time for us to discuss a depression game plan."

I must look a little puzzled because he continues, "It's our game plan for what we do should you begin feeling depressed. We've talked about the warning signs. Are you keeping that sleep journal like we spoke about?" I nod-lie. "Good," he says warmly. "Now I want to talk about coming up with a plan in the event you begin to feel depressed. I'm talking moderate to severe depression. Remember, patients with bipolar can get depressed again after a period of stability. Even when they're doing all the right stuff."

I think it's starting, but again, why bother saying anything? He can't cure me. He can't tweak my DNA, make it all better.

"It can be really discouraging," Dr. McCallum is saying. "I want us to have a game plan so you know there are many, many options."

"Are you saying we should have steps written down? Like if I get depressed, we'll do X, Y and Z?"

He nods. "Exactly. I'll tell you what I'm thinking and then you give me your thoughts, okay?"

I nod. How many freaking options can there be?

"First, in the event of a more moderate to severe depression, I'd highly recommend that you start on lithium again."

"You know my mom will veto that idea," I say immediately.

"I know, Catherine," Dr. McCallum responds. "Your mom connects lithium to your suicide attempt. But you had been taking it for only a week or so at the time of your attempt, right?" He opens my folder. "Yes, it looks like it was a new prescription. I've explained to your mom that lithium greatly decreases the risk of suicide in bipolar patients.

It's a no-brainer in my book." He takes a big sip of his coffee. "Seeing how you responded to the Lamictal, I think the right dosage would be effective. Next, we'd amp up the psychotherapy. You've done well at the IOP. And I'd also like, at some point down the road, for the three of us to talk about other therapies that are out there. Things that you should be aware of. Some new things, some old, tried-and-true therapies." He pauses, and I get the feeling something big is coming. "Like ECT. Electroconvulsive therapy."

Holy shit.

"I know, it sounds extreme," Dr. McCallum continues. "And in movies it looks inhumane and primitive. But there are many studies showing it to be highly effective for patients who are severely depressed. Catherine, please listen. Lithium and psychotherapy would be my first response. But we have other options. Maybe a different medication. Maybe two different meds. There are different routes we can take medicine-wise, different combinations." He leans forward in his chair, shortening the distance between us. "I'm only mentioning ECT because I want you to be *aware* of it. I want you to know about it if in the event you get severely depressed, another therapy besides meds and counseling exists. There's also something new. For the more acute, severe cases of depression, some doctors are using ketamine injections. Ketamine has been used generally as an anesthesia, but it can lessen symptoms of depression for short periods of time." He sits back again. "I'm in no way suggesting any of this for you now. I'm happy with how you're doing on the Lamictal. The only reason I'm telling you this is because I want you to be aware that there are other ways to get relief in the event of a severe episode. Any questions so far?"

I shake my head, but he doesn't speak. Five, ten, fifteen seconds go by.

"Catherine," he finally says. "I know you are extremely perceptive, extremely observant. I can see that this label of bipolar causes you anxiety. That you worry about the quality of life you can have with it. Many of my patients with bipolar tell me this. It's a common fear."

Again, I am nodding. I force myself to hold still.

"I'm telling you this to *inform* you. There are a number of different therapies to help you. You can manage this, Catherine. You *are* managing this."

I want to say, sure, I can manage it now with Zero still at arm's length and my phone alive and still breathing incoming texts. But what happens when my world implodes, when my second round of friends evacuate, and Grandma's absence resumes its presence as a yawning hole in my gut? Zero is an opportunistic mother and I doubt a million electrical volts ripping through my skull will help me "manage" it.

34

The school library is quiet and cool on this Tuesday before Thanksgiving. I've just finished the chicken salad I made for Mom's and my lunch. Mom was painfully grateful this morning when she came into the kitchen to find me finishing up our sandwiches, her flowered tote already packed with an apple and a pack of cheese crackers. "I could get very used to this," she had said, reminding me that no one has cared for her since I've been on this planet. "Maybe we can start taking turns?" she asked brightly.

I said yes, but I was thinking that Bill could return once I am gone. He could make her lunches. There'd be nothing in the way, then—no Catherine with all the incessant and unrelenting worry her existence demands. No twenty-four-hour monitoring of moods and meds. Mom would be free, her life open to so many possibilities: a new job, maybe something that would utilize her accounting degree and isn't based solely on flexibility; money for better clothes and hair color at a nice salon, not from a box from ShopRite; and Bill. Companionship. Love. Marriage. A new part-time family, mothering Bill's adorable, *normal* kids.

Inside my cubby, my phone vibrates with a new email. It has to be from Jenna. She's the only person who communicates with me via email instead of text. I hope she's located another Jane letter. I scan her message. She has a partial letter—only the bottom half. I type back a quick thank-you before allowing myself to read the letter. Knowing Jane's story, her tragedy, makes the reading almost unbearable.

And now, popping uninvited into my head is the image of freshman me locked in Michael's phone, dancing and dancing forever.

That girl and Jane are equated in my mind somehow.

My eyes run along Jane's sentences and immediately I sense the difference in her writing and tone. The 6888th has been transferred from England to France and Jane doesn't seem too happy about it.

don't clean up like the British do. The rubble was everywhere, like they're all just waiting for the war to be over to start sweeping. We took a train from Birmingham to Southampton, where we crossed the Channel in the tiniest boat you ever saw. At night, we slept on canvas shelves basically, four or six high, stacked so tight I couldn't sit up without bumping my head on the one above me. Like I said, Le Havre was a pile of rubble. And just when I thought our troubles were over, they put us on a train with big holes in its roof. I guess we should've been grateful for those holes because the cars had not a single window. When we finally got to Rouen, there were hundreds of our boys, Mama, all waiting to welcome us. In cars, in trucks, on roofs, waving from any place you looked. Most of the girls were laughing and carrying on, but others did not like it one bit. Those boys **were** helpful, Mama. They carried our bags and helped us get settled at the Caserne Tallandier (Napoléon's troops slept here—that's how old it is!). It was a very lively scene, with many of the French coming to greet us. But deep down, it made me sad. Because most of these welcoming soldiers were Negroes. Coming over here, seeing how the British people treated us—how nice and kind they were, it kind of makes it harder now to see the prejudice. There's other stuff too. Hurtful stuff they say about some girls, how they don't like men, they like women. Or that most of us get pregnant and have to go home. It is shameful. Because we WACs, we're proud of what we're doing here. The girls always say that they picked the best of us to come overseas. But it feels like no one recognizes it, at least not too many Americans do.

Sorry to be complaining so much. It's hard sleeping on a mattress stuffed with straw. The ends keep poking into me every time I roll over. I barely get *any rest. I can see you smiling as you read this, Mama. You know I turn into a bear without my rest. Not too much longer now I'll be writing to let you know when I'm coming home. Give Mari and Petey and yourself triple, no, quadruple hugs from me.*

Your loving daughter,
Jane

I feel aggravation dangerously close to rage building. I know what happened to Jane was ages ago, but the prejudice she suffered is making my heart thump angrily. Maybe it's leftover emotion from history this morning with Farricelli hissing "cunt" and "dyke" at me throughout class. I didn't dare do a thing. I don't want to get Michael in any more trouble. Tyler got a one-day in-school suspension, but Michael slid by with just a warning. Probably because of his prior history with Farricelli. So I just sat there and absorbed Farricelli's stream of hate. Is that why I'm so infuriated for Jane right now? Or maybe it's the fact that this institutionalized racist bullshit is still going on today.

Overheating with the unfairness of it all, I unzip my hoodie. How could they treat Jane like that? How could they treat any of them like that? She was there doing her part. For the very country that was shitting on her. All because she was black and a woman. But mainly because of her skin color. A white woman would never have been treated that way. Tears blur my vision as I think of Jane. Joyous, adventurous Jane. She couldn't help when or where she was born. She was innocent.

The word echoes in my head.

Innocent.

Innocent.

Innocent.

And then something deep inside me shifts—it is a major, tectonic-plate kind of shifting, the type that creates new landscapes. I have to rest my forehead on the desk and take deep breaths. I am shaking, but I understand something now. Something good.

I'm innocent too. Just like Charlie.

35

This knowledge purrs through me a full twenty-four hours, a steady current of something warm and sweet like reassurance or exoneration or both. It soothes me and prompts me to return the briefest of smiles to Olivia in the hallway at the end of school on Wednesday.

"Happy Thanksgiving, Cath," she says, uncharacteristically alone at her locker, her smile expanding upon spotting my abbreviated one.

Michael is waiting for me at my locker, and I have to fight the urge to plant a very public kiss on him.

"So you can come over on Saturday?" he asks me, his hands fidgeting with the zipper on his backpack. He's been different since he brought me to school on Monday. Mechanically, the same—waiting for me in the morning, walking out of history class together, texting at night, making plans for the weekend. But he's more reserved now. Like he's disappointed.

"I'll be there," I say as Tyler approaches.

After greeting me with a hello plus direct eye contact, Tyler says to Michael, "We better get going. Gonna be a long line."

Wait. What? Are they doing something?

Michael turns to me, a flush creeping up his neck. "We're gonna check out that zombie movie. . . . It's . . . it's that special deal. You know, five-dollar shows before five o'clock."

The reality slaps me. Hard. Because the three of us had already planned on seeing it together. In two days—the Friday after Thanksgiving, when the theater would be packed with fellow zombie fans.

He changed the plans and didn't ask me to go with them.

"Today's the premiere. Can't wait!" Tyler says. "Catherine, you sure you can't come?" He is clearly under the impression that Michael already asked me and I said no.

Michael's whole face is red now, but he stays silent, watching me like we're playing chess, awaiting my move. What's with him? He should be fumbling an excuse my way as to why he didn't include me. I could've gone on Friday, or even tonight. But Michael's just waiting along with Tyler for my answer.

Of course, I can't divulge that today is my last IOP at St. Anne's and I would never miss it. Instead, I stutter-lie, "No, I—I'm . . . I'm working."

"I feel like a slacker next to you," Tyler says to my deceitful face. Another dart.

Michael, clearly uncomfortable, throws his backpack over his shoulder. "Let's get going, Ty."

311

Awkwardness is thick and sludgy between Michael and me, and Tyler senses it. But he misconstrues the heaviness, probably thinking that Michael and I want to be alone for some dramatic good-bye or something. "So, Mike, I'll . . . I'll meet you at your car?" Tyler asks.

Michael nods and waits until Tyler is out of earshot. The hallway is still hellishly full of kids who laugh and flutter by, the looming four-day Thanksgiving weekend ratcheting up their energy level. But not me. I am stunned, flattened by Michael's exclusion.

"Cath, I didn't ask you because I knew you wouldn't be able to come," Michael says, the expression on his face a weird mixture of guilt and defiance. "Work, right?"

This time I can't lie. So I say nothing as my heart beats triple time. God, please don't let me cry in front of him. Michael must see my bewilderment, because he suddenly pulls me close and buries his face in my neck. An edge of the Band-Aid on his chin hurts me, but I hug him back anyway.

"Cath, don't be sad," he says. "I didn't ask because I didn't want you to . . ." He stops.

"You didn't want me to what?" I whisper, my lips pressing against his ear.

"I didn't want to make you feel bad," he says, pulling away just enough to look at me. "I don't want to hurt you." And then, in the middle of the crowded hallway, he gives me a very public kiss. It's a complicated kiss, layered with hurt and apologies and something else on Michael's part, maybe frustration, but he keeps kissing me. And the fact that he doesn't stop kissing me tamps down the hurt and fear about what just happened.

But not all the way. Both Michael and I know this kiss is a short-term patch job. Because what started in the car ride to school on Monday is not a product of my imagination. This change of plans is undeniable proof that I'm losing him.

36

"Congratulations!" Mom cries minutes later when I slip into the Accord. "It's your last IOP!" She retrieves a Dunkin' Donuts bag from behind my seat. "Let's celebrate!" She places the bag in my lap before shifting into drive.

I can still feel Michael's kiss vibrating on my lips, but I feel numb, lidocained by his zombie-movie betrayal. Before, I would've been walking on air right now, jubilantly scarfing down the contents of this bag of doughnuts. But now the fragrance wafting out of the waxed bag is wrong—too sweet. I swallow drily. I can't eat.

"What's wrong?" The lightness in Mom's voice is gone, instantly replaced with worry: doughnut rejection is a big red flag in Pulaski Land.

"I just had two candy bars." The lie sails smoothly from me.

"Two? *Two?* What'd you get?" Mom asks, so happy

all is okay in Appetite-ville that she ignores my egregious nutritional blunder.

"Reese's."

"They should add a third peanut butter cup to the package. Two just doesn't cut it, hunger-wise," she says gamely. She guides the Accord through downtown Cranbury and past the Green, where the huge Christmas tree and jumbo menorah take center stage. Red bows and baskets laden with evergreen boughs adorn every faux antique black lamppost, each quaint "shoppe" tastefully decorated for the shopping bonanza that Christmas has morphed into. Strings of white lights loop every storefront, restaurant window, shrub and tree. Even Rodrick's is festooned up the wazoo. Cranbury prides itself on having one of the best-decorated small-town New England greens, an award that probably originated from our hokey non-news newspaper, the *Cranbury Courant*.

Unaware of the holiday skeptic beside her, Mom murmurs, "I just love this time of year. Do you think you and Michael will exchange gifts?"

"We agreed not to." Again, the lie soars effortlessly into the interior of the Accord. I need to prep her for what's ahead.

Surprisingly, Mom doesn't dissect this, interrogate me or overanalyze my and Michael's "decision" not to exchange gifts. She gives me a quick glance, nods and then changes the subject.

"Catherine, do you think Kristal would be able to drop you off at home next Friday? Dominic asked me to help with a private party and Aunt Darlene is going to Boston for the weekend."

I text Kristal right away with the request. My phone choos with her immediate reply: "Yes! Yes! A 1000 times yes! ☺ Let's do chipotle 🌶 🌶. And where are you??? Get your ass here asap! Last day party!!! 💃 💃 💃 "

And just like that, her one text extends like a strong and solid tree branch to the slowly sinking-in-quicksand Cat Pulaski. Because right now, right this moment, Kristal is still here.

It's definitely party mode in Room Three. Holiday music plays softly in the background and today's snacks are candy canes, gingerbread cookies and hot chocolate. After we complete our DBT forms, Sandy opens group by thanking us.

"I am so proud of you all," she says, her eyes getting misty. "You are all warriors. Heroes. Bringing your intelligence, your honesty, your courage, your warmth and humor and making our group exactly what it should be—a supportive, safe, nurturing zone. It's not easy, baring your souls, exposing your fears. If there's one thing that I hope you've learned from our meetings, it's this: that you are never alone and that everyone—*everyone*—experiences pain. You have the tools to manage that pain. Honesty with yourselves and honest communication with those around you—your parents, your friends, your doctor, your therapist. You'll be okay if you remember this one rule: *stay* honest and *say* honest."

Lil' Tommy lets out a "woo-hoo" and then suddenly stands, thrusting a small, red, chafed hand over the coffee table and keeping it there, palm down. "C'mon, everybody, group huddle!" he yells.

Garrett hops up and places his hand in the air above Tommy's. John smacks his hand on Garrett's. Alexis, Kristal and I follow. "On the count of three," Tommy whoops like a little cheerleader, "everybody shout 'Go . . . go . . . um . . . ' " He stops, looking stymied.

What do you call our group?

Garrett supplies the cheer. "Go Room Three! IOP!"

Tommy beams his gratitude at Garrett. And then yells, "Okay, on the count of three! One! Two!"

He pauses and looks around. This is beyond dorky and stupid. Something outside these four walls we would all vehemently deny ever happening. Yet each one of my comrades is completely into it. Fully invested. Garrett with his blond baby dreadlocks, his blue eyes crinkled in laughter; bulky John in full Red Sox regalia, smiling and shaking his head in amusement; Alexis with her peppermint candy cane clamped between grinning candy-sticky lips; and Kristal the loudest one, cheering us all on, her free hand warming my shoulder. Sandy throws her hand on top of mine.

And in the second before we all act like the ridiculous bunch of damaged teenagers that we are, Tommy's other red, raw hand roars down on top of Sandy's, the slap reverberating through the room. His little face, with those glasses that constantly slide down his nose, smiles up at all of us. A laugh gurgles inside me, its source both that sense of exoneration I discovered yesterday afternoon in the library and this group bonding, this acknowledgment of what we've all been through, the pain that's brought us here and, for the briefest of moments, the safety and healing of this circle. I laugh out loud as Tommy shouts, "Three!"

At the top of our lungs, six kids with a buffet-worthy selection of mental health issues and their fearless leader, scream, "Go Room Three! IOP!" and then collapse, laughing and high-fiving, on the sofas.

With a smiling eye roll, Garrett needlessly reminds us, "Mum's the fucking word on that scene, folks."

My favorite therapy dog, Lucky Boy, prances in for our final hour of IOP. As we hang out on the floor, playing with him, Sandy reviews next week's step-down program schedule. We'll meet in Group Room B on Wednesdays and Fridays from three o'clock to five o'clock.

Thanks for the memories, Room Three.

Sandy scratches Lucky Boy above the base of his tail, his favorite scratching spot, weirdly enough. "We've changed the timing a little," she tells us. "The new group I told you about won't be starting until five-thirty. This way, we can try to protect the privacy of those of you who aren't comfortable seeing other people here."

We settle into small pockets of conversation, and John moves his large frame to the carpet beside me.

"Hey, Catherine," he says softly. "How you doing?"

I smile at him. I feel a kinship with John. Besides Kristal, he's the one I'm closest to here. "Pretty good," I say. "How about you? How are things with your father?"

"Better," he says. "My dad is finally coming around." John had been sharing with us the aftermath of his decision to quit the wrestling team and how pissed his father was because it eliminated all chance of a wrestling scholarship for college. "What about you? With your PTSD or depression or"—he shrugs—"whatever, from your grandmother?"

The answer doesn't come easily. I have so strenuously trained myself to censor all responses, it takes me a moment to find the truth and not just formulate what I think John wants to hear. "Better. For sure," I say. "Lighter. Like I don't have this big secret anymore. But . . ." I stop. *It's okay,* I tell myself. *Keep going.* I need to start doing what Sandy said—"say honest." It's about fucking time. "But kind of worse too," I continue. "Like . . . I don't know. Because it doesn't hurt quite as bad, I feel like I don't remember her as well. She feels further away." I look at John to gauge his reaction. Does he think this is totally wacked?

"I get it." John nods, absently stroking Lucky Boy's head. "Not that this is anywhere near the same, but when my dog died, it was horrible, but once that intense sadness lifted . . . I don't know, I felt like I was moving on and kind of forgetting him in a way."

I nod, a little shell-shocked. That is precisely it. And all this time, I was worried my feeling was strictly a bipolar thing. I grasp his forearm, the material of his track jacket smooth under my fingertips. "Thanks for everything, John. I really mean it. Thank you."

Kristal and I stand next to her car as the St. Anne's parking lot empties out. Mom is running late and texted that she'd be here in ten minutes. Music is blasting out of Kristal's car window and she dances around in the cold air, keeping me company until Mom arrives.

"Oh God, I hope I love it. I'm freaking out a little!" she says. "What if it sucks? It's too late to withdraw my ED application."

Kristal's dad works with somebody whose daughter attends Vassar, and the daughter, Stephanie, invited Kristal to spend Saturday night with her. Stephanie and a bunch of her friends are returning early to school from Thanksgiving break. Kristal leaves first thing on Saturday morning for Poughkeepsie.

"It will be great! And if it isn't, you can text me all night," I offer.

"*If* you have your phone on," Kristal chides. "Seriously, Cat, do not do that to me again. It sucked. I really needed to talk to you." She stops dancing and holds my gaze. "Okay?" There is a challenge in her tone, a veiled threat that I need to hold up my end of this friendship bargain.

"I will sleep with my phone on," I say, holding my fingers up as if to swear on a Bible. "On my pillow, okay?"

Kristal spontaneously hugs me. "I wish you were coming with me!"

Mom pulls into the parking lot and into the spot next to Kristal. She waves and I can see she's on her phone.

"Happy Thanksgiving!" I tell Kristal as she gets behind the wheel of her car. "And remember, on Saturday, text or call me whenever! Even if it's in the middle of the night."

Kristal nods, her body brimming with excitement. Again, I feel a jolt of abandonment, that sense that she can and will go on with her life.

I stand on the curb as Kristal backs her adorable Volkswagen out of the parking spot. Her car stereo is still blasting and she's waving to me instead of checking behind her. The parking lot is empty but for one pickup truck, which has been idling in the row behind Kristal. Kristal starts to dance inside her car, bouncing on the seat and clapping both hands over her head, leaving the steering wheel unmanned. All for my entertainment.

I laugh until I see the pickup's brake lights come on. The truck backs up, fast, its bed piled high with leaves tacked down by a tarp, obstructing the driver's rearview mirror. There's no way the driver can see Kristal. They are headed for a direct hit.

I rush forward, into the spot Kristal has almost vacated, and I can see her eyes widen in surprise at my charge. I bang both hands on the hood of her car, screaming "Stop!" just as the pickup truck screeches to a stop.

Their two rear bumpers are almost touching. As I rush to Kristal, still seated in her car, I catch a glimpse of movement inside the dark cab of the pickup truck. Its passenger-side door cracks opens just a couple of inches. I can barely see inside the truck, but it looks like two people. Is the passenger going to get out? Bitch at Kristal? Shit. But then suddenly the door slams shut and the pickup truck peels away, escaped leaves dancing in the air in its wake.

Kristal lowers her car window. With an embarrassed smile, she says, "Now your mom is never going to let me drive you home next Friday. Tell her I will never dance and drive again."

It's Wednesday night, 1:16 a.m. So technically it's Thursday morning—Thanksgiving. I can't sleep. Like a few nights ago, my body refuses to unwind. I should record this in my sleep journal, if I actually had one. I've transported the troops downstairs already to Grandma's room. So all should be well.

It was a good day, I tell myself. The last session of group was a riot with that ridiculously corny circle time.

I text Kristal again: "You will have a great time at Vassar!!! Don't worry!" I am pathetically proud of my little cheer of support. Catherine Pulaski is thinking of other people for a change! It's a start at least.

But the movie thing with Michael keeps intruding on all the good: St. Anne's circle time, my heart-to-heart with John, Kristal's hug. In the dark silence of my bedroom, Michael's withdrawal overshadows all of it. He's started the checkout process from Hotel Catherine.

One hour later, I am only a little tired but also jittery. Fuck. Has it started? Has the stress triggered another chemical miscue in my head? Which will lead to another manic episode? What will it be this time? I've already done the home improvement and vacation disasters. And now there'll be a whole new cast of witnesses to my freak show, lacing up their sneakers and getting ready to run.

I force myself to lie down. To take deep breaths. *Relax, Catherine. Relax.* I think of my self-soothing collage from group. The one Kristal and I had almost peed in our pants laughing about. In addition to the joke pictures, I had also cut out from magazines photos of a fluffy white comforter and an apple pie and an ad for dryer sheets because they remind me of Grandma. I hum "You Are My Sunshine" softly and, finally, drowsiness descends. My limbs feel weighted in a blessed way and my mind slows. That current of exoneration, the one I had first felt outside the library, thrums softly through me. It had gotten muted by the debris and clutter of the day.

I am still innocent.

I remember Dr. McCallum talking about Grandma and her death and my disorder. This was sometime back in July, when we were first getting acquainted and I was still unaccustomed to his blunt questions. I was startled when, with no warning, he opened with something like, "I believe your grandmother's death played a role in the onset of your depression and bipolar disorder. I think we need to talk about your grandmother, what happened that day, how you're coping, how you feel now. I think it would be enormously helpful."

"What?" This was the first time any doctor had linked

Grandma's death and my sickness. "Are you saying because Grandma died . . . I mean, the way she died, *gave me* bipolar disorder?" I asked.

"No. I am not saying that at all, Catherine." Dr. McCallum leaned forward. "Let me be very clear," he said slowly. "I do not believe grief or trauma *causes* mental illness. We know that grief can be a severe *stressor*. That *stressor* can trigger the *onset* of a mental illness. Do you understand that?"

"So I would've gotten sick even if she hadn't died?" I already knew the answer.

He took a deep breath before speaking. "Probably. Catherine, most studies indicate that there is a strong genetic factor for bipolar disorder. So, the answer is yes, it's likely you would have gotten sick. If not after your grandmother's death, then maybe as a result of some other stressor, or else it would most likely have developed on its own."

That stung, as it always did. I despised that my fate was determined when I was only a zygote.

But I understand now what Dr. McCallum was saying, and I can finally put the guilt for that malfunctioning aside. I am a victim of genetic roulette.

It's not my fault.

37

Mom wakes me at eleven on Thursday morning. My eyes are gritty and my muscles ache. I slowly sit up and take a groggy self-inventory. I'm not jittery anymore; now it's the opposite. I feel completely and totally wiped. The warmth of my white cocoon draws me back down until Mom wakes me again at noon.

"Happy Thanksgiving. Baby, you okay?" she asks, smoothing the hair at my forehead. "How do you feel?"

It's a double-edged question. We both know it. I don't want to worry her. I won't tell her I couldn't sleep last night and that when I did, it was fitful, with vivid dream scenes I couldn't understand. I am scared something is starting to happen with me. That the Lamictal is losing its footing, and my defenses are weakening.

I force myself up and scoot to the end of the bed. "I'm tired, that's all. What time are we leaving?"

We've been celebrating Thanksgiving at Aunt D's since I was born.

Mom studies me. She doesn't quite believe me but doesn't push. "I'm already done with the pies, and we don't have to leave until four. Uh . . . I was thinking that maybe we could go through some of Grandma's things? Clean out a little?"

My heart picks up its pace. The suitcase. "Did you start yet?"

"No. I'm not touching a thing until you're okay with it."

I exhale. Disaster averted. But I am so not equipped for this discussion right now. I busy myself with throwing on some socks.

"Cath, hon, we could really use the space," Mom says, standing to make my bed. "We'll keep a lot of her stuff. I promise. It's just that if, *when* you have friends over and you want some privacy, we could have a little study or den. You guys could hang out there, or I could go there when you want to hang out in the living room."

The hope on Mom's face subtracts ten years and I catch a glimpse of what she looked like as a young woman. Without me shackled to her. And now she's feeling like things are okay, that we've found a new equilibrium, that it's fine to start making plans and moving forward to a future with friends again. Guilt presses down on me, and I find myself nodding.

"Really, Cath? You think you're ready?" she asks. "I don't want to push you."

"It sounds like a good idea," I respond slowly, not

wanting to age her any more than I already have. "But can we do it together? Can we do it over Christmas break? Can you wait for that?"

"Of course."

I know I can delay this cleanout for a long time. "So you won't touch anything until I'm ready?"

"Scout's honor," Mom says. "I won't take one crappy tchotchke off her dresser without your consent."

38

Michael would almost seem like his old self this Saturday night—warm and affectionate—if not for the current of weirdness between us. There's no trace of the angry, humiliated boy who couldn't connect on a punch, or the boy who blew off his girlfriend on Wednesday. He doesn't bring up the movie and neither do I. But that weirdness is affecting our timing with each other and we've fallen out of rhythm.

Lorraine and Tony are dragging Nonny out to dinner, but they left pizza warming in the oven for Michael and me. Anthony is also a no-show, out to dinner with his landscaping buddies to celebrate the almost end of their season.

The house is silent after the departure of the three elder Pitoscias. In the kitchen, Michael shuts off the oven. "You ready to eat?" he asks.

I shrug. We have the entire house to ourselves. I just want to be with him. I need him to pull me close, put his warm hands on me, tell me I'm beautiful and that he's liked me since freshman year, and kiss me. Like Wednesday at school. Like last weekend in the basement. But I also don't want that. Because it's not right anymore.

I guess I don't have to worry, though, because he doesn't walk toward me and take my hands. We don't sneak off to his bedroom to undress one another. Instead he turns around and slides oven mitts onto his hands. "I'm starving," he says, and pulls the baking trays with their bubbling-hot pizza slices out of the oven.

"*Mangia!*" he announces proudly.

He kissed me once tonight. Inside Lorraine's Subaru before he walked me to my front door. One time.

Once.

Huge opportunities had appeared like open sets of double doors, beckoning Michael to touch me, but he ignored them. After his parents and Nonny had left, he parked his long, lean body at the kitchen table and worked his way through both trays of pizza. When the clan returned, Michael suggested playing Taboo with everyone. When Anthony arrived home at ten, even he seemed surprised to see us playing a stupid game with his parents. I saw him exchange a look with Michael. It was like Anthony was embarrassed or something, and he had scurried upstairs muttering an excuse. But the worst was when Taboo ended and we still had an hour to spare before my eleven o'clock curfew.

Lorraine, my boyfriend's mother, suggested we play

foosball in the promised land of the basement. Michael said no. *No.* He wanted us to watch a movie on the Tuskegee Airmen for our project. Sure, he pulled me close under the blanket on the sofa in the TV room and kissed my forehead and cheek, but that was it.

I was silent as Michael drove me home, all doubt about his intent erased. I thought about what would happen next. How the texts would lessen, how he would start being busy on weekends and then, finally, maybe after Christmas because he's good and sensitive and wouldn't want to dampen my holiday vibe, he would come by in the white Subaru, red-necked and red-faced, and explain that he really likes me but he's just not ready for a serious girlfriend. And can we still be friends? And I will nod numbly and wonder at precisely what point he deleted the holiday talent-show video of freshman me from his phone. In school, he will stroll out of history class with only a slight glance my way, leaving me to fend off Farricelli alone, exposing me to the taunts of Riley's crew, who will see that I am once again unguarded and pounce.

"You okay, Cath?" Michael had asked after pulling into my driveway.

"Yeah," I said. "How about you? Everything okay?"

He broke eye contact then and looked at a spot above me. "Yes."

I began tugging on the cold door handle. I needed to get out.

"Wait," he said, his hand on my arm. "You sure you're okay?"

I turned and looked straight into his face, at those beautiful brown eyes and lips and the awful, angry red scar that will permanently mar the sweet smoothness of his chin. My hand instantly went to it and my index finger softly traced the raised line.

"I'm just so tired," I said. *Of my life,* I added in my head. "That's all."

39

The clock on Grandma's dresser reads 1:36 a.m. It's been exactly two hours and twenty-one minutes since Michael dropped me off.

The amber prescription bottles on Grandma's carpet gleam subtly. I just took an inventory of the troops. All this time, I've blindly recruited and have no real idea of the troops' strength. I still don't really. Who the fuck knows if seven Lexapro of unknown dosage combined with a motley assortment of a few Celexa, Abilify, Paxil, Zoloft and Lamictal will be sufficient. And I'm not even sure about the Tylenol. I think swallowing a whole bottle is more likely to kill only my liver.

I'm finally starting to get tired. I lie on my side and rest my head on my left arm. The back of my snowflake earring pierces the soft skin behind my ear and I take it out. Then the other one. I sit up, the silver snowflakes barely glinting in my palm. They seem lightweight and dull now. I can't wear these anymore. I push down hard on the Lexapro cap and twist to open the bottle. Tilting my hand, I let the earrings fall inside. I close the bottle, tuck everything inside their Capezio shoe box home and pack it away under Grandma's bed.

It's reckless to keep them here, especially since I've agreed to a cleanout of this room. But maybe it's symmetry I'm going for. Grandma basically died in this room. It feels right in some way that my partners in death should stay here too.

Instinctively, my fingers straighten the ruffled eyelet bed skirt. I remember buying this with Grandma at Target a month before she died. I don't want to think about her now. She'd be disgusted with me. I also avoid all eye contact with the impaled mega-Jesus over Grandma's bed for the same reason. But neither Grandma nor Jesus can stop me from climbing onto this bed and pulling the yellow afghan over me. Fatigue laps at me with dark soft waves, but I can't fall asleep yet. I need to check my phone for any texts from Kristal.

She had texted me a few times earlier tonight saying she was having a good time. Then a great time. And then she'd-better-freaking-get-into-this-school time because it was beyond amazing, and the people were so cool, and smart, and hipster-y but not in the "clichéd hipster way." Her last text was to say that they were leaving a party and headed back to the dorms. She said she'd text me all about it once she was in bed. And I waited because I wanted to hear, but also because I wanted to tell her about Michael and how he didn't like me anymore.

But she never texted.

I text her now: "You ok???"

There's no choo in response. I imagine her happily asleep in a single bed, and opposite her, another girl in a twin bed, in a room inside an old stone building that was converted into a dormitory, surrounded by other sleeping college kids who will all get up in a few hours and trudge to the cafeteria to relate last night's events. And like the thousands of other Sunday-morning kids in the hundreds of noisy college cafeterias that hum with conversation and utensil clatter, they will eat and laugh and be normal. This is where Kristal will be.

And where I won't. Ever.

I click on Notes and find my D-day List. Zero tells me to delete the entire thing. I do.

40

There are three things about the step-down program that are different from the IOP: we meet two days a week instead of five, two hours instead of three, and we are assigned to Group Room B, a space that reeks of new carpeting and whatever carcinogenic gases are being emitted by the pleather sofas. On Wednesday, our first day, most of us walked straight past the offices and restrooms in the familiar route to Room Three. Vanessa had to redirect everyone but Tommy.

"You want Chipotle or Panera?" Kristal whispers to me as the last minutes of group wind down. It's Friday, and despite witnessing last week's near collision, Mom is still allowing Kristal to drive me home after group.

"You choose," I say softly, "I like both." I want Kristal to decide because I don't want to put any food pressure on her.

"Chipotle," she says, and gives me a quick grin.

These dinner plans have buoyed me the entire uneasy week. Things are very awkward with Michael. I am quiet with him and I think that unnerves him, because he is fumbling again, stuttering and flushed. He holds my hand at school, though, and surprisingly, the clasp is still warm and sure, as if to power through what our minds cannot.

After school today he texted, "Can we get together on Sunday?" and added the death-knell sentence: "We need to talk." I haven't responded yet. I'm not ready for him to officially leave me yet. I plan on talking to Kristal about it over dinner. I know she'll help me.

The interior of Kristal's car is immaculate. It looks and smells brand-new. "Give me one sec," Kristal says. She's texting the girl she stayed with at Vassar about some fresh-man guy she met: Eli from Greenwich, who she says is funny and who I know is gorgeous—Kristal had sent me a couple of pictures of him on Sunday.

"Fuck," Kristal says. "She thinks he has a girlfriend." Kristal stares at her phone and I can see the frustration etched on her face. "Like there could be anything happening with me, a *high schooler*. Plus, I'm not even gonna get in." She makes a big show of clicking off her phone and zipping it into her bag. "There's a Fro-Zone in Cranbury, right?" she asks with false brightness. "Should we hit that for dessert? Or maybe just get coffee and doughnuts?"

I'm sensing a binge-eating episode coming on. "I don't know," I say. "Why don't we see what we feel like after dinner?"

The atmosphere inside the Volkswagen instantly sparks

as Kristal catches on. "Jesus Christ, Cat! Not you! Please tell me you're not watching every goddamned thing I put in my mouth! Are you gonna become a bathroom Nazi like my mother?"

"No," I say softly. "It's just that . . ."

Do I tell her what I know?

"What?" Kristal demands. "It's just what, Miss PTSD?"

I shake her insult off and take a deep breath. "I know that you're still doing it. I heard you in the bathroom when I slept over." Kristal's silence roars at me, so I continue, "I'm not passing judgment. You're my best friend. I want to help you."

"Well, isn't that nice?" Kristal's voice stings with its sarcasm. "Maybe you and your boyfriend can join forces, sell bulimia ribbons, host a 5K for me? It's so fucking easy being Catherine Pulaski, isn't it?"

This is it. My open door. I can tell her now. I want to tell her. "No. Not at all," I say. I am starting to overheat. "And I . . . I don't have PTSD. Or maybe I do, but I was never officially diagnosed with that. I have . . ."

Oh my God. Can I allow these words to leave my lips? Publicize *this* pain? Riley's reaction to my bipolar confession flashes through my head. No, no, no. Don't think about that. Kristal's different. She'll be okay with it.

Kristal asks, "What? You have what?" She's still angry.

"I'm bipolar." The words are out now. I cannot take them back. My heart slams against my ribs as I study Kristal's face. At first, there's no change of expression; she watches me, steely-eyed.

But then she slowly shakes her head and turns to stare

337

out the windshield, and I know my secret is sinking in. She seems stunned.

I continue, "I was diagnosed after my grandmother died. They think her death was a stressor that might have triggered it."

Kristal doesn't say anything for at least a minute. There's no air in here. Then she asks in a strangely flat tone, "You have manic depression, right? That's another name for it?"

I nod, my body temperature flaming as the realization slams me in the gut. This confession was a big, big no, the hugest fucking mistake.

"So you have depressions and then the opposite, right?" she says in that robot voice. Without waiting for an answer, she asks, "Have you tried to kill yourself?"

It doesn't matter now. "Yes," I say. "Last year. In September. I swallowed lithium and Prozac. My mom found me."

Kristal turns to me and I can see the glistening streaks on her cheeks. She is crying. "All this fucking time I have spilled my guts to you, telling you everything. *Everything*. Including the greatest humiliation of my life. The deepest, darkest, rawest part of my life. And you couldn't confide in me? Ever? Not just that you're bipolar, but that you *attempted suicide*? That's kind of major shit, Cat! And you couldn't tell *me*? Not one, not *one* fucking thing? I'm an idiot. I thought we were best friends. Jesus, now I don't even know if we're friends at all!" She slams the steering wheel with her fists.

"I am so sorry," I say, guilt and remorse racing through me in equal parts, jacking up my heart rate a millionfold.

"I was afraid to tell you because my other friends couldn't handle it. They left. It's like . . . I don't know. I still can't believe that this is my life now. It's like someone turned everything upside down and told me to walk on the ceiling, that I'd get used to it. But everybody else still uses the floor. And I thought if I didn't tell anyone else, they wouldn't see me up there."

"You know what?" Kristal says, wiping her eyes with the back of her hand. "We all fucking feel like that. I keep telling you, Cat, as much as you want to believe you're special that way, you're not." She rests her head on the leather headrest and looks up through the moonroof. "I'm just going to drop you off at home. I don't want to do dinner"— her voice catches on the word "dinner"—"with you anymore."

Her rejection pours over me like boiling wax, scalding me stiff. I cannot cry. "I'll get my own ride." I fumble with the car door and have to wait for her to unlock it before I can escape. Woodenly, I step onto the sidewalk in front of St. Anne's as she peels away into the night.

41

I stand on the sidewalk. I have no one to call for a ride besides Mom and Aunt D. No one. And this fact suddenly staggers me as much as Kristal's words. I almost had Kristal, and I almost had Michael, but now I have no one.

I turn off my phone to prevent Mom from tracking me. I decide to walk home in the cold black air. To my empty house.

As I step off the curb, that old pickup truck that almost hit Kristal speeds into the parking lot. It slams on the brakes as if the driver recognizes me. I take a step backward, toward the entrance, and the truck slowly pulls into the same spot it was parked in last week. The passenger's-side door opens. Something tells me to go back inside, to the safety of the foyer. It's empty, the door to Room Three wide open, with bits of conversation floating out. I catch a glimpse of movement in the parking lot, so I rush to the women's restroom. I wait a good five minutes until all is quiet and then swing open the bathroom door.

I am in the hallway when our eyes meet. My body registers the surprise before my brain does. He sits on one of the plastic chairs in the foyer, wearing the Paoletti's Landscaping jacket that I borrowed on Halloween. My brain finally permits the identification. *Anthony Pitoscia. Anthony Pitoscia. Anthony Pitoscia.* He stands and gives an awkward nod. "Hey, Cath."

I can barely hear him over the roar of white noise in my head. He is saying something about starting therapy. Today at five-thirty. Court ordered. Something about alcohol and drinking. It's hard to focus on what he's saying, because there are facts and meanings connecting inside my head, sliding the Michael puzzle pieces into place. I understand now.

Anthony was in the truck that almost plowed into Kristal last Wednesday. Anthony, who doesn't have his license, was sitting in the passenger seat and got a good look at me that night. It was Anthony who told Michael about seeing me here, at the St. Anne's psychiatric outpatient facility. Learning how fucked up I am must've sealed the deal, because Michael had already started pulling away. And that is why Michael could not bear to touch me last Saturday. That is why, despite the wealth of opportunities, he politely declined, passing on exploiting the sick girl's mind and body. He wouldn't go *there* anymore with her, because it's just not the right thing to do.

341

Anthony touches my arm, his face a mask of concern. "We're cool, right, Cath?"

I nod and my mouth responds, "Sure." I shuffle past him, desperate to get outside and hemorrhage in private.

I walk fast, like the thoughts ricocheting in my skull. I don't feel the cold. In fact, I'm working up a sweat that drips down the sides of my face, mixing with my tears. I bring my pace to a run, and before long, I'm all the way past the strip mall, finished with the lonely strip of blacktop that connects commercial Cranbury to quaint Cranbury. I run past the high school and down historic Main Street, into downtown Cranbury. I only slow when I hit the Green, which glows festively under the starless sky. Then, finally, I stop and sit on the bench between the town Christmas tree and menorah. There's no one around me. My heart slows.

We were supposed to do this, Michael and I. He wanted to walk the decorated Green one night but really, really late, after all the stores and restaurants had closed and everyone had gone home. He'd done it last year by himself, and he said it was a little surreal, but beautiful. Romantic. He wanted to do it with me this year.

Now, that will never happen. Sorrow for the loss of him engulfs me. Michael. A true connection. Yes, it was prompted by some bogus losing-my-virginity goal. But it pushed me to allow Michael inside at least a portion of my life. And it's over now. Along with the dinners at the warm, garlic-scented Pitoscia home. And Nonny. I swallow a sob. Even if in some unknown universe Michael still wanted me, I can never set foot inside the Pitoscia home and show my lying face.

The truth is that I hurt everyone around me. Mom, who's aging at warp speed and needs therapy to lasso her anxiety. Kristal, who tried to be my friend, my best friend, only to get a trifecta shafting: no support, no confidence, no honest camaraderie. Michael, who wanted that freshman dancer in the red skirt, only to discover *me* hiding in her shell.

But I realize all of that isn't even the worst part. It is this: that maybe I've been blaming everything on Zero and my diagnosis. Maybe the truth is that I'm just a selfish asshole who happens to have bipolar disorder.

I am aware of that darkness hovering, sniffing blood in the water, ready to strike. I stand suddenly. I need to move.

I am afraid.

I can't bear the black weight of Zero again. Infiltrating my world and sucking all energy and light and emotion from it. He will always be with me, waiting in the wings, ready to pounce when my foundation cracks. I don't know if I have the strength to fight him for the rest of my life.

I walk past the cupcake shop and shoe store and pharmacy. It's not just fear. I am bone-tired of the shame. And buckled by the knowledge that I will be a perpetual child, never completely independent because of my unstable mind; I will have to moor myself to others to keep safe.

But who do I have? Michael and now most likely Kristal will be joining the exodus from my life. I will be alone again. Just like September of sophomore year. But a low tide of something good runs through me. Because I am realizing now that that profound sense of loneliness is missing. That cored-out sensation is absent. Is it because I no longer feel guilty about my disorder? That I no longer believe I am unworthy?

Zero is not here.

My feet stop, and I'm filled with an unexpected sense of elation. The worst has happened, yet my world is not crashing in on itself. I am Zero-less. And I do not want to die.

I want to live.

Even with this disease, my bipolar life can be good. Isn't that what my D-Day List proves? That great times and experiences are still possible? More than possible—I've been fucking doing it! I've been *living,* with meaning, purpose and joy.

Maybe Kristal didn't leave because I'm bipolar. Maybe she was just pissed I never confided in her. It might be the same with Michael. I knew what he was asking for when he drove me to school. He was *begging* me to confide in him. I keep blaming the illness for constraining me, but maybe I'm the one who's been limiting myself. Out of fear.

This sudden clarity hits me like a lightning bolt, and I wonder, is it the Lamictal holding the line? Or God? Or Grandma? Maybe it's Jane. Is she here with me? If this were a movie, I'd see her reflection in a storefront window, catch a fleeting glimpse of a uniformed young woman gazing at me with a look of determination, that steely strength inside her somehow touching me, saving me.

But there's no one else in the reflection of Rodrick's on the Green's picture window. Except someone is looking at me. From inside. It's Rodrick. Waving at me. Dear God, is he my guardian angel? Are you freaking kidding me? Impeccably groomed in black leather pants and silky black shirt and slinking to the front door with the grace of a panther?

Rodrick opens the door. "What was I? A one-night stand?" he asks teasingly. "Where have you been? And who is doing your hair?"

This is beyond bizarre. "I . . . I do it myself. My mom does the back," I say, self-consciously running a hand over my head.

"Not bad, but why don't you come back next Saturday? I'm training somebody and we could use your head. No charge."

My response rises up, honest and true. "I want to let it grow out," I say. I no longer need to wear my hair this way as penance.

Rodrick nods, his eyes studying me intently. "Yes. But I'm seeing a layered bob, grazing your jaw. Nothing longer. We need to show off that gorgeous neck." He winks at me. "So come in and we'll clean it up so it grows in right. How's nine-thirty? It's Catherine, right?"

"How do you remember me? I was here, like, six months ago." I can only imagine manic me, chattering incessantly and vibrating in his chair.

"Because I was having one of the worst days ever and you basically saved it," Rodrick says, and runs a hand over his smooth, clean-shaven head. "Coming in like that, demanding the Hepburn cut and completely crushing it." He smiles. "I needed that. So, see you next Saturday?"

I nod, and I actually feel calmer. For now, maybe this is what I will have to survive on: small acts of kindness that I never fully savored before, like Sabita's thoughtfulness, Alexis's compassion, John's concern, Aunt D's perpetual support. Even Olivia with her tiny olive-branch smiles. And Dr. McCallum. My prying, probing ally who has probably saved my life. Alongside my mother.

My mother.

I take my time walking past the shops, my body and mind drained. I am still sad about Kristal and Michael, yet strangely hopeful in a way and also a little scared. Because if I didn't have to walk, if I didn't have that cushion of time and physical exertion to absorb the grief and hurt, what would I have done if I had gone straight home? In the heat of anguish, would I have pulled out my shoe box and washed down the troops with a few cold gulps?

I don't know, but I don't *think* so.

But it doesn't matter now. I am dumping that box. I am fucking dumping the entire thing, with its pills and nasty notes and harsh reminders of what the last two years have cost. Tonight. As soon as I get home. Because that box makes it too easy and I am too erratic. It's no different from a loaded gun.

I pick up the pace and turn on my phone. There are seven voice mails: four from Michael, two from Dominic's and one from Aunt D. She's supposed to be in Boston. Why would she be calling me? I listen to her voice mail: "Catherine, it's Aunt Darlene. Hon, I'm sorry to bother you, but I'm . . . I can't reach your mom. Dominic called me tonight. He said she never showed up at work and isn't answering her phone. Can you just call me and let me know what happened? Thanks, honey. And call whenever you can. It doesn't matter what time." I click on the most recent message from Dominic's. It should be Mom, explaining the mix-up. Instead, a husky, masculine voice says, "Uh . . . hello . . . hello, Catherine. It's Dominic. I'm looking for your mom. She was supposed to help out tonight with a private party at five. But she never showed up, and your mom never misses without calling. I'm a little concerned. Can you have her call me when she gets a chance?"

It's almost seven now. With icy fingers, I click on Mom's number. It rings and then goes to voice mail. Just as I am certain that I am standing on Main Street in downtown Cranbury, I know something is very wrong with my mother. The sidewalk tilts under my feet as I begin to sprint the last mile home.

42

The Accord is still in the driveway, but the house is dark. With trembling fingers, I unlock the front door. "Mom?" I call out, panting. No answer. From the foot of the stairs, I can see up into the darkened second-floor hallway. The bathroom door is open, and light streams into the dark hallway. "Mom!" I yell, pounding my way up the steps. My heart beats triple time. Please, God, make her be all right. Please let her not have had a stroke. Please let me not find her, a fallen redwood, on the pink chenille rug.

The bathroom is empty. I race into her bedroom. She's not here. The black skirt and white blouse, her Dominic's uniform, lie posed on the bed, imitating her. Scaring me.

My legs feel uncoordinated as I stumble downstairs. There's that stillness. The silence that screams. I walk through the living room and stop at the entrance to the dark kitchen. Grandma's door is open a crack and her bedroom light is on. I have a sick sense of déjà vu, but it's inverted, reversed somehow.

*Because this is what my mother would have felt. Had I
killed myself.*

I slowly enter the kitchen. "Mom?" I call out.

Is she dead?

No answer.

*Please, God. Please, God. Don't let her be dead. Not now.
Not yet. Not this way.*

I'm afraid of what I'll find in Grandma's room.

I enter. Mom is here, seated on Grandma's bed, wearing only a bath towel wrapped around her. Her shoulders
are slumped, her head hangs. The plaid suitcase lies open
on the floor. On Mom's lap, cradled in her hands, is my
shoe box.

No. No. No. Not that. Not now. Not this way.

I freeze. "Mom?"

She doesn't move. She doesn't acknowledge me.

Dear God, is this a stroke? Did the discovery blow an
artery in her brain?

Don't go. I need you. I need you. I need you.

Finally, she blinks and tilts her head, and I rush toward
her. She takes my hands, kissing each one and then squeezing them both in her cold, worn fingers. I look into her
eyes. She is here, but stunned by a grief too big to compre-
hend. Its depth staggers me.

In a ragged whisper, she asks, "Are you leaving me,
Catherine?"

And another truth breaks on me. One that I feel in my
bones. It is incontrovertible, immutable and, now, so very
fucking clear.

If I had killed myself, I would have killed her too.

43

Seconds-before she stepped into the shower tonight, Mom remembered Grandma's gold watch. It's an expensive piece and Mom worried that in our upcoming cleanout of Grandma's room, we might forget about it and mistakenly donate it to Goodwill. So with a towel hastily flung around her, she went downstairs. She knew the watch was in the plaid suitcase, wrapped in a hankie and secured inside an old glass Gerber baby food jar. At first, she was thrilled to find Uncle Jack's old uniform jacket. *Catherine can use this for her project,* she thought. But when she pulled the jacket out, my shoe box tumbled to the floor.

Once I helped Mom dress, we called Dr. McCallum. I explained what had happened and that Mom wanted to take me to the ER. In another strange turn of events, Dr. McCallum just happened to be shopping at the Cranbury Costco and drove straight to our house.

He spent two and a half hours with us. First talking with me and then with Mom and me together. For the first time, I followed Sandy's advice to "stay honest and say honest." I told Dr. McCallum everything about my stockpile, how and when and why I collected the pills, my nighttime ritual of taking them out and lining them up and my safety protocol in rotating their location from under my bed to under Grandma's bed. He asked if there were other stashes or if I had made additional plans besides the shoe box.

No, I told him. This was it.

At least four times he asked me if I wished I were dead or if I was thinking of killing myself. Each time, I honestly answered no. I told him everything that had happened with Michael and Kristal and Anthony. And that it wasn't bullshit that I had planned on dumping the shoe box tonight. I explained why I thought I needed it. How the worry about Zero's return and the harsh truth of what my future held crippled me at times. How I felt this was the only way to deal with it. How having an escape plan reassured me. How I felt like it was impossible to say these things out loud.

He listened and nodded and listened. "You know, everyone thinks the hardest part is the *asking* for help. I'd disagree. I think for most of my patients it's getting to that point right *before* you take the leap of verbalizing it, and then working up the strength to actually say it out loud, that's extraordinarily difficult."

When Mom joined us, I repeated a lot of what I had told Dr. McCallum. She was still pale and crying a little, but she visibly relaxed when Dr. McCallum told her he thought I was safe. He wanted the pills destroyed tonight and said that Mom had to supervise me doing it.

So now Mom and I are sitting on the kitchen floor, with a ziplock bag between us. We've tossed the old ballet shoes, the unopened packages of tights and crumpled recital flyers. I showed Mom the notes from Riley Swenson's crew.

"I was wondering what those were," she says, and stares at them, something cold and hard in her eyes. "I despise that family." She rips the notes up angrily and tosses the pieces into the baggie.

My shoe box is empty now but for the bottles. "I'm glad you're here," I tell Mom. "I want to do this together."

Her eyes fill with tears. She nods and picks up the Celexa bottle. I take it from her cold fingers, unscrew the cap and dump the pills into the baggie. I thought I'd feel something, like fear that my escape route was no more, or the sadness of letting go. But I don't—not at all. With each pill that falls out, I feel lighter. Mom opens the last bottle, Lexapro. I take it from her and retrieve the snowflake earrings and empty the bottle. Then I seal the bag and hand it to her.

"What happened?" Mom asks. "Why were your earrings in there?"

I explain why I put them in there and what happened tonight with Anthony.

"Fuck," my Catholic mother breathes. "We both had really shitty nights."

And we start to laugh.

*　*　*

352

It's a no-brainer. We both choose the condo on the Oahu beach. How can you beat walking right out your back door and onto smooth white sand and into the glorious ocean? HGTV is running a *Hawaii Life* marathon, and in bed beside me, Mom snorts as a couple on the show chooses the fixer-upper a good three miles from the water because it had room for a garden. It's 11:30 p.m. and we're on our third episode.

Tonight, I couldn't say good-night to Mom. She seemed fragile and I felt raw and sad but also relieved. So I got into my pajamas, grabbed my pillow and walked into Mom's room. She was sitting on the bed, hunched over, rubbing moisturizer into her hands.

"Can I sleep in here tonight?" I asked.

For the rest of my life, I will never forget the smile that lit up her face.

We watch another full episode and then start a fifth.

Under the covers, Mom's hand rests lightly on my forearm. "Cath, honey, I'm starting to fade. Wake me up if you need anything."

That sense of inverted déjà vu lingers. Our mother-daughter roles had reversed and then righted themselves, but some maternal vestiges remain in me. Either that or she has awoken my dormant maternal instincts. For the first time, I really understand that the mother-daughter dynamic changes. I guess there will always be a psychic umbilical cord linking us, going both ways now, sustaining us. She will always live my pain, and as I grow older, I will live more and more of hers.

I stroke the hair off her forehead before kissing it. "Good night, Mom. I love you."

44

On Saturday morning, I dial Michael's number. I still haven't listened to his voice mails or read his texts from yesterday. He picks up in the middle of the first ring.

"Can you come outside?" is the first thing he says.

"What?"

"I'm here. Parked outside your house. Can we talk? In the car?" Michael's voice is raspy and he sounds tired.

I tell Mom where I'm going, throw on my winter coat and slide into the Target version of Ugg boots. I grab the snowflake earrings off the kitchen table, slide them into my coat pocket and walk outside. My heart races as I approach the Subaru. Michael hops out to open the passenger-side door. Before I slide in, our eyes catch. He looks fried, with mussed-up hair, dark shadows beneath his eyes, and stubble. Somehow, he's still painfully cute, though I know he's here to break up with me.

Oh God. That sense of loss hangs over me. I just want to get this over with and return the earrings without breaking down in front of him.

Michael gets back in the car. His entire face and, from what I can see, his neck are bright red. "Yes, Anthony told me about seeing you at St. Anne's," he starts. "But, Catherine, I had a feeling before that. I . . . I knew you didn't have a job."

He *knew* I didn't have a job? He knew I was lying? Is that why he stopped waiting with me for Mom to pick me up after school? Why he was awkward every time my alleged employment came up in conversation?

Michael is saying, "I knew that your mom was taking you somewhere. I knew you had some stuff going on last year—"

"Wait," I interrupt. "How did you know? That I wasn't working?"

"That day you left your phone at school. I took it and went to the law firm. I saved that paper, the law firm's messed-up letterhead, from that time at the library. I asked for you and they thought I meant your mother. One of the attorneys said she was taking her daughter to the day clinic and that she'd be right back, she just had to drop you off."

Jesus Christ. That was in October. He knew all this time? I want to bolt from the car.

Michael must understand that I'm humiliated, because he grabs my hand. "It's okay, Cath. It's *okay*. That doesn't matter to me."

I shake my head. He doesn't fully get it. "I'm not just

going to the doctor's," I say, fighting back tears. "I had to go to an IOP. That stands for intensive outpatient program. I went five days a week. Three hours a day. Group therapy."

Michael shakes his head. "I told you, I don't care about that."

I could just let it be. Let him think that's all there is. But I'm so done with my usual modus operandi. I pull my hand away and sit up straight. I will watch his reaction to my secrets and I will bear it, whatever the fuck it is.

"I didn't just go through some 'stuff' last year. I have bipolar disorder. I have to take medicine for it. Every day."

As I'm waiting for his response, it starts to snow, as if on cue. The white flurries swirl outside the car, present at both the beginning of our relationship and at its end. But Michael is shaking his head.

"So what, Catherine. So what?" Michael asks. "I'm a fucking wimp. I can't fight to save my life and I collapse at the sight of blood. You didn't run from *me*."

I am blown away by the absurdity of his statement—a blood phobia and a missed punch?

"That *stuff* I had going on last year?" I say again. "I tried to *kill myself*, Michael. I tried to OD on my meds because I was depressed, so depressed that words can't describe it. But the bitch of bipolar is that it's not just these soul-sucking, zombielike depressions. There are also manias, these episodes where crazy ideas take hold in my mind. They seem reasonable at the time, but they're totally bizarre and out of control. I have to live with this for the rest of my life, and it's hard to wrap my head around a future with it. Because up until my grandmother died, everything was fine. I was just like everybody else. Like you. Normal." I stop to take a deep breath and study his face, searching for the flustered reaction, the pulling away.

But it doesn't happen. His brown eyes are holding mine intently.

"Go on," Michael says, taking my hand again. "Don't stop."

"Look, I get that you had some really rough times. Being bullied, that's beyond brutal. I know that kids kill themselves because it hurts so badly. I'm really sorry you went through that. But don't you understand? We"—I point at each of us—"*you* and *I* . . . *you* and *I* . . . " I want to tell him that we are different. That Louis Farricelli is external. That he won't always be with Michael. That there's an end date on the time Michael has to be near him. But that my problem is internal. It will always be a part of me. We are not the same. But then I realize that the cause of pain makes zero impact on how it feels. Like Sandy said, "Pain is pain." I can no longer rank who is entitled to hurt more.

I glance down at my coat pocket with its secret cargo and then return my gaze to Michael. He needs to understand this part. "Bipolar is chronic. It's never going away. It's genetic. Do you get that?"

Michael nods. "Cath, I already knew about you being bipolar. And about your overdose. That fucking Riley told anyone who would listen."

Michael knew. He knew but he still came after me. Still wanted me. But now he doesn't.

I can't tear my eyes from that face. "So what happened, then?" I have to ask this. "What made you stop liking me?"

"What?" Michael asks, astonished. "I never stopped liking you."

"You changed our movie plans. After you drove me to school that morning, something changed between us. And then last Saturday, at your house, you . . . you didn't even want to touch me."

Michael grabs my hand again. His voice is soft, husky, the hint of a small, sexy smile on his lips. "Cath, I want to do everything with you. Everything. Believe me on this one."

He's not lying. I can see it in his eyes. I begin to unclench, a warm hum filling me.

"The truth is . . . I . . . I didn't want to go any further with you . . . like that . . . because I knew you were holding back . . . not . . . I don't know, sharing your life with me. Not to sound like a cheesy Hallmark card. But our relationship felt kind of fake at times, because I knew you were lying about your job, and I knew there was stuff going on in your life that you didn't trust me enough to talk about. I didn't want to . . . you know, go any further. It wasn't easy." Michael runs his free hand back and forth on the steering wheel. He's flushing again. "You'd never expect a guy to say that." He locks eyes with me. "But it's different with you. And it was getting to me more and more that you kept lying to me. Especially after Farricelli and the hospital. That's why in the car, I was, like, begging you to open up and you wouldn't. It just really pissed me off. I was going to bring it up with you this weekend. That's why I texted you that we had to talk."

I nod. "Look, I'm sorry I didn't say anything earlier. But, Michael . . . you have no idea how hard it is. I feel humiliated, having this. I told Riley and Olivia and they left, and now they want nothing to do with me. So do you get why I'm scared? I figured you wouldn't like me if you knew the truth. I'm just starting to accept it myself."

"How do you feel now? With it out in the open between us?" he asks.

I shrug. "I'm not sure yet. Weird. A little nervous. How do you feel?"

He smiles and pulls me close, burying his face in my neck. "Great." He suddenly pulls back. "Where're your earrings?"

I pull them out of my pocket. "I thought we were breaking up. I was going to return them to you."

"Hey, Cath," he says, "we, *you* and *I*"—and he imitates my earlier action, pointing first at me and then at himself— "*you and I* are definitely not breaking up."

45

Mom waits for me at the front door as Michael drives off. She doesn't say anything, just opens her arms, and I walk into them.

"It went great. I told him everything," I say.

She squeezes me harder and then pulls back. "Your phone chooed at least four times while you were talking to Michael." She pulls my phone out of her robe pocket. "It's Kristal."

I call her and she picks up on the first ring. "Can I come over, Cat?" Kristal's voice trembles. "I need to talk to you."

"Yes," I say, and give her my address.

"I'll be there in a half hour. . . . And, Cat . . . do you hate me?" she asks.

"No fucking way."

We talk for hours on the floor of my bedroom. It's an apology free-for-all, with Kristal agonizing over how she reacted to my admission, and me trying to explain why I had held back, about Grandma and my old friends, and how my world had crashed all at once and I couldn't separate the reasons why, so I connected everything to my diagnosis.

Kristal listens, squeezing my hand a couple of times. "I'm so sorry, Cat. I was just so pissed that you never told me anything, I couldn't think of anything else. My mom always says I barrel into relationships, overshare and expect too much of people too soon, and that's why I always get hurt." She leans back against my bed. "But I get it. All last night I kept thinking what a hypocrite I was, lighting into you while I was doing the exact same thing. Lying about bingeing. And maybe it's worse because I lied right to your face."

"Well, so did I," I say. "You asked and I didn't answer." I wait a beat. "So how are you? Really?"

"I called my eating coach as soon as I got home last night. We talked for about an hour and I've got an appointment on Monday with her."

"I'm glad. I'm here for you. Whenever you're stressing or are tempted, I'm here." I think about Dr. McCallum last night in our living room and start to smile. "Jesus, our therapists really earned their money last night. Listen to what happened after you left St. Anne's."

And I tell Kristal everything—about seeing Anthony, walking to the Green and then coming home and finding Mom with my shoe box.

Kristal's eyes fill with tears. "Cat, you weren't going to do anything to yourself, were you?"

"I was planning on it, for the next time I got depressed," I say. "But I don't feel that way anymore."

Our eyes hold. "Promise me, Cat," Kristal says, leaning forward and taking both my hands. "Let's promise each other if . . . when . . . we ever get to that place, we'll call each other. It doesn't matter what time. We won't do anything until we talk. Let's have a password, okay? Only to be used in that situation, okay?"

I nod. I am beginning to cry. Moved by this girl and her gift of friendship. "What should the password be?"

She gives me the same smile she did on the first day we met. Tentative, scared, but one that connects us. "Anne," she says.

46

Mom is driving me to the Pitoscias' this Saturday night to celebrate Nonny's birthday. It fell midweek, on December 18, but the family party is tonight. Lorraine has cooked Mom's chicken and mushroom dish. This is the first time I'll have been at the Pitoscias' since seeing Anthony at St. Anne's, and I'm nervous. Now all the Pitoscias know I go to St. Anne's, because Nonny was eavesdropping when Anthony told Michael.

"You okay?" Mom knows the situation. "Should I just hang out around the corner in case it's too weird?"

"No. I can always ask Michael to take me home," I say. "Go to dinner with Aunt D."

"I think it will be fine, Cath," Mom says, pulling into the Pitoscias' driveway. Michael waits for me at the front door. "They seem like a nice family. Lorraine was very sweet when she called for the recipe. She said Nonny insisted that you be there."

That makes me smile. I lean over to kiss Mom. "Keep your fingers crossed," I say. I take a deep breath and step out of the Accord. I really don't want to go inside. I don't want to face Michael's family, knowing it will be awkward.

Stop it, I tell myself.

The anxiety over this dinner is normal. Mom and Dr. McCallum and Kristal have drilled that into my head. But it was Kristal who did the best job of putting it into perspective.

"This freak-out, Cat," she had said yesterday at group, "it's what I call a 'luxury' anxiety. I'm not criticizing you, but for people like us, with serious fears, this ranks pretty low on the shit-to-worry-about list. Just put it out of your mind. We've got bigger fish. And fuck them if they can't handle it."

My phone vibrates with her text now. "BIGGER FISH. REMEMBER THAT!"

I wave to Mom as she backs out of the Pitoscias' driveway. In the ten seconds it takes me to reach their front door, Nonny has zipped past Michael and stands on the stoop in just her sweatshirt and leggings. She's clapping and calling, "C'mon, Catherine!" Michael and I barely have time to make eye contact because Nonny is hustling me inside, down the hall heavily infused with the evergreen scent of a lit Yankee Candle and straight into the kitchen.

"Hey, Michael's friend! Nice to see you," Michael calls from behind me.

Lorraine's at the stove, and she rushes toward me. Her hug is its usual intensity, but she holds on longer than normal. She just whispers, "Catherine," but her tone tells me she knows it was tough to come over and she's glad I'm here. Tony gives me a two-second pat on the back before winking at me and telling me to take a seat.

And then Anthony comes in. He walks straight over to me. "We good, Cath?" He holds his hand up for a high five. I smile and when my hand connects with his, he holds on to it. "Really?" He's smiling too, but his eyes are asking if I'm mad at him for telling Michael. If I'm mad that his entire family knows my secrets now.

"Really," I say, squeezing back.

Nonny pulls out a chair. "Sit, Catherine," she commands. "What's the matter with you? Why you go to that place, St. Anne's? You drink too much like Anthony?"

Michael, Lorraine, Tony and Anthony instantly object. "Jesus, Nonny," Michael snaps. "I told you not to do this."

Nonny sits next to me, so close our knees touch. She takes my hand, her worn-smooth, spotted fingers warming mine, her mega eyes wide with concern and affection. I shake my head. "No, it's not drinking."

"Then what? You think you fat? You want to be skinny like those models? Men like women with meat on them." She stands and slaps her plump hips. "My husband, Nico, he called these his handles. He use these to hold on."

"Okay, I just threw up in my mouth," Michael moans.

"Is that it?" Nonny persists. "You want to be skinny?"

"No," I say as the kitchen grows heavy with silence.

"It's okay, Cath," Michael says. "You don't have to talk about this anymore." He sends Nonny a warning look.

Nonny takes off her glasses and leans forward. "Are you sad, Catherine? That it?".

"Sometimes. Sometimes I am."

All the Pitoscias have frozen in place except Michael. He slides into the chair next to mine and places his hand on my back.

"Why?" Nonny asks. "What make you sad?"

"I have . . ." My God. Am I going to release this into the Pitoscia stratosphere? I know only one thing right now: that I want to stay honest and say honest. It's the only way. "I have bipolar disorder. It makes me sad sometimes, and sometimes it makes me hyper. I take medicine for it."

Nonny stares at me. Her eyes search my face for clues, I think, indications of my brain defect. She says nothing but stands suddenly, drops a fierce kiss on my forehead and charges out of the kitchen in her Crocs.

Anthony drops his head to the table. "Jesus. I'm still reeling from the handles image."

"Catherine, you come here now," Nonny calls from her bedroom.

Michael and I enter to the sound of Mitzi squealing in her crate, and I see a pile of *People* magazines strewn across Nonny's bed. She pushes it aside and pats the mattress for me to sit.

"Look," she says, passing me a magazine featuring some movie star on the cover. "This one, she got bipolar. And she got an Oscar and married to that actor from *The Godfather*. Ooh, he's a nice one. Makes lots of money. That's pretty good, huh?" She flips open another magazine, points to a former Disney pop princess gone bad. "And her too. She got it too. But now look. She in medical school. She gonna be a doctor." She brings a third magazine close to her face. "And this guy. This rock-and-roll guy. He got bipolar too." She beams at me. "Everybody got it. Don't you worry. You just live with it. That's all."

Michael looks at me and grins. "Don't you feel so much better now?"

I do.

47

FEBRUARY

"Doing anything for the long weekend?" Dr. McCallum asks at the end of our session.

"We're going over to the Pitoscias' on Friday night. They're having a little party," I tell him. "But we might be late. That's Mom's first day of manager training at one of the Dunkin' Donuts in Cranbury."

"And how about you? I thought you told me that your aunt had offered you a job."

"Our step-down program ends this Friday, so I'm starting next week. Not at the same place as Mom, though. Neither of us thought that was a good idea. But you'll like this one: we started running together. It's gonna be tough being around doughnuts all the time."

Dr. McCallum nods. "Good for your head and your body. And what's happening with the history project?"

I'm psyched to tell him that our paper on Private First

Class Jane Talmadge was chosen to be the first biography featured in both the local paper and the county's online *Patch* publications. Bev Walker was totally pumped because Michael and I included info on the exhibit at the museum. We also took a chance and submitted it to a couple of military journals, and one accepted it for publication in May, which makes me so freaking happy. Because unlike our first soldier, Jonathan Kasia, our research uncovered no public tributes to Jane: no books or websites, no annual parade, no athletic field named in her honor and no statue of her on the New Haven Green. Nothing. We couldn't even locate a relative. So it was all on us to get her story out there and give her some of the honor she deserves.

"So things at school are pretty good," I tell Dr. McCallum. "And I'm reading again."

Mrs. Markman, the school librarian, is only too happy to provide recommendations. She usually has a pile of books waiting for me when I stop by between classes—I'm eating in the cafeteria now during lunch. Sometimes at Michael's table, sometimes at Sabita's, where I'm not the only new member: Olivia showed up a few weeks ago and asked if she could sit in the empty chair next to me. She hasn't said what caused the breakup between her and Riley, and I'm not asking yet. Friendship baby steps are fine for right now.

The first book I read or reread was *The Perks of Being a Wallflower*. After all this time, I had to see if I would feel the same way about it. And only in our new den with Grandma's yellow afghan hugging me.

The den is great. We placed a desk inside Grandma's closet after taking off the doors and wallpapering the newly created alcove—just one of the handy design tips Mom and I picked up from HGTV. The room also has a new love seat and recliner, along with new carpeting. The mega-Jesus over Grandma's bed is gone, taken down when Michael and Mom and I painted the walls a soft blue. Mom donated him to St. Stanislaus, a small Polish Catholic church in the next town, the same church we now go to on Sundays.

The room gives me a sense of peace. Because I swear, there have been a few times, when I was alone doing homework or talking on the phone, that the scent of peppermint, Grandma's favorite candy, softly swirled around me. That's what made me feel safe reading *Perks* again in there.

I found the same story radically different this time around. Before, I could only focus on guilting myself for my genetic disorder while exonerating Charlie for being an innocent victim. That's wrong, I know that now. And before, the absence of Grandma and my friends made the support of Charlie's family and friends seem fake. But with Michael and Kristal in my life, I'm seeing that people don't necessarily run from me. They seem to want to be a part of my life. At least for now.

But what really struck me was how skewed my perception was that first Saturday of September, sophomore year. The fucked-up lens of my depression transmitted a version of the story that just wasn't there. *Perks* is a story of hope. The message is that yes, we get dealt some horrifically shitty cards, but despite the hand, we still have choices, decisions to make about where to go from here. There is still some control.

I tell Dr. McCallum what I've discovered: this distorting effect of depression.

His eyes hold mine. "Remember this, Catherine. Because that is exactly why we have a depression game plan," he says. "For that very reason."

The knowledge that Zero will come back doesn't cripple me anymore. I'm getting used to the idea of cycles. My mind is tidal, and I think I can learn to accept that. I will have to learn to ride out the extreme episodes, even the apocalyptic Zero. And I get that our game plan to deal with it hinges on one thing: staying honest and saying honest. I need to become my greatest advocate. Especially at the first signs of my shit going south.

It's dark as Mom drives us home from the appointment. The houses fly by, each window flashing the quickest view of lit interiors, glimpses of the lives within. I used to think that only my house was a house of pain, but now I know that every house has its share. Like Bev Walker pacing in her high-end kitchen as the shower in Kristal's bathroom runs; or Lorraine and Tony Pitoscia staring at Anthony's DUI court papers spread out on the dining room table; and even Farricelli's parents, whose dream of a college football scholarship fractured like the vertebra in Louis's neck. Not to mention all the others whose pain I cannot see.

Not everyone is chronic, but I know no one is immune.

48

JULY

"Dear God, Catherine! Brake, for Christ's sake! And move over!" Mom shouts from the passenger seat. "Center! Center! Move! You almost sideswiped those parked cars."

My driving lessons with Mom are going pretty darn good but for my tendency to hug the right side of the lane. On the mornings she's at Dunkin' Donuts, I drive her there, and usually Michael or Olivia picks me up. I'm scheduled to take the test for my license in three weeks, and the Accord and Bonnie Raitt are waiting for me, since Mom just bought herself a two-year-old Subaru.

It was Mom who decided it was time. Between our work schedules and my internship at the New Haven Museum in the visitor services department, Mom was constantly chauffeuring me around. That and the fact that my Lamictal has kept me stable, along with my "stay honest, say honest" mantra, Dr. McCallum, Mom, Aunt D, my sleep journal, Michael and Kristal.

It takes a village.

"Catherine, see those two parking spots ahead. Pull into the first one and keep going to the second," she says unnecessarily. "This way you don't have to back out of the spot. A pull-through parking spot is always the way to go." Mom glances at me before starting to laugh. "Duh, I know. You don't have to say it."

Mom and I walk in together. I get an iced decaf with two sugars and wait for Michael to arrive. High Honors student Michael has already started writing his Common App essay. He's chosen the "what has been your greatest challenge" question and he's writing about being bullied.

I know I will be using the same prompt for my application. And I know only too well what my answer will be.

We've already started the college tours. The first was with Kristal to Wesleyan, where she's headed in thirty-seven days, four hours and sixteen minutes—she texts me the freshman move-in date countdown every morning. Turned out that she fell more in love with Wesleyan than Vassar. Michael came with Mom and me to UConn for an info session and campus tour. The main campus in Storrs is huge and surprisingly beautiful. Mom, of course, freaked out over the size of the school and has made me agree in advance to a substance-free dorm wherever I wind up.

I have no problem with that. How can I? I never thought I'd be here, walking into student unions, libraries, athletic centers and cafeterias, checking out dorm rooms and bathrooms. Me, Catherine Pulaski, headed to college.

My life resumed.

49

MARCH, SENIOR YEAR

"Cath!" Mom calls from the front door, her tone carrying both elements of shock and excitement. "Cath! Where are you?"

"I'm in the den!" I yell back. I'm at the desk, finishing up an AP English paper on *Beloved*.

Mom hurries in. "Cath." The word is heavy with meaning. Because she's holding out a light brown envelope. Addressed to Catherine Pulaski. From UConn. It's about half the size of an eight-by-eleven envelope. This doesn't look like good news. I've heard acceptances come in large envelopes thick with admission info.

I stare at the envelope and then open it with shaky fingers. The papers are folded in half. Slowly, I unfold them. And read.

Dear Catherine,

Congratulations! It is my pleasure to inform you of your admission to the College of Liberal

Arts and Sciences as a psychology major at the
University of Connecticut Storrs Campus . . .

Mom pulls me into a bear hug, screaming and crying, "My baby's going to college! My baby's going to college. You did it!"

I cry. Hard. Because I can't believe this is a reality—me, going to college.

I am going to college.

I pull back to look at Mom. "*We* did it," I say, my voice cracking on the "we." I want this to be our moment. I need her to know that I know I couldn't have done it without her. That she's my anchor, and that I'm so infinitely grateful. But the words aren't coming. Instead I repeat, "*We* did it."

Mom nods—she understands—and then pulls me close again. She buries her nose in my neck and breathes in, her voice muffled. "You smell like peppermint."

I inhale the scent that has floated over us. Closing my eyes, I allow myself to see. A future. *My* future, unspooling before me: college, job, friends, marriage and maybe, *maybe* even kids. It's there. It's been there all the time. Definitely not perfectly rosy and bright. But mine for the taking. All mine.

Author's Note

HISTORY

Private First Class Jane Talmadge is a fictional character, but her experiences are based on the recollections of real women from the 6888th Central Postal Directory Battalion found in Brenda L. Moore's wonderful book *To Serve My Country, to Serve My Race*, as well as in *One Woman's Army*, the amazing autobiography of the commanding officer of the 6888th, Lieutenant Colonel Charity Adams Early. Both books, along with Cheryl Mullenbach's *Double Victory: How African American Women Broke Race and Gender Barriers to Help Win World War II*, were instrumental to the writing of this story. I was incredibly moved by the courage and perseverance of the 6888th. Kristal's mom put it best: "You think about what these ladies were facing. It was a double whammy of prejudice—they were women and they were black." Despite the discrimination and danger, the 6888th persevered and triumphed.

Early in the writing process, I knew I wanted Catherine to be inspired by a figure from history, someone who had moved forward despite overwhelming odds. That idea led me to think about the first waves of soldiers who stormed the heavily fortified beaches in Normandy. It was complete serendipity that while doing research on the Normandy American Cemetery and Memorial, I found an article about the four women buried among the 9,383 men. Three of these women were from the 6888th: Mary H. Bankston, Mary J. Barlow and Delores Browne. They were killed in a jeep accident in Rouen, France. Their tragic story, as well as the overall courage of the 6888th, gripped me and became the inspiration for Jane Talmadge.

WHY I WROTE THIS BOOK

High school is a strange, surreal and sometimes intensely difficult four years when most of us, for the first time, take a long, hard look at ourselves and our parents, family and friends and start to see cracks or flaws. These years seem like a recipe for turmoil—huge physical and emotional changes are experienced within a very contained community. It can be destabilizing, but when our world has contracted, when our sense of self is often defined by the labels of others, it can be brutal. Let's throw in social media that can publicize on a large scale the slightest incident. It jacks up the consequences of every action and increases the pressure.

Now let's add more: anxiety, depression, eating disorders, drug abuse and addiction, alcoholism, obsessive-compulsive disorder, cutting and bipolar disorder and other disorders or afflictions, physical or mental. In addition to all the usual turbulence of these years, there are now these great, deep pockets of pain, of more pressure, many covered with a stinging layer of stigma. My heart is with those who bear this heavy weight. Know that this story exists because of you.

I wrote this book because I wanted to talk about handling pain: We need to acknowledge it out loud. We need to tell someone. We need to *stay honest and say honest*. I worry that we are programmed not to discuss pain; we manage our profiles with only our best photos and our happy times, and this filtering seeps into our personal interactions out of fear. Fear that too much disclosure will result in different treatment or outright rejection. But pain is a constant in life. The only way to get through it is to talk about it. To not keep it locked inside. Because not talking about pain means it doesn't go away. And by talking about it, we may find others who share a similar pain. Who understand. Who can help.

There are many resources out there. If you are suffering or if you feel the urge to harm yourself, *please* tell someone. Let your pain out. And if the first person you contact doesn't hear you, *don't quit*. Talk. *Keep talking*.

—

Call 911 if you are in immediate danger of harming yourself.

Call 800-273-TALK (8255) (National Suicide Prevention

Lifeline) if you are in crisis or having suicidal thoughts. It is a twenty-four-hour, toll-free, confidential hotline.

Contact the NAMI (National Alliance on Mental Health) HelpLine at 1-800-950-NAMI (6264) or info@nami.org. The NAMI HelpLine can be reached Monday through Friday, ten a.m. to six p.m. EST, for answers to questions about mental health, including symptoms of mental illness, treatment options and support groups.

Sources

Association of Recovery in Higher Education. *RECOVERY PROGRAMS*. http://collegiaterecovery.org/programs/

Devlin, Philip R. "Connecticut Women and the Battle of Normandy: Can You Help Solve a Mystery?" *Simsbury, Connecticut Patch,* June 5, 2012, patch.com/connecticut/simsbury/connecticut-women-in-world-war-ii-and-the-battle-of-n6b0c8a5457.

Dunkins, Brittney, "Students with Depression Fight to Stay on the 'Path,'" *GW Today,* http://gwtoday.gwu.edu/students-depression-fight-stay-'path'.

Earley, Charity Adams. *One Woman's Army: A Black Officer Remembers the WAC*. College Station: Texas A&M University Press, 1989.

Jamison, Kay R. *An Unquiet Mind: A Memoir of Moods and Madness.* New York: Knopf, 1995.

Jamison, Kay R. *Night Falls Fast: Understanding Suicide.* New York: Knopf, 1999.

Khan, Amir. "Dating With a Mental Illness," *U.S. News & World Report,* December 5, 2014, health.usnews.com /health-news/health-wellness/articles/2014/12/05/dating -with-a-mental-illness.

Moore, Brenda L. *To Serve My Country, to Serve My Race: The Story of the Only African American WACS Stationed Overseas During World War II.* New York: New York University Press, 1996.

Mullenbach, Cheryl. *Double Victory: How African American Women Broke Race and Gender Barriers to Help Win World War II.* Chicago: Chicago Review Press, 2013.

Williamson, Wendy K., and Honora Rose. *Two Bipolar Chicks Guide to Survival: Tips for Living with Bipolar Disorder.* Franklin, Tennessee: Post Hill Press, 2014.

"6888th Central Postal Directory Battalion (Women's Army Corps)," *6888th Central Postal Directory Battalion,* history .army.mil/html/topics/afam/6888thPBn/index.html.

Acknowledgments

After I finished this manuscript, I went online and ordered myself a pair of silver snowflake earrings, the same ones my research had uncovered while writing about Michael's anniversary gift to Catherine. Soon after taking them out of the package, I lost them in my house, yet I couldn't order another pair. I had linked some cosmic significance to the earrings, believing that the story's publication somehow rested on their reappearance.

Two months later, on a late January morning, I found them deep in a kitchen drawer. Twenty minutes later, my phone chimed with an email from agent Sara Megibow offering me representation. The stars had aligned. Sara understood the story instinctively. Brilliant, sharp, enthusiastic and genuine, she is a continual advocate and support. This book would not have been possible without her. I am beyond grateful.

Editor Kate Sullivan transformed this story and deepened it in ways I could have never done on my own. It blossomed under her guidance. With Kate, no sentence was left behind, and she always seemed to catch—on instinct, I think—themes I had meant to expand upon but never actually did. I had no idea how collaborative the revision process would be, and I can't imagine going through it on this story with anyone other than Kate.

Diane Cohen Schneider is a gifted writer and friend whose insight and skill shaped the story from page one. Darlene Beck-Jacobson's insight and suggestions were spot-on. Arriving in the eleventh hour at the request of our agent, Miranda Kenneally's suggestions proved pivotal and inspired me to write one of my favorite parts of the book, Chapter 45.

I'd also like to thank the Society of Children's Book Writers and Illustrators (SCBWI) for the very generous grant that made this story possible. And Kathy Temean, former SCBWI regional advisor to the New Jersey chapter. It was at one of Kathy's Avalon Workshops that she urged me to write something new. That something new was the first page of this story. Thank you, Kathy!

I'd also like to thank Regina Brooks of Serendipity Literary. Winning the 2013 YA Discovery Contest was my first professional validation as a writer, and it turbocharged the writing of this story. I am also grateful for another professional boost from the Shoreline Arts Alliance; this story was a finalist in the 2015 Tassey Walden Awards.

To my parents, thank you for always being in my corner and always ready to embrace my latest adventure. And for instilling deep love of reading and writing in me.

To Jenna and Frankie, thank you for your endless patience while I was writing this book. Thank you for repeating yourselves all those times I was still lost in the story and staring at you with glazed eyes. Thank you for pushing me to keep going. Jenna, your intelligence and sharp eyes made me fear your critique! Getting your stamp of approval was—in a word—priceless. Frankie, I am grateful for your technical advice on dialogue and texting and zombie apocalypse information. Thank you also for pointing out the quote from Otto Frank that day we visited the Anne Frank House and for telling me how you thought it was one of the most meaningful things you read.

And finally, to my husband, Frank: you were the inspiration for Dr. McCallum—an intuitive, caring and dedicated child psychiatrist. This story is being published in large part because of you. From technical advice and general editing to continual support and encouragement, I could have never written it without you. Thank you.

About the Author

Karen Fortunati is a former attorney whose experiences on the job with children and teens and personal experiences witnessing the impact of depression, bipolar disorder, and suicide inspired her to write this story of hope for those who struggle with mental illness. She wanted them to know that they are not alone in navigating the shame, stigma, and anxiety that often complicate the management of this chronic condition. Karen graduated from the University of Scranton and Georgetown Universtiy Law Center and attends graduate school at Trinity College in Hartford, Connecticut. She works part-time as a museum educator and lives in Connecticut with her family and rescue dogs.